Deborah Carr, *USA Today*-bestse[...]
and *An Island at War*, lives o[...]
Channel Islands with her husba[...]

Her Mrs Boots series is inspired by another Jersey woman, Florence Boot, the woman behind the Boots (Walgreens Boots Alliance) empire. Her debut First World War romance, *Broken Faces*, was runner-up in the 2012 Good Housekeeping Novel Writing Competition and *Good Housekeeping* magazine described her as 'one to watch'.

Keep up to date with Deborah's books by subscribing to her newsletter: deborahcarr.org/newsletter.

www.deborahcarr.org

facebook.com/DeborahCarrAuthor
instagram.com/DeborahCarrAuthor
pinterest.com/DeborahCarr
youtube.com/@DeborahCarrAuthor

Also by Deborah Carr

THE WITCHING HOUR

DEBORAH CARR

One More Chapter
a division of HarperCollins*Publishers* Ltd
1 London Bridge Street
London SE1 9GF
www.harpercollins.co.uk
HarperCollins*Publishers*
Macken House, 39/40 Mayor Street Upper,
Dublin 1, D01 C9W8, Ireland

This paperback edition 2025
1
First published in Great Britain in ebook format
by HarperCollins*Publishers* 2025
Copyright © Deborah Carr 2025
Deborah Carr asserts the moral right to be identified
as the author of this work

A catalogue record of this book is available from the British Library

ISBN: 978-0-00-866404-6

Printed and bound in the UK using 100% Renewable Electricity
by CPI Group (UK) Ltd

To my mother, Tess Jackson, for all the good times, the laughter and her delicious apple pies.

The Witching Hour

The fear of witchcraft was rife in the 16th and 17th centuries and the Channel Islands have been described as 'proportionate to their size, the witch-hunting capital of Atlantic Europe'.

The island of Jersey had a population of approximately 10,000 people and out of that number over 65 islanders were sent to trial for witchcraft before the island's Royal Court.

Prologue

June 1642

A hum of excitable voices decreased as we ran from the castle green. I clung onto Xavier's hand as we hurried to Old Mother Dorey's cottage a short distance away, my legs shaky from fear. The jeers increased with the heavy thud of wooden wheels bearing another unfortunate accused of sorcery from the keep to the road.

'Witch! Sorceress! Burn in Hell!'

'Don't look,' Xavier insisted when he caught me glancing over my shoulder. 'Now do you understand my insistence that you leave as soon as possible?'

I wanted to argue with him but had to admit he was right. I was a stranger to this time. Different. This place wasn't safe, especially now the Witchfinder was after me.

'Can't we just go away somewhere and hide?' I asked, desperate not to leave him.

We turned a corner, and he stopped, pulling me into the shadows. He took me in his arms. 'My beloved, if there was any other way don't you think I would choose it?'

He put his finger under my chin, lifting it slightly so that I looked deep into his dark blue eyes. His handsome face blurred as tears filled my eyes.

'Yes,' I said, my voice barely audible.

He pulled me closer and enveloped me in his arms, then kissed me. 'I love you more than life itself, Briar. The thought of not having you with me is unbearable, but I would rather know you were back in your own time, and safe, than in danger here.'

He tensed, his eyes shifting to the right. I felt his heart pounding against me. 'Someone is coming,' he whispered. 'We must keep going.'

We moved on again, arriving shortly afterwards at a small, low-roofed cottage. Smoke rose gently from the chimney. It seemed dark inside, and I wasn't sure I had the courage to go in.

Xavier knocked once on the door. Within seconds it drew back, revealing an elderly woman, her heavily lined face giving her a permanent frown.

'Inside.' She waved us in with an urgency that heightened my fears even further.

It took my eyes a few seconds to become accustomed to the lack of light but I was soon able to make out a small black candle in a low silver candlestick on a table near the back wall.

'Thank you for helping me,' I said, remembering my manners and that I had come here for her help.

Old Mother Dorey shook her head impatiently. 'No time for talk.' She lit the candle, murmuring something to herself.

I glanced at Xavier and he gave me a reassuring smile. My heart raced. I tried to steady my breathing, certain I was about to pass out from fear. I wasn't sure what frightened me most, leaving him or the spell the elderly witch was about to cast upon me.

Xavier's hand tightened around mine, comforting me. I must be brave. I might be about to leave the love of my life, but I wasn't the only one suffering. I needed to be strong for Xavier's sake. After all, I was returning home to my beloved mother, whom I had missed terribly each of the sixty-three days I had been here with Xavier.

I still didn't know how it had happened, but presumed one of my mother's spells must have gone awry. She would be suffering agonies not knowing what had become of me, while I had been rescued by my handsome, dark-haired privateer who had managed to keep me safe. Until yesterday when the Witchfinder had discovered me and ordered my arrest.

The witch coughed, dragging my mind back to the present. I watched as she picked up the black candle. Then, taking a small glass amulet with a cork pressed into the top she slowly turned it, letting the wax drip onto it so it completely covered the lid.

She blew gently on the wax and held it out to me. 'Take this in your hand.'

'What is it for?' I asked quietly, my voice trembling.

'It will protect you when you leave us.'

I stifled a whimper. This was happening too quickly.

'Do as she commands, Briar.'

I reluctantly let go of his hand and took the warm glass container from her.

The older woman took a satisfied breath. 'I shall give you a moment to bid your farewells, but then I must send you on your way.'

Panic washed over me. I looked at Xavier. 'Please, don't send me away. I'm sure we can think of a way to keep me hidden from that man.'

Xavier took me gently by the shoulders and gazed at me silently. 'You heard the jeers and baying for the blood of those poor women who were executed last week.'

'Yes,' I said, unable to stop tears from running down my cheeks.

'I will not let that happen to you.'

I reached up and rested my free hand against his cheek. 'But I'll never see you again.' Never kiss him or lie in his arms again. My heart broke at the prospect.

He took me in his arms and, turning his back to the old woman so she couldn't see me, kissed me as if our lives depended on it.

'Now,' he said, gently taking my wrists and moving them from around him. 'We must be brave, Briar. Who knows, we might one day see each other again.'

I almost laughed at the ridiculousness of his comment, but reasoned that I had gone back in time, so maybe it was possible.

'Even if you did,' Old Mother Dorey said, 'she won't remember you.'

'What?' I stepped to the side and stared at her. 'I couldn't possibly forget Xavier. What we've shared.'

Her lined mouth drew back in a pitying smile. 'You have little choice.'

When Xavier didn't seem alarmed by this information, I looked up at him. 'You knew about this?'

'I did.'

'But I don't want to forget about you,' I cried. 'About us.'

The witch tilted her head to one side. 'Why the fuss? If you have no memory of your time here you will have no reason to be upset.'

She made sense but I hated to think of those beautiful memories vanishing. Then something occurred to me. 'What about Xavier?'

'I'm not going anywhere.' He gave me a sweet smile. 'Fear not, beautiful girl. I shall remember our love for both of us.'

Still shocked, but somewhat placated, I sighed. 'I suppose that will have to suffice.'

Someone shouted outside on the street. We all glanced at the door as footsteps ran in our direction. We couldn't be caught with Old Mother Dorey and especially not with her magick tools on display.

'I'm sorry,' I said, realising I was putting us all in danger. 'Please continue.'

She looked at Xavier. 'Step away from her.' Her voice was gentle, and I sensed she felt a deep sadness for us.

Once he had done so, she closed her eyes and, picking up her wand, waved it in a clockwise motion over the top of the candle. She began to chant.

'Protect this woman, keep her safe, send her back to leave no trace. As I will it, so mote it be.'

The amulet seemed to heat up in my hand, but even though I wanted to let go of it I daren't do anything to mess with her spell. Instead, I focused my attention on Xavier. Our eyes locked, his heartbreak mirroring my own.

'I love you,' I whispered.

'I love you, too.'

5

I heard her repeat her spell several times, but each time it became more distant. Then slowly Xavier seemed to fade away, and all my fears faded with him.

Chapter One

DIANA

Midsummer's Eve 1943

'I don't understand why you persist in refusing to join the coven,' I said, trying my best not to allow my daughter's choices to diminish any of the joy I always felt creating my flower crown in anticipation of tonight's Summer Solstice celebration in the woods. I looked forward to every part of this preparation, feeling it brought me closer to my female ancestors who had passed their practices down to me.

'I don't mean to be difficult, Mum,' Briar said, resting her head on my shoulder. 'And I am grateful to you all, but I struggle to follow something blindly simply because it has been expected of us down the generations.'

I was tempted to tell her how I suspected it was one of our ancestors, or a friend of theirs, whose spell had returned her to me a year ago, but since Briar seemed to have no recall of what had happened or where she had been for those weeks after her disappearance, I didn't think it wise to put thoughts into her head that could potentially trouble her.

I watched my daughter as she picked up and studied a perfect ox-eye daisy I had picked to add to my crown. I couldn't quite put my finger on what it was exactly, but Briar had changed in some way. I wished I dared delve into what might have happened but knew well enough that to do so would only cause her pain.

She had endured enough upset over the years, thanks to the bullying she had received growing up from those ignorant of the truth about how we lived our lives.

'I understand your reasons, but I don't want you to allow others' nastiness towards you to cause you to miss out on the sisterhood that means so much to me and did so to your gran. One of these days those who judge us harshly might discover our coven only ever use our powers for good, or to protect ourselves and those we love. Never to hurt others.'

'I know that, Mum, but I doubt others will be open-minded enough to even try to understand anything about us when it's easier for them to just be mean-spirited.'

She was right. Many people who came to me for potions to alleviate ill health visited my home when they were least likely to be spotted by neighbours. But that didn't change how I felt. Being a witch was my birthright as far as I was concerned. For my daughter to reject gifts bestowed on her pained me daily and I had no intention of giving up my quest to bring her into the coven.

I looked up from my pestle. 'Pass me that jar of moon water, will you?' I asked. Although most of my mixtures were medicinal, some required a spell to be woven into the mixture, and for that I often needed water energised by the moon.

Briar picked up the jar and placed it on the table. 'Here you go, Mum.'

I saw her watch as I unscrewed the lid and poured a little into the granite mortar. I didn't like to remind Briar yet again that our usual thirteen members were reduced these past three years after seven were evacuated with their families just before the island was invaded by the Nazis.

Determined to focus on my preparations once more, I counted the different types of flowers I had picked and so far threaded around the wire fashioned to fit my head. 'Rose, lavender, elderflower, camomile, yarrow, calendula, St John's wort, delphinium.' What had I missed?

'Mum.'

Realising Briar was speaking, I turned to her questioningly. 'What is it?'

Smiling, Briar held out an ox-eye daisy. 'Is this what you're looking for?'

It was. 'You see?' I said, satisfied. 'You are one of us, whatever you might think.' I took the daisy from Briar's tanned hand. 'You really would gain so much from joining us.'

She went to argue, so I raised my hand. 'I've said my piece and I'll leave it there.'

I fastened the daisy into the crown and held it up, turning the beautiful display slowly to study each flower. Satisfied, I placed it carefully on my head. 'What do you think?'

'Beautiful – and there are the requisite nine flowers. It's perfect.'

'Thank you.' I placed the garland in my copper bowl filled with moon water, my excitement about the evening ahead increasing.

Unable to help myself, I said, 'There's time for me to make one for you.'

Briar smiled and shook her head slowly and hugged me. 'Thanks, Mum, but when I'm ready I'll make my own.'

'I'll fetch my coat, then I'd better get going. I don't want to be late.'

'I'm aware you'll be out all night,' Briar said. 'I'll make your deliveries tomorrow.'

'You're a good girl,' I said, grateful to her for all her help. 'There are a couple in particular that I need you to make sure are taken tomorrow.'

I lifted the garland carefully from the copper bowl, then, draping a tea towel onto the wooden worktop, placed the dripping flower crown onto it. I waved for her to follow me to the other end of our galley kitchen. Picking up a small bottle, I handed it to her. 'I need you to take this to Mrs Aubert.'

She carefully unscrewed the lid from the bottle and sniffed. 'Rosemary. A nerve tonic? She has been working hard lately, I noticed.'

I nodded, picturing the forty-something lady who had struggled ever since her husband had died suddenly after being arrested by the occupying forces for some minor indiscretion the previous year. 'I promised to give her something to help.'

Briar smiled. 'That's kind of you, Mum. But then you're always thinking of others.' She replaced the lid and lifted a sachet. 'May I ask what this one is for?'

Wanting to make the most of any opportunity to show my daughter how useful her powers could be, I suggested she tell me.

She smelt the contents lightly, then looked up at the

feathery-leaved plant I had hung in bunches at various places in the room to decorate the kitchen and living area for midsummer. 'Fennel?'

I nodded. 'And why does she take that?' I asked, testing Briar's knowledge and yet again trying to prove my point that she was wasting her powers not making the most of her inheritance.

Her expression changed and I knew she was thinking of the young woman who had been one of her closest friends since meeting on their first day attending the parish school. 'Poor Clara.'

I also felt sympathy for the girl, who seemed to have suffered the shame of giving birth to a young soldier's baby. The gentle boy had soon been sent back to Germany in disgrace and Clara had been left bereft with a bulging tummy and ruined reputation, not that Briar or I had changed towards her, apart from offering our support in whatever means we could. And now that supplies were becoming fewer over the months, my way of helping was with my herbs.

'If I recall correctly,' Briar said, 'Clara infuses it in hot water and drinks the tea.'

Proud of my daughter's knowledge, I added, 'That's right. This way she'll be able to pass on useful nutrients to her sweet baby through her breast milk.'

Briar sighed heavily. 'I'll stay with her for a while when I take this to her.'

'Thank you. I doubt she has too many visitors now. I know how time can run away from you,' I said, thinking of the few occasions Briar had been home late and almost broke curfew. 'Please don't forget to leave in good time to be home before curfew begins. You know how nasty some of those patrol soldiers can be.'

'I won't, Mum.' She gave me a kiss on the cheek. 'Anyway, never mind me, you're the one who will need to be careful tonight.' I could tell she was concerned. 'If they catch you, who knows what they might do?'

She was right. It was one thing to break curfew and another entirely to be caught dancing and chanting around a bonfire deep in the woods throughout the night. I knew that if we were caught there was only so much our High Priestess Babette Le Dain's husband, our parish Connétable, would be able to do for us. But Babette had insisted it would be fine if we were careful.

'Will you take Tula?'

At the mention of my familiar – a Jersey toad, or *crapaud* as we referred to them here, that I had inherited from my grandmother – I glanced out of the window and smiled, spotting her sitting in her favourite spot under a large *Pontederia cordata* leaf overhanging the side of my pond.

I shook my head. 'No. We each agreed to leave our familiars behind. Some of them don't get along and it can be distracting.'

Briar laughed. 'I can imagine.'

My seriousness returned. 'If you do go out in the evening please remember to take Pippin with you. She'll protect you.'

'I will, Mum, I promise.'

'Off you go then,' I said, wishing to continue with my preparations and cast a spell protecting my home before I left.

Briar kissed me on the cheek and left the kitchen. I thought of the tiny pipistrelle bat with its dark golden brown fur that my daughter had inherited from my mother, and wondered why she found it completely natural to have her own familiar and still doubt her place in the coven. I sighed heavily, deciding that the next spell I cast would be one to help her see sense and finally do what was meant for her.

I thought of the women waiting to start our celebrations in the woods above Anne Port and, hurriedly putting my coat on over my white dress that I had made for this special evening, carefully placed my flower crown in my basket, and went to the door.

'Have fun, Mum,' she shouted after me as I hurried outside.

It didn't take too long for me to join my friends in the woods. I slipped off my coat and placed my crown carefully on my head. I loved it up here, sheltered from onlookers but still enjoying a perfect view of the solstice sunrise.

I loved meeting with my coven but this extra meeting with my sisterhood to celebrate Litha was always special.

'You're here,' Babette said, waving me over to join them. 'And your flower crown is beautiful as ever.'

'As is yours,' I said honestly, looking from our High Priestess to each of the other women. 'All so colourful and pretty.'

As soon as I had completed our circle around the sticks and logs some of the women had collected earlier that day, Babette took a metal bowl of smoking embers kept from the previous year's fire and scattered them carefully onto the tinder-dry straw and kindling.

Jeanne, our youngest member and Babette's daughter-in-law, handed each of us a glass of mead. My heart swelled to be here in this magickal place, with these women who were as close to me as sisters.

'We raise our glasses to Litha,' Babette said, toasting this perfect midsummer's eve. 'And remember those women who went before us and who passed all that we know and treasure down through the ages to enable us to protect ourselves and those we cherish.'

'To Litha,' we said before taking a sip of the potent, sweet liquid.

Then, placing our empty glasses to the side, we began dancing around the fire as it took hold. Joy washed over me. One day, I was certain, Briar would be here with us, and I couldn't wait to share this happy, perfect evening with her.

Babette brought our dancing to a standstill as she raised her hands to the sky. We watched as she removed her flower crown and held it up. I carefully lifted mine, missing the gentle weight of it on my head, as did the other women. Babette smiled at each of us then cast hers into the fire. I threw mine at the same time as the others, watching the flowers being consumed by the flames and the smoke from them rising into the night sky.

We began our chanting as one.

'We celebrate Litha with the sun at its peak and embrace this summer solstice filling our souls with the joy that it brings us and strength it beholds.'

I lost myself to our chanting as we danced around our fire, absorbing all that Litha gave us as the sun set and skies darkened, only stopping a few hours later to drink more mead. I became aware of a passing storm strong enough to bring lightning and thunder, and was grateful that the thick canopy of trees protected our fire from most of the rain, as we prepared to continue chanting and dancing until sunrise.

Chapter Two

BRIAR

June 1943

I flinched as another fork of lightning illuminated the night sky and, potentially, my whereabouts to the Nazis patrolling the area, as it crashed against one of the castle's turrets high above me. I could almost hear Mum chanting with her coven, but I was aware I was being fanciful. They were too far away for me to hear them, and anyway I knew they would have to take care to keep their voices low so as not to be heard by a passing patrol.

I wondered if she had cast a protection spell around me that I didn't know about. I could do with one now. It occurred to me as I ran from the Nazi chasing me that if I had agreed to be inducted into the coven I might have been able to cast my own protection spell.

Mum was going to be furious if I was caught and arrested, especially as she had reminded me not to stay out after curfew, and even more so if she discovered I had left Pippin at home.

At least my familiar offered me some protection, even if all she could do right now was try to distract the soldiers or set off and warn Mum that I was in danger.

'Halt!'

I tensed instinctively, aware the order was directed at me. The castle grounds loomed high over the village and Honey Bee Cottage where I was supposed to be. Hearing him shout the order a second time, I peered frantically through the rain for somewhere to hide. I spotted a curved wall to the side of the castle. It wasn't ideal, but I couldn't see any other option.

I broke into a run, almost breathless with terror, and although my legs felt as if they weren't moving, I eventually made it most of the way across the long stretch of grass that made up the castle green.

'Stop, now.' Hearing a second voice closing in on me as the two soldiers called out to each other, I took a steadying breath.

Come on, Briar, you can do this I insisted, though I wasn't sure I could. Then, too frightened not to move, I made a dash for the rundown building ahead, forcing my shaking legs to go as fast as possible.

I hurtled in through the gap in the wall, tripping in my haste and only just managing to right myself by grabbing hold of the remaining piece of a ledge. My finger stung as part of my fingernail tore off against the stone. Breathless, I was relieved to spot an alcove at the back. I hurried over and crouched behind a mound of stones next to the remains of a dividing wall to a narrow hallway.

I recalled Mum telling me that this was an old cell that had once been part of the Mont Orgueil dungeons. Right now, though, I was just relieved to have a place where I could hide.

No one followed me inside. After a couple of minutes I

tentatively stepped out from behind the mound of stones and walked over to the open doorway.

Another loud crack of thunder overhead made me jump. Why hadn't I kept an eye on the time? I would then be at home in Honey Bee Cottage, lying on my bed reading, rather than stuck here and wet in this miserable shelter.

Summer storms were often inconvenient and this one had certainly taken me by surprise.

Barely daring to breathe, it dawned on me that I hadn't heard anything further from the soldiers. I strained to hear their voices above the din of the storm. Then, unable to hear anything other than rumbling thunder and rain. I wiped my face with the hem of my blouse. I might be soaked but for the time being I was out of the rain, thanks to the partial roof shielding me. It was something to be grateful for, I supposed.

I flinched as a fork of lightning slammed against the ground outside. As much as I yearned to be at home, I had no wish to be struck by lightning. I hoped the soldiers had decided to forget about me and retreat into the castle until the storm blew over. There would be little chance of me making it across the green and on to the village if they continued to patrol outside.

I shuddered, unsure why. Rain dripped from me, but I wasn't cold. The hairs on my forearms stood on end and an icy trickle ran down my spine. I stilled, sensing for the first time that I wasn't alone. Terrified, I closed my eyes, desperate to keep control of my panic.

'What are you doing here?' a voice boomed from the darkness behind me.

My breath caught in my throat. I covered my mouth to stop a scream from escaping. It dawned on me that although

I didn't recognise the man's deep voice, he didn't have a German accent, so at least he wasn't a soldier. Hoping I was about to see another local who had also carelessly been caught out after curfew, I took a steadying breath and forced myself to turn slowly to face him.

For a split second, I thought there was something familiar about him, but I presumed I must be wrong because I had no recollection of ever meeting him before.

He seemed surprised to see me. His eyes widened and his mouth dropped open as he slowly raised a finger to point at me. 'It's you.' He closed his eyes and shook his head before opening them again. 'How can this be?'

I had no idea what he might be referring to, so I didn't respond. I stared at the grubby, unshaven but well-built and, I had to admit, even if only to myself, rather handsome man. He was dressed oddly, though, in what appeared to be a red woollen fitted jacket with a torn, filthy shirt underneath. I recalled seeing men wearing similar clothes in school history books but couldn't fathom why anyone might be dressed like this now.

He didn't speak, seeming as bemused by my appearance as I was by his. I studied the rest of his clothing.

He was staring at me with an intensity that made me step back. Had I met him somewhere before? I couldn't think when, but there was something about him. What, though?

He took a step towards me, causing the soles of his boots to clunk noisily on the stone floor. I instinctively moved away from him but couldn't miss the shadow of sadness that swept across his face. His expression softened. 'You do not remember.' He seemed to be speaking to himself rather than asking me a question.

Another clap of thunder startled us both and made me focus on the matter in hand. 'Please stop talking,' I said, keeping my voice as low as possible, although still needing to be heard above the din of the storm. 'We mustn't be overheard.'

'Who will hear us over this?' He stared up at the partial roof, then frowned and stepped back. 'What is happening?' He looked from side to side, searching for something.

What was wrong with him? I hoped I hadn't managed to land myself in worse danger trapped with this stranger than I had been at the mercy of the soldiers.

He was breathing heavily as if he had been running. Not running, I realised. He was in shock.

'Are you quite well?' I asked, not confident in my nursing skills should he collapse.

He kept glancing at the walls, then the partial roof. 'What has become of the cell?'

'Pardon?' What on earth was he talking about?

'The walls,' he snapped, waving his arms in frustration. 'The door. The roof. The—'

'For pity's sake keep your voice down,' I snapped, baffled by his odd ramblings. 'I have no idea what you're talking about. You must be quiet, otherwise you'll draw attention to us.'

He walked over to the doorway. Fearing he might be spotted and hating to think he might draw the soldiers' attention to us both, I leapt forward and grabbed him by the arm.

He stopped and stared down at my hands, a sad expression on his face. Did I remind him of someone? Not wishing to cause him any further consternation, I let go.

'You'd better come and hide here near me if you don't want those Nazis out there finding us.'

'Nazis?' He said the word quietly as if trying it out for the first time. He peered at me through the gloom. The constant lightning all around sporadically illuminated the space and the strain on his face. 'What, pray, are Nazis?'

This was all I needed. Since many islanders and children were evacuated just before the Channel Islands were invaded, the numbers of locals still living in Jersey were greatly reduced. Despite some sense of familiarity, I couldn't place the man. I knew I wouldn't forget a face as handsome as his, nor his odd way of behaving. It was unusual to come across a stranger on the island since the invasion three years before, at least one that wasn't wearing a German uniform.

'Stop messing about,' I pleaded, ignoring the hurt expression on his face. I felt mean for a second but was frustrated with his silliness, and struggled to contain my rising temper. 'Now really isn't the time. Come and crouch next to me. You must make yourself less conspicuous if we don't want them to spot you.' I tapped the top of the pile of rocks in front of me.

'Hide? Behind there?'

Why was this man not listening to me? 'They could come looking in here at any time,' I explained in case he really didn't understand the magnitude of the danger we were in.

He stared at me for a moment. 'Why would I hide when I am free to walk away?'

'Free?' This man was incredibly annoying. I glanced at the door, realising he was intending to make his escape. 'Do not go out there,' I whispered through gritted teeth. 'You'll draw attention to both of us and I'm not going to jail for your carelessness.'

His mouth tightened into a thin line. 'You've changed.'

What? I went to ask how he felt able to make such a comment, but I was beginning to feel intimidated by his strange behaviour, so I kept quiet.

I pictured Mum with her coven and wondered how they could still have a fire with the rain. I knew she would still celebrate Litha, but Mum didn't need to be with her coven to do that. I hoped she hadn't gone home and already discovered I wasn't there. I hated to think of her alone in our tiny cottage fretting about me, especially on what was supposed to be a special day for her.

I took a steadying breath, aware I needed to find a way to make this man listen to reason. 'I didn't mean to insult you, but there are soldiers outside. Well-trained ones. They are searching for me.' I chewed the inside of my lower lip, willing him to take what I was telling him seriously.

It occurred to me that I had thought myself alone in the ruin when I had entered it. 'How did you get in here?'

He didn't seem to hear me and instead of answering my question went to go outside. At once, a soldier screamed at him. I tensed. The stranger immediately stepped backwards into the room, and turned to me with a horrified expression on his face.

He swallowed. 'What are they?' he asked, his voice barely above a whisper.

'You'd better come and hide here with me.' I waved him over to where I was hiding behind the tumbledown wall and waited as he crouched beside me. He was trembling, as if he had seen a ghost.

'Do you honestly expect me to believe you've never seen a member of the Wehrmacht before?'

He shook his head. 'I do not know what that means.'

Either he was mad, or… A terrifying thought occurred to me. 'Where have you come from really?' I hesitated for emphasis. 'And why are you here?'

He looked as thunderous as the storm outside. 'I was in this cell awaiting my execution.' He looked around once more as if he couldn't believe what he was seeing. 'Why are you hiding in this place?'

'I think it's obvious.'

'Not to me. Explain, if you will, Briar.'

I stared at the glowering man, who, I noticed for the first time, wore his hair in a much longer style than any man I had ever seen before. As another flash of lightning illuminated our hiding place, I saw how dark his blue eyes were and it dawned on me with a pang that in any other situation I might find him rather attractive. Oh, hell, I did find him attractive, I realised, as my insides somersaulted.

'How do you know my name?'

His eyes shifted away from mine. 'You must have told it to me. I'm Xavier,' he said, gazing at me for a couple of seconds as if waiting for me to react in some way. 'Xavier Givroye.'

Had I told him my name? I didn't recall doing so, but then my mind was racing and I could barely think straight.

'You haven't answered my question.' I explained about visiting my friend and missing curfew. 'My mother will be furious.'

He rubbed his face with his dirt-ingrained hands and groaned wearily. 'Do you think we should leave before the storm ends?'

It made sense for us to use the driving rain as cover. It was difficult to see very far. Why hadn't I thought of it before now? 'That's a good idea.'

Then, unable to help myself, I said, 'May I ask why you're dressed in those odd clothes?'

He seemed indignant at my question, tired even. 'These are my clothes.' He looked down at them and slapped the once cream material of his breeches. 'They were not always in this sorry state.'

I listened, bemused, as he explained that he had been a privateer before falling out with his superiors and being forced into the recently banded Parliamentary Army. He hesitated every so often as if waiting for me to speak, continuing when I didn't. He obviously believed everything he was telling me. It was staggering and not a little unnerving. I wasn't sure why I felt as if I was in a strange dream. Maybe I *was* dreaming, I thought, wishing that to be the case but knowing it wasn't.

I scrutinised his clothes. Underneath the grime they seemed authentic as far as I could tell. They were certainly well worn. Then I studied the sincere expression on his face and thought about his unusual hairstyle.

'Where are you really from?' I asked, nervous at pressing him. There was something dangerous about him that scared me. Or was it the way he kept staring at me every so often as if waiting for me to give him information I didn't have? I decided I had little choice but to voice what was niggling me. It was an odd question but I hoped it would give me some answers about his being here. 'What year do you think it is?'

The pitying gaze he gave me was annoying, but I waited for his reply. 'I have been contemplating asking you the same question,' he said eventually.

'Me?' I asked surprised. 'Why?'

He waved his hand up and down in front of my body. 'Your clothes. Although I have seen something like these before, haven't I?'

'I don't doubt it.' I looked down, embarrassed at my worn woollen skirt and mis-matched jacket. 'I know they're shabby, but there's little chance of finding anything new now.' I sighed, recalling how smart I had been before the Germans invaded and all our lives changed. 'Our priorities have changed. We're lucky to have food or anything to heat our homes, let alone decent clothes to wear.'

Again, that strange look. Was I the one losing my mind? Could my earlier confrontation with the soldiers have sent me into shock? Was that why everything seemed slightly off kilter? I needed to find out more, because right now nothing made any sense at all.

I decided to persevere. 'I'm sorry, Xavier, I know it's a strange question. I need to understand why you're dressed that way and where you think you are right now.'

His look made me want to shrink away from him, which I would have done if my bottom wasn't already pressed against a wall.

He sighed. 'It is the year of our Lord 1643,' he said matter-of-factly.

I heard the resigned tone in his voice. He seemed sincere, and I wanted to believe he was answering as honestly as he could, even though he wasn't making any sense.

Irritated that my lazy timekeeping had been the cause of me being stuck in here with a deluded man for company and Nazi soldiers outside, I wondered: why hadn't I done as my mother insisted and kept an eye on the time?

'Briar?' His deep voice was gentle now; something in it suggested a familiarity between us, and I frowned.

Thrown by his change of tone, I looked at him. 'Yes?'

'What year do *you* think this is?' His eyes bored into mine.

I decided to be as courteous in my answer as he had been. 'I'm certain it's 1943.'

He laughed wearily, shaking his head. After a few seconds his amusement vanished. 'You believe what you are saying, don't you?' The puzzlement on his face deepened. 'But it does not make sense. It can't,' he whispered, looking as if he was about to throw up.

'Why not?'

'How is it possible for me to travel three hundred years into the future? To a world more terrible than the one I know?'

My fear of him was turning to sympathy when my thoughts were interrupted by soldiers shouting, their voices coming closer to our hiding place.

'I have no idea, Xavier,' I replied, trying my best not to give in to my panic. 'I wish it wasn't possible, for both our sakes, but I'm afraid it is 1943. If we are to stand any chance of keeping our freedom, we need to escape from here before it's too late.'

Chapter Three

DIANA

Midsummer's Day

Elated, I walked home to the village with the other six women from the coven. It was almost five-thirty and we parted ways early to each quietly make our way home, hoping to go unnoticed by any patrolling soldiers. The last thing any of us needed was to draw suspicion on ourselves.

I opened the door humming to myself and stepped inside Honey Bee Cottage.

As I passed the living-room window I sensed movement in the shadows across from the cottage. I assumed I would see Hauptmann Klein, one of the officers who seemed always to be hanging around the village, but was relieved to find no one there.

'Infuriating man,' I grumbled.

I had noticed several officers watching my daughter, who I knew had given none of them any encouragement. Even though I was her mother and probably biased, I couldn't deny how pretty she was with her shoulder-length dark hair and green eyes, but I was still surprised that an officer of the Wehrmacht didn't bother hiding his interest in her. Life under German rule was worrying enough without his beady eyes ever alert for Briar, and I knew his unwanted attempts to watch our cottage bothered her – and not only because of herself. She was protective of me and had admitted she worried that his attention on us might end up with him discovering my witchcraft practices.

I had reminded Briar that all our neighbours knew I grew herbs and made up sachets and tinctures, using them to help ailments. Most of them benefitted in some way. None knew I was a witch, though.

Apart from the civic head of our parish, our Connétable's wife, of course. But then Babette Le Dain wasn't only his wife, she was also High Priestess of the Gouôrray Coven. Somewhere back in time, whoever had brought together the first coven had decided to use the Jèrriais spelling for Goray, where most of us lived, which was especially useful since none of the Germans knew our local patois.

I glanced upstairs to where I assumed Briar was still sleeping. I had half hoped she might be waiting for my return like she did every year at this time. She might not be ready for her induction into our coven but she always enjoyed seeing me happy, and each midsummer's morning had greeted me with a prepared breakfast.

I would have loved to wake her. We had all day to sit and chat and I didn't want to be selfish. I decided instead to harvest my herbs while the droplets of midsummer dew still glistened on them.

Presuming I didn't yet need my large straw hat to shade my

neck from the early morning sunshine, I spent the next hour carefully selecting and picking my herbs and placing them in my basket. I loved doing this task, planning, as I picked them, which ones I would tie into small bunches and hang up to dry, and which I would keep to be steeped in oil. A wave of joy coursed through me. How lucky I was to have been born into a family of witches, to have grown up as I had done, learning the traditions passed down through my family. It was a heritage worth more than any other as far as I was concerned.

I loved helping others, and despite all I had learnt at my mother's and grandmother's side as I helped them in their own gardens, I knew I still had much more to discover. Along with pride I felt the usual pang in my heart each time I remembered my ancestry, aware that Briar's choosing not to continue our traditions meant she was missing out on so much. There was still time, though, I told myself, as I picked a few stems of lavender and carefully placed them in my trug.

Back inside the cool of my kitchen I cut small lengths of twine and neatly tied my herbs into bunches, hanging each, as I completed it, upon one of the small nails hammered sometime in the past along one of the beams. The sight and aroma of these herbs and those hanging from my living room mantle comforted me as I thought of Clara. The poor girl needed a friend especially now when so many others had turned their backs on her.

A bumblebee flew into the room, distracting me.

'Aren't you beautiful,' I said opening the back door and waiting for the bee to exit. 'Are you here to let me know a visitor will be coming to the cottage?'

The bee flew out and, feeling better, I went back to my

kitchen and collected ingredients from my many jars. Then, picking up a small bottle and taking a black candle from a box in my pantry cupboard, I walked back to the living room, making sure I kept away from the window and any prying eyes.

I needed to cast a protection spell against the negativity of the Nazi soldiers. I shuddered, then set my tools out on my small table to the right of the hearth. I began to ground myself by taking a moment to stop, breathe and push away negative thoughts, but I found I couldn't shift the sense that something was wrong. What, though? I thought for a moment, unsure what it might be.

Deciding my anxiety was caused by a lack of sleep and too much mead the previous evening, I cleansed the area near to the hearth by lighting the candle. Focusing my attention on my spell, I took a pinch of dried raspberry leaves, another of ground black pepper, one of dried rosemary and another of chopped dried pine needles which I had gathered from the Jersey pines on my way to St Catherine's wood the month before. I carefully fed each into the bottle and added the lavender oil.

I placed the lid on the bottle and carefully screwed it into place. 'May this oil protect those anointed with it. May it defend Briar and me, protecting us like a shield, and repel all that intends to harm us. So mote it be.'

Comforted to have cast some protection around us against that ghastly soldier, I placed the bottle behind the curtain on the windowsill, where the moon could shine on it that night and energise the concoction. Satisfied with my efforts, I blew out my candle and placed it on the mantlepiece. I covered my mouth as a yawn began to take hold and decided to go and wake Briar. She never slept in this late.

'Briar?' I called as I walked to the stairs. When there was no reply I sensed for the first time that I was alone in the house.

Panicked, I ran upstairs to check her bedroom. I opened the door. My heart dropped when I saw her bed was made and Pippin sleeping above it in the rafters.

'Where is she, Pippin?' I asked, though knowing she would only answer to Briar. 'You need to go and find her. Quickly.'

I opened the window for the tiny bat to fly out, willing her to do whatever she could to bring Briar back home safely.

Chapter Four

XAVIER

I t was almost dawn but, unsure whether the soldiers were still there, Briar and I kept ourselves hidden. Despite her not recognising me, her slightly frosty demeanour, and the fact she clearly suspected I might not be sane, I had no wish to bring our meeting to an end any earlier than necessary. I relished being in the same room as her once more.

Nonetheless, I was struggling to understand how I had come to be here. I thought back to discovering Briar in my own time, frightened and bewildered. It seemed that it was now my turn to experience the unexplainable.

I still couldn't believe the cell had partly crumbled. How unfortunate that I was still unable to leave and walk away to my freedom. None of this made sense – not my surroundings disintegrating in the blink of an eye, nor the oddly named soldiers supposedly chasing Briar and who were no doubt waiting outside somewhere for us. How had I come to be here? The only person I knew of with the magickal powers to send me here was Old Mother Dorey, but why would she do such a thing if I hadn't asked it of her?

Briar's elbow touched mine lightly as she stretched. She flinched and looked askance at me. 'Sorry. I didn't mean to touch you.'

'Do not concern yourself.'

She sighed. 'We need to get away from here somehow. It's still early but more people will be getting up and moving around soon and I don't want them finding you. You're a stranger here and I daren't become involved in anything that might put my mother in any danger.'

I was unsure why she was more concerned about her mother at this moment, but didn't ask why.

'What would you have us do?' I asked, resigned to making my escape. I decided to leave worrying about what had led me to this place until I was safe elsewhere.

She glanced at the doorway and inched closer to me, her voice low. My skin heated to have her next to me. I forced myself to listen to what she was about to tell me.

'I live not too far from here. If we can cross the green without being spotted and make it down La P'tite Ruelle Muchie, we can hopefully sneak along Le Mont de Gouray and down the hill to the village and my home. My mother will know what to do after that.'

She seemed doubtful despite her assurances.

I pictured the route. 'Would it not be better to make our way along the shoreline?'

She shook her head. 'I don't think that's wise. There are Germans patrolling all along there and the road above the sea wall is visible from the castle. There's a gun emplacement up there now, as well as one at the end of the houses on the pier.'

Road? Sea wall? Houses? I pictured the rotting wooden structure that made up the pier. It hadn't been solid enough to support a cart, let alone a row of houses, when I had seen it last. It seemed that much had changed and that I had little choice but to go along with her suggestion.

My thoughts vanished as a small bird flew into the cell. It flew straight over to Briar and I realised it wasn't a bird but a bat. In the daytime?

'Pippin,' Briar whispered happily as she used to do when seeing me unexpectedly, when we had been together in my time. I longed to be back there when she loved me as much as I loved her now.

I realised she was speaking to the tiny brown animal now sitting in her hand. 'You must help us escape from here,' she said, her voice soothing.

I heard voices coming from somewhere outside and tensed. We were running out of time.

Briar raised her hand slightly and the bat flew outside. I barely had time to give her a questioning look when we heard shouting.

'That'll be Pippin,' she said proudly. 'She'll be making trouble.' She laughed. 'You've no idea how many people are frightened of a tiny bat.'

I nodded. 'We must make haste if we are to make our bid for freedom.'

Briar gave me a withering look, reminding me she had been the one to make the suggestion. I longed for her eyes to fill with the love I had been used to seeing.

'I don't know if I'm more frightened hiding in here or about taking our chances out there,' she admitted. 'But I believe this is our one chance to make a dash for it.'

I recognised her fear only too well. I had fought enough battles to understand trepidation. Resting a hand on her slight shoulder I had to force myself to concentrate and not think about the last time I had done that. Her shoulder had been naked then. A groan escaped my lips.

She tensed. 'What is it?'

Hoping she mistook my reaction for concern, I gave her an understanding smile.

I noticed her gaze upon my clothing once more. 'Why do you stare?'

She frowned. 'If we are caught, I'm not sure how you'll explain your clothes.'

'Then we will ensure they do not catch us.' I cocked my head in the direction of the doorway. 'I have no weapon with which to fight. I shall do my best to protect you.'

Clearly unmoved by my gallantry, Briar stared at me. 'The soldiers have guns, Xavier. You should concentrate on saving yourself. I'll take care of me.'

The only other woman I knew to be this bold was Ember, but she was an experienced and fierce warrior. Neither woman had taken to the other, and despite my devastation at losing Briar I had at least been relieved to have her away from Ember's ire when Old Mother Dorey had worked her magick.

Focusing on the present, and determined not to show my shock at her rebuff, I asked: 'Would you wish for me to go first?'

Briar narrowed her eyes. 'Do you know which way we must go?'

'I live here also,' I reminded her. 'Have done so for many a year. I am well acquainted with the island.'

'Maybe back in the 1640s you were, but there have been

many changes in the past three years, let alone the past three hundred.' Glancing at the doorway, Briar said, 'I suggest you do as I say, if you want us both to get out of here in one piece.'

I wanted to protest, but she was right. I was a stranger in her time. Seeing those men had proved that to me. 'I shall do as you ask.'

Briar stepped past me without another word. She pressed her back against the wall to the right of the door and peered over her shoulder to the outside. The early morning light illuminated her face more clearly as she gave a satisfied smile. 'Pippin is chasing them.' She laughed. 'Two grown men, soldiers, frightened of a tiny bat. Whatever next?' She waved for me to move closer to her. 'When I make a run for it, follow me.'

I nodded.

'Now.' Her voice was quiet but urgent. She then bolted out of the door and I ran after her.

She was perhaps thinner than when I had seen her before, I mused as we hurtled across the green, but thankfully she was fast. Within thirty seconds we reached the cover of the narrow steep lane leading down the hill. Once at the bottom, I knew we needed to run up another hill for a short way to reach the next part of our route, which would finally take us down to the village with its small cottages where she lived.

I stumbled as we neared the wall of the first cottage, my boots slipping on the smooth granite cobbles. Briar stopped, grabbed my sleeve and pulled me back into a narrow alleyway.

Not daring to speak, I listened to the sound of heavy boots running in our direction and pressed myself back against the alley wall.

My heart pounded as Pippin flew past, the two soldiers thundering after her as they did their best to catch her. I had faced many foes but none as startling as these impressive-looking men with their metal helmets and deadly guns. What had I come to? And why?

I felt another tug on my sleeve. 'We had better go this way,' Briar whispered as she pulled me down to her, the warmth of her light breath stirring emotions in me I hadn't felt since we had parted. 'I daren't risk going that way in case they come back, or someone spots us and turns us in.'

I had little choice but to follow her, keeping close to the left-hand wall. Life in my own time had been dangerous, but this was enough to drive godfearing people into apoplexy.

Briar's warm hand found mine and I clung onto it tightly, realising she would believe I was afraid. She led me down another narrow alleyway, one barely wider than my shoulders. I spotted something dart to the right and supposed it was her bat having lost the soldiers before returning to Briar.

Briar's fingers still gripped me, and the intimacy of her smaller hand in mine calmed me slightly, reminding me this was unsettling for us both.

She stopped suddenly and I slammed into her back, sending her flying forward. Instinctively, I reached out with my free hand and wrapped my arm about her waist, stopping her from falling and only just managing to keep upright myself.

'Forgive my clumsiness,' I murmured, mortified at my carelessness. I realised I was still holding her tightly against me and let my arm drop from around her.

'Um, we're almost there,' she said after a moment's hesitation. 'This way.'

Chapter Five

XAVIER

I barely registered the door before Briar opened it and pulled me inside. The little bat flew past my ear just before she closed the door quickly behind us. I went to thank her but was distracted by a woman who was waving a bunch of smoking herbs that smelt of lavender. A witch?

The woman noticed me and yelped. As she leapt backwards her elbow caught a bowl, knocking it off the small table and onto the floor. What appeared to be salt and dried herbs tipped out. She scowled at us. 'Look what you made me do.'

'Sorry, Mum,' Briar said, drawing a heavy curtain across the front door. 'It couldn't be helped.' She bent to scoop up the smattering from the floor. 'I hadn't meant to interrupt.'

What had I walked into? Whatever it was I didn't want Briar scolded on my behalf. I noticed the window was open and saw the bat fly in and dart behind a vase on a high shelf at the back of the room.

Briar's mother smiled. 'Pippin found you then?' she said in

37

a satisfied voice that told me she had been the one to send the bat after Briar.

'She did.' Briar looked in the direction of the vase. 'You're a clever girl.'

Briar's mother glared at her.

'I beg you, madam, not to scold her. The fault is mine alone. Your daughter only sought to help me.'

The woman seemed to notice me properly for the first time. 'That's as maybe,' she said narrowing her dark green eyes. 'Anyway, who are you and what are you doing with my daughter?'

Before I could respond, she turned her attention to Briar. 'Have you been out all night?' Then back at me. 'Surely you're aware of the consequences if you were discovered roaming the streets after curfew?'

I had not been aware but was loath to antagonise the woman further by admitting as much. 'I—'

'Mum, calm down.' Briar stood up and brushed the mixture she had picked up from the floor into the bowl, which her mother had retrieved. 'Do you want a passing patrol to hear you?'

This warning silenced her mother. She shook her head. 'Of course I don't. How do you expect me to react when you do exactly as I asked you not to? I've been beside myself with worry. Frantic.'

Briar stepped forward and drew her mother into a loose hug, taking care not to spill more of the precious mixture. 'Sorry, Mum, I hadn't meant to upset you.'

The woman seemed to calm slightly. While they hugged, I took a moment to look about me. I was in a small, low-ceilinged cottage, lit by the glimmer of a fire in its small hearth, with bunches of drying herbs tied with twine hanging from small hooks dotted along the mantle. There was a pine table, four chairs and what appeared to be a well-padded seat I would give anything to collapse into, succumbing to the tiredness that suddenly seemed to sweep over me.

'This is my mother, Diana Le Gros,' Briar said. I looked over at the women and saw Briar's mother staring at me, her face ashen and eyes narrowed in suspicion. Not that I blamed her for being unsure of me. I pictured my attire and dishevelled appearance. I too would be unhappy should a stranger in my state burst into my home with my precious daughter. Diana studied me and didn't hide how unimpressed she felt. 'Mum, this is Xavier Givroye.'

Diana didn't react immediately but turned her back on me and set the bowl on a windowsill, I presumed to do something as she gathered her thoughts. She then began tidying a nearby table of small bottles that looked as if they contained tinctures.

Eventually she addressed Briar. 'Why is he dressed that way?' Her voice was quiet but loud enough for me to hear.

Why my clothing was more disconcerting to this woman than my unexpectedly accompanying her daughter I could not fathom. Did she not wonder why Briar had brought me to their home?

'I'll explain everything in a bit, Mum.' Briar took off her jacket and hung it on a hook from the mantelpiece although there was little heat emanating from the barely glowing embers in the grate. 'Xavier and I bumped into each other at Mont Orgueil.'

'What were you doing up there?' Her mother's expression darkened and all at once she appeared to waken from her strange stupor. 'You do realise how dangerous it was to go there?'

'Yes, I do. I'm sorry.'

'Sorry?' She shook her head rapidly, clearly beside herself. 'I had imagined you locked in a cell somewhere by now. Or worse—' Her voice broke, and she glared at me. I dared not speak for fear of upsetting her further.

She walked over to the dining table and pulled out a chair. I watched as she slumped onto it. Should I perhaps leave them to their privacy? Unsure where to go, I decided to await instruction from either of them. She wiped her eyes with the back of her fingers and motioned for me to join her at the table. Grateful to finally be seated, I did as she asked.

'Would you like some tea?' Mrs Le Gros asked wearily. 'It's camomile.'

'Tea?' I asked, unsure what she meant.

'A tisane. Um, an herbal infusion,' Briar said helpfully. I hadn't noticed her leave the room, but as my mouth was dry, and I assumed the three cups Briar was carrying to the table were to be used for the drink, I nodded gratefully.

'You are both too kind.'

'If you are caught here,' Mrs Le Gros said as Briar busied herself moving the pot slowly, her eyes shifting to the front door before returning to me, 'we should probably act as if we know each other.' She waited for Briar to serve the dark yellow liquid.

I was about to reply that I hoped I wouldn't be here long enough to come across many people, when Mrs Le Gros continued, 'You should both change out of those wet clothes. And the sooner the better if you don't wish to catch a chill.'

Reminded of my wet state and concerned for the state of their chairs, I stood abruptly, almost knocking Briar's arm.

Mrs Le Gros sighed. 'The chairs are wooden, they'll be fine. Briar will find some of my late husband's clothes for you to wear until yours have … dried.' She shook her head slowly. I wasn't sure if it was because she was still trying to come to terms with my appearance in her home, or if the thought of parting with her late husband's clothes to someone she didn't know or trust explained her reaction. 'Although I'm not sure you should wear yours again. You won't blend in with the locals wearing what you have on now.'

I was growing weary of the insults being thrown at my attire, then reasoned she had a point. 'I appreciate your kindness, madam.'

'Please, call me Diana. If we are seen it will be better if people assume we are well acquainted. Safer too. First, though,' she added, 'Briar will fetch a towel for each of you. Once you have dried off you can both drink your tea and tell me why you've been out all night.'

Briar disappeared for a moment then returned with two pieces of rough-looking fabric that I presumed were the towels. She handed one to me and I was surprised to discover the fabric was soft and how efficiently it absorbed the water from my skin.

Briar explained how I had unexpectedly appeared behind her. Mesmerised by the steam rising from the hot drink, I wondered what was to become of me and hoped my presence would not cause trouble for Briar and her mother. Needing an explanation for my hostess, I attempted to find a way to explain my situation.

'Mistress, I am at a loss to explain my presence.' I shook my head and, indicating my clothing, added, 'Despite my dishevelled appearance, I assure you I am a man to be trusted.'

She stared into my eyes with such intensity, I felt as if her gaze was boring into my very soul. I had to force myself not to divert my eyes, certain that to do so might confirm her suspicions of me. I was holding many secrets, most not suitable for ladies' ears, and was concerned that her study of me should not alert her to any of them.

'I understand how disconcerting it must be for you to have a stranger arrive with your daughter,' I continued in an attempt to distract her. When she didn't respond, I wondered how I might define my travel through time. How could anyone explain away the unexplainable?

I decided to try and change the subject once again, to one more familiar to her. 'May I ask what was in the spilt mixture?' I suspected I was testing her patience and risked being thrown out but if she was a witch then I needed to know if that meant Briar was also. I had never knowingly spent a night in a witch's home and wasn't sure how much safer I would be here than elsewhere.

Her gaze became steely. 'Why would you ask such a question?'

'My apologies, Mrs Le Gros, I did not mean to offend.'

'Whether you meant to or not, Mr Giv-, Giv—'

'Givroye, madam.'

'Don't you know it's rude to poke your nose in another person's business? Especially at times like these?'

I sensed her fear and it dawned on me what she had been doing. 'You were casting a spell?' I whispered without thinking.

I heard a gasp from the doorway.

'Why would you ask my mother such a question?' Briar snapped. Something that appeared to be an undergarment dropped from the mound of clothes in her arms.

I realised my mistake. Witches had powers I didn't understand. I thought of Old Mother Dorey and her ability to send Briar forward three hundred years. I had been foolish to ask such a thing. I knew well enough how dangerous it was to accuse someone of sorcery.

'My apologies. I didn't think.' Desperate to explain myself further, I added, 'You told me this was a different time to mine, Briar. I'm unsure why but I had assumed witch hunts no longer existed here.'

Diana's gaze shifted to her daughter. 'Briar?' Diana's voice was tight, her right hand resting on her neck. 'Why did you bring this man with you?'

I caught the look of anger in Briar's eyes and could tell she was wondering the same thing.

'I'm sorry,' I said quickly, concerned about the damage they could do should they choose to use their magick on me. 'I did not mean to frighten you or offend in any way.' I shook my head. 'My only defence is that I have not slept for a couple of days and maybe my mind isn't working as it should be.'

They both stared at me. Then it dawned on me. They weren't horrified because I had mentioned a spell; they reacted that way because I had been right.

'You are witches.' It wasn't a question and neither took it as one.

Nor did they answer me. 'I think you had better change now,' Briar said wearily.

'Thank you.' A thought occurred to me. 'I must retain my

clothing for when I return to my own time,' I said, catching Diana giving me a doubtful look.

An ache filled my belly at the thought that I might never find a way to return home. Then again, I reasoned, would that be such a terrible thing if it meant I spent the rest of my life alongside Briar? The happiness that thought brought me soon vanished when I saw the way she looked at me. There was no love in her eyes for me now.

Briar indicated the clothes she had laid on a chair next to me. 'Here are some of my father's things. There's a shirt, trousers,' she said, holding each item up before draping it over the back of the chair. 'This is one of his jackets, and I thought you would need socks.' Her face reddened but he wasn't sure why.

'Socks?'

'For your feet.' She held up two woollen items. I watched as she pointed to a pair of uncomfortable-looking shoes.

'They might not fit, but they'll be far less conspicuous than your boots.'

I studied my beloved footwear. We had been through much together. They were scratched, muddy and rather worn but after years of use extremely comfortable. I would miss wearing them. However, I knew she was right. I needed to push aside sentiment and learn to wear the correct clothing for the time being.

'I am in your debt.' I was. These two women, whom until an hour ago I had never met, at least as far as they were concerned, were now doing their best to help me survive.

'Mum,' Briar said waving her mother to her. 'Shall we go to the scullery for a few minutes to give Xavier some privacy?'

I realised Diana Le Gros had not averted her gaze from me.

She still seemed offended by what I had said, and I didn't blame her.

'Hmm. I suppose it's only proper we should.' She raised a finger. 'I don't know who you really are, but if you think for one minute I won't notice if you steal something, then you'd be wrong. Any nonsense from you and I'll be calling out to alert the patrol. Understand?'

I pressed my right hand over my heart. 'I swear to you I am no thief and would never repay your hospitality by stealing from you.'

'I should think not.'

'Mum, come along.' I heard tiredness in Briar's voice and guilt coursed through me. The sooner I found a way to return to my own time the better for everyone's sake. 'I'm sure Xavier is as shocked by his being here as we are.'

I waited for them to leave the room, then exhaled. If this was a nightmare, I prayed something might wake me from it. And soon.

Chapter Six

BRIAR

'Pass me my boline,' Mum said with a nod to her right.

I looked around for the white-handled knife she kept especially for cutting herbs. I had also observed her carving symbols with it when she was preparing her space to cast a spell. Spotting it tucked slightly behind the enamel bread bin I picked it up and held it out to her.

'Thanks for sending Pippin,' I whispered.

'Was she helpful?'

I nodded.

'What's going on?' Mum asked, almost snatching it from me. 'Who the devil is that man anyway?' I took a breath to answer but she wagged a finger in front of my face. 'And why in heaven's name did you think bringing him here was a clever idea? And don't think I've forgotten about you missing curfew, young lady,' she added before I had a chance to respond. I wasn't sure what question to address first. Mum lowered her hand. I had little choice but to be honest.

'This is going to sound far-fetched,' I began nervously.

'Firstly, I'm truly sorry I forgot the time and was late coming home, but I was on my way back from visiting Clara when I was spotted by a soldier.'

'You must have been out after curfew for that to matter.' Mum shook her head in frustration. 'Silly girl. Go on.'

'I spotted a tumbledown ruin at the back of the castle and ran to hide in there. That's where I met Xavier.'

'He was hiding too?'

I shrugged. 'That's the thing. When I was first in there, I was certain I was alone. And as far as he's concerned so was he. One minute he was by himself in a cell in the castle dungeons, the next he was standing in the ruin behind me.'

I decided to leave out about Xavier being there because he was awaiting execution. The last thing I needed to do was confirm her suspicions about him being dangerous. I couldn't possibly know for sure, but I sensed there was something trustworthy about him. Or was it simply that I wanted to feel that way? I wasn't sure, but it was too late to worry about that now he was in her home. Ordinarily I would never lie to Mum, but for some reason I felt compelled to help him, although for the life of me I wasn't sure why.

'Cell?' She glanced at the partly open door to the living room and lowered her voice. 'How did you manage to help him escape from a locked cell?' she groaned. Taking a few pieces of lavender, she pinched off the flowers and set them to one side, then began cutting the stems into short pieces. 'You're not making much sense.'

Typical of Mum to pick up on the one word I shouldn't have used. I cringed inwardly at not taking more care when I was speaking. 'That's the thing. The cell was the same ruin I was sheltering in from the storm.'

'And hiding from the soldiers,' Mum added, one eyebrow raised reminding me she still hadn't forgotten about me being out after curfew. She shook her head and closed her eyes wearily. 'You're telling me you believe he travelled through time?'

I sighed. 'I can't think of any other explanation. His clothes, his genuine bewilderment. He told me the year was 1643, but it's not, is it? It's 1943?'

I waited for her to speak but she just stared at me blankly. A look of – what? She had an odd expression on her face. One I hadn't seen before. It wasn't disbelief, it was more a dawning of some kind. I had no idea why that might be and didn't dare annoy her further by asking.

'I know this sounds far-fetched, but if you had seen the shock on his face when he saw me, you'd believe him too. I mean who in their right mind would go around in those breeches – and that weird jacket? Especially now.'

Mum nodded. 'That's true. Perhaps he is telling the truth,' she said, softening. 'And perhaps he has somehow come here from the past.'

Wanting to make the most of her lack of argument, I quickly said, 'Which is why I brought him here. I thought if anyone could help him return to his time, then you could do it. You and your coven.'

She stopped what she was doing and stared at me again.

'I see. So after insisting you have no wish to join us you now want to call on our help?'

I shifted my gaze guiltily. 'Yes, I suppose I do.'

She frowned.

'Briar, you know how depleted the coven has been since seven of us were evacuated with their families just before the invasion.' I did. 'We need you now more than ever. I think it's about time you accepted your place with us, don't you? You know it's what your grandmother would have wanted for you above anything else.'

I wasn't surprised she was using this opportunity to attempt to persuade me. I loved my grandmother deeply and still missed her even though she had died almost a decade before. I thought of my familiar Pippin whom I adored and inherited from her. I always felt safer knowing Pippin was nearby, watching out for me. It was almost like having my grandmother watching over me still.

I had known I was on borrowed time when I initially rejected Mum's invitation to join her and her friends, three years before when I was eighteen.

Mum was right; I should do my bit if I was to expect these women to help Xavier, but surely I needed to immerse myself entirely in magickal practices if I wanted to accept my heritage and be initiated as a witch?

'I'm sorry, Mum,' I said, wishing I felt able to do as she asked. 'I know my reluctance pains you but you and Gran always said you couldn't partially be a witch. I need to be completely sure before I agree to my initiation.'

Mum gave a resigned sigh. 'Yes, that's true and you must do what's right for you,' she said eventually. 'You might not be ready but there's no harm in continuing to learn about our practice.' She pointed to the rosemary, half of it chopped, the other placed in a small bag. 'I want you to tell me what you think I prepared this for?'

I didn't even need to think before replying. 'The chopped rosemary you'll burn and the small bag containing the rest will be hung above the door.'

She gave a satisfied nod. 'And why would I do that?'

'For protection.' I sighed, understanding why. 'It's because of Xavier, isn't it?'

'It is.'

Needing to know what she intended to do about helping him, I said, 'Will you go and speak to the coven yet? Or should I take a message for you?'

'I need to think.' She frowned and stared out of the kitchen window at her herb garden, where Tula still sat near the small pond. Mum loved the warty toad. She was typical of those seen in children's storybooks but most people seemed repelled and tended to stay away from her.

Neither of our familiars was at risk of being eaten by the Nazis, which was a relief. And I reckoned that even though food was becoming scarcer by the month, no one else would bother trying to steal them, as toads and bats were hardly appealing as a meal.

'I've never tried to send a man back three hundred years, Briar,' Mum said thoughtfully. 'If I could work out how to do that, I'd send these damn Nazis back three years across the channel.'

Mum had a point. I had seen her do many things others would find suspicious, like healing a neighbour's lingering ulcer, or growing herbs and vegetables in our small garden when others' produce failed. I knew she kept much of her magick from me, working her more complex spells in secret because I hadn't yet been initiated.

'If you can't help him, what will we do? We barely have food for ourselves, and it'll take no time at all before one of the locals notices there's someone new in the village.' I thought of

Hauptmann Klein, avidly watching our home, far too much for my liking.

Mum said, reading my thoughts, 'It doesn't help that that German officer seems to be lurking near this house so often.'

'I agree. We can't leave Xavier to his own devices, not with soldiers on every street corner. He doesn't have anywhere else to go, though, or'—I thought with a sudden dash of sadness— 'anyone else to turn to for help.' It saddened me that everyone he knew was long dead.

'We'll think of something,' Mum said, putting her arm around me and giving me a hug. 'I'm sorry if I've been harsh, but you've had a nasty shock what with one thing and another.'

I felt guilty. If only I had done as I was supposed to and returned home on time, but then Xavier would have stepped out of that ruin and been arrested, or worse.

'Whatever we think of this situation, I believe I was meant to find him before the Nazis did.'

Mum thought for a minute, then nodded. 'I believe you're right.'

'Thanks, Mum. I know you'll do all you can for him and I know you can work your magick and send him back to where he should be.'

Mum tutted. 'You have more faith in my abilities than I probably deserve. I'll do my best to find a way to make it happen. Until then, we must keep him inside the cottage, away from prying eyes.'

'You're going to help me?' Xavier asked from the doorway, making us both jump. 'You are gracious ladies indeed.'

Mum folded her arms as she turned to face him. 'I don't know how much you overheard, but I only agreed to try.' She shook her head. 'Right now, though, I have no idea how to do it, or if it's even possible—'

'It is. I assure you.'

I couldn't understand his certainty, or why he looked at me as he spoke, especially as Mum was the one he was responding to. And why didn't she meet my gaze when I looked at her? I turned back to Xavier and saw him staring at me intently, as if waiting for me to understand something, or... I shook my head, certain my tiredness was giving me fanciful thoughts. 'You must promise to stay out of sight.'

He gave me that disappointed look again.

He bowed, then, straightening, he looked at each of us in turn. 'I meant only that if I came here, there must be a way for me to return.'

I heard the determination in his voice and suspected he was trying to be brave. He was from a different time, after all, and who knew how people dealt with difficulties back then?

'It makes sense that there should be a way,' I agreed.

Mum turned back to her work and finished filling the small bag. She tied it neatly with some garden twine, careful to make a loop. 'Let's hope you're both right.' She indicated our almost bare pantry. 'We have little food as it is,' she said, passing him as he moved out of her way. We followed her to the living room. 'Briar and I will share what food we have with you.'

She lifted the small bag and hung it on a nail above the front door.

Xavier frowned. 'I—'

She shook her head. 'No need for gratitude, just please do as we ask. You're unused to the Nazi regime currently in charge of the island. We might not like it but we have had time to become used to their rules and ways of doing things.

There are many regulations we must abide by and these change often and with little notice. The most important thing you must do is remain hidden. If, for any reason, you do venture outside with one of us, you must be as inconspicuous as possible. With everyone's suspicions as high as they are now, it is difficult to know which locals to trust. If we were caught harbouring you, we would risk being imprisoned or deported to the Continent.' She shivered. 'And neither Briar nor I would want that.'

'I understand. I shall do as you wish.'

I caught Mum's side-eyed glance in my direction and knew that if there was any way Diana Le Gros could cast a spell to send Xavier back to 1643, then she would find it. And it couldn't happen soon enough, as far as I was concerned. If I had thought our lives in danger before this evening, then coming across Xavier had made our chances of surviving this war a hundred times more difficult than they had ever been.

Chapter Seven

DIANA

Later that evening, I tried to make myself comfortable in bed, exhausted after all that had happened. I reminded myself how much I loved my daughter more than life itself.

She was right to save Xavier's life, and I had to admit to myself that I would have done the same thing. There was something about the way he looked at her, though, and the undercurrent of sadness that seemed to encompass him. I couldn't help wondering whether he had anything to do with her disappearance for those six weeks while I had been on the mainland visiting friends, several months before the island was invaded. I had only discovered she was missing when one of my neighbours asked whether Briar and I had enjoyed our trip away. I had asked Briar about it but she insisted she had no idea why the neighbour would say such a thing, and in the end I had given up questioning her and pushed the incident from my mind, trusting my daughter and knowing that if she had had an answer she would have given it to me. Since then,

I had been alert to any danger as I struggled to keep her safe, fed and warm.

Her denial made more sense now, though. Had something happened to her, like it had to Xavier? Had she slipped back in time? As odd as this situation was, I couldn't shift the feeling that Xavier had been sent here for a reason. And despite not knowing why, Briar's senses had told her that she needed to rescue him and bring him to our home. Could he be here as some sort of warning to us? A message from our ancestors? Was he a protector we hadn't known we needed? The thought intrigued me.

If Xavier had travelled forward three hundred years – and going by his clothes, hair and the way he spoke I had little reason to disbelieve him – then I wondered if he was the first time traveller I had met. Whoever he was, I had to be vigilant until I knew him better. I certainly needed to understand more about this strange, charismatic man I was harbouring in my home.

I thought back to my childhood, when my older brother sat on the end of my bed each night before I slept, reading excerpts to me from his favourite book, *The Time Traveller*. How I missed him. My throat constricted at the memory of happy times with him, always feeling safe when he was around. He had been such a kindly man.

He succumbed to ill health in his early twenties. A weak heart, our family doctor had said. I still recall the physical pain in my own heart when I heard the shocking news that he didn't have long to live. I missed him still, even though he had been gone almost ten years now. My one consolation was at least he hadn't lived to witness what the Nazis were doing to our beloved island.

I wiped my eyes with the backs of my fingers and punched my pillow several times to try and make it more comfortable. Our guest was asleep downstairs on the sofa, and I hoped Briar was asleep in the bedroom next to mine. I lay back and gazed at the ceiling. It was too dark to see clearly but the darkness made the perfect canvas for me to picture the fear on my daughter's face when she and Xavier had burst into the cottage.

I closed my eyes, willing sleep to find me, and soon. I needed to find a way to help Xavier, and in turn free my daughter and myself from the responsibility of caring for him.

Right now, though, I needed to plan the best way to untangle this mess we had inadvertently found ourselves in. I had no idea how. I hoped my dreams might find the answers.

Chapter Eight

BRIAR

I woke after a restless night's sleep feeling more exhausted than when I had gone to bed. Nonsensical dreams of time machines and monsters had kept my mind busy. I presumed the monsters represented the German soldiers. At least that's what I hoped. The thought of them being a sign of something even worse was too terrifying.

Could my dreams be my subconscious trying to warn me about Xavier? No, if I were to help him then I needed to trust him, to a certain extent at least.

I tried to work out what it was about Xavier that drew me to him. The strange thing was that it wasn't simply an attraction but something deeper, something I didn't understand. I pictured his dark blue eyes, the colour of deep sea, and his dark wavy hair reaching almost to his shoulders. My stomach did a somersault as I recalled how it had felt to have my hand in his and how taut and muscled his chest had been when he slammed into the back of me.

It dawned on me now that although I had been the one to

rescue him, I'd sensed for some reason that he had come here to protect me. From what, I couldn't fathom. Mum and I had looked out for each other well enough since the island's invasion and we were used to no longer having a man about the house for protection, so it was doubly strange that I picked up this energy from Xavier.

I stopped thinking about it. There was more to Xavier than I knew, and right now all I needed to focus on was helping Mum to help him.

Hearing movement downstairs, I wondered if Mum was already up. Not wishing her to be left to look after Xavier when I had been the one to invite him into our home, I washed, dressed and went downstairs.

Xavier was standing with his back to the tiny fire even though he couldn't have felt much heat coming from it. His face was pale, and he looked as if he had been awake all night – which wouldn't have been surprising after all he had experienced the evening before.

'Did you sleep at all?' I asked him.

He shrugged and gave me a weak smile. 'A little. Did you?'

'The same.'

'Your mother is in there.' He indicated the kitchen, and I went to see if there was anything I could do to help her.

'Morning, Mum. How are you today?'

She stilled, then looked over her shoulder at me. 'As well as can be expected,' she said, 'with all that's happened.'

I wondered if she had come up with a solution for how to help Xavier but didn't like to ask. Not before she'd had her morning tea.

'I've made us all mint tea,' she said. 'There's still a little mint in the garden. It's all we have, apart from a small amount of bread each, but it'll have to do.'

'I'm sure Xavier will be grateful for whatever we can spare him.'

A cough behind me alerted me to his presence in the kitchen doorway.

'I am beholden to you both for the kindness you have already bestowed upon me,' he said.

'We're only doing what anyone else would do in our place.'

He gave me a look that suggested he wasn't convinced.

I served out our meagre breakfast before taking a seat. Mum and I watched as he drank the tepid tea.

'It is pleasant,' he said thoughtfully, and I wondered whether he might have ever tried mint tea before.

Mum took a sip of her tea before placing her cup on the table. 'I've been giving your problem some thought, Xavier,' she began, sending my hopes rising. 'I told Briar I'll do all I can to help you, but I'm presently at a loss about how to do that.'

He looked as disappointed as I felt.

'You don't think your, er, friends in your group might be willing to help?' I asked tentatively, making sure not to mention the words 'witch' or 'coven'. I knew I was labouring the point and that if Mum felt this was something she could approach them about, she would do so. Yet, for some reason I couldn't fathom, she seemed unwilling to take that step.

'The thing is, my friends more than likely would help, but —' She gave Xavier an apologetic look. 'I don't mean to offend you, but the reason I don't want to go to them just yet is because I don't know you.'

'I understand,' Xavier said.

'I appreciate that.' She shifted slightly in her chair.

There was something else troubling her. 'What is it, Mum?'

She stared at me, frowned, then looked down at her hands clasping her teacup.

'If I might interject,' Xavier said quietly. 'Is it that you are embarrassed to tell them about my presence and how I came to be here, in case they do not believe you?'

I watched Mum consider his question. 'Yes, that, too, I suppose.' She gave me a bemused look. 'And the questions people will ask.'

'You mean people wondering who he is and where he's come from?'

She nodded. 'Yes.'

Xavier looked from me to Mum. 'I assure you I will take the utmost care when venturing outside.'

'I'm afraid that won't be enough.' Mum sounded adamant. 'Xavier, you have no idea how careful you must be. These are treacherous times. People who were friends before the war are now suspicious of each other. We wouldn't simply be thrown in jail if you were discovered here. You don't have identity papers. There's no one other than us to vouch for you, and if you were caught the authorities would assume you were a spy.' She shook her head. 'No, there's no way around this, Xavier. You'll simply have to stay indoors at all times.'

His eyes widened. I couldn't blame him for not liking the idea. This was a small cottage and who knew how long he would need to remain here out of sight?

Nonetheless, I had to support Mum on the matter. 'It's true,' I agreed. 'We've heard rumours about people writing to the German authorities tipping them off about other locals hiding radios or breaking other regulations simply because of some minor disagreement they might have had before the Occupation. It's horrible.'

'It is.' Mum sighed, clearly deeply saddened by this dreadful turn of events. 'We have to watch every word we say outside this house, or even in the garden, in case we're overheard by a passerby. Some people, not many, I must add, but a miserable few are acting out of character, probably through fear. But their actions are hurting those they betray. My heart breaks more each time I hear another story.'

I didn't want Mum upsetting herself and patted her hand lightly. 'It'll be fine, Mum,' I assured her.

'I hope you're right,' Mum said. 'We are all frightened and worried about who's watching us.' She looked at the two of us before continuing. 'Gossip is rife, especially among the locals. No one wants to be caught doing anything they shouldn't. The repercussions if I'm discovered out after curfew, let alone in the woods with my friends, would be horrendous.'

'You mean being sent to prison?' I asked.

Mum didn't answer straightaway, and Xavier spoke instead. 'Worse?' He glanced at me, his dark blue eyes sad. My sympathy for him increased momentarily. Poor Xavier, I thought sympathetically, he had arrived here and swapped one threat for another.

'I can't take the chance of Briar or me being sent to one of the camps in Germany,' Mum explained. 'It's hard enough having these men on our doorstep, and'—she groaned—'in some cases, having our homes requisitioned for the officers to live in.' Xavier sat in silence as she spoke. 'Thankfully our cottage isn't much to look at and as it's tiny it's easily hidden in this village. We've yet to draw attention from the authorities, and I'd like to keep it that way for as long as possible.' She gave Xavier a worried smile.

'I understand. The locals must be fearful,' Xavier murmured.

'They are.' Mum drank more of her tea. 'There is also the fact that one of my friends in the, er, group is married to a man who has no choice but to speak with senior German personnel almost every day because of his position on the island. I've always thought of him as a good man, and'—she raised a hand —'I have no reason to think otherwise, but since the invasion he has less power, and if we were caught doing anything there would be little he could do to help us.

'I'm going to need more time, Xavier,' she said thoughtfully.

'We don't have much time, though, Mum,' I reminded her. Xavier gave me a grateful look, clearly desperate to return to the life he knew and get away from all the strangeness he must be feeling now.

Mum's cheeks reddened and I could tell I'd annoyed her. 'I'm well aware of that, Briar.'

Chapter Nine

XAVIER

I paced back and forth in the kitchen. I had been ensconced inside the cottage for three days and although it was a quaint home, and the company pleasant, it wasn't easy to be around Briar and have to behave as though I hadn't once known her intimately. I needed to get out, if only for a few hours.

'Whatever's the matter?' Briar's voice sounded behind me as she entered the kitchen.

I hadn't heard her come in and I felt my cheeks heat at being discovered acting in an agitated fashion. There was no point in denying how I felt. 'I must go outside.' When she didn't immediately argue I continued, 'I could help with your deliveries perhaps?'

Briar sighed. 'I know being cooped up in here day and night must be a struggle for you, Xavier, but you heard what Mum said. It's just not safe for you to be seen out. I'm sorry.'

'I have the correct attire now. Surely, I will not be noticed?'

She shook her head. 'No, it's too dangerous, and not just for you.'

I recalled what Diana had said and realised how selfish I was being. 'I understand. It's wrong of me to make a fuss, and be ungrateful.'

She watched me thoughtfully. 'If Mum can help you return home, then this might not last too long.' She walked over to her jacket which was hanging on a hook by the door, took something out and brought it to me.

'Anyway, you'd need one of these.'

I stared at the folded thick paper in her hand, unsure what I was looking at. 'What is this?'

'An Occupation Identity card,' she said. 'Everyone on the island has to be registered and carry one at all times.'

I took it from her and studied it. There was writing, but in the top right-hand corner I saw a likeness of her more exact than any portrait I had ever seen and peered closer at it, fascinated. 'How is this achieved, this portrait?'

'With a camera.' She shook her head. 'I don't have one anymore, not since they were banned. I'm not really sure about the science behind taking and developing a photograph or how to explain what one is.'

'A photograph,' I echoed. 'What a strange word.'

I handed her back her card, bemused yet again by the newness of all these things I was discovering.

She put the identity card back into her jacket pocket. 'I've been thinking. You might not be able to go away from the cottage, but as long as we don't speak loud enough for anyone passing to hear you, I'm sure it'll be all right if we spend time in the garden. The granite walls and hedging keep it sheltered from passersby.'

'I'd like that,' I said, my mood lifting at the thought.

Briar smiled. 'And I'll find ways to keep you busier while you're inside, too.'

'That is kind of you.' It had been impolite of me to behave ungratefully towards Briar, especially after all she and Diana had done for me.

Outside the back door of the cottage, Briar took a straw hat and placed it on her head. 'Do you want me to go and find one for you?'

I almost laughed, then remembered she recalled nothing about my life, so I stopped myself. 'I don't, thank you.' When she seemed doubtful, I added. 'I've been at sea for several years and am accustomed to being out in the sun without shade.' I indicated my swarthy complexion. 'As you can see.' I smiled to ensure my meaning was understood.

Her eyes lowered briefly as though she was embarrassed.

'You cannot offend me, Briar. I am used to spending most of my life surrounded by uncouth men, and—' I stopped, not wishing to mention Ember.

Briar frowned suspiciously. 'Would I be right in thinking you were going to mention a woman?'

I nodded. 'I was.'

She didn't speak for a moment. 'Your wife?' Her look was one of concern.

Thinking she thought that there was a woman back in my time, I shook my head. 'I am not married.' I smiled to lighten the mood. 'It would not be fair for me to take a wife when I spend most of my life away from home. Spent,' I corrected myself. Those days were behind me, at least for now.

The moment passed and Briar reached out to a selection of gardening tools leaning against the wall. She picked up a trowel and handed it to me. I felt the now-familiar ache of knowing she did not remember me. Hoping for a sign that she did remember me, at least in some small way.

'It's probably just as well then,' she said, walking over to a small makeshift structure that seemed to pass for a greenhouse and taking up two small trays of seedlings. 'You plant those over there.' She indicated an area in the vegetable garden to my right and handed me one of the trays. 'They're carrot seedlings. I'll plant these beans against the wall by the netting.'

I watched her push the trowel into the soft earth, making a space for the first seedling. She looked over her shoulder at me. 'If you did have a wife she would only be concerned for you and wondering where you were.'

Is that how Briar would feel for her husband? I supposed so. I thought how joyful it had been between the two of us back then, and my heart ached. I missed that time with Briar when she loved me deeply. Before Old Mother Dorey had cast a spell to send her forward to her own time to escape the clutches of that madman, Roger Dankworth. I clenched my jaw at the memory when the Witchfinder had discovered the woman I loved.

'Xavier?' I heard Briar saying my name and saw she was staring at me. 'What's wrong?'

I must have seemed pensive, which wasn't surprising when I had been thinking of all I had lost. Losing Briar three years ago had been agony, and every day since I had missed her. Being close to her now and unable to show the depth of my feelings for her was so much worse.

'I'm sorry,' I said, forcing my mind back to the present. 'I was lost in thought, nothing more.'

She rested a hand on my arm. 'Perhaps being outside has

not been such a good idea. Shall we go back inside and fetch a drink?'

I had no wish to return to the small living room. 'No, I'm happy out here,' I insisted. Suspecting Briar might need to be reassured, I added. 'I was thinking of my family.'

'Of course. You miss them.'

I nodded. 'I do. Although my parents are no longer alive. I only have my sister and my aunt, who took my sister in. I often stay with them when I'm on the island.'

Briar seemed content to know I had family who cared about me. 'They must be worried about where you are.'

I shook my head. 'I have escaped my death sentence. They will assume I have sailed elsewhere and will be glad of it.'

'Yes, I suppose they will.' She looked down at the seedlings.

'Let us continue working out here,' I suggested, keen to change the subject.

'All right,' she said, smiling. 'Let's do that.'

As we continued planting, I asked, 'May I enquire what you plan to do once this war is over?'

She gave an amused laugh. 'If it ever is.' She grinned wryly at me. 'No, I must be more optimistic. *When* the war is over.'

I wondered whether she would remain on the island, but supposed that unless she married a man from another place, she would have no reason to leave.

Briar planted the next seedling as she considered her response. 'I don't want to marry and settle down to have children,' she said eventually. 'I want freedom to travel and see other parts of the world.' She sighed. 'If there's much left of it worth visiting.'

I frowned, hoping that Briar's low spirits were not due to my reminiscing about my family. 'There have always been wars,' I said, 'and countries usually find ways to rebuild when peace comes. Hopefully that will be the case after this one and you will be able to travel as you wish.' *Preferably with me*, I thought but didn't dare add.

'Hopefully, yes,' she said, a gleam in her eyes. 'How about you? You said you were a privateer. I always thought that was the same as a pirate. I don't mean to be offensive, if what I'm saying is insulting in any way.'

'It is not,' I said, smiling to reassure her. I had my own vessel. It wasn't a large one but with all the piracy in the channel, the Governor of the island called for men with military expertise to offer their services. I had been a soldier in the army for a few years and, with my sailing experience, I decided I was well placed to earn a living by helping the island. It was dangerous much of the time but I enjoyed the excitement.'

'You must miss it being stuck here then?'

I took a moment to reply. I did miss it, but 'being stuck here' was not entirely miserable either. 'Somewhat,' I said. 'I will try and make the best of my situation.'

'That's very stoic,' Briar said. 'Wartime spirit, and all that.' She laughed, and it felt like music, uplifting and joyful. I looked down at the ground to hide my delight.

She finished planting the last seedling in her tray, stood up and turned to me. 'May I ask why you ended up in a cell about to be executed?'

I groaned. 'An interaction between my vessel and another, which I was certain was crewed by pirates, went awry. The captain, although acting illegally, was well-connected. Before I had a chance to report him, he sent word lying that I had been the one practising piracy and insisted I was using my position as a privateer to cover my illegal antics. He somehow managed to arrange for liquor to be hidden on my boat. Government inspectors came on board to search my vessel, while I watched them, amused at the waste of their time. As you can imagine, I was shocked to my core to see what they discovered.'

She gasped. 'But that's horrendous.'

I sighed, the pain still raw. 'It was. I was arrested, accused of betraying the island of Jersey and sentenced to hang.'

She shook her head slowly. 'Oh, Xavier, you poor thing.'

Not wishing her to feel pity for me, I shrugged. 'Not so. I am here with you, am I not? In this beautiful little garden, working in the sunshine. I am far better off than I could have been.'

Over the next few weeks we often worked side by side in the small garden, enjoying cold drinks when the weather allowed, and I became used to the restrictions that were now part of my life. I was with Briar. We exchanged memories of our lives, even though it again pained me that she recalled nothing of those sweet, precious weeks we had shared, back in my time.

'When this is over,' Briar said one day, 'I will show you every inch of this beautiful island and you can tell me how different it is from your time.'

'I'd like that very much.'

Chapter Ten

XAVIER

As time went on, I wondered if Briar would ever know how much I looked forward to being out of this cottage and alone with her.

Meeting her for the first time had felt much like being hit by a bolt from heaven. She was the most beautiful woman I had ever seen. I still felt the same powerful pull towards her. Only this time I had no choice but to restrain my emotions so that she would not feel uncomfortable around me.

When she wasn't out making deliveries, or foraging for Diana, I would gaze at her as she snipped away at some mint Diana had asked her to fetch, wondering how long I could cope with my tormented thoughts. Was it possible for Briar to feel nothing for me, yet have loved me the last time we were together? I had not changed; at least I didn't think I had. Perhaps her experiences of the past three years living under Nazi rule had changed how she trusted others?

'What's wrong?' she asked when we were outside in the garden.

I hadn't realised she was watching me. I tried to find an excuse for my introspection. 'I was thinking about my home,' I lied.

She took the few steps over to me and rested a hand on my forearm. Her eyes lowered to her hand, then rose to meet mine. 'It must be hard not to be with those you love.'

I had to avoid looking into her eyes to reply. 'It is. I miss my family and closest friend Andre, but as I have said before they will rejoice at my not having been put to death.'

'That's a good point.' She put the small bunch of mint in the trug she had placed on the low wall. 'Being a privateer must be a dangerous profession.'

'There is a chance of being injured or killed whenever we're at sea and challenging another vessel.' Seeing the look of shock on her face, I added, 'I am always armed, though, and able to defend myself.'

'Doesn't it worry you that you could be hurt?'

I leant against the back wall of the cottage. 'Not really.'

'No?'

I tried to put my daily life into some context for her and thought about how hers must be, with the Nazi soldiers running the island. 'No more dangerous, probably, than it is for you and your mother here since the invasion.'

She sighed. 'I suppose not. Do you miss your work?'

I nodded. 'I miss the excitement of confronting other vessels and not knowing what will happen when we try to take over. Some pirates are extremely well armed and fight back with great expertise.' I recalled the sensation when every nerve in my body had come alive at the thrill of combat. 'I miss being useful.'

'I imagine you must do.' She sat, patting the space next to

her on the low wall. 'Please tell me about your friend Andre. Is he a privateer like you?'

I nodded. 'He was for a while. Andre has more sense than to continue going to sea as I did. He prefers working on dry land as a stonemason, like his father before him.'

Briar crossed one leg over the other and leant forward, her hands clasped around one knee. 'Is he like you?'

'Like me?'

She laughed. 'I mean, is he tall, well-built?'

I frowned. 'I'm not sure what you mean.'

Her cheeks reddened. 'Broad-shouldered,' she said hurriedly and I wondered why she was suddenly being coy.

I pictured Andre. 'He's taller than I am,' I explained thoughtfully, 'but not as broad, I believe.'

She didn't speak for a moment. 'How did you meet? Do you recall?'

'It was through Ember.' The unfamiliar clothing suddenly felt restrictive. I fidgeted, unused to wearing such a tight shirt and wishing I could remove it. The mere thought of Ember reminded me how difficult life had been for a long time, until she finally accepted that I no longer cared for her. I liked excitement but she was too unpredictable and volatile and I couldn't imagine her ever changing.

Briar stilled. Only for a second, but long enough for me to notice. 'You've mentioned her before, I think. Is she Andre's sister?'

I shook my head. 'Ember is his cousin. They are opposites in every way. He is kind whereas she is—' I struggled to think of the best way to describe the wild, determined woman who fought better than most men and who for several years had insisted was the only woman for me, until she finally accepted that I was not in love with her and that she should turn her attention elsewhere. 'Ember is strong. She wields a sword better than most men, but not someone you would choose to cross.'

'She sounds like a force to be reckoned with.'

She stood and fanned herself with her straw hat. 'I think it's time we went inside and had a drink of water, don't you?'

'I agree.' Picking up her trug, I carried it inside. Once in the kitchen I poured us both a glass of water. While we were drinking, the need to speak to her about something that concerned me became too great for me to hold my tongue.

I thought of a conversation Briar and I had shared three years before, when she had confided that her mother wanted her to be initiated as a witch but she did not feel ready. I had overheard enough of their conversations recently in the small confines of the cottage to know that Briar was still reluctant.

'Briar? I said, keeping my voice low, not wishing her mother to overhear should she return without us noticing.

'I have something I feel I should say to you, but I don't want you to think I'm interfering.'

She scowled. 'Go on.'

I explained about hearing her and Diana arguing about Briar accepting her heritage. I saw her face cloud over in annoyance.

'And you think I'm wrong, is that it?'

'I know it's not my business.'

'It isn't, Xavier.' She gave me a pointed glare. Ordinarily I would have relented but I had no way of knowing how long it would be if Diana succeeded and we parted forever, and I believe that if you care for someone and think it important, you must have that difficult conversation.

'I know. Will you hear what I have to say, though?'

She hesitated before leaning back against the worktop and folding her arms defensively. 'Fine. What's bothering you?'

I braced myself, aware that what I was about to say might anger her. 'I apologise for being forward, but you and your mother have been very kind to me and I feel it would be remiss of me not to say how I feel about something important to both of you.'

Briar raised her eyebrows then smiled. 'I'm intrigued. What is it?'

I took a moment to choose my words. 'I have overheard several conversations between you. You are reluctant to be initiated into your mother's coven.'

Her expression darkened. 'You've been listening to private conversations between my mother and me?'

I held up a hand to stop her. 'Not intentionally. But you must admit it's difficult not to overhear when others are talking, especially if voices are raised.'

She narrowed her eyes as she stared at me silently for a moment. She took a slow, deep breath and exhaled. 'I suppose you're right about the lack of privacy here sometimes. Not about my choices.'

'Do you mind me continuing?' I asked, unsure whether to go on.

She waved for me to do so. 'May as well, I suppose.'

'I promise I only have your best interests at heart. Ordinarily I would not involve myself in others' affairs.' When she didn't speak, I asked her the question that had been bothering me. 'Why are you set against embracing your heritage?'

She frowned. 'You know something of witches?'

I shook my head. 'Only the danger people risk by practising witchcraft.'

'Then why the concern?'

'I feel I owe you something after you both took me in.' I shrugged and held my arms out. 'I have nothing to offer either of you but my thoughts.'

Her eyes dropped briefly before she looked at me once again. 'I'm frightened to be initiated, if you must know. To take that final step.'

Confused, I asked, 'As they no longer burn witches, I am unsure what scares you about it? Isn't your magick something that's been handed down through the generations?' She nodded. 'It's your birthright, Briar, isn't that how your mother feels?' Again, she agreed. 'What is frightening about something that comes naturally to you?'

'Because once I'm initiated, I'll be committed to the other women completely.'

I didn't understand and it must have shown on my face.

'What if I feel trapped? Or if I discover being a witch isn't something I need in my life?'

I began to understand her reticence. 'But Briar, you're already a witch. From what I've seen about this house and your mother's daily rituals and work, you've been living this way your entire life. I don't see that much will change after your initiation apart from your powers increasing?'

She stared at me as if I had enlightened her about something she had not considered before. 'Um, I don't know.'

I had spoken freely but now it was time to stop and let

Briar make her own decision about her fate. At least I had shared thoughts I felt were important for both women.

'I will think about what you've said.' Briar smiled. 'Thank you for caring enough about us both to broach the subject with me. I appreciate it.'

I realised my shoulders were tight with tension and relaxed them. 'Thank you for allowing me to say my piece.' I took another drink of water. I hoped that, whatever happened, Briar and Diana would always remain close.

'I'm sorry you've been stuck in here for so long,' Briar said, snapping me out of my reverie.

'It is no fault of yours,' I assured her. 'I am grateful to you and your mother. Neither of you asked to be in this situation.'

'On that note,' Diana announced, startling the pair of us as we realised she had joined us, 'I'm glad I have the two of you together. I may have come up with an idea.'

The delight on Briar's face mirrored my own.

'Really? Tell us more,' Briar insisted.

'I've heard from one of our neighbours that a storm is on its way across the channel.'

'A storm?' I asked, unable to contain my excitement as I realised what this could mean. 'Are you saying you intend performing your magick tonight?'

Diana put a finger to her lips. 'Hush, you never know who might be listening.'

'There's no one here but us, Mum,' Briar reminded her. Seeing Briar's delight at the thought of me leaving hurt deeply. 'Tonight, though? Are you prepared yet, do you think?'

Diana sighed. 'I pray for all our sakes that I am. I have done much preparation since Xavier's arrival, in case this very thing happened. We have little choice but to try. Keeping Xavier hidden here is becoming more dangerous with each passing day. Eventually someone will overhear him in the garden, or pass the living room window at the wrong moment.' She groaned. 'Although trying to reach the cell in the castle isn't going to be easy either, but I have a feeling tonight has to be the night we give it a go.'

I caught Briar's eye. I had no wish to return to my jail cell, but maybe the women could find a way to send me back on the other side of the wall, where I would have a chance to evade the guards. 'Tonight then. What do you need me to do?'

'We must return to the castle as soon as it's dusk,' Diana explained. She sat at the table and motioned for me to join them. 'I've been thinking about everything you told me,' she continued. 'And even though it's not ideal, I believe you both must be in exactly the same place as you were for any spell to work.'

Briar groaned. 'What if this storm isn't an electric one, though, Mum? Will you need one of those to make it happen?'

I was intrigued by her answer and waited for Diana to speak.

'I suspect so.' She gave me a sympathetic look. 'I'm sorry, it's not ideal but we must make the most of this opportunity.'

Briar frowned thoughtfully. 'But the castle is guarded.' Was she resigned to this failing? Unlike me, she knew how far her mother's powers reached. If she doubted Diana had the power to help me, then I had little hope of returning to my time.

'I'm aware of that, Briar,' Diana said. She turned to me. 'You'll need to change back into your own clothes before we leave, of course.'

'I'll go and fetch your handkerchief,' Briar said. 'Who

knows, it might not work if you don't have absolutely everything you came with.'

It was a relief to finally step outside into the street once again as we hurried along the lane past cottages later that evening. Diana was carrying a thick cloth bag, which I offered to carry for her.

'No, I'll keep this close to me for now.'

It looked heavy but I presumed she didn't trust me to carry it for her. I followed close behind the two women. At the end of the row they turned left and just as I was about to, something to the right of me caught my eye.

I stopped and, turning to look more closely, noticed a man in the shadows. He moved slightly forward and seemed to be studying me as I was him. Moonlight caught his face but not enough for me to see if I recognised him.

'Xavier,' Briar whispered from around the corner. I turned to answer, conscious that I needed to quicken my step if I was to catch up with her and Diana. I glanced back at the soldier but he was no longer there. Could he have gone to report seeing a stranger in the village?

I wasn't sure whether to mention him to the women as I rushed to rejoin them.

'You must stay close to us,' Diana said. 'Now, come along, there's no time to waste.'

We eventually reached the castle green. The little bat Pippin, which I now knew to be Briar's familiar, was flying around us again. Then Briar gasped and I spotted several soldiers patrolling the area. The bat darted off. I grabbed the women's arms and hastily pulled them behind the hedging at the top of the steep lane.

'It's around the back there,' Briar whispered, pointing near where the soldiers had stopped to light cigarettes and talk.

I began to be frustrated by their presence.

Diana held out a hand, palm up. 'It's just starting to rain.' She handed me the bag she was carrying. 'You can take this now, Xavier,' she whispered. 'You're stronger than me and your legs are much longer. If anyone can get my things to the castle it's you.'

I took the bag from her hands. It was heavy and I was intrigued by what could be inside. 'We should go one at a time,' I suggested, carefully hoisting the bag onto my shoulder, not wanting to damage its contents or make a sound to alert the soldiers. 'It isn't raining heavily yet and our footsteps might be overheard if the three of us go together.'

'Good idea,' Briar agreed. She smiled and lowered her voice. 'Your training is coming into good use tonight.'

'I'm glad to be of help for once.'

She leant in closer to me and whispered in my ear. 'Is this the excitement you felt when you confronted those pirates?' she whispered, her warm breath reminding me of sensations I had felt with her, and making me wonder whether leaving her again was something I could bear.

'It is like it, yes,' I admitted.

'I thought so.' She took a deep breath. 'I think I can understand the attraction.' Before I could utter a word in response, she asked, 'Would you like to go first, Xavier?'

Happy to do so, I waited for the soldiers to turn their backs, then rose to my feet and without hesitation ran until I reached the ruined cell. I stopped and waited in the shadows for the women to reach me. I heard Diana panting slightly before she came into my line of vision. Once all three of us were inside the cell a dreadful thought occurred to me.

'I must not be in here when you send me back,' I insisted, desperate to step back outside. 'If I am, you will be signing my death warrant.'

Briar gasped. 'He's right, Mum. We'd be responsible for Xavier being executed.'

'What choice do we have?' Diana argued as she took her bag from me and lowered it to the ground.

'I would rather remain here than return to a locked cell,' I argued. 'At least here I can live some sort of life. Back there, if I am caught again, I will immediately be executed.'

The women looked at each other. 'He has a point, Mum.'

Diana sighed and waved her arm towards the opening. 'You can hardly be outside, though. What if you're spotted before the spell is cast?'

'Now Mum has a point, Xavier.'

I thought briefly. 'Then I will stand in the shadows immediately outside this room while that is done.'

Diana gave a resigned shrug. 'Fine. Now, please let me concentrate, otherwise you'll be going nowhere.'

I heard her mumble something under her breath. I wasn't sure but it sounded like she didn't have much confidence in me going anywhere.

Briar stepped forward. 'Why don't we go somewhere safer and try there?'

Diana crossed her arms, looking furious. 'Like where?'

'Witches Rock?'

Diana shook her head. 'No. That's the sacred place of another coven. I wouldn't be welcome there.'

'Then how about the wooded area above Anne Port where

you meet the other women?' Briar suggested. 'There's more shelter and it's closer.'

Diana shook her head. I sensed her refusal was because of something she wasn't sharing with us. I moved closer to them. Diana stilled and tilted her head slightly to one side as if she were listening for something, probably to reassure herself that we were out of earshot of the soldiers.

Diana scowled. 'Let us focus on sending you back to your time.'

I glanced at Briar, wishing that my going home wouldn't mean being parted from her once again. 'I appreciate your help. Thank you.'

'I'm sorry, Mum. I didn't mean to upset you,' Briar said quietly.

'I need to concentrate, Briar,' Diana snapped. 'We'll discuss this when we're alone later.'

One of the soldiers looked up at something or someone I couldn't see. A voice shouted what sounded like an order and the three of us withdrew further into the shadows.

'We do not have much time,' I reminded them.

A rumble of thunder sent a tremor through the ground and seconds later a fork of lightning lit up the bay.

'Wonderful,' Diana exclaimed.

I watched in anticipation as Briar hurriedly helped Diana unpack the contents of the bag. A jar containing herbs of sorts and an oil was placed on the ground. A short candlestick holder was set down next to it and a black candle placed in it upside down. I gave Briar a questioning look.

'It's to reverse what's happened,' she said knowledgably. 'To hopefully undo whatever was done to bring you here.'

I supposed it made sense.

Wanting to make the most of every second I had left in her presence, I watched her, trying to memorise every tiny feature of her face. She was my soulmate, although she didn't seem to know it.

Finding the situation too painful, I willed Diana to finish her preparations, not daring to ask how long I must wait.

'There,' Diana said, giving a satisfied sigh. 'I am ready. If this does not work, I have no idea what might.' She sat back on her haunches.

I was desperate not to end up back in the locked cell. 'As I said before, if I stand outside the door at the given time, hopefully your spell will work,' I said. 'If the soldiers see me, it will only be for a split second.'

I saw Briar's face light up in the moonlight in a way that made her eyes shine and my heart ache. She was so beautiful and kind. My heart contracted painfully at the thought that I was spending my last few moments with her.

'That's a good point, Xavier.' She patted her mother lightly on her back. 'Let's give it a try, Mum.'

Hearing voices from above us on the keep, Diana raised a finger to her lips. 'Good luck, Xavier. I wish you well.'

Diana lit the base of the candle. Then she poured the herbs and oil from the jar into a small copper bowl and, raising it in one hand, tilted the candle until the flame ignited the mixture. I watched as everything turned to ash. Taking a stick, Diana drew a tiny X and a G to mark my initials in the powdery substance.

Transfixed, I saw her close her eyes and begin chanting the same words several times over.

'Hear these words, accept his name, send him back to

whence he came. More importance I cannot convey, send him now without delay. So mote it be.'

Snapping out of my reverie, I took a small step back so as to be sure that I was standing outside the cell.

'Oh,' Briar gasped, stepping forward. 'I almost forgot to give this back to you.' She reached out to pass me my handkerchief.

I instinctively went to take it, the skin on my hand grazing hers as a bolt of lightning slammed against the castle.

I heard Diana's cry of anguish as everything went black.

Chapter Eleven

BRIAR

June 1643

Had I fainted? I opened my eyes slowly, frightened by noises that sounded as if they came from below on the green. Sounds that hadn't been there seconds before. Were those jeers? I went to ask Mum what was happening but couldn't see her.

My breath quickened. Something had gone wrong. Had her spell failed? Panicked at the thought, I forced myself to remain calm as I attempted to get my trembling legs to work.

I presumed I must be dreaming. Yes, that's what was happening. I gazed down towards the cacophony of noises, reasoning that my mind was playing tricks and showing me how it must be for Xavier now he had returned to his own time. The smell of horse manure filled my nostrils and I stepped back against the wall as two horses passed, one leaving a trail of dung in his wake. I wrinkled my nose then thought of how Dad had taken a trolley to one of his friend's homes to collect horse manure for his roses.

A soldier yelled at a group of people to move back from the castle gates. I did hear jeering. I peered back along the path, trying to make sense of what was happening, but crowds of people now surged forward from the market stalls and for a moment I couldn't see what had claimed their interest.

A louder yell distracted me. Turning quickly, I stared in disbelief at the spectacle nearby. Crowds of people were dressed in clothes similar to Xavier's. I gasped, noticing I was standing outside what had been the ruin but now was a solid curved wall.

Giddiness washed over me. This was no dream. A few seconds passed before my brain caught up with what I was seeing. If I was here, then where was Xavier? Had my mother sent me back instead of him? My breathing quickened at the horrifying thought. To be alone here in this unfamiliar, terrifying place, with nothing recognisable to me apart from the castle looming high above, was more than I could stand.

Could something even worse have happened? Was Xavier here, but on the other side of the wall? If he was inside the cell there was no way I could get him out, or even see him.

Hysteria welled up inside me but I knew instinctively that to give in to it would be the most dangerous thing to do. I needed to do something.

A hand grasped my wrist and pulled me backwards. I attempted to snatch my hand away but the grip held firm and tugged, almost unbalancing me. The next thing I knew, my back hurt as I was forced against the uneven granite wall. I looked up into Xavier's almost dark blue eyes and felt my legs go weak for a second time in as many minutes.

He let go of my wrist and slipped his arm around my waist. 'You've had a shock,' he said quietly, steadying me. The heat of his body against mine soothed me and I only just managed to contain my relief that he was here with me.

I wasn't sure what he was doing at first, until it occurred to me that he was shielding me from being seen by others. 'You're here,' I said, unable to keep the sob from my voice.

'I am.' His eyes bored into mine and I saw fear. He was as shocked to find me there as I had been to find him. 'We must make haste away from prying eyes.'

The urgency in his voice was unmistakable and I tried to move but my legs took a moment to work.

'Whore!' a man's harsh voice bellowed.

People pushed and shoved, jeering at some poor soul. I leant to one side to peer past Xavier's shoulder and saw that the route to the castle entrance had been cleared to make way for a cart, on which a dishevelled, terrified middle-aged woman stood. I watched her standing with her chin raised, trying to appear strong, as people threw bruised vegetables at her. Her shaved head jarred sideways as half a cabbage hit her on her left temple.

My throat tightened. 'What are they doing to that woman?' I asked, appalled. 'She needs help.'

'If I thought there was any way to aid her, I would,' Xavier said miserably.

The cart stopped briefly before it began to move on again, the crowds following shrieking insults at the poor soul.

Iciness trickled down my spine. 'They think she's a witch, don't they?' *Like Mum and Mrs Le Dain and all the others in the coven*, I thought, feeling sick. Now I understood why Xavier was trying to hide me from these people. 'Where are they taking her?'

'Market Place in town.'

Market Place? 'I don't know where that is.' I caught the woman's gaze and for a second her eyebrows furrowed. They seemed too large for her face, and it was clear she was in shock and had endured more than any human should be expected to. Deep sorrow swept over me. What had she done to deserve this cruelty? Nothing, I imagined.

'What will they do to her when she gets there?' I whispered, unable to drag my eyes from her.

'I'll tell you when we're away from here.' He looked around us. I followed his gaze and noticed several people watching us. Xavier must have seen them too.

'Xavier?' I whispered, terrified. 'Those people…'

'Do not speak. Your appearance is making them curious. Hearing your voice will only add to their intrigue. We must not tarry.'

I knew enough about history and how witches had been treated in the sixteenth and seventeenth centuries to be aware that anyone looking, sounding or acting differently from what people were used to was at risk of being accused of sorcery. It was why my mother and her coven still practised magick to protect themselves and those they loved. Seeing what they did to women accused of such practices made me understand better why they felt the need to do so.

I kept my head down and held Xavier's hand tightly as we pushed our way through the crowds. Several people turned to look in our direction, their eyes narrowing on me. I could barely breathe for fear of what they might do, given the chance, but then another jeer went up and they were distracted once more.

'We must hurry,' Xavier said.

I didn't argue but forced my legs to move even quicker to keep up with his increased pace.

Chapter Twelve

XAVIER

I gripped Briar's hand as I led her to the village. I was still shocked at finding she had travelled back in time with me. Just when I thought things couldn't be worse than having to leave her – now this. As much as I had dreaded not seeing her again, that was preferable to her being caught here. I thought of the determined, mean-spirited Witchfinder, Roger Dankworth. His fascination with Briar three years before had been the reason why I had sought out Old Mother Dorey to help return Briar to her time. The old witch had been dead a while now, though, and I had no idea who to ask for help.

As I had come to expect, Briar was doing her best to appear stoic, but she needed more than that if she was to survive being here for a second time. She had to find a way to become invisible.

'You need suitable clothes,' I said when we were some distance away from the castle and heading towards Gorey village. This time, though, I was the one rescuing her. We reached the village and, relieved to be away from prying eyes,

I pulled her into a side street behind a row of cottages, some of granite like her home, Honey Bee Cottage, others built of wood.

'It's odd being near to my own home yet it being unfamiliar,' she said.

Having recently gone through the same thing but in reverse, I realised how disconcerted Briar must be now she understood my own confusion better.

'I often wondered what the village looked like in the past, but I must have pictured it through nostalgic eyes. It never occurred to me to think about the poor unfortunates locked away in the castle,' she added thoughtfully. 'That poor woman, Xavier. I can't bear to think what will lie ahead of her in Market Place.'

Now we were away from immediate danger, I slowed my pace, giving her a chance to catch her breath. She looked around her, attempting to take in the scene.

'The only thing that's the same is the castle up on the hill.'

I stopped in front of a cottage and, not wishing to shock the inhabitants, knocked lightly on the front door before opening it and stepping inside, pulling Briar in with me. I closed the door quietly behind us.

Briar looked up, hearing the footsteps of someone running into the house from out the back. She gave me a questioning look.

I barely had time to catch my breath before my sixteen-year-old sister ran into the room. Her hand flew to cover her mouth when she saw the pair of us standing by the door.

'How can this be?' She stared at me as if she had seen a ghost. Then turned her gaze to Briar, before flying towards me and leaping into my arms. 'You're free.' Tears ran down her cheeks. 'I don't understand,' she sniffed. 'Aunty heard you were to be executed some weeks since. How are you standing before me now?'

Realising I was still holding Briar's hand, I let it go and wrapped my arms around my sister's back, hugging her tightly as she clung to me, sobbing.

'It's a long and strange story, little Wren. One I shall share with you someday. For now, sweet sister—' I took her by the waist, lifted her from me and set her feet on the wooden floor. Wren wiped her eyes and, taking a handkerchief from the pocket in her skirt, blew her nose. 'This is my friend Briar.'

Wren looked Briar up and down, not seeming as friendly as I would have liked. She scowled up at me. 'Why does she dress'—she raised her hand to the side of her face and whispered—'in such a shameless fashion?'

Recalling Briar and Diana's expressions when they had first met me in my strange apparel, I understood my sister's confusion. 'You wouldn't believe me if I told you. Now, I need you to fetch clothes for her to change into. Some of our aunt's will do. Or, if we still have them, our late mother's.'

Briar opened her mouth to speak when we heard footsteps outside. I tensed.

'Hurry, Wren, there's no time to waste.'

Hearing the urgency in my voice, my sister immediately ran out of the living room without another word.

'You have a sister,' Briar said. 'No wonder you wanted to return to your time so badly.' She looked towards the door where Wren had gone. 'She's sweet.'

Amused, I frowned. 'Only on occasion.' I listened to the footsteps, willing them to pass the cottage, and shook my head. 'She is a good girl, though, and loyal.'

Hearing the footsteps pause outside, I took Briar's arm. 'You had better remain hidden until you are wearing less conspicuous clothing. It is too dangerous for you in the living room should someone arrive unexpectedly.'

I led her into the back room and opened the door of the small pantry. 'In there.'

She gave me an unhappy glance before she stepped inside. I closed the door, aware there was no window, and hoped she wouldn't panic. The only light would be through a hole high in the door to let in air. I hoped Briar didn't inadvertently make any noise. It was a small space and it would be easy for her to accidentally knock over a candle, jar or another of the items stocked in there.

I tensed again, hearing someone outside the house. 'I will be as quick as possible.'

I hurried back to the main room to see who had come to the cottage, hoping word hadn't already reached the Witchfinder that a stranger had arrived in the village.

I kept out of sight as Wren raced back into the room, grumbling under her breath, her hands holding a pile of clothing. She opened the door and spoke to a voice I recognised as belonging to one of our neighbours. They passed on a message from our aunt, letting Wren know she would be away from the village for another few days.

Relieved the visitor did not expect to come inside, I waited while Wren thanked them and closed the door.

'Aunty must be having a better time at her cousins than she expected.' She raised the pile of clothes slightly. 'I'll take these to your friend.'

I stayed out of the way, not wishing to embarrass Briar

while the women spoke of underclothing, and tried to work out how to keep her hidden.

'A smock,' I heard Wren say, before explaining when it should be worn. I recalled my own confusion when Briar had handed me her father's clothes.

'Hose?' I smiled, picturing Briar's confusion at the knitted items that looked like the long socks her father had worn.

They discussed petticoats and the skirt Wren had found for her, then Wren added, 'I shall find a jacket to go with them but these should suffice for now, and these shoes will have to fit.'

Poor Briar, I thought, as she admitted to Wren that she had no idea how to wear the garments. I left my sister helping her and went to sit and think. It had been a busy few weeks and I was more tired than I had realised, not that I had time to give in to my weariness. Not while Briar was in danger – and she surely was, with Roger Dankworth on the lookout for anyone he could accuse of sorcery.

Chapter Thirteen

DIANA

After a frantic search by Tula, Pippin and me, I had to concede that I had done the worst thing possible and sent my daughter back in time with Xavier. I needed to leave the castle green without being seen. I hastily packed my bag and lifted it. However I looked at this, my Briar had little chance of surviving. The only certainty was that Briar had no chance at all if I was arrested for being out after curfew and prevented from finding a way to help her.

The irony of being furious with Briar for being out after curfew occurred to me and I pushed it away. If only she were here for me to be cross with her. I brushed tears from my cheeks, knowing that there was nothing my daughter could ever do again that would cause me to be angry with her. All I wanted now was to have her back where she belonged and the sooner the better, for all our sakes.

First, though, I needed to go home. Once there I would be free to think of a way to make a plan to sort out this horrible mess. I hurried back to Honey Bee Cottage, barely able to see through my tears, trying to work out what could have happened. Briar wasn't silly enough to have gone outside while I was casting my spell, not when there were soldiers around. I recalled her speaking to Xavier. Had she reached out and touched him just as the lightning struck the castle as I finished my spell? She must have done. There was nothing else I could think of to connect them and send them back in time together.

I had to stop walking. I reached out and grabbed the top of a wall. That must have been what happened. I whimpered. I needed the privacy of my home if I was to come to terms with this horrendous situation.

I staggered into my cottage with Pippin and Tula immediately behind me and only just managed to close the front door before my legs gave way. I sank heavily to the floor. What had Briar been thinking? Why had she reached out to him at that precise moment? Surely, she knew better? My heart pounded painfully and my vision swam. For a moment I suspected I was having a heart attack. I had sent my precious daughter back to the most dangerous time in our island's history. How could I ever forgive myself?

I needed to be strong, for both of us. Wherever Briar was, she would be relying on me to find her and bring her home. If I allowed my heart to fail at this moment I would be leaving her to a terrible fate. I waited for a wave of nausea to rush through me. No one apart from me knew what had happened, and it was up to me to make things right.

What had I been thinking, letting her persuade me to attempt to send Xavier back? Why hadn't I refused? Or asked my sisterhood for help? Why was I blaming Briar? I had been the one to insist I could do this alone. I had been such a fool.

I had to calm down. I forced myself to inhale slowly through my nose, then exhale through my mouth. I needed to think.

I got to my feet, went to my stock cupboard and, taking a phial of lavender oil, dabbed it on my temples and wrists. Then, opening my biscuit tin, I took out two of the small camomile-and-lavender-infused biscuits I had made the previous day. My poor girl was going to have to find a way to survive for as long as it took me to bring her back and I had no intention of giving up until I saved her from the horrors my spell had cast her into.

Chapter Fourteen

BRIAR

Wren waited while I dressed in the hose and smock, then helped me with the bodice before fastening the wool skirt and showing me how to wear the neckcloth over my shoulders. Satisfied with her efforts, she handed me a piece of linen with ties at either end.

'Your forehead cloth,' she said, giving an irritated sigh and tying it on my head when I looked bemused. She then covered it with a cloth cap. 'Your coif,' she said before she walked away and left me to put on the worn leather shoes.

Poor Xavier, I thought, *having to dress in the clothes that to him must have seemed very strange when he arrived in my time.* It was now a shared experience between us that no one else could possibly understand.

I folded my own clothes neatly, hoping to have an opportunity to wear them again, and left them on one of the lower shelves of the cupboard. Hopefully, if they were seen by anyone, the person would assume they were dustcloths or for mending. As long as no one unfolded them and discovered their strangeness, they should be fine where I left them, until the time came when I could return home.

The shoes were too small and pinched my feet but I had little choice but to get used to wearing them. Never mind feeling sorry for myself. My thoughts returned to the unfortunate woman in the cart on her way to be executed. I would never forget the fear in her eyes.

Then my thoughts returned to how I had got here. It had to be Mum's spell. She must have made a mistake. How could that have happened? She was always extremely careful when preparing and casting spells. I supposed it must have been the first time she had cast a spell to return someone to another time in history.

If that was the case, then why hadn't she approached Babette Le Dain for help before attempting to send Xavier back? She must have known there was a greater chance of her spell working with the aid of the other members of the coven. Now I was stuck here. My throat tightened as my fear increased. What would happen to me now?

I instinctively looked around for Pippin, and panicked when I was no longer protected from those wishing me harm. I rarely went anywhere that made me feel anxious without her.

Feeling lightheaded, I tried to steady my breathing. There was little point in fretting. I needed to think practically about what to do next. The only person I had to rely upon was a man I barely knew. A condemned man at that. I thought back to the weeks I had spent in Xavier's company, getting to know him slightly. I recalled his frustration being cooped up in the cottage, his desire to help, and his gratitude. Then there was Wren's reaction to seeing him again. She had known him all her life and no one was that delighted to see someone they didn't adore. I had little choice but to trust him.

But how much could Xavier realistically do to help me? He was a wanted man, after all. Having grown up with a grandmother and mother who practised witchcraft, I had studied enough history to know that in Xavier's time the Channel Islands were known as the witch-hunting capital of Atlantic Europe. I shuddered at the thought.

It hit me with a jolt that, only hours before, I had thought my life difficult because I had to deal with Nazis at every street corner, watching our every move. *How preferable was that scenario now*, I mused miserably. It never occurred to me that I might choose to live that way rather than another. Then again, I had never reckoned on being transported back in time to the seventeenth century.

I hoped Mum would ask for help now, and that her coven could draw me back before it was too late – before someone accused me of being a witch. But there was little point worrying when I could do nothing about the situation, so I decided to do as Xavier had done and concentrate on keeping safe until Mum managed to rescue me.

Noticing a linen cap on the worktop, I wondered how to arrange my hair under it. Having no clue, I carried it through to Wren to ask for her help once again.

Xavier was sitting at the table, his head in his hands. I couldn't help feeling sorry for him. It wasn't as if he didn't already have enough to deal with as an escapee. There must be a warrant out for his arrest. Someone must be searching for him, intending to make an arrest and carry out his execution.

Both of us were in danger, Xavier even more than me right

now. I felt sick at the thought that neither of us had much chance of surviving here for very long.

He must have heard my footsteps because he raised his eyes and stared at me. He didn't speak and seemed lost for words.

'Is everything all right?' I asked, confused at his reaction.

'You look different,' he said thoughtfully. 'You'll fit in better dressed this way.'

'I'm glad you think so.'

'Please, sit.' I did as he asked, my legs still wobbly from the shock of all the changes that had happened so quickly.

'We must hope no one spotted either of us,' Xavier said matter-of-factly. 'A stranger wouldn't be noticed dressed as you are, but people know me well. It will be common knowledge that I escaped from prison. Suspicions will be raised about you, too, should someone see us together.'

'People are certainly curious.' As they were during the Occupation, I reminded myself. 'And suspicious, no doubt.'

Wren brought us cups of wine and a plate of what looked like bread and some cheese. It smelt delicious and I realised I was exceedingly hungry. It was more cheese than I had seen since the island was invaded three years before, and my mouth watered at the familiar tang. I ate hungrily, relishing the creamy softness upon my tongue.

'That was delicious,' I said gratefully, relaxing slightly. I was beginning to feel less frantic about being here and more willing to let things happen at the pace they were meant to. I might not have known Xavier long but now I was calmer I listened to my instinct that I could trust him.

Xavier drank from his cup, then, placing it down on the table, opened his mouth to speak when someone banged heavily on the front door. He leapt to his feet at the same time as me.

'Quick, come with me.' He turned to Wren. 'Delay as long as you can before opening the door.'

She nodded, her pretty face pale with fright.

'Quick, that way.'

Xavier grabbed my hand for the second time that day and we ran out of the room. He pushed me into the cupboard, then crammed himself in with me, our bodies pressed against each other in the darkness as he closed the door with difficulty behind him.

A feeling of warmth and protection washed over me. I didn't recall experiencing it before, but something flashed through my mind in the near darkness. It was like waking from a half-remembered dream – one in which I had dreamt about Xavier, loving him, being physically close to him. Intimate.

I gasped, shocked.

'Are you quite well?' he whispered, sounding anxious.

I sensed him looking down at me. Did our proximity disconcert him as much as it did me? I had never been this close to a man before, though I had a faint memory of lying naked beside Xavier in a dream.

He put his arms around me. 'All will be well,' he soothed, trying to comfort me.

I had little choice in the confines of the cupboard but to slip my arms around him too. I did feel comforted ... but also something else. I had noticed Xavier's muscles before but hadn't felt them against me – hadn't realised how firm his chest and stomach were.

He cleared his throat, then moved as far back as the small space allowed.

I heard brief murmurings, then the footsteps of someone who didn't care about being heard. A woman's voice rang out, demanding to know where Xavier was.

I wondered who she might be. I felt him tense. He knew her.

'Stay here,' he whispered, his voice hoarse for some reason.

The smell of the wine on his warm breath calmed me. It was a relief to be in here with him, if only for a little while.

'I see two plates, Wren,' the woman snapped. 'I am aware your aunt is away visiting her sister, and Xavier was seen coming here. With a woman.' The last words were said with malice. I stiffened. What was this woman to Xavier? Did he have a wife he hadn't mentioned? I was surprised when the thought stung.

My eyes had become accustomed to the darkness and I looked up at Xavier. 'Who is she?' I whispered anxiously, shocked by the woman's aggressive tone toward his sister.

I saw Xavier close his eyes and grimace before answering. 'That is Ember.'

I hesitated. 'Is she your wife?'

He made a sound like a laugh mixed with relief. 'No, thankfully she is not.'

Before I could react, he pushed open the door.

'Xavier?' Where was he going?

'Stay here,' he said, giving me a reassuring smile. 'Don't come out until I fetch you.'

He closed the door behind him, leaving me in the darkness listening to his heavy footsteps march through to the living room.

'There you are,' Ember announced triumphantly. 'I knew you couldn't be far from here. Where in the devil's name have you been hiding? Everyone thinks one of your old seadogs whisked you away to the Continent.'

'What do you want, Ember?' I heard him ask, his tone cold.

There was a moment's silence. 'Where have you come from?' she said suddenly. 'Who is with you?'

'It's no business of yours. You wanted to find me and now you have.'

'I'm not ready to leave yet, Xavier,' the voice said, filled with sarcasm.

I presumed he must have gone to open the front door, hoping the woman would leave, because then I heard hurried steps coming in my direction, with Xavier's heavier ones following.

'Ember, don't you dare.'

His booming threat was one I doubted many would risk ignoring – but not this woman, I realised, as the door was wrenched open. A tall, fierce-looking woman with black hair and piercing green eyes, not dissimilar to my own in colour, looked me up and down before doing the same to Xavier. She glared at him, then at me, and I saw flecks of gold that seemed like tiny flames in her irises. She was not happy.

She pointed a long finger at me, her eyes narrowed. 'Who are you and what are you doing here?'

She wasn't dressed like me or Wren. She had the appearance of a warrior and was unmistakably powerful and didn't bother hiding her possessiveness over Xavier. I was too shaken by her ferocity to respond to her question.

Her steely gaze moved to Xavier, who, though several inches over six feet in height, wasn't much taller than her.

'Give me one reason why I shouldn't kill you, and this'—she glowered at me with a sneer—'mouse?'

'I'm not a mouse,' I snapped, shocked into action. 'Anyway, why would you want to kill either of us?'

She glared at Xavier. 'Yes, Xavier, why do you think I would want to do such a thing?'

'Ember, watch yourself.' The threat in his voice was unmistakable. It was obvious they were used to sparring with each other.

Ignoring him, Ember stepped closer to me and lowered her head until her nose almost touched mine.

'Tell me. What would you do if you discovered your man hiding another woman from you?' she asked, her voice low and menacing.

She had a point, if that's what we had been doing. I pushed aside the feelings Xavier's closeness had stirred in me and stood as tall as I could. 'You've made a mistake,' I argued, instantly aware when she raised her hand to hit me that I had said the wrong thing.

'Liar! I don't make mistakes when it comes to my man.'

'I am not your man, Ember,' Xavier growled. 'And don't you dare touch her.'

Chapter Fifteen

XAVIER

It seemed that no matter how many times I told Ember there was nothing between us any longer, she refused to listen. I glanced at Briar's sweet face as she glared at me angrily and thought of how it had felt having our bodies pressed against each other once more. I sensed by her reaction in the cupboard that she had remembered something from our time together, before she had been sent back to her own time, her memory wiped.

I wasn't sure what, or how much, she remembered, if anything, but now wasn't the time to focus on that. We had to wait until we were alone to delve into our past, and I had to wait for her to bring the subject up, in case I was wrong to imagine she had recalled anything.

Unfortunately, Ember, who had an uncanny sense for these things, hadn't been mistaken about the depth of my feelings towards Briar. She was a witch, after all, and a woman who, I knew only too well, would have no qualms about harming anyone she saw as competition.

I had loved Ember once, years before, but had ended the relationship because she was far too volatile for my liking. Since falling in love with Briar three years ago, I hadn't touched another woman. I had begged Old Mother Dorey to send Briar back to her time not because I didn't love her with my entire body and soul, but because she had come to the Witchfinder's attention. I knew too that even if I kept her from his clutches, there was still a chance that Ember would discover that Briar had replaced her in my affections.

And now Briar was back here, trapped without Old Mother Dorey to help her, and Ember had discovered her. It was only a matter of time before Ember's newly ignited misguided jealousy, quiet for the last three and a half years, sparked trouble for Briar. I just had to hope Diana and her coven rescued Briar before Ember managed to do her worst.

'Ember, we both know there is nothing between us and hasn't been for a very long time.' It wasn't a lie, I thought miserably. Briar might have felt something in that cupboard, but the way she looked at me hadn't changed. My heart pinched with pain to know that the love that had once shone for me from her beautiful green eyes hadn't returned.

Briar also didn't know that my reason for rushing to hide us was because this wasn't her first time here. If I had, she would have understood my fear that the Witchfinder had already been informed and might come to arrest her. Was I saving her by keeping our past from her, or could I be putting her in danger by not giving her information she might need? It was something I must consider and deal with, and soon.

Ember's eyes darkened to the shade of a stormy sea. There had been a time when I was younger when those eyes had enchanted me, but I knew her better now. I had learnt the hard lesson that surface beauty could hide the darkest heart. I was in no mood for her dramatics now and had no intention of standing by and allowing her to strike Briar.

'Why don't we join Wren in the other room where we can sit in comfort?' I suggested, wanting to defuse the tension. After a brief hesitation Ember turned on her heels and led the way. I gave Briar a reassuring smile, hoping to persuade Ember to leave before her insinuations made Briar dismiss whatever vague memories our closeness might have stirred in her.

Briar might not possess Ember's prowess at deception, or her height or strength, but it was clear she wasn't someone to be walked over, I thought with admiration.

After a light refreshment provided by my sister, during which Ember had sniped and sneered, I decided I would not entertain her or her nonsense further.

'It is time for you to leave, Ember,' I insisted.

She shook her head. 'You might think you have no need of me, Xavier, but you forget you're a wanted man. You need all the friends behind you that you can muster. She gave Briar a pitying smile. 'No, I can't see her helping to keep you safe. She will have enough problems of her own being a stranger here, especially with the Witchfinder on the prowl.'

Damn Ember. She has a point. I would need help if I were to ensure Briar's safety until it was possible to send her back home. I leant back in my chair and sighed heavily. 'What do you suggest?'

'Xavier?' Briar snapped. 'Why are you listening to her?' She gave Ember a pointed glare before turning her focus back to me. 'I've only just met this woman and even I can tell she is no friend of yours. Or mine,' she added angrily.

I groaned. 'You're right. Unfortunately, though, so is Ember. If we are to survive this ordeal we will need help from others.'

Briar frowned. 'Surely you have other people you can trust to help?'

I did, but no one better than Ember at the moment. I thought of Briar and Diana's predicament. 'How many people do *you* trust to share your secrets with? Or Diana?'

I saw by the droop of her shoulders that I had struck a nerve.

'I'm sorry, Briar, but I don't see we have much choice but to trust Ember.'

'I am still here,' Ember grumbled.

Briar and I looked at her silently, each as miserable as the other.

'Now we've established what's what,' Ember said, a note of triumph in her tone, 'why don't you start by telling me exactly where you've been, Xavier, how you escaped and who exactly this woman happens to be.'

'I'm not sure how much you'll believe about what I shall tell you,' I began.

'Tell me.' She leant back in her chair.

She listened silently, then, when I had finished, frowned. 'What do you want to happen?' She looked from Briar to me.

'I need to go back to my own time,' Briar said.

'And I have to clear my name.'

'You don't wish to go back with her?' Ember asked, testing me.

I did, but this was where I belonged, however much I didn't want to be here without her. I took a moment to respond.

'Briar has a life in the 1940s and I have one here.' I hid the sadness that came over me at the thought of not seeing Briar again. 'At least I will if I find a way to avoid the executioner.'

'We will find a way to save you, Xavier,' Ember said.

I saw something in her eyes that left me in no doubt how much she was enjoying being in charge of the situation.

I cast my eyes down briefly before looking directly at her once more. 'Thank you.'

Ember looked thoughtful for a moment. She had an idea. 'I know what to do.' She looked at Briar. 'First, we must hide you. Even I do not have the powers to send another person forward in time.'

Briar blinked and I could see realisation dawning. 'You're a witch?' Briar asked, shocked.

Ember frowned. 'Don't say that so loudly. I am, not that many people know it. I need to find another way to help you if your mother is unable to succeed. I presume it goes without saying that you watch what you say to everyone.'

'I realise that,' Briar said quietly.

Briar sounded as exhausted as I felt but at least we had Ember on our side. For now. 'You said you knew what to do?' I reminded her.

She grinned. 'Andre.'

'My oldest and dearest friend.' We had been at loggerheads on many occasions, but I knew him to be a kind and honest man and one I trusted wholeheartedly. 'He owes me a favour.'

Ember stared at me silently for a few seconds. 'There's no time to waste if we are to do this. I'll take you both to Andre's home immediately.'

Chapter Sixteen

BRIAR

'Where is this place?' I asked as I placed the clothes bundle under my arm.

Ember gave an impatient sigh and replied to Xavier as if he had been the one to ask the question.

'Not far. I trust my cousin to take care of you until I find a boat to take you both off the island.'

Not wishing to leave and ruin any chance of Mum finding me, I gave my head an emphatic shake. 'I'm not leaving Jersey.'

Ember's steely gaze turned on me. 'I do not care whether you live or die. I do care about Xavier surviving. If you wish to remain with him, then you'll do as you're told.'

I looked at Xavier. I could see he believed Ember was right. We had little choice but to leave this house. Worrying about being taken far away from Mum's help was something I must deal with another time. Right now I needed to be somewhere safe.

Wren appeared from another room and hugged Xavier tightly. 'Come back to us, brother.'

'I will do my best,' he said, giving her a kiss on her head. 'Please let our aunt know you've seen me and that I am no longer awaiting execution.'

'I will,' she said, sniffing away tears. She let go of him and turned to me. 'I suppose I should thank you for bringing him back,' she said, not looking at all grateful. 'If he is caught trying to help you escape the Witchfinder's clutches, I will never forgive you.'

I heard the word 'Witchfinder' and barely managed to contain a shudder.

'That's enough, Wren,' Xavier said, though his voice was gentle.

'Enough talk,' Ember grumbled. 'Wait here. Be ready to leave at a moment's notice.' She slipped out of the house. In what seemed like no time at all, she was back again and waving for us to follow her. We hurried down a side alley and passed more houses. A door opened and Ember pushed me inside, pulling Xavier after her.

It took a moment for my eyes to acclimatise to the dimness in the room. I saw movement out of the corner of my eye and turned to see a tall man standing, arms folded, with his back to a fire that was struggling to take.

'Andre!' Xavier stepped forward his arms outstretched. 'I'm so happy to see you.' He turned to me. 'Briar, this is my friend Andre Touzel.' He smiled at the man whose face I couldn't make out very clearly in the dim light.

Xavier stepped forward, his hand outstretched. 'Andre, my good man. How grateful I am for your kindness in taking us in.'

Andre peered over Xavier's shoulder and saw me. 'There is no need for thanks between friends.' Taking a sidestep, he passed Xavier and walked over to me.

'And who, pray, is this fair maid?' He studied me thoughtfully. 'I do not believe I have seen you before.'

Unsure how best to answer, I smiled. 'I'm Briar Le Gros,' I replied, shaking his hand just as the fire in the hearth noisily crackled into life. Andre had piercing blue eyes with an unmistakable glint in them. What with his strong nose and beautiful mouth, his looks made my breath catch in my throat. He wasn't ruggedly handsome like Xavier. In fact, though his features were impressive, he somehow missed being handsome, but only just. Unlike Xavier, whose unkempt hair and sun-kissed skin had awakened something in me I still didn't quite understand.

There was something intriguing about Andre, though, although I wasn't sure what it might be.

Ember laughed for some reason.

What a strange reaction, I mused. Maybe it was the oddness of my situation. I was known for being sensible and proud of that fact. I had never lost my head over any man. Then, in the space of a couple of hours, I had felt a torrent of emotions, one minute excited, the next shy when pressed up against Xavier in the cupboard. Now I was thinking about people's looks. This was not the time to be distracted. I was acting irrationally and needed to keep my thoughts focused. I stifled a yawn, not wishing to seem rude but unable to help myself.

'Where are my manners?' Andre said, taking my arm and leading me over to the table, where he pulled out a chair and waited for me to sit.

'Hester,' he called. 'We need sustenance for four people.'

Andre took two candlestick holders, lit the candles and placed them on the table. A middle-aged woman brought a tray into the room and set it down on the table before Andre. He set a bowl of food down in front of each of us, and a pottery tumbler, then poured what looked like wine into each of the tumblers and sat.

'Thank you, Hester. You may go now.'

She didn't seem to notice us, or maybe she was used to strange people coming to the house. Either way, I realised welcoming people in the dead of night was something that didn't faze Andre, and I wondered why. Who was he, apart from Ember's cousin, and what part was he going to play in helping Xavier and me escape?

'It's only broth,' Andre said, picking up a loaf of bread from the tray and pulling off chunks which he passed to each of us to dunk in our food. 'It will taste good, though. Hester has been with me since I was a boy,' he explained when he caught me looking at the door she had just left through. 'I trust her with my life.'

'Yes,' I said, unsure what else to say.

I ate in silence, listening to the three of them discuss sleeping arrangements. I could barely keep my eyes open and a few times my head dropped as my eyelids closed. I didn't much care where I slept, as long as it was somewhere dry and safe.

'Briar?'

I heard Xavier say my name and jerked my head up once more. 'Sorry?'

'Ember will be leaving soon. I wanted to ascertain whether you are comfortable sleeping in this house alone with Andre and me, or if you would rather Hester return to spend the night?'

Smiling with gratitude at their thoughtful consideration of my feelings, I shook my head. 'There's no need to call for Hester,' I assured them. 'I trust you both to be gentlemen.' I didn't add that I was too weary to worry about anything at all. I yawned. 'Sorry. I'm struggling to stay awake. If you could let me know where to sleep, I'll go to bed.'

Andre went to get up, but Ember put her hand on his shoulder and pushed him back into his seat. 'I'll show her the way.'

I swallowed the last mouthful of my meal and finished the wine. I suspected she intended to warn me off Xavier once more. Not caring, I focused instead on the thought that in a few minutes I would be able to give in to sleep.

'Thank you for taking us in, Andre,' I said as I rose to my feet.

'It is my pleasure. I trust you will sleep well.'

I wished the two men good night, hoping that my exhaustion and the wine would help me catch up on some much-needed sleep. I followed Ember out of the room and up a ladder-like staircase to a mezzanine. There was one bed. I assumed Andre had given up his room for me.

'This is Andre's room?'

'It is,' she said simply. I opened my mouth to tell her that I couldn't possibly take the only bed in the house, but she took my arm. 'You are to spend the night here. The men will make do downstairs.'

Her tone didn't allow argument. I waited, hoping she would leave me, but she stood at the top of the ladder and glared at me.

'We will find a way to send you back,' she said with an assurance I was coming to recognise. Her voice was low, presumably because she didn't want the men to hear what she was saying. 'You will not return again, or you will feel the coldness of my blade.' She said it as a matter of fact rather than a threat. 'Xavier is a good man, but—'

Tired and irritable at her assertiveness, I interrupted. 'We are only together now because of circumstance, and I can assure you that as soon as I return home I will make a point of staying there.'

Even in my exhaustion I knew I didn't have the experience to become involved with someone as worldly as Xavier. If this was the kind of woman he was used to associating with, then I had no business allowing myself to imagine any closeness between us.

'I am glad you understand.'

I didn't add that maybe Xavier should have a say in the matter. What he chose to do with Ember was nothing to do with me. 'If you don't mind, I'd like to go to bed.'

She turned and left without another word.

I lay down, not caring that I had nothing to change into. I simply felt relief at finally lying down on a bed. I closed my eyes and heard Andre and Xavier's deep voices coming from downstairs as they quietly discussed our next steps. I was happy to leave plans for our future in their capable hands.

I dreamt about being back at home with Mum and helping her harvest some herbs. Then I dreamt I was in Xavier's arms, kissing his chest as he told me how much he loved me and would never let me go. What seemed like seconds later, I woke, startled at how Xavier's warm flesh had felt against my lips. My cheeks burned and it took a moment for me to realise where I was and that I had been dreaming. It had seemed very realistic, more so than any dream I had ever experienced.

It took a while for me to gather my senses, and I decided to repress any thoughts of what it felt like to lie with Xavier. I had been too disturbed by the realism of my dream to think clearly.

The house was silent but, despite my exhaustion, I couldn't manage to fall asleep again. Eventually I got up and ran my fingers through my messy hair, trying to make myself as presentable as possible. Then I went downstairs, creeping into the room as quietly as possible. I smiled to see the two men asleep at the table where I had left them, their heads resting on their arms, the jug of wine empty. These men had the power to save me, or at least I hoped so.

I looked around the room and it was then I noticed the fireplace. I gasped.

Both men sprang to their feet, giving me a shock and making me shriek.

'Sorry, I didn't mean to wake you,' I said, panicking at their battle-ready expressions.

Both relaxed instantly. Xavier came over to me. 'Something frighten you?'

I shook my head, embarrassed to have caused a scene. 'No, it's the fireplace.'

The men looked at each other. 'Something is wrong with it?' Andre asked, frowning as he walked over to inspect it.

'No, it's not that.'

'Then what?' Xavier pushed his hair back from his face and retied it with a thin leather lace.

I struggled to come to terms with what I was seeing. 'It's exactly the same as the one at Honey Bee Cottage,' I said disbelievingly.

Andre rested his hand on the heavy oak beam that made up the mantelpiece. 'How can that be possible?'

I wasn't sure but as I studied it further, I knew – despite the darker, more basic decor, the lack of a lean-to at the side of the house where our kitchen stood, the different front door – that I was right.

'I'm sure this is my house.'

Chapter Seventeen

XAVIER

'Your house?' Andre and I asked in disbelief.

She gave me a pleading look. 'You've stayed at Honey Bee Cottage. Surely you must agree with what I'm saying?'

I gave her comment some thought. The village was very different now to how I had found it in the future but, wanting to help her, I studied the room carefully. 'I've visited Andre many times, but it feels smaller here than your home.' She went to speak, but I shook my head. 'I'm not saying it isn't possible, but the chance of this building still standing after three centuries is doubtful, do you not think?'

The look of resignation on her face saddened me. I didn't want to take away the connection she had made to her life. Her expression changed and I could see she wasn't one to give up easily.

'No, I don't. There are plenty of properties still standing in Jersey from this period.' Although her voice sounded determined her eyes held a look of doubt.

'You could be right,' I said, happy to relent.

She grimaced. 'There must be a way to prove it, though.' She pointed to the fireplace. 'What about that? You must recognise it as being the same one as ours.'

I studied the fireplace trying to recall Mrs Le Gros's. 'It is similar, I grant you.'

'I'm certain it's the same one.' She walked over and, stepping into the inglenook fireplace, peered up the chimney. She ran her hand over one of the stones, her face lighting up suddenly. 'It is.'

'You can tell?'

She waved me over and pointed. 'Look, there's a chink missing from that corner of the granite stone.' She took my hand and placed it on the stone. 'Feel for yourself.'

Understanding how the connection between future and present comforted her, I felt the roughness of the missing corner piece and smiled. I studied the room afresh. The windows were in the same places, as was the door. The more I looked, the more familiar the room became, and I had to agree that the cottage could indeed be Mrs Le Gros's home. I recalled only too easily how out of place and out of control I had felt when time had shifted me forward, and I was happy that she had discovered this connection.

I turned to Andre. 'My friend, meet one of the future occupants of your home.'

He clapped his hands together cheerily, seeming unfazed by my comment or Briar's insistence. 'If that is true, then I am honoured. Why don't we acquaint ourselves with stories of our home over breakfast?'

'I'd like that,' Briar said, shooting a cheerful smile in my direction.

Andre left the room and called for Hester.

I reached once more into the chimney to find the chink. 'This is extraordinary. Maybe we can pass a message to your mother this way?'

Briar's immediate delight vanished as she gave my suggestion some thought. 'The paper would catch alight before she saw it, I imagine. Mum has a fire in the grate every day. It's where she works with her herbs, preparing them for her tinctures and balms.' She frowned. 'Although now we have so little fuel, we are lighting fires less frequently.' She crossed her arms. 'Maybe there is a way. I know she will be frantic about me and I'd love to let her know I'm safe.'

Hearing footsteps, we turned to find Hester carrying a tray of food to the table. 'Let's sit and eat,' I said. 'We'll think more clearly with full stomachs.'

Andre strode back into the room. I was relieved to be able to relax and talk more freely than we could have done with Ember present.

As soon as we were seated and each of us served with food and drink, I told Andre about wanting to send a message to Diana. 'How do you think we might go about this?'

'If we can't communicate with her from here then I imagine my mother will attempt to contact me through Mont Orgueil somehow,' Briar said thoughtfully.

'It is the obvious place,' I agreed. 'I would probably do the same thing. There is little reason for her to suspect you would spend time in your own home, albeit at a different time.'

Briar stopped eating and I wondered if she was imagining being in this room, lighting the fire or even eating her own breakfast with her mother nearby.

'I know this will sound odd,' Briar said, a pink tinge to

her cheeks, 'but I can't help sensing her presence. It's as if Mum has just left to fetch something from the kitchen, or is in the next room where Hester is now, and I just can't see her.'

I stilled, wondering if I could pick up a sense of Mrs Le Gros. For a moment I thought I felt her presence, then decided I was being fanciful. I barely knew the woman and I doubted whether it was possible to feel the presence of someone not to be born for several centuries – unless, like Briar, one was related to her.

Briar closed her eyes. 'I'm imagining Mum humming to herself as she works,' she explained. 'I can almost hear her, I'm certain of it.'

I caught Andre's eye and saw he was as unsure as I was about how to react to Briar's comment. He was a kind man, though, and kept his doubts to himself.

She opened her eyes and caught us looking at each other. 'You think me silly, don't you?'

'No,' we both said – too quickly to be believed.

I saw Andre's expression alter slightly. 'If I can accept you and Xavier meeting as you did and returning to this century, then I have to trust what you are suggesting.'

'You don't believe we've come from the future, do you?' I asked without thinking, wishing now that I had introduced Andre and Briar when she had last been here. I had been too frightened to share her presence with anyone lest Ember discover her whereabouts.

Andre flinched and I saw something I hadn't expected in his eyes. Guilt. 'Is there something worrying you, Andre?' I asked, concerned.

He cast his eyes downward for a moment. Returning his

gaze to mine, he said, 'I believe I am the reason you were sent forward in time, Xavier.'

I shook my head. 'That doesn't make sense. Unless you have special powers,' I joked, to show how little his comment fazed me.

He leant forward. 'It's true.'

Seeing how troubled the thought made him, I shrugged. 'Tell me how you believe you brought this about.'

He took a deep breath. 'When you were condemned to death, I was desperate to find a way to help you. I recalled you mentioning Old Mother Dorey being able to help people at their wits' end.'

I didn't remember saying anything to him but supposed I must have done. 'Go on.'

He folded his hands in his lap. 'I spoke to anyone I thought could help you, but when you were to be executed the following day, I knew any chance of you being rescued had gone.'

'What did she say?'

He studied his hands and shook his head. 'She was gravely ill, Xavier. I should not have gone to her, but I did and there's nothing I can do now to change that.'

'Andre, what happened?' I asked intrigued.

He looked me in the eyes once more. 'Her daughter told me she was too unwell but the kindly old woman insisted she would do whatever she could to save you. I thanked her and left.'

I could tell there was more. 'And then?'

'Her daughter showed me to the door. She was angry with me for bothering her mother, which was understandable.

She explained her mother was hours from death and told me not to expect her to have the strength to do anything for me.'

My heart swelled to know this dear woman's last act had been to send me into the future to be with Briar. I reached out and rested a hand on Andre's forearm, grateful to my friend for his intervention. A thought occurred to me. 'You said she was gravely ill.'

'She passed on the following morning.'

I opened my mouth to speak when Ember entered the room, a frown on her angelic face. The atmosphere of the room dipped. I suspected she had bad news to impart. I wished she had kept away for longer to give Andre and me a chance to talk further.

Ember stopped at the end of the table and looked from one of us to the other. 'Something has happened.'

It wasn't a question.

Chapter Eighteen

DIANA

I couldn't shift the sense of panic, nausea and loss that accompanied my every waking minute. How could I have been this careless? I recalled how I had scoured the ruin immediately after Briar and Xavier's disappearance, frantically searching for a message from my daughter and almost getting caught twice by patrolling soldiers.

They were probably alerted by the sound of me sobbing as I pulled stones from the walls, looking for a note I prayed she had left me. I was desperate for proof Briar was still alive somewhere. Briar was resourceful. She would find a way to contact me somehow, of that I was certain. I had to be. It was all I had to keep me from giving in to the hysteria welling up inside my chest.

After my fruitless search, I had made my way to Witches Rock, only returning home when curfew was nearing. It was now the next morning, following a sleepless night desperately scouring my grimoire for spells or ideas and wondering why the answer couldn't be found. It wasn't safe to keep my grimoire out in the open, so I decided to return it to its hiding place.

I took a fork and prised up the short floorboard in the corner of the room, to the right of the inglenook fireplace, rewrapped my grimoire in the ancient linen cloth from my grandmother's shawl, and slipped it back inside before replacing the board.

Satisfied my book of shadows was safely stored from prying eyes, or German soldiers should they decide to search my home, I got to my feet and resumed pacing back and forth across my living room, desperately trying to think of a way to rescue Briar before it was too late.

I forced that notion to the back of my mind. I couldn't bear to even contemplate such a scenario. I had two choices. Either I found a way to bring my daughter back to me, or I accepted the fact that my stupidity had caused her death. I had no idea how to make the first option happen, and refused to accept the second. There was nothing for it but to go to my coven and admit to casting a dangerous spell without my High Priestess's permission.

I glanced at the wall clock and, seeing it was twenty minutes after the end of curfew, slipped on sturdier shoes and lifted my coat from the hook behind the front door.

I had barely buttoned it up when there was a light knock at the door. While I debated whether to answer, or ignore it and hope the visitor went on their way, the person knocked again. Clearly, I needed to speak to them if I was going to be able to leave the house.

I opened the front door and was taken aback to see Babette Le Dain standing there. My High Priestess. Had she sensed what I had done?

'Babette?' I said, bemused to see the woman I had known since we met on our first day at kindergarten. We hadn't spent much time together other than as a group in the coven, since a falling-out over a matter that now seemed ridiculously trivial compared to losing Briar. Our previous High Priestess had passed away after a sudden illness six months before, and Babette had been chosen to take her place, which had ignited my feelings of unfairness. Just because she was a lady of standing and the wife of the civic head of our parish didn't mean it didn't hurt that she had been chosen over me.

Her face bore no amusement; indeed, it was clear she was angry about something. Surely, she hadn't already heard what had happened? Had she?

'Good morning, Mrs Le Dain,' a woman said from nearby. Babette raised a hand to wave at her. 'Good morning, Mrs Le Neveu.' Still smiling at the woman, she said out of the corner of her mouth, 'I suggest you ask me inside.'

Wishing I had an alternative, but aware that if our conversation was to remain private it needed to take place in my cottage, I moved back and waited for her to enter. Once the door was closed and we had privacy I offered her a seat.

'I don't have time to stop for longer than a few minutes,' she began.

I waited for her to continue, trying my best not to look as tense as I felt. She looked me in the eye and folded her arms across her chest. 'I see you have no intention of admitting what you've done, Diana. Although I suppose I shouldn't be all that surprised.'

I gritted my teeth, determined not to let her goading make me snap back at her. 'Why don't you share what's on your mind, Babette?'

'Very well.' She sighed. 'I had intended to come and ask you if you knew about it, then reasoned it was none of my business. I discovered that you, Briar and a strapping young man were seen walking up to Mont Orgueil last night.' She stared at me, for a moment looking unsure of herself. 'And only you returned.'

As irritated as I was to discover others were gossiping about my daughter and me, I knew Babette well enough to sense her concern.

'Whoever spoke to you this morning was quick off the mark. It takes you ten minutes to walk here from your house and they must have run to your place immediately curfew was over to pass on this news.'

Babette rolled her eyes. 'I won't mention names but you're lucky it was someone I can trust not to share the information with anyone else.'

Pacified slightly, I nodded. 'I was going to call on you, as it happens,' I admitted. She looked doubtful. 'It's true.' I indicated my coat. 'You arrived here before I had a chance to leave.'

'Coming to see me, you say?'

I nodded, indicating the armchair. 'I think you'd better take a seat.' When she had done so, I added, 'I've done a silly thing, Babette.' I explained how Xavier came to be here, what I knew about him, and my attempt to help him return to his time in history.

She stared silently at me.

'Are you all right?' I asked, hating that I had shocked her deeply.

'I will be.' She shook her head. 'What you did wasn't silly, Diana, it was utterly reckless. Poor Briar. She's heaven only knows where. At least she'll probably be with someone she knows, which can only be a good thing.'

I hoped she was right. 'I need your help to rescue her. Will you do that for me?'

Babette stared at me, disappointment oozing from every pore, and I realised that instead of asking for her help I should have first apologised for what I'd done. 'You don't have to look at me that way, I know I'm in the wrong. And I'm sorrier than you can imagine.'

'You know it's not safe to cast spells of this magnitude without the coven's support, Diana.'

'I do,' I admitted realising she was more hurt by my secrecy than angry. 'I promise I've learnt my lesson. I have no intention of doing anything like this again.'

Babette leant forward and rested a hand on my knee. 'Never mind that now. I am here to help you, not reprimand you, although I don't know why you didn't feel you could confide in me about this Xavier chap.'

'I thought that with all you have going on, supporting your husband, you had more than enough to cope with.'

'Not where friends' daughters are concerned, Diana.' She sighed. 'The others will help us find a way to resolve this and bring Briar back to you.'

'Thank you,' I said, hearing my voice break with emotion. 'I'll never forgive myself if any harm comes to her.' It was true. My daughter meant everything to me. I needed her back, where I could at least watch out for her.

'We will do our best to make sure she comes back safely.'

Relieved to hear her assurances, I relaxed slightly, and the sobs I had been holding forced their way out.

Chapter Nineteen

BRIAR

E mber's powerful presence filled the room. She wasn't as tall or as broad as either of the men, but there was an unmistakable strength about her that was difficult to ignore. I tried to imagine what might have happened in her past to make her this way. She stood silently in front of us, arms by her sides, contemplating something she hadn't yet shared. It was clear she made a far better friend than enemy, and I was going to have to follow Xavier's lead and find a way to befriend her.

Another thing she didn't bother hiding was her possessiveness of Xavier and Andre. She clearly considered me to be an unwelcome guest she would not have entertained, given the choice. I shifted my gaze to Xavier. He was charismatic and I had to admit, if only to myself, that I was attracted to him. There was something about him that niggled away in my brain, though: a familiarity that, despite my best efforts, I couldn't put my finger on. Did I feel as if I knew him because he reminded me of the hero in one of those films I enjoyed watching at West's Cinema before the war, or for some other reason? But what? I probably felt connected to him, I thought, because of the strange experiences we now shared. Ember's reaction to us both showed me I needed to remember my place and be careful not to overstep any boundaries.

I noticed Andre stare at me thoughtfully. He had a knowing look on his face, and I wondered what he was thinking. I decided not to worry about it. My focus should be on finding a way to send a message to Mum, and the only chance I had of doing that was with the help of these three people.

Even though Xavier was a condemned man he had proved to me that I could trust him. He was, after all, my closest ally. Ember was no friend of mine, that much was evident. I hoped her affection for the two men would keep her in check and be enough of an incentive to help me succeed in my endeavours. There was something about Andre that made me feel I could trust him. I supposed it was the kindness that shone through his eyes.

When none of them spoke, I decided to take the lead. 'I think we can all agree that the best way for everyone to get back to their normal lives will be to find out how to send me home.'

'The issue is how we make that happen.' Andre yawned. 'If you believe this was your home then the obvious solution would be to find some way to send a message to your mother by leaving one here.'

'Her home?' Ember smirked. 'Now *that* I am interested to hear about.'

Andre explained why I had come to that conclusion and raised his hand when Ember began to speak. 'Not now, Ember. It is not the time.'

Relieved she didn't argue for once, I decided to let Ember know what we were doing. 'I'm trying to think of a way to make contact with my mother.'

Ember grimaced, clearly thinking me ridiculous.

'The message will need to be left where Diana will find it easily,' Xavier said thoughtfully, leaning forward resting his forearms on his thighs, his hands hanging loosely between his legs. 'Does your mother have a place she might hide private papers or jewellery do you know?'

I was about to shake my head when a memory sprang into my mind. I thought back to several years before, when I saw her hiding what I eventually discovered to be her spell book. I gasped, unable to hide my excitement. 'I do know of somewhere.'

I leapt to my feet, delighted to have recalled the only time I had caught her secreting the book in a hole under the floorboards. She had taken care never to go to that hiding place again when I was around, probably hoping I hadn't noticed what she was doing, since I never referred to it. Aware of the value my mother placed on her privacy, I never dared take a peek.

Now, though, I couldn't wait to have a look. I picked up a two-pronged fork from the table and walked over to a corner on one side of the fireplace, hoping I recalled correctly where the secret hidey-hole was. Willing it to be there, I stuck the prongs between the two floorboards, trying not to damage either utensil or floorboards. But I was unable to shift them.

'Let me try,' Andre said, eager to have a go. He took the fork from my hand and, withdrawing a dagger from a sheath at his side, knelt on the floor and carefully manoeuvred both instruments into the narrow gaps.

I was beginning to give up hope that there was a hole this far back in history. 'Maybe the floor has been changed since you lived here,' I said, aware how odd that sounded.

The three of them looked askance at me. 'What I mean is—'

Andre cheered triumphantly. 'Success.'

We watched as he pulled up a shorter floorboard and put his arm into the hole until it disappeared up to the elbow.

'What's that?' I asked as he withdrew a sheet of paper.

'Is this paper?' he asked, holding it up between his thumb and forefinger.

'Yes, of course,' I said, unsure why he couldn't recognise such an everyday item. Seeing each of them look at me with disdain I realised that what they were used to writing on must be very different to the twentieth-century sheet in his hand.

'Please give it to me,' I said. I unfolded it, my hands shaking, excited to read my mother's familiar cursory writing. She had held this, I thought, relishing the unexpected connection to her.

'What does it say?' Ember asked impatiently. Either she couldn't read my mother's modern writing or she was illiterate. Pushing thoughts of Ember aside, I began to read.

Darling Briar, I leave this note in the hope you remember seeing this secret place. Please know I am trying all avenues to find a way to bring you home. Babette Le Dain and the rest of my e...

Briar realised the crossed-out 'c' was the start of the word coven, and was relieved her mother had had the sense not to use such an inflammatory word. She read on.

...group of friends. I have been to Mont Orgueil searching for a message from you, but to no avail. Witches Rock is also somewhere I've looked for clues from you. If you find this, please write on the back of this note so I have confirmation you have read it. All love, Mum. XX

I couldn't speak for a few seconds. Even the air in the room seemed to still. Then Xavier grabbed hold of me, lifting me up, and spun me round laughing.

'You are clever like your mother,' he cheered. 'We now have a way to communicate with her.'

'We do,' I agreed not caring that tears were running down my face as I stared into his eyes touched by his delight.

Andre coughed and the room felt cooler as Xavier's gaze left me. He lowered me to the floor, his arms dropping from around me. I stepped back, instantly missing his touch but comforted by the knowledge that Mum was doing all she could.

My thoughts raced as I tried to make sense of how our communication had spanned three hundred years. Maybe she had cast a spell to make this happen. I tried to imagine what that spell might look like but, exhausted from all that had happened in the previous twenty-four hours, closed my eyes, deciding to simply relish the knowledge that it had worked.

I smiled, aware that when Mum read my reply, she would be beside herself with relief, as I was now.

'Do you have ink and a—' I struggled to think what the correct name might be for a writing implement.

'Quill?' Andre said, leaving the room briefly before returning carrying a small bowl of what seemed to be ink, and a goose feather, its end fashioned into a nib.

I sat down to write, making a dreadful mess. 'This isn't easy,' I mumbled, biting my lower lip and giving it another try. I wished Mum hadn't expected me to reply on the back of her own message because I was running out of space with all the inkblots among my attempts to set words down. In the end I decided the most important thing was giving her proof I was still alive.

Overjoyed to find note. Am well. Desperate to come home.
Know you will make it happen. Surreal to be staying in the same
house we live in. Is a comfort. Much love, Briar xx

I went to fold it up, but Andre's hand pressed down on my wrist. 'Wait. It must dry first.'

I sat back, staring at the sheet of paper and my badly scrawled reply while Andre sprinkled a fine powder over the ink. Soon Mum would be reading my words. It occurred to me that both she and I had touched the piece of paper and a warm feeling seeped through me, calming me for the first time since my unexpected arrival.

Eager to return the note to the secret place so Mum could find and read it, I stood. 'Is it possible to return it to the hole now?'

Andre shrugged. 'Take care not to touch the ink and smudge it any more than it already is.'

The amusement in his eyes and the knowledge that my mother would soon read my reply cheered me and made me laugh. 'I would never survive here with my writing skills.'

'Not everyone needs the skill to write,' Ember said huffily. 'Some people believe possessing the knowledge of survival more useful.'

I didn't respond. My writing, however rudimentary it was with the tools I currently had at my disposal, was everything to me now. It was the only way I could converse with my mother, and the miracle of that happening was almost more than I could bear without crying.

A harsh voice called for someone outside in the street and the three of us stilled.

'What's the matter?' I asked, seeing their horrified expressions. 'Who is it?'

'That's what I came to tell you,' Ember whispered. 'I heard that the Witchfinder had discovered a new witch in the area and called his men to begin searching the village.' I wasn't certain, and it was over in a split second, but I thought I spotted a look of excitement flash across Ember's face.

'And you didn't think to tell us immediately?' Andre snapped.

'Quick,' Xavier said, his face pale. 'Hide the message before he comes here.'

Xavier must have seen my horror and shook his head. '*If* he comes here,' he said, correcting himself.

Andre picked up my note and ran the few steps to the corner of the room. I held my breath as he set the note deep into the hole, willing him to hurry. There was another bang on the door.

'Open this door,' a voice demanded.

'Quickly,' I whispered, my heart pounding so hard I was certain everyone must hear it.

Andre replaced the floorboard and stamped on it, then strode to his front door.

'Mr Dankworth,' we heard him say. 'Do please come in.'

Chapter Twenty

XAVIER

Fear flashed in Briar's eyes. Wanting to remind her I was there for her, I took hold of her wrist and gently pulled her to my side, stepping forward to shield her. It wasn't much protection, but it was all I could do at that moment.

Roger Dankworth, the Witchfinder who had arrested Briar the last time she had been here, strode purposefully into the house. He took his time studying each of us in turn. He wasn't a local man, but everyone on the island knew of him, speaking in hushed tones about his expertise at hunting down women assumed to be involved in sorcery. I had seen the depths he would go to to prove someone guilty. Witnessing Briar's distress when he had interrogated her was enough for me.

It pained me to think how much terror he had sent through our small community, but whatever my thoughts about him, it wouldn't bode well to rile him – not if I wanted to keep Briar safe until her mother worked her magick. I concentrated on keeping my anger at bay.

I prayed he didn't recognise her. A man as arrogant as the

Witchfinder was, I hoped, far more recognisable to others than we were to him. If he was aware of my death sentence, then Briar would be at Ember's mercy, and that was something I couldn't let happen.

His eyes narrowed as his gaze fell on Briar. 'Who is this?' He pointed to her with a leer that made me want to step between them, but to do so would only antagonise him.

'I'm Briar Le Gros.' I heard the terror in her voice. I noticed he did too and hated him even more, seeing his enjoyment at her show of fear. He turned to Ember, probably because he recognised Briar's surname as being local.

'You.' He reached out and poked her hard in her chest.

I cringed inwardly. I had never witnessed anyone treat Ember disrespectfully without her retaliating. On this occasion she had the sense to keep her expression blank. No show of fear, or rage, or anything, for that matter. If I hadn't been more concerned for Briar's safety I would have cheered her fortitude.

'Ember Touzel.'

He frowned. 'I believe I know you.'

She didn't respond.

His eyes narrowed. 'What sort of ungodly name is Ember?'

Without flinching, she answered. 'There is nothing ungodly about me or my name, sire.'

By the look on his face, he couldn't decide whether to be impressed or infuriated by her response.

The man turned to Andre, then to me, but didn't ask us to reveal our identities. He seemed far more interested in the women. Then, without another word, he turned and walked to the door. Before leaving, he turned back to us and pointed his stick at Briar. 'I have you in my sights, maid. You are known to me and I will recall how soon enough.'

Briar tensed, but didn't make a sound. We stood in silence as he left the house.

Andre hurried to close the door behind him, then puffed out his cheeks. 'That was uncomfortable.'

Ember said, 'I'd say it was far more than that.' She stared at Briar before speaking to me. 'She needs to leave, for all our sakes. It's not safe for her to stay.'

'But where will I go?' Briar glanced at the corner where her mother's letter was hidden. 'If I go, I won't know how my mother responds.'

'She has nowhere else to go,' I argued.

Andre came closer to us, keeping his voice low, careful, no doubt, in case the Witchfinder was still lurking outside. None of us needed him to overhear our conversation lest we tip him off in any way.

'I believe Briar is safe here, for now,' I assured them despite my uncertainty. 'If her mother replies with instructions she might not need to be here for much longer.'

Briar sighed. 'That's what I'm praying for.'

'We all are.' Ember's eyes filled with disdain. 'A witch's daughter who prays? I'm shocked,' she added spitefully.

'That's enough,' I snapped, glaring at her. 'We must support each other, Ember.'

'I do not have to do anything,' she reminded me. Then shrugged. 'However I shall refrain from sharing my thoughts. For now.'

She was infuriating, but I had no intention of rowing with her and giving her the attention she craved.

Ember avoided my angry gaze. 'How long do you expect your mother to take?'

Briar shrugged. 'I have no idea if she will find a solution.'

'Surely you have faith in her abilities?' Andre asked, seeming worried.

Briar's eyes filled with unshed tears. 'Yes.' She hesitated then took a steadying breath. 'Mum helped Xavier return here and she'll have a better chance of rescuing me with the help of her sisterhood.'

Briar needed my backing. 'I know Diana Le Gros a little and Briar's right,' I said quickly before Ember had a chance to argue. 'I believe she will succeed. We have no choice but to wait and hope we hear from her again shortly.'

Ember flung her arms wide, glaring at me. 'What if he comes back and arrests you? Or us? What then?'

I understood her fury. By backing Briar I was putting the rest of us in terrible danger, but if I wanted to help the woman I loved then it was what I must do.

'I'm sorry, Ember, but we need to read any message Mrs Le Gros sends and we can't do that if Briar and I are hiding elsewhere.'

'Briar. Briar. Briar,' she snapped glancing at Briar with a fierceness even I hadn't seen before. 'This woman only came into your life a few days ago yet already her wishes must come before any of ours.'

'Before yours, you mean.' I was relieved Briar's previous visit to this time had been when Ember and Andre had been staying on the other side of the island with family. I doubted Briar would still be free if Ember had suspected the closeness between Briar and me then. Anything Ember and I had shared before I first met Briar was long over, but she was a jealous woman who didn't take kindly to another woman taking attention from her.

'I know it seems that way,' I began.

'It doesn't seem it,' Andre replied firmly. 'It is that way, Xavier.' Ember took a deep breath to continue her rant but Andre continued. 'Don't argue, Ember. Even if you don't, I understand Xavier's loyalty to Briar.' He gave Ember an apologetic smile. 'It is not her fault Xavier ended up in her time. It is thanks to her and her mother that he has been returned to us.'

She didn't look appeased. 'It is due to her mother's carelessness that we are hiding this woman who could end up leading us all to the hangman's noose.'

Ember turned her back on Briar and walked to the door, waving her hand over her shoulder to emphasise her boredom with the conversation. 'I've had enough of your whining.'

The three of us watched her go, none of us bothering to plead with her to stay. I wondered if Briar and Andre felt as much relief as I did to see the back of her.

Andre picked up his cup and took a mouthful of the contents. 'We must discuss our options.'

'Options?' Briar seemed confused.

'Indeed.' He sat at the table again. 'We know the Witchfinder will return. He has a nose for lies and never wavers or gives up on his prey. Unfortunately for us, he has discovered your whereabouts, Briar. He will have his spies watching you. If your mother is unsuccessful in her endeavours, you will have to move away.'

'For how long?'

I did not know and had no intention of lying to her. 'Either for good, or until your mother succeeds.'

We fell silent, none of us caring to voice the third option. I shrank from the thought of Briar being arrested and tried as a witch. I saw her stare at the corner of the room where the message was hidden.

I saw Andre watching Briar as I had been. I sensed his fear for her future, as did I.

Ember, we both knew, could not be trusted to do the right thing. Where had she gone? I wondered, a troubled sense of doom seeping into my mind. Was she capable of tipping off the Witchfinder or his cronies about Briar's mother? Telling them where Briar had come from? Giving them proof that Briar's mother, if not Briar herself, was a witch?

I hoped that even Ember would not stoop low enough to cause the death of an innocent woman.

Chapter Twenty-One

DIANA

I t had been three hours since I had come up with the idea of writing a note and placing it in my hidey-hole, and two since Babette Le Dain had helped me devise a spell to send it back to Briar. She had gone to speak to the other members of our sisterhood immediately after leaving me to cast the spell and wait to see what happened.

I couldn't settle, deciding to steep camomile, lavender and verbena and add it to heated oil to make a soothing balm. I sensed I would need one over the next few days and my personal supply was running very low. I stirred the oil, unable to resist for very long the need to check whether Briar had seen my note.

I leant over the oil infused with the herbal mixture and breathed in slowly to steady myself. Calmer, I locked the front door in case Babette returned unexpectedly with someone else, then hurried to the corner of the room, kneeling and impatiently working the floorboard. Reaching into the hole I felt the piece of paper and stilled, breathless at the thought of this attempt to reach my daughter not working.

Was I expecting too much that this would work? Did Briar even remember seeing me at this private place of mine? And even if she had discovered it, why would she ever think to look inside? Panic coursed through me as it dawned on me I didn't know whether the floor even existed back then.

I checked myself. This cottage was a couple of hundred years old, but three hundred? I didn't know. I reassured myself by deciding that even if the floorboards had been replaced over the centuries, it was possible for the hidey-hole to have been dug out all those years before. Then again, for all I knew this could have been someone's garden back then, or common ground.

I pushed my doubt away. I had to try whatever might be possible to reach her and I wasn't going to find out the results if I didn't summon up the courage to look. I lifted the sheet of paper out and saw my handwriting. Taking a steadying breath, I slowly turned it over to check the reverse, hesitating in case my attempt had failed. I cried out. There was writing.

I stared at it. It was terribly messy with blotches all over it. I couldn't even recognise whether it was Briar's writing. I studied it and saw her name at the bottom. She had written it. I covered my mouth with my hand to stem another cry of delight. I didn't need to alert that damn Nazi who was probably snooping around outside as usual. I looked at the writing once more, aghast at the difference, and supposed she must have used a quill. It would explain the almost illegible scrawl.

I sat back on my haunches and read, the words blurring

through my tears. Frustrated, I brushed them away, blinked, then attempted to reread what she had written.

Briar had replied – that was all that mattered. Against all the odds my darling daughter had found my message and answered me.

My heart raced as I closed my eyes, lightheaded with relief. She knew I was searching for a way to rescue her. I had succeeded in my first goal. Now all I needed to do was find a way to bring her back.

I clutched the sheet against my chest, then noticed my right thumb had a smudge of dark ink on it and gasped. I touched one of her words. The ink was still slightly wet.

Tears flowed freely down my cheeks, and I knew that if I could bridge the divide of three centuries this way, I could succeed in my quest. I had no idea how, but I would do it. And with the help of my coven nothing was going to stop me.

Knowing my daughter as I did, I knew she would be waiting impatiently for me to reply. I quickly grabbed my fountain pen and wrote a hurried reply.

Briar, my dearest child, the ink from your words has smudged on my thumb. I feel closer to you than I ever dared hope I might again. I have spoken to Mrs Le Dain who has promised to help me. Stay strong, darling girl. Know without doubt that I will find a way to bring you home. Your loving mother. XX

Hearing one of my neighbours being questioned by a soldier outside, I quickly secreted the sheet of paper back in the hole. As I was about to replace the floorboard, it occurred to me to try and send back my fountain pen with it. It would help Briar with her responses. I smiled to myself. It would also help me decipher them. I had several pens, but Briar knew this one had been gifted to me by her father on our first wedding anniversary. It was silver and she knew how I valued it. I placed it carefully onto the sheet of paper and replaced the floorboard before standing and moving back to gather my thoughts.

Being involved in witchcraft all my life I had learnt about the abhorrent treatment of witches by witch-hunters centuries before. It was partly why we remained secretive. *Another way to keep women in their place*, I thought with irritation. Now was not the time to become angry about things I could not change. I needed to focus on bringing my daughter back to the relative safety of the island as it now stood.

Chapter Twenty-Two

BRIAR

I was still trembling from coming face to face with the Witchfinder despite him having left Andre's home almost an hour before. He looked nothing like I had expected. Not that I had a clue what a Witchfinder should look like, but it certainly wasn't this man with his long light brown hair, a black dusty hat covering the top of his head. I thought of his sharp features and dark brown eyes and shivered.

The way he had taken his time to silently study each of us, stopping at me, staring into my eyes for an inexorably long time, bothered me. I wasn't sure but I had thought he sniffed when he came to me. As if I was a flower or spice of some sort he was trying to place. It was disconcerting.

My attention kept being drawn to the corner where my reply waited for Mum to find and read it. I tapped my foot impatiently as I sat at the table, oblivious to Andre and Xavier's conversation.

'Do you think it's too early to take a look in case Mum has replied yet?'

Xavier and Andre glanced at each other before smiling.

'Do as you wish,' Andre said. 'She must be as anxious to hear from you as you are from her.'

I picked up the fork and knife and walked quickly over to the corner of the room. The floorboard wouldn't budge. 'It's stuck.' I panicked. 'Please help me.'

I reasoned that whatever Mum might say she would not have had time to put any plan to rescue me into action. The thought saddened me but I needed to be realistic.

Andre took the implements from me and managed to lift the floorboard. 'What in heaven's name is this?'

Xavier and I stepped forward, fascinated to discover what had caused Andre's excitement.

Andre peered into the hole for a moment longer before reaching in and retrieving something. Desperate to know what it might be, I watched as he held it up. The three of us stared at it, aware that it had not been there before. 'What is this?'

'I believe I saw this when I was with you and your mother,' Xavier said.

I bit my lower lip, not wishing to give in to my emotions yet again.

'Briar?' Xavier asked.

'That is my mother's silver fountain pen,' I said studying the familiar briar that had been engraved along the length of the pen and was the inspiration for Mum choosing my name.

I saw their confused expressions and realised I needed to explain further. I took the pen from Andre, unscrewed the cap and showed them the nib. Then, unscrewing the barrel, pointed to the converter. 'That's where the ink is stored.' They exchanged doubtful looks. 'It's a writing implement.' I took the note from Andre and wrote my initials to show them.

'Like a quill,' Andre said in a hushed tone as he watched me replace the cap on the barrel and hand the pen to him.

He studied it in awed silence.

I took the note from him and read it, my heart swelling with joy to read Mum's words. 'She has been offered help, Xavier,' I told him. I reached out and, smiling, rested a hand on his forearm. 'You'll all soon be rid of me.' I did my best to sound jocular but living in this nightmare was proving too much. 'You won't be in as much danger with me out of the way.'

Xavier didn't smile. 'I am still to be executed,' he reminded me.

I wished he hadn't. I hated to think of him no longer walking the earth.

'Sorry, I shouldn't have said that.'

He smiled but it didn't reach his eyes. 'I will be happy to know you are safe. Your mother's news is what we need to hear.'

Andre was still studying the pen. 'It is a thing of beauty.'

'Mum treasures that pen more than any of her possessions,' I explained, wanting them to understand how important this message was from her. 'She's showing us how determined she is. I've never known her to part from it before, ever since my father gave it to her when I was born on their first anniversary. She never lets anyone else use it.'

'Then we are honoured,' Xavier said, taking the pen from Andre and studying it for himself.

I noticed Andre's expression lighten. 'What is it?'

He pointed to the hole. 'The hiding place must hold a passage between now and the future,' he said thoughtfully. 'Although I do not understand how.' He stilled at hearing his own words. I suspected he hadn't meant to voice them. He glanced nervously towards the window.

'There must be a portal there,' I suggested.

'We must take care not to share our thoughts with others,' he whispered. 'Even, I fear, from my own cousin.'

'You don't trust her?' I asked, shocked to hear my own doubts about Ember being voiced by someone close to her.

His shoulders slumped. 'I do not.' My heart ached at his admission. 'If I am to ensure your safety, and as your host I believe it is my duty to do so, I have no choice but to be alert.'

I felt the weight of their troubles on my shoulders.

Xavier noticed and took my hand. 'Do not blame yourself. You were being kind wanting to return my handkerchief to me. It was our timing that was remiss not your actions.'

'Now is not the time for recriminations,' Andre reminded us. 'You are not safe here. I sense it. Xavier, you must take Briar somewhere secure.' He closed his eyes briefly. 'Where Ember will not look for her.'

'You really do not trust her?' Xavier asked seeming surprised.

'But the messages,' I argued.

'I shall forward any on to you,' Andre promised.

Hearing footsteps outside in the lane, I felt my pulse race. 'Where should we go?'

Xavier gave my question some thought as Andre handed my mother's pen back to me. 'We do not wish to put anyone else's life in danger, but we dare not travel too far from here.'

He crossed his arms and, even through my fear, I couldn't miss the outline of his muscles through his linen shirtsleeves. He sensed me staring and glanced at me, a question in his eyes that I couldn't make out.

I turned away, pretending to study my mother's pen, desperate to hide my mortification.

Andre walked over to the window and peered outside. 'I know somewhere.'

'Tell us,' Xavier said.

'There is a boat shed along the beach in between two of the shipbuilders' yards. You can hide in there for a few hours, at the back under sacking.'

Xavier seemed surprised. 'How do you know this?' He raised his eyebrows. 'Do you refer to Pierre Thebault's yard?'

Andre nodded.

Intrigued, I asked. 'Who is he?'

'A relative of mine,' Xavier answered. 'We do not get along well but he is a good man and would never betray me to the guards should he find me in his quarters.'

'You're sure?' I asked, uncertain.

He nodded. 'I am.'

I wanted to know more about this plan of Andre's. 'What will we do after that?'

Andre went to speak, but Xavier rested a hand on his shoulder. 'We will wait while Andre secures funds to pay for us to be taken to France. Is that not correct, Andre?' he asked with a confident smile.

Andre laughed. 'You know me well. I shall go ahead and arrange everything with Pierre.'

'I'm not sure,' I said, frantic about leaving the one place where I could communicate with Mum.

Andre rested his hands on my shoulders. 'I shall check the hiding place often. If your mother requests you to be at a certain place, I will send word to Xavier and a passage back to the island will be arranged immediately. You will only be a couple of hours away. Please trust me. All will be well.'

Nervous about what lay ahead, I had little choice but to trust Xavier and Andre's confidence in this man they had mentioned. My need to return home was stronger than ever but there was little I could do to speed things up apart from keep myself safe. I reached inside my skirt pocket and was calmed by the cool touch of my mother's silver fountain pen.

One day I would return this to her, I vowed, feeling comforted by my promise.

Chapter Twenty-Three

XAVIER

Andre, true to his word, arranged for us to hide at Pierre's boat shed. The sacking Briar and I were resting on was relatively comfortable. It felt good to be by ourselves once more, although I would have preferred something less rustic. I held out one of the apples and a cube of cheese Andre had wrapped up in a cloth for us.

Briar took it gratefully. 'Thank you.' I watched her bite into the red peel before eating the cheese. 'This is delicious.'

'I believe they're from the orchard at the back of Andre's family home near St Martin's Village. I recognise the taste.'

A dribble of apple juice ran down her chin and I had to resist wiping it away with my finger.

Briar apologised and drew the back of her hand across her chin. 'They're so juicy,' she laughed, keeping her voice low. 'What must you think of me eating so messily?'

I daren't reply. I enjoyed seeing her a little happier. Tomorrow morning before dawn we would be in a small boat crossing the channel on our way to the French coast. I had many acquaintances that I'd built up from my ventures over the years. Once we were safe I'd then plan what to do next.

Her expression changed.

'Something is troubling you?' I asked.

She cast her eyes down, staring momentarily at her hands. 'Do you think we'll be able to return here again?'

Not wishing to dash her hopes, I nodded. 'Maybe not for a while, but I will bring you back as soon as it's safe, or if Andre sends word from your mother.'

'Thank you.' She continued eating her apple. 'That's a relief. I know this is odd for both of us, but I feel better having you nearby. Knowing Andre's looking out for communication from my mother is also comforting.'

I replayed her words in my mind. 'You feel safer around me?' I couldn't help asking, relishing the feeling of being needed by her.

She finished her apple. 'I do.'

Watching her full lips move, I felt compelled to kiss her. I missed the pressure of her lips on mine. I looked deep into her eyes, trying to gauge if she would mind. Then, without further thought, I put my hand behind her head and drew her to me. She didn't hesitate and, encouraged by her response, I pressed my lips against hers in a kiss.

Briar gave a gentle groan. Her arms circled my waist and, relieved she wanted this too, I pulled her tightly against me, continuing to kiss her.

Someone called out a name outside the shed. Startled out of our passion, we held our breath. Our eyes locked and neither of us spoke as we waited to see what happened next. Footsteps sounded on the stony pathway and the man shouted again but this time from a distance.

Briar's arms dropped from around me. She pressed her fingertips against her lips, making me want to kiss her again.

'I don't know what came over me,' she whispered, her cheeks flushed.

'I instigated it.' I studied her face and seeing no regret in her expression, smiled. 'I don't know what came over both of us, but I'm glad it did.'

She looked up at me from under her long dark lashes. 'So am I.'

I had hoped our kissing would ignite memories of us together in the past, but couldn't see anything in her reaction that told me they had, and struggled to hide my disappointment.

Hearing more voices, I focused on the present, not willing to take any chances with her safety. I motioned for her to move back closer to the wooden side of the shed, hoping that if someone did look into the barn they would be less likely to spot us. She shuffled backwards but seemed concerned.

'We should be fine here for now,' I said.

'I was just thinking how much I enjoyed getting to know you better at Honey Bee Cottage,' she whispered. 'I was thinking about you and Wren living with your aunt, and wondered about your parents.'

I took a mouthful of the beer from the bag Andre had left. 'They died over a decade ago, in 1631, from an outbreak of typhoid fever.'

She frowned. 'I'm so sorry.'

It had been a terrible loss, but I had no wish to dwell further on it. 'My aunt is my mother's sister. She welcomed us into her home. I've been away at sea for most of that time but Wren is like a daughter to her.'

'I'm glad the pair of you had someone close to care for you.'

'We were lucky,' I said. 'Others weren't so well cared for.'

I thought of my mother, so gentle and sweet, and my rowdy father, who intimidated her when he had been drinking. 'It was terrible for us at the time, but my parents would have wanted to go together.' My heart ached at the thought of the volatile couple and their deep love for each other as well as their love for Wren and me. 'They were opposites in all ways, but adored each other.'

Briar sighed. 'I enjoy thinking of people in love, don't you?'

'I, er, don't really think about it.'

Her cheeks flushed and she looked away. 'I don't know why I said that.'

Not wishing her further discomfort, I changed the subject. 'We should try to sleep while we can. We will be woken early and tomorrow promises to be a long day.'

Making ourselves comfortable on the sacking, we turned our backs to each other. I felt the warmth of her body against mine and ached to turn around and hold her. The last time Briar and I had shared sleeping quarters we had been in the same bed. I wondered whether we would ever make love again. Pushing the thought away, I heard her gentle breathing. She was still awake. Could she be as troubled by our closeness as me?

Not wishing to embarrass her, I determined to catch some sleep, doing my best to banish thoughts of the sensations I'd felt when we kissed. Eventually I drifted off.

Chapter Twenty-Four

DIANA

I closed the front door to the cottage behind me and turned right along the lane, hoping I would find something vaguely nourishing in the village at Rosedale Stores. A hand rested on my shoulder, making me jump. I heard a gasp and turned to see Babette's daughter-in-law Jeanne panting and red-faced behind me.

'Sorry, Mrs Le Gros, I hadn't meant to startle you.'

I forced a smile. It wasn't the poor girl's fault I was edgy today. 'It's fine, Jeanne. And it's Diana, remember? We've spoken about this.' Many times, I thought. 'Is anything the matter?' Had Babette discovered something about Briar's return? My heart pounded as dread coursed through me. 'Tell me quickly,' I added trying my best not to panic.

She shook her head. She took a piece of folded paper from her coat pocket and handed it to me. 'Babette said to give this to you as soon as possible.'

I unfolded the piece of paper and read Babette's note.

Please join me for a cup of tea at my home this morning, B

Intrigued, I reread it. 'Did Babette say why she wants me to call on her?'

'Only to make sure you came as soon as you could.' She leant closer to me and lowered her voice. 'Babette didn't want to write that bit down in case it was misinterpreted by someone, if you know what I mean.'

I did. We all knew to be careful. Most islanders were good people but I'd heard gossip about some reporting neighbours to retaliate for old grievances from before the invasion. A disgusting way to behave, as far as I was concerned, but as Babette was the wife of our Connétable, someone harbouring bad feelings towards her husband for a fine or other punishment could still be resentful and want to get back at him. What better way to hurt the man than to bring shame on his wife by reporting her for some imagined misdemeanour?

Not wishing to waste any time, and uncertain whether there would still be food left at the store, I pointed in the direction Jeanne had come from.

'Let's go then. We don't want to keep Babette waiting.'

We walked to the other side of the village, partway up the hill and then along the pathway towards Babette's grand front door. Her home was a beautiful white Georgian house and much smarter than mine. The paint wasn't as perfectly white any longer after several years not being repainted, and the garden had fewer flowers, but it was still majestic and imposing.

I went to raise the heavy lion's-head knocker when the front door opened.

'I'm glad you came so quickly,' Babette said, welcoming us

in as she turned and led us through her pristine hallway. 'I hoped you would. I've sent my maid out on an errand. I'm hoping she'll be out for at least an hour.'

I tried to hide my impatience and willed her to have progressed in finding a way to rescue my daughter. 'Is this about Briar?'

'Hush.' She raised her finger to her lips and glanced upstairs. 'My husband is upstairs changing for an important meeting. I'd rather he didn't know you were here.'

I squashed my indignation. Babette would have her reasons for keeping my visit a secret.

'This way.' She opened one of the doors off the hallway and I was surprised to see a staircase leading downwards. 'Hold onto the handrail, the steps are rather steep.'

Jeanne closed the door quietly behind her, then followed us down.

I did as she asked, wondering where we were going. I glanced over my shoulder at Jeanne and could tell she had been down here before by the lack of surprise on her face.

Once in the basement there were three other doors. 'My word, what a place,' I said, wishing I had a basement in my cottage. It would be useful for so many things.

'You haven't seen anything yet,' Jeanne whispered, closer behind me than I had realised.

Babette stopped in front of the door to the left, lifted a gold chain hanging around her neck and retrieved a gold key. She bent slightly, slipped the key into the lock and turned it.

Jeanne nudged me lightly in the ribs. 'Wait till you see this.'

'Hush, Jeanne,' Babette said as she opened the door and hurried us through, closing and locking it behind us.

I immediately sensed a change in the atmosphere. It was

colder than in the other room we had just been in. She switched on the light, and I gasped.

'What is this?' I asked, unable to take in such an incredible sight.

'It's my secret library,' Babette said. 'It's where I keep my artefacts and everything I need for my spells. Do you like it?'

'Like it?' I stared at her aghast. 'It's the most magickal place I've ever seen.'

Chapter Twenty-Five

BRIAR

Xavier's breathing had altered. He was asleep and, although our backs were against each other and he wouldn't have been able to see me, I felt more able to think clearly without him awake.

I withdrew my mother's fountain pen from my pocket and stared at it, still stunned that she had parted from it. Having it helped me feel connected to her and able to cope with all I was going through. I knew that whatever happened I would always be grateful to her for her insight in finding a way to send it to me, and I was determined to keep it safe for her.

I was still gazing at the delicately engraved briar curving around the pen when I heard a shout and footsteps running in our direction. It took a moment for me to gather my senses and understand what was happening.

Xavier, ever alert, immediately leapt to his feet. How he had gone from a deep sleep to readiness for a fight, I had no idea. Then I saw him fly backwards, slamming against an oak pole and groaning in pain when a hefty guard crashed into him.

Another man grabbed my wrists and hauled me to my feet. Where had they come from? I wondered, realising these two must have crept into the shed before the others. I had thought coming face to face with a Nazi officer terrifying but nothing prepared me for the dead-eyed glare of the Witchfinder as his eyes settled on me. I almost felt myself wither under his gaze.

'What, pray, is this?' he said snatching my mother's fountain pen from my hand.

I had clutched onto it as tightly as I could, furious at not having anywhere to hide it when I heard the footsteps, but he was stronger than I was and the cool silver pen slid from my grasp. 'That's not mine.'

'A thief into the bargain,' he mocked. 'Interesting.'

'No. You don't understand.'

Xavier looked at me. 'Hush, Briar. It won't do any good to argue. He has made up his mind.'

'About what?'

I stared up at the Witchfinder and his smug satisfaction. Did this man have a quota of witches he needed to arrest each month? Was he paid by the number he incarcerated?

The vile man held up the pen. Moonlight coming in through a split in the shed wall caught the engraving and almost blinded him. He snapped his head to me, and a gnarled finger with a yellowing fingernail pointed close to my chest. 'Arrest this witch.'

'What? No. I'm not a witch,' I insisted, conscious that it was only partly true. Two soldiers I hadn't noticed before grabbed hold of me roughly.

The back of the Witchfinder's bony hand smashed into my cheek, sending me reeling. I heard Xavier's anguished yell.

'She attempts to cast a spell on me, on my eyes, with this wand.'

'That's nonsense,' I argued, and received another smack to the face for my stupidity.

My mind raced despite the stinging pain to my face. How did he know where to find us? Did someone tip him off, or was it his spies that I gathered lurked in every shadow?

'Silence. I have seen with my own eyes the power of this spell enhancer.'

'Spell—?' I tried to regain my senses and went to lift my hand to my cheek to shield it from further attack, forgetting for a moment that my arms were being restrained. Desperate not to give in to the tears threatening to spill down my cheeks, I swallowed, squeezing my eyelids shut.

'Stay strong, Briar,' Xavier shouted after me. There was a tremor in his deep voice and even though I heard his distress his words gave me strength.

Andre arrived from somewhere nearby, breathless and frantic. 'Try not to fret, Briar,' he shouted. 'Know we are doing all we can for you.'

We? I wondered if that meant him and Ember or him and Xavier's relative who owned this barn. I winced as shackles were placed around my wrists, pinching the skin as they were locked. Then the indignity of being hoisted over one of the guard's shoulders and carried outside before being unceremoniously dumped onto the back of a trailer like a sack of potatoes. The Witchfinder climbed up onto the front seat of the cart.

'Remain calm if you can,' Xavier shouted from inside the

barn. I went to respond but his words were immediately followed by the sounds of punches and groans. What were they doing to him?

'Leave him,' I heard Andre plead as the cart drew away from the beach, several soldiers following behind on foot.

Confused and terrified, I tried to keep my head down, although why I bothered when no one would recognise me, I wasn't sure. Maybe it was three years of oppression and living under Nazi rule and learning to be as inconspicuous as possible.

Poor Xavier. I hoped he was all right. I thought of Andre's earlier assurances but instead of feeling comforted I knew he had little chance of rescuing me from whatever fate the Witchfinder had determined would be mine.

A rotten tomato hit my cheek, sending its juices into my right eye. My eye smarting, I blinked rapidly, trying to rid myself of the sting. Others began cursing me and threw foul-smelling vegetables in my direction. I hadn't even been found guilty yet. Hadn't been charged with an offence, yet already my fate seemed to have been decided.

I realised that despite my innocence I would almost certainly be found guilty. I had little choice but to keep my wits about me as best I could if I were to stand any chance of surviving long enough for Mum and the coven to rescue me.

Chapter Twenty-Six

XAVIER

I had never wished to kill a man more than when the Witchfinder slapped Briar. Rage coursed through me. That man would pay for damaging her sweet face if it took me a lifetime. I doubted I'd ever forget the shock in her eyes at his unexpected brutality. She had given him no excuse to resort to such violence. It was clear to everyone in the shed that Briar posed no risk to him.

My ribs ached from the punches his brutes had relished giving me. Despite my best efforts I had been unable to go to Briar's aid, thanks to the guards holding me back, until I heard the cart's wheels were well away from us.

'Be on your way,' one of them said, his gruff voice irritated probably from being woken to make the arrest. I thought about disobeying his order but reasoned that he and his even larger comrade would be watching me until I was out of sight and that to disobey would only result in me possibly being arrested, or worse – and then what help would I be to Briar?

'We'd better do as they say,' Andre whispered, mistaking my silence.

I followed him back inside the shed and helped collect the remnants of food and drink Briar and I had been enjoying only a few hours earlier. I picked up my jacket from the heap of straw that was still warm from us sleeping on it and held it against me briefly before walking outside, trying to plan her rescue.

'And where do you think you're going?' Andre asked, following me. He snatched the jacket from my hands when I didn't answer.

'Give it back to me.' I tried to retrieve it but he held it away from me, knowing I'd never hit him.

'I asked you a question.' He glowered at me, fear and concern on his face, then draped my jacket over his forearm and rested his free hand on my shoulder. 'Xavier.'

'You know where I am going.'

He groaned. 'Be sensible. Think before reacting.'

I had no intention of being dissuaded. 'I must help her. If I had only acted earlier and taken her from here. Why didn't I insist we leave last night?'

'You'd have already been too late,' Andre insisted. 'This man is powerful. He has contacts everywhere and most islanders are too frightened of him to lie to him or his minions if questioned about someone.' He sighed heavily. 'He probably has the ports watched too, knowing him.'

He was right but I was too frustrated to agree.

'We must focus on what we can do to rescue her, but sensibly.' Andre's expression softened. 'Running headlong into the fray will only bring attention to yourself, and if you're rearrested how will that help her?'

'I must do something. Briar has no recollection of being here before. What if he remembers her?' I said, suspecting the man already had. 'What if he tells her and she discovers I lied to her?'

Andre shook his head, confused. 'Been here before? When? Why wouldn't she recall it?'

I explained what had happened, how Old Mother Dorey had cast a spell returning Briar to her own time after I had rescued her from the castle, and how the consequences of that were the loss of her memory from that time.

Andre stared at me, open-mouthed. 'Are you telling me there was something between you then and she has no idea?'

I closed my eyes and nodded, regretting my decision not to tell her, realising now that it had been foolish of me. 'Yes.'

'For the love of all that's holy, Xavier. What have you done?'

I gritted my teeth. 'I will rescue her, Andre. Somehow.'

'Xavier. Think.' He glared at me. 'As a condemned man there is little you can do. That man might not have recognised you but guards will be searching for you, asking questions. There are those at the castle who will know you. Other islanders. How far do you expect to get before you're rearrested? And if they do find you your sentence will be carried out without delay. What will Briar do then if you're dead?'

As frustrated as I was, I knew he was right. I had assumed Roger Dankworth had gone to the barn to arrest me because he had discovered who I was. When he had arrested Briar instead it only increased my guilt.

'I understand your misgivings, Andre.' I relented wearily.

'You are a true friend. I know what you say makes sense, but I must do something.'

'Don't be foolish. Who will save her if not you?'

'You, my friend. That's who.'

His hands rested on each of my shoulders. 'I would do everything I could for her, I promise you that, but I would rather we consider all our options first. Will you at least attempt to do that?'

He made good sense. I groaned, impatient not to be able to race off after her immediately. 'I will. What do you suggest?'

Andre frowned. 'We know where she's been taken.'

I thought back to what I had heard from others' arrests. 'Before the Connétable.' I pictured the rotund, florid-faced man known for his lack of humour. I might be affected by Briar's gentle voice and pretty face, but I doubted he would be.

'That's right,' Andre said. 'As with any case when someone is charged with something that might ultimately end with a death sentence.' I winced at the thought. 'She will be taken before him and six Sermentés.'

I tried to work out what he meant. 'You mean six sworn men to make a jury?'

'Yes. An informal one. Then, if they agree to send Briar for trial, she will be indicted before the Cour de Cattel.'

'The Bailiff and three Jurats,' I said recalling what this meant. 'At Mont Orgueil Castle,' I said almost to myself, knowing she would be put before a jury of twenty-four landowners made up from her own and adjoining parishes.

'Yes. She'll be kept there and await the next sitting of the Court.' He grimaced. 'I know it's overwhelming but try not to panic. Twenty of them must find her guilty for her to be condemned, don't forget. She still has a good chance of being released. Only five people are sufficient for her acquittal too.'

I knew he was trying to reassure me but his words had the adverse effect. 'But she's a stranger, she doesn't know five people,' I reminded him. 'Or have a parish. She has no living family, or even a home.' As I spoke, my despair for her safety increased. This was hopeless. 'How can Briar expect to be found innocent if the only people who can speak up for her are a condemned man and you?'

Andre frowned. 'I will do my best when I go before them,' he insisted, his voice drifting away. I saw his confidence fade. Like me, Andre was waking up to the pointlessness of it all. 'You are right, Xavier. If they discover she has no history here, no one to vouch for her, they will surely conclude that she is, if nothing else, a curiosity.'

We stared at each other. 'Which is exactly what we don't want.' I tried to remain calm. 'They would not be wrong,' I said miserably. 'Would they?' I rubbed my face with my hands, desperate to come up with a useful idea. 'We must do something. I can't let her die when the only thing she's guilty of is trying to help me.'

Andre rubbed his chin. 'I know, my friend. I want to help her too. We will find a solution.'

'I wish I knew how.' I could hear the desperation in my voice.

He thought for a moment. 'We must use all the knowledge we have. Don't forget you've already escaped the cells at the castle. Not many people can say that. If anyone is capable of a successful plan it will be you.'

'Have you forgotten the only reason I escaped was because I went forward in time? The cell disintegrated around me.'

My fury increased. 'Briar will be inside those walls, with no chance of escape without us.' A thought occurred to me. 'Our only chance to help her will be to reach her before she's taken into the castle.' Feeling slightly better, I added, 'I'm going to follow the cart up to the Public Hall. I'll attempt to see her before she's taken in front of the Connétable.'

'But she left a while ago.'

I grinned. 'Yes, but the cart is slow and I know a shortcut that will take me ahead of her.'

'And when you do get there?' he asked as we reached his home.

I did not know. 'I haven't thought of that yet. I must let her see I am nearby. It will give her hope, remind her she is not alone.' I tried to keep my voice low but realised that wasn't the case when a villager turned and stared in my direction.

Andre nodded. 'I'll accompany you. But—' he said, reaching his front door first and standing in front of me. He cocked his head to one side. 'Listen. I can still hear the cart's wheels going up the hill. She isn't too far away.'

He was right. The hillside road doubled back on itself, making the cart seem closer. I strained to hear more. My heart leapt at the sound of her voice. 'She's asking the guards something.' I couldn't quite hear what it was, though. 'If only I could get to her and take her from them.' I peered down the lane but my view was blocked.

Sensing what I was thinking, Andre pulled me back by the arm. 'No, Xavier. The crowd has amassed around her and it's too big for any hope of you taking her.' He pointed towards them. 'That must be why they haven't gone too far up the hill yet. None of those people will recognise her and most will be suspicious of Briar because of it. Others will be relieved her arrest has taken the focus from them or someone they know. We must bide our time.'

'Until what?' I asked impatiently through gritted teeth.

'Until there are fewer witnesses.'

He opened his front door and pushed me inside before I could argue further.

Chapter Twenty-Seven

DIANA

I gazed around Babette's basement in awe, trying to take everything in. Bookcases filled with leather-bound tomes ran along each wall, and a huge table in the middle of the room held what I assumed to be her grimoire, lying open next to a sheet of thick paper and a fountain pen. There were shelves holding jars filled with all sorts of things, ranging from herbs to what looked like small bones. Candles at various stages of use stood along one edge of the table and the windowsill. I noticed that each pane of glass had been painted over with a dark liquid, a good idea if Babette wanted to keep prying eyes from peering inside.

On one wall was an inglenook fireplace with a cauldron hanging from a tripod over a low fire, from which steam gently curled up. I wondered what concoction she was in the middle of making.

Babette noticed me looking. 'I've started heating some water in readiness for when we find the right spell.' She sighed happily, arms outstretched. 'What do you think of my special place?'

'I'm envious to the point of being almost speechless,' I admitted. 'And honoured to have been invited here.' I wondered why it had taken her so long.

She seemed pleased with my response and gave a satisfied nod. 'I promised to help you rescue Briar and I'm a woman of my word. As your High Priestess, I believe it's my duty to do all I can for you and your lovely girl.'

'She must be scared witless,' Jeanne murmured half to herself.

Babette glared at her. 'I'm not sure how you think that thoughtless remark will help Mrs Le Gros feel better?'

I noticed she had addressed me formally and supposed it was to remind Jeanne of the seriousness of the task at hand. 'It's fine,' I said, not wishing the poor girl to feel bad on my behalf. 'I've had the same thought, many times.'

Babette led me to the end bookcase. 'There's no time to waste. I believe we should start our search here. You work from this side.' She gave Jeanne an impatient wave. 'You from that end, Jeanne. And do pay attention. I know the spell is in here somewhere because I recall my mother talking me through it.' She frowned. 'Not that I ever imagined I might need it.'

'Thank you both for helping me this way,' I said. 'I appreciate it more than you will ever know.'

Babette gave me a sympathetic smile. She indicated the rows of books nearest to her. 'I thought I'd found the spell I'm looking for.' She placed her fingertips on an ancient-looking open book next to her grimoire. 'But it isn't quite right. With help from you and Jeanne we should succeed in less time than it would take me looking by myself. And, as we all know, time is very much of the essence.'

It certainly was.

Jeanne walked over to study the books on one shelf. 'Do you recall what the book cover looks like?'

Babette glowered. 'If I remembered that, Jeanne, I would have found it by now.'

Jeanne's cheeks reddened. 'Sorry, I didn't think.'

Not wishing the poor girl to think I didn't value her contribution, I smiled at her. 'I was about to ask the same thing,' I fibbed, glad when she seemed less embarrassed.

We began our search. I enjoyed losing myself in the heavy, intriguing books filled with fascinating words. After what seemed like about an hour but must have been much longer, Babette cleared her throat to grab our attention.

Jeanne and I looked over to her. 'Have you found it?' I asked, unable to hide the desperation in my voice.

'Unfortunately, no.' Her slumped shoulders showed her disappointment. 'I'm afraid the time has run away with us. You need to leave straightaway if you're to be home before curfew starts. We can't risk you being arrested if we want any hope of helping Briar.'

As reluctant as I was to stop, Babette's reminder was enough to make me close the book I was holding and slide it back into the gap from which I had taken it.

'Don't worry,' Babette assured me. 'I'll send a message to my son and let him know I need Jeanne to stay here for the night. He won't argue and it will give her and me the chance to keep looking. I'll call in on you tomorrow to let you know if we've found it.'

I clasped my hands together 'Thank you.' Babette went to

show me out but, not wishing to waste any of their time, I raised a hand to stop them. 'Please don't worry, I can find my own way.'

As I hurried home, I willed one of them to find the spell. The sooner my precious daughter was back home again with me, the better I'd feel.

Chapter Twenty-Eight

BRIAR

I tried to hide my panic but it was difficult when strangers were yelling profanities at me and throwing stinking vegetables. 'Where are you taking me?' I asked, my teeth chattering in fear.

'Quiet.' It was the man who had hoisted me onto his shoulder and deposited me in an undignified heap onto the back of the foul-smelling cart before climbing up next to me, while the other took his seat at the front next to the Witchfinder.

When we reached the bottom of Gorey Hill and began the slow ascent I thought about the many times I had walked this way to deliver one of Mum's packets. The roads were nothing like the tarmacked ones I was used to. Muddy from rain during the night, the ruts in the ground and stones made the journey bumpy and extremely uncomfortable.

I shuffled backwards on my bottom until I was leaning against the front panel of the cart. At the top, I waited for the cart to turn right towards the castle, but it turned left, continuing up the hill instead.

I wished I'd paid more attention in history classes and had some idea about what was in store for me. 'Please tell me.'

He bit one of his dirty, chewed nails and spat it out. 'You're being taken in front of the Connétable. Now shut your mouth.' The horse broke into a slow trot.

I did as I was told, relieved that I wouldn't be going straight to the castle cells. I presumed it would take us about an hour to reach the Public Hall at the speed the cart was doing especially if the road there continued to be as uneven as it had been to this point.

I tried to focus on the scenery around me, the orchards and fields we passed. There were one or two small farms, from what I could see, but I was too shocked by my arrest and too sick with fear about what would happen next to take much of it in. I had no way of defending myself and couldn't see how I could escape – or think where I would go, if I did manage to get away. I might have been born and raised on this part of the island but I barely recognised this place.

I thought of the main road leading from town to Gorey pier and how that was little more than sand now, with boat builders dotted along where, in the future, a road and trainline would exist. It was like visiting a place you had dreamt about and it appearing far different in reality. But what was my reality? The 1940s or the 1640s?

I would give anything right now to be transported back to the Occupation. I smiled to myself, thinking how ridiculous I would have thought this if someone else had voiced it to me a couple of weeks before. At least I knew how to behave in my own time, what to expect and what not to do. I also had friends, and Mum.

Why did the Witchfinder come for me? Was it simply because I stood out from most people because my hair was shorter, or something else? The way I spoke maybe? Could it simply be because no one recognised me on the island? I decided I needed to know more.

'What will happen to me at the Public Hall?'

The driver snorted, then spat, making me nauseous. 'You'll be presented to the Connétable,' he said in an accent so strong even I barely understood him. 'Then six Sermentés will determine *plutôt coupable qu'innocent.*'

The only word I recognised was Connétable. Babette's husband was the Connétable now and I hoped the man I was going to be presented to was fair, as I had heard Mr Le Dain to be.

'What does that mean?'

The one sitting on the bench above me rolled his eyes as if I were stupid. 'Whether you're more guilty than innocent.'

'I see.' I didn't, not really, but I reasoned that at least someone would be giving me a chance and not simply assuming I was guilty. It was small relief but better than nothing.

By the time we reached the Public Hall I was ready to step down from the cart. My backside felt bruised and my head hurt from the bumps in the muddy road. I didn't need to touch my cheek to know it was swollen, and I felt utterly miserable.

The officer jumped down and waved for me to go to him. Movement caught my eye to my right. I peered through the long grass at the edge of the field but saw only trees. I noticed the guard peering in the same direction to see what had distracted me. Being more vigilant, I let him lift me down. The driver climbed down from his seat and said something to him. As he spoke, I took the opportunity to have another look, hoping I had been right and that there was someone watching.

My heart leapt when first Xavier then Andre stepped out from behind the tree and waved at me. They had come for me. My heart soared. Then several honorary policemen appeared from inside the hall and shouted. Someone had seen Xavier and Andre. Four Honoraries took off after them. I was alone. Again.

Chapter Twenty-Nine

XAVIER

'Her face,' I said angrily as we made our way through the quieter lanes back to Andre's home. 'I can't forget how her delight in seeing us turned to panic when those bastards came after us.'

'We had no choice but to run,' Andre said sounding as fed up as I felt. 'At least we escaped and are free to try and reach her again.'

It wasn't much consolation. Once inside he poured us both a brandy. We sat at the table nursing our drinks, each lost in his own misery. An image of Briar's mother came to me along with an idea.

'Fetch a quill and ink,' I said, a sense of hope flickering as my mind raced. 'I will write to Diana. She needs to know what has become of Briar.'

Andre's mouth opened in astonishment. 'You wish to torment the poor woman?'

I didn't like to remind Andre that it was Diana's pen that had given the Witchfinder reason to believe his suspicions about Briar being a witch. 'What other choice is there? If she's to help Briar, she needs to know everything that's happening.'

I saw his doubt and had to admit to myself that even I didn't really know what I was doing. I just needed to do something. Anything to help her.

Andre nodded and left the room. He returned moments later holding a bottle of ink in one hand with a quill and paper in the other. 'Writing implements.'

We sat at the table. He watched in silence as I struggled to put into words what I wanted to write. I needed her to understand the urgency of the current situation. We did not know how long it would be until Briar's trial but if it was soon and she was found guilty, which I suspected she might, then that evil man could have her death on his hands before Diana found a way to rescue her daughter.

The front door opened, surprising us both. Andre and I leapt to our feet, ready for another onslaught by the Witchfinder, but it wasn't him.

'Ember.' I saw her eyes narrow at my dismissive tone. I had not meant to annoy her, but it dawned on me at that moment something I had not allowed myself to suspect before. I might only see her as a friend now but even those feelings had cooled to ice.

'Yes, it was me,' she said, displaying an arrogance I had never witnessed before.

'What was you?' Andre asked looking bewildered. When neither she nor I answered, he looked at me. 'Xavier, what is it?'

I shifted my gaze from my friend to Ember. 'Do you wish me to tell your cousin what you've done? Or will you?'

She shrugged a tanned shoulder. 'Xavier is angry with me

for bringing the Witchfinder to your door.' She sneered at Andre's horrified expression.

'You did what?' He seemed astonished. I wasn't sure why I was so surprised by his reaction, when even I had been shocked by Ember's revelation.

She sneered at him. 'She's clearly a witch.'

Andre looked stunned. 'You don't know that. She is not even from—'

'You don't even have the words to explain why she is here, or where she has come from,' Ember shouted. 'Do not accuse me of misdeeds when it's clear there's something unnatural about her.'

I clenched my fists. 'If you were a man, I would—'

Ember's green eyes appeared to deepen in colour. She stepped in front of me, her face almost touching mine. 'You would what, Xavier?' She sniggered. 'You know as well as I do I am a match for most men. Possibly even you.'

I had witnessed Ember flooring many a man with a sword in her hand. I relaxed my hands. I was not in the habit of fighting women. Any woman. Even one as aggressive as her.

She shook her head. 'Are you in love with the baggage? Surely not, Xavier?' She laughed. 'I always imagined you to have higher standards.'

She was attempting to rile me with her mocking, determined to entice me into a fight. As the realisation occurred to me my fury waned.

'You are to be pitied,' I sneered, keeping my tone level, wanting to infuriate her.

'Pitied?' she spat.

'Yes,' Andre snapped, stepping forward. 'Why else would you do something this disgusting to that innocent woman?

She's never done anything to harm you.' He folded his arms across his chest. 'Or is all this because you're jealous of Briar? Of the affection Xavier clearly has for her?'

'What?' She spun round to face him. 'Why would I be jealous of that mouse? Or have feelings for Xavier?' She almost spat my name.

'Then why do it?' I asked, unable to resist. 'If I mean nothing to you, why bother?'

She turned back to me. 'Because she's dangerous,' she said after a moment's hesitation.

'One minute you call her a mouse, the next she's supposed to be dangerous,' Andre laughed. 'What is it to be, Ember?'

I agreed. 'If anyone is dangerous, Ember, that person is you. I warrant Briar does not have any man's death on her conscience. We both know that not to be the case where you are concerned.'

'I agree,' Andre said. 'You tattle-tale-ing about her to the Witchfinder proves you are the one who is not to be trusted,' he shouted. 'My own cousin. I am ashamed of you.'

I saw her anger dissipate, to be replaced by something resembling shame. She stared at Andre in silence, her shoulders tense.

Remembering that the message I had been drafting on her arrival was still lying on the table for her to see, I took the opportunity of her eyes being locked with Andre's to pick up my jacket from where it was draped over the back of the chair and dropped it onto the paper hiding the evidence.

Andre must have sensed what I was doing. The next thing I knew he stepped forward and took Ember by the arm and led her to the front door.

'What are you doing?' she asked, attempting to shrug off his hold.

He wasn't having any of it. 'You are no longer welcome in my home.'

'Why are you siding with him?' She held her free arm out in my direction. 'He is not your family. He should be the one to go, not me.'

'Xavier has not betrayed me,' Andre answered quietly as he pulled her towards the door.

Ordinarily we both knew Ember would push anyone away if they tried to force her to do something she didn't want to. This time she relented and went quietly, her respect for her cousin clear. He opened the door, and she stepped outside, turning to face us both.

'I do not regret my actions.'

I wanted to hate her at that moment but like Andre, I saw how pitifully she was behaving. I turned my back on her.

'You see,' she said quietly. 'I am right.'

Without another word, she strode down the lane and Andre slammed the door.

In an instant he went to the table, lifted my jacket and retrieved the note, taking my message to hide it for Diana to find, while I focused my thoughts on the most important mission I had ever taken on. To rescue the woman I loved before it was too late.

Chapter Thirty

DIANA

'They are in this house right now.' I often spoke my thoughts aloud when I was alone, unable to shake the habit of speaking to my husband despite him having passed years before. Startled by a noisy clanging on the floor, I spun round to see Babette's timid daughter-in-law, Jeanne, staring wide-eyed at me, her mouth open and a mass of broken pottery and glass at her feet. Tears started running down her cheeks.

'What are you doing, Jeanne?' Babette snapped, causing me to notice her presence for the first time. 'For pity's sake take more care.' Babette looked at me apologetically. 'Very clumsy, that one.'

I wasn't sure when they had arrived and presumed it must have been while I was in shock after reading Xavier's words. The girl was clearly distressed but I wasn't sure what to say.

Noticing a carpet bag by Babette's feet, I looked up. 'Does this mean you've found something?'

Babette arched an eyebrow. 'I believe so.' Her dark eyes

twinkled with excitement but instead of telling me, she pointed at the note in my hand. Jeanne took a tentative step towards the space in the floor and peered into it.

Still unsure how long the two women had been in my home, it dawned on me that Jeanne must have been sent to the kitchen for drinks, returning to the living room just when I had spoken about Xavier and Andre being in the room. No wonder she had been startled enough to drop the tray holding my favourite water jug and glasses.

'Stop gawping, dear,' Babette said, giving the young woman a weary sigh. 'Find something in the kitchen to clear up that mess.'

Jeanne went to do as she was told. I noticed her mouth move slightly before she hesitated.

'What is it, Jeanne?' I asked, feeling a duty to calm her although I was impatient to find out about Babette's discovery.

Jeanne looked about her. Realising she was looking for the men I had spoken about, I said, 'I didn't mean they were physically here right now.' When her expression didn't change, I closed my eyes briefly to steady my light-headedness after reading Xavier's alarming note. 'They were here three hundred years ago.'

Jeanne's brown eyes wrinkled up at the sides as she tried to understand my meaning. 'You mean they are … ghosts? Here?'

Babette patted her on the shoulder, her lips pursed thoughtfully. 'Don't concern yourself, dear. Leave that mess for now. First, I need you to go to my home and'—she lowered her voice to a whisper—'you know where my grimoire is hidden?'

'Yes, Babette.'

'Fetch it immediately. Be careful not to be followed.' She forced a smile. 'Don't show any panic if you are. And do try not to appear as if you're doing something you shouldn't. Now be quick about it.' Babette steered Jeanne towards the front door, opened it and gently pushed her outside. 'We need to leave enough time to plan our next steps before curfew begins.'

'Yes, Babette,' Jeanne replied looking bemused.

'Good girl. Now hurry.'

As soon as Jeanne had run off, Babette pulled out the chair next to me at the table. 'I'm sorry about your glasses and jug. Naturally I'll replace them as soon as possible.'

I didn't like to say they were irreplaceable, having been a gift from my late husband. We had far more pressing matters to deal with if I wanted Briar back home before it was too late. 'Please, don't worry about those. I'm more interested in why you're here.'

She didn't answer my question. 'Now Jeanne's gone, why don't you let me read that note. I can see that it has troubled you for some reason.'

I slid the note to her and explained about Xavier communicating with me via the hole in the floor.

She stared at me silently for a moment before reading the news that Briar had been arrested. I saw her pale, just as I must have done.

I watched her, too impatient to wait any longer. 'You didn't say what you found. Please tell me it's the spell,' I pleaded, breathless with fear that she might not have done. I wasn't sure how much longer I could hold my nerve before giving in to the hysteria building up in me.

'This is worrying indeed,' Babette said, rubbing her top lip with her finger.

'The spell, Babette?' I reminded her.

'What? Oh, yes, we might have located the correct spell.' She gave me a reassuring smile. 'At least I believe so.'

I cried out, pressing my hands against my chest. 'You have?'

She nodded, then rested her palms on the table and leant slightly forward. 'You must stay strong, Diana, especially now. Try not to give in to your emotions,' I heard her add as my mind raced. 'Briar is relying on you to keep a cool head. She needs us both to remain calm and do this properly.'

I nodded, forcing myself to calm down. 'I understand.' I didn't need her to elaborate further. I had no option but to succeed.

'From what I gathered in that note, your Briar has been arrested by some witchfinder.' She shivered and looked into my eyes. Neither of us spoke for a few seconds. We knew about the dreadful tortures and deaths our fellow witches had faced back then. She continued reading. 'Briar has been taken before the Connétable at the Public Hall up in St Martin,' she read almost to herself. Babette frowned thoughtfully. 'But that building wasn't built then.'

I pictured the date above the front door of the Public Hall. 'Maybe not the one your husband works from, but clearly something must have preceded it.' I thought back to all I knew about the history of witches on the island and what happened to them after their arrest.' I presume they'll take her to Mont Orgueil castle to be put on trial.' I pictured the ruined cell where she and Xavier had vanished. 'Briar will most likely be locked up in one of the cells by now. Where Xavier was kept and where she first met him.'

I didn't add, 'and where I had last seen her'. I swallowed hard to clear my throat.

'I imagine so,' Babette replied.

I waited for her to consider our options.

'You mentioned he was a soldier,' she said thoughtfully.

I nodded. 'Some sort of privateer. I gather he was locked up because he had fallen out with the Governor of the island, or a senior person in charge of things back then.'

'As a military man I imagine he will have experience of planning assaults, if not some fighting.' She gave me a reassuring smile. 'He will know how to defend Briar and I think we can be certain Xavier will be doing everything in his power to rescue her.' Babette pointed to a few words. 'I'm guessing he will attempt to take her back to the last place you saw them, to give you a chance to bring her back from there.'

I had thought the same thing. 'If I had the spell to hand when she was still staying in this house before her arrest,' I moaned miserably, 'it would be much simpler to bring her back. It is going to be far more difficult with her incarcerated at the castle.'

'Maybe so, but ifs and maybes aren't going to help us,' Babette said matter-of-factly. She rubbed the base of her neck thoughtfully. 'Where is that confounded girl?'

I didn't like to think of her being cross with Jeanne. 'I'm sure she's doing her best to be quick. I did give her rather a fright, don't forget.'

'I suppose you're right, but she can be such a trial sometimes.'

I frowned.

'Sorry, I'm being mean.' Babette looked at me, her sympathy unmistakable. 'Briar is a strong, brave girl, Diana. Never forget that. I know the circumstances aren't how we might wish them to be, but we have no choice other than to work with the cards that have been dealt to us.'

Babette was right. I just hoped she knew what to do next and asked her to explain her plan, hoping she had one.

'The most difficult part of this is going to be casting the spell without being seen by one of the soldiers patrolling the castle.' She checked her watch. 'We're not going to have much time if Jeanne doesn't get a move on.'

'But what is your plan?' I asked frantically, wondering if it might have been better for all of us to meet in Babette's basement and work together to create the right spell.

Babette gave me a reassuring smile. 'We don't have time for me to go through everything. I'll give you all the instructions you need when I'm ready.'

I had the horrible feeling she was still trying to work through a few things and struggled to hide my panic. I didn't think I could stand failing a second time.

Before I could fret further, the front door opened and a panting Jeanne pulled out a small thick book with a worn, tooled leather cover from her large coat pocket. She held it up triumphantly. 'Here it is.'

'Finally.' Babette stood and snatched the grimoire from her daughter-in-law. 'There's no time to sit down and rest, Jeanne,' she said when the girl pulled a chair back from the table. 'We have to leave right away.'

As we made our way to the castle, ducking into doorways and trying to remain unseen by both locals and soldiers, it occurred to me that the weather might not be right for this to work.

'It's a clear night,' I whispered as I followed Babette.

She hesitated and turned to me, shaking her head

impatiently. 'And what has that to do with anything, apart from the moonlight making us less inconspicuous?'

I swallowed nervously. Hadn't I mentioned the weather before? 'The night Xavier arrived and when I inadvertently sent them both back there was a thunderstorm. Lots of lightning.'

'Why didn't you say?'

I'd been too busy worrying about Xavier's note, but didn't say so. 'I'm worried our attempt won't work because those aren't the conditions now,' I admitted, hating that I had put her to all this trouble, and it could be for nothing.

Babette stared at me from the gloom of the doorway where we were hiding. She puffed out her cheeks. 'Oh, Diana.'

Aware we were risking being caught acting suspiciously, but not wanting her to give up without trying, I quickly said, 'We mustn't let that stop us.'

She frowned, then shook her head. 'I don't know if it's worth us risking being arrested when so much is against us.'

Why had I been so foolish? 'Babette,' I pleaded, grabbing her wrist.

She looked down at my hand, then into my eyes. 'Let go of me, Diana.' Her voice was calm with a steely determination. 'I understand your fear, but I have a family too. I'm already risking my liberty helping you.'

My heart raced. She was right. 'My daughter is almost certainly going to be executed and for all we know it could be soon,' I reminded her. 'If you don't feel able to continue with this, please let me borrow your spell book and accoutrements, so I can try to cast the spell myself.'

I saw her contemplating whether it was worth risking her

liberty for the sake of a spell that had a high risk of failure. I willed her to give it a go.

'Babette?' I urged, struggling with my impatience and fear that she would return home without helping me. 'What do you want to do?'

She groaned. 'I won't hand over my book of shadows, it was my great-great-grandmother's. In all honesty, I don't intend passing on anything else for that matter.' She gave me an apologetic half-smile. 'I did offer my help, though,' she relented. 'I will do what I can. I'd rather the rest of our ladies were with us to add strength to our chanting but it'll be too dangerous for seven women to try and stay inconspicuous.'

'As long as we try something before it's too late,' I said, barely able to keep control of my panic.

She sighed heavily when I didn't respond further. 'Fine. We'll have to do our best, but we must hurry.'

Relieved she hadn't given up, I followed her up the long narrow lane and the rest of the way to the castle green.

After having to wait for the patrol to move away, we ran to the ruined cell. Stepping inside, I touched the wall with both hands, closing my eyes and trying to send my love and strength to my daughter. Was it even possible to send emotions across time? I pictured her hugging herself, frightened about what to expect.

'Hurry,' I whispered.

The thought that we were racing against time, yet three hundred years in the future from what Briar was experiencing now, was baffling. I shook my confused thoughts and panic away. There was no time for that now.

Babette closed her eyes and slowed her breathing as she grounded herself. Knowing I should do the same, I copied her.

Then she cast a circle with sea salt, indicating where Jeanne and I should stand when it was complete. Before setting out her ingredients for her spell, she placed her book of shadows on the ground and opened it, then took two candlesticks from her carpet bag and set them down on either side with an indigo candle in one of them.

'For transforming Briar's world into a different one,' Babette explained quietly as she worked. 'To this one.' She took a gold candle and, inserting that into the top of the second candlestick, said, 'To intensify my spell.'

She reached out a hand to Jeanne. 'Pass me the cauldron.'

I watched as her daughter-in-law took a small iron pot whose base could fit into the palm of my hand. I had never seen one this size before and marvelled at its perfection.

As I watched I kept alert to any sounds or movement in my peripheral vision by the doorway, not wishing to be caught off-guard by soldiers on patrol.

Babette opened a jar and poured a mixture of oil, herbs, black pepper and what looked like mugwort into the cauldron. Then taking a match, she lit the gold candle, picked it up and lit the second candle and then the mixture.

'I need to call on our ancestors to help us,' she said quietly as the small area filled with the scent of lavender, herbs and candle smoke. Taking a scrap of paper from her pocket, she dropped it into the flames. I had noticed words written on it but not what they were.

With these words, I call upon our ancestors for help. May our dear daughter be brought back to us across the ages, quickly and unharmed. Hear my words. So mote it be.

She looked up at me and Jeanne and together we recited the words again and again. As often happened, an otherworldly sense came over me as I lost myself to the chanting. The three of us recited the words over and over, our voices quiet for fear of discovery.

The bright moon darkened and, unable to help myself, I glanced up at the sky through the broken roof to see thin clouds thickening and slowly covering the moon and sky around us. I willed our ancestors to do their best for Briar and help us in some way, but despite our best efforts nothing happened.

Minutes later we were still standing next to the ruined, empty cell, the smoke vanished from the cauldron and the clouds dispersed until the sky and moon were bright once more. Jeanne looked as if she was about to pass out from fear.

Hearing voices, Babette and I exchanged glances. She snapped her spell book closed while Jeanne and I hurriedly blew out the candles and gathered Babette's tools, returning them to the carpet bag. Devastated not to have succeeded, but conscious that if I had any chance of helping Briar I needed to keep out of sight and remain free, I brushed my feet over the salt to erase the circle.

'Quick, they're coming,' Babette whispered.

Jeanne took off and ran along the green, disappearing towards the top of the lane without waiting for Babette or me to follow. The poor girl was clearly terrified, as were we all. I gathered my wits, took Babette's hand and ran.

None of us spoke until we were back inside Honey Bee Cottage, the door closed behind us and the three of us panting and out of breath.

'I'm sorry we couldn't save her,' Babette admitted, her voice shaky and eyes filled with unshed tears.

She seemed almost as devastated as I was at that moment.

'I know. Thank you for trying, I really am grateful. It was brave of you both to do this for me and I'll never forget what you've risked tonight to help me.'

Babette groaned. 'I think I know what went wrong.' She placed her carpet bag down on the living-room floor.

'You do?' I hoped she was right. I couldn't bear to leave it at that. I was going to find a way to save Briar, if it killed me doing it.

'I hope so. I know we don't have time to waste as far as Briar's concerned. I'm also fairly sure this spell is the right one.'

'Why did it fail then?' I asked tearfully.

Babette took my hand in hers. 'Because we now know the weather conditions must be perfect for the spell to work.'

She was right. There had been an electric storm both when Xavier appeared and also when he and Briar vanished. Miserably, I agreed with her. 'Does that mean you'll help me try again the next time we have a storm?'

She gave me a reassuring smile. 'I will do my best. It must be an evening when my husband is busy and I can slip out without him knowing.'

'The weather has been humid lately and we're forecast a few hotter days,' Jeanne said thoughtfully. 'I'll keep a lookout for thunder or lightning. As soon as I see any I'll call for you.'

My relief was palpable. It wasn't perfect by any means – only having Briar standing in the cottage with us would have achieved that – but it gave me hope. 'As will I. Thank you both.'

I hugged them again and showed them out of my cottage. Now all I needed to do was hope that a storm would come to the island before it was too late.

Chapter Thirty-One

BRIAR

I had managed to remain stoic, at least to others while facing the Connétable's officers and even when I first arrived at the castle to await trial. But it had been days now since they had thrown me into this dark, damp cell and I felt my spirit begin to splinter.

None of the ten other women even looked at me, their spirits already broken, and the only future I could see for myself was being condemned as a witch. Aware that this must have been how Xavier had felt the second before he was transported forward in time made me admire his courage even more.

It took all my resolve not to collapse in a hysterical heap. Although that was probably helped by the fact that I had no intention of voluntarily lying down on the disgusting flagstone floor if I could help it.

Desperate for fresh air to alleviate the putrid stench of bodily fluids on the floor and unwashed bodies around me, I edged closer to the window for relief. It took time because the stronger of the women had commandeered the area and I had to wait until the guard came and the women pushed towards the door to grab what passed as food. Taking my chance, I rushed forward, breathing in as much of the outside air as I could. Even though it wasn't cold outside, the damp seemed to permeate my bones. I wrapped my arms around myself but it made little difference.

I wasn't sure what was worse, hearing the screams of women who had been dragged from the cell hours earlier as they begged for mercy, or the nauseating fear that I was soon to receive the same treatment. Again, I cursed myself for my stupidity in instinctively reaching out to Xavier when my mother had sent him back that night. I would have saved everyone so much heartache and trouble if only I had done as Mum instructed.

Mum. I thought of her messages. I wasn't alone, despite how it appeared at that moment. Determined to keep hope alive, I pictured Xavier when he had waved to me from next to the apple tree by the Public Hall. He looked as anxious as I must have, despite his forced smile. It was kind of him to rush there and show he was nearby. It calmed me slightly to know he and Andre had not given up on me, and I knew without any doubt they were doing all they could to find a way to rescue me.

Then I remembered that as an escaped convict Xavier's chances to do much were drastically reduced. I squeezed my eyes together, determined not to cry. Even I knew that to show any weakness in this hellhole was dangerous. I was already watched suspiciously by the other women in the cell. I wasn't sure what it was about me, but the clothes and bonnet covering my hair that Wren had given me clearly didn't hide whatever it was that made me stand out and cause their distrust. If women in the same dire situation as me reacted this way, then why should I expect the court to treat me with any mercy? I shivered at the thought that, when I was brought in front of those in charge, they might even take the opportunity to use me as an example to deter other witches from practising.

I wished Pippin were with me. I always felt comforted to know she was nearby. But she wasn't here and there was no point in using up valuable energy wishing for the impossible.

I noticed several women watching me. A familiar fear crept down my spine and I immediately looked away. I had learnt not to catch Nazi soldiers' eyes, since any glance from me could be misconstrued. I didn't need these women using me as a scapegoat. After three years of Occupation, I knew that people in fear for their lives might act in a way they would never ordinarily do. All it would take for me to be condemned was one of these desperate women offering false information about me. I had no wish to be their sacrificial victim.

I had only been in this place for a night and most of the following day when the sound of a heavy key in the lock was followed by deep voices talking rapidly to each other. I strained my ears to hear, but they spoke too quietly for me to make out what was being said. The cell door opened and the taller of the two guards stood in the doorway and scanned the room. They were looking for someone. I lowered my gaze and tried to appear smaller by dipping my shoulders slightly. I had no wish to be their next victim.

'Her, there,' one of the men shouted.

I daren't look up, willing them not to come for me. Women around me moved away until their backs were against the damp walls to make room for the guards to pass and grab their prey. Each of us was filled with dread in case we were chosen to replace the poor soul whose pleading cries we had heard earlier as they were being tortured.

They moved towards us. I kept my eyes down, trying not to breathe as sour breath came closer. A dirt-encrusted hand gripped my shoulder. My legs buckled beneath me but he must have been used to this reaction because his arm quickly encircled my waist and he half-dragged, half-carried me out of the cell. I heard the door slam behind us and the key turn in the lock and wished I was back there with the other women.

'Where are you taking me?' I hoped he would explain I was to be presented at court, or even let go. Anything other than having to face the Witchfinder. I had heard enough women begging for mercy, their voices carrying along the stone corridor between the cell where I had been held and from where he carried out his interrogations, and had no wish to discover what heinous things he did to cause such distress.

'Please, I haven't done anything wrong. This is a mistake.'

The hand on my waist clasped my skin tightly. 'Quiet, witch.'

'But I'm not,' I argued, my teeth chattering with fear.

'That's for the Witchfinder to decide.'

My stomach dropped and my mouth went dry as I tried to think of a way to escape what lay ahead of me. Aware I had little chance of getting away from the guard, I realised I had nothing to lose. Twisting in his arms, I grabbed at his grubby face with one hand, my nails digging into his cheek, and kicked him as hard as I could.

He yelped in pain and dropped me onto the flagstones, then kicked me in the stomach. 'Whore,' he spat at me, only just missing my face.

I saw him draw his foot back ready to kick me again, so curled up into a foetal position to protect myself from the next blow, only vaguely aware of heavy footsteps coming our way.

'What is the meaning of this?' Roger Dankworth's voice boomed through the echoing corridor.

I wasn't sure what was worse, this bully or the Witchfinder, and stayed where I was on the cold floor.

I heard fist against bone and assumed the Witchfinder's punch had connected with the man's face. 'I said bring her to me, not mete out your own justice on the wench. Now carry her through.'

Rough hands lifted me and hoisted me over a shoulder, winding me, as the guard carried me the rest of the way to the Witchfinder's interrogation chamber.

I winced as I was unceremoniously dumped onto a wooden chair and my arms strapped onto each armrest. The guard stepped back to the side of the room, where I saw another scowling silently. Neither of them would be rescuing me from what was about to happen.

Roger Dankworth removed his tall, faded black hat and placed it on the end of some sort of contraption that I didn't want to imagine might be used on inmates.

He stared at me with his dark, almost black eyes, bending forward, his hands resting on his knees, until his face was close enough for me to smell his rancid breath. He leant even closer and breathed in through his nose slowly and deeply before standing upright again, a satisfied smirk on his thin face.

'I hope you're going to make things easy for yourself and confess.'

'To what?' I knew well enough what, but had no intention of letting him off the hook that easily.

His brows lowered. 'To being a witch.'

'But I'm not,' I insisted.

He shook his head slowly. 'You are. I smell your magick on you.'

Did he? I clenched my teeth, determined to stand up to him despite my terror. 'I told you I'm not a witch and that's the truth.'

Could he really smell it on me? I might not have been inducted into the coven but all the women who had gone before me in my family back to the sixteenth century had been witches. Was it possible for me to reject my birthright and everything that had been handed down to me through the centuries?

A hard slap to my left cheek brought me back to the present. My cheek stung and my eye watered as the pain registered. 'I'm really not a witch, whatever you may believe.'

He stepped back and folded his arms, a strange, satisfied expression on his face. 'If you do not wish to make this easier for yourself, you leave me no option.'

Option? For what? I was about to ask, when he turned to the men near the door.

'Bring in the surgeon and the midwife.'

One of the men immediately left the room.

What?

'Why?' I asked, terrified about what they might do to me.

He didn't answer but stared at me.

A couple of minutes later a tall middle-aged man entered the room followed by a woman who wouldn't meet my eye.

'I'm not a witch,' I said although I was unsure why I bothered. Looking at their faces it was clear neither of them had any intention of defying the Witchfinder.

The Witchfinder waved for one of the guards to come over to me. 'Untie her.'

Once the leather ties were removed and my hands freed, I rubbed my wrists to alleviate the pain.

Roger Dankworth's eyes narrowed as he addressed me. 'Remove your clothes.'

I shook my head, horrified. 'No.'

He clicked his fingers at the woman. 'Strip her.'

I pushed her away. 'No, you can't do that.'

He waved for the two guards to leave the room.

'Over there,' Roger Dankworth instructed, indicating a corner where a wooden screen stood blocking off a small area, where I was to go to remove my clothes.

I walked over to it followed by the woman and the surgeon. I stared at each of them defiantly for a moment, trembling in fear and shame. I had never been naked in front of anyone before, apart from my mother when I was younger.

I turned my back on them and slowly began to remove my clothes, hoping to leave the bonnet on and hide my hair that was much shorter than that of other women I'd met.

Finally, having stepped out of the skirt and removed the shift, I draped them over a low stool and stood, arms crossed over my chest, and slowly turned to face them.

'And this,' the midwife said, pulling the cloth bonnet from my head. She seemed momentarily taken aback to see my hairstyle.

The following minutes while each inspected every inch of my skin were excruciating. I wanted to cry, but refused to allow them to see how they made me feel. This would be over soon, I kept telling myself as the time passed.

Finally, they stepped back, whispering to each other. 'You may dress,' the surgeon said.

I hastily pulled on the clothes, grateful to be covered once more. At least the Witchfinder hadn't watched, I thought. It was unnerving enough to be under that man's scrutiny fully dressed.

They went to join him, waiting for me to follow.

'Well?' he asked, his booming voice commanding as usual.

'Nothing, sir,' the surgeon said.

The Witchfinder's eyes slid in my direction. 'Are you certain?' he asked without blinking.

The surgeon coughed nervously. 'Yes, sir. We checked everywhere.'

He finally turned his gaze from me, picked up his hat and placed it back on his head. 'You may leave.' He yelled for the guards.

I stood in front of him willing him to send me back to the other women.

The guards returned to the chamber.

'Take her back to the cell.'

The same man who had brought me here grabbed my arm roughly and began leading me from the room. I relaxed slightly but before I could step out of the doorway, the Witchfinder's hand landed on my shoulder, restraining me.

I felt his warm breath on the back of my neck and gave an involuntary shudder. 'You can't fool me, I recognise your scent only too well. I will see you again.'

He let go and I dared not look back as the guard half-dragged me out of the room and along the corridor away from him and his threats. As we walked it occurred to me that if I had done as Mum asked and been initiated into the coven two years before, I would have spent that time practising my craft. What a fool I had been not to listen to her. If I had, I might have been able to cast a spell to get me out of this mess.

Chapter Thirty-Two

XAVIER

Andre checked the hiding place and brought back a note from Diana. He read it briefly before handing it to me, closing his eyes, his sadness obvious.

'Diana has been to the castle with two friends.' He shook his head. 'They tried but were unable to rescue Briar.' He looked stricken.

I thought back to when I was locked up in that formidable place. 'Briar will probably be kept with others, which is never pleasant, but at least she won't be alone with her thoughts to torment her.'

I wondered what might have happened if Diana's spell had worked, and she had unexpectedly rescued a dozen or so other convicts with Briar. I supposed she wouldn't care, as long as Briar was safe.

We must find a way to get into the castle, I mused.

'No.' Andre shook his head even though I hadn't spoken my thoughts aloud. 'It's too dangerous.'

'I haven't said what I was thinking yet.'

'I know you well enough, Xavier. You're considering giving yourself up to get inside those damn walls, aren't you?'

I was. Aware he wouldn't stand back and allow me to do something like this without a fight, I added, 'Briar's life is at stake and I can't live any sort of life knowing I didn't do all I could to save hers.'

'You are a condemned man, or have you forgotten?'

I hadn't. 'Andre, I've lived a longer life than she has.'

'Hardly more than two or three years.' I saw the annoyance on his face.

'Maybe, but I have lived those years to the full – experienced many things, both good and bad. What has Briar seen of life apart from the war that the island is living through? She is a young woman. She deserves to…' I was embarrassed to continue, realising that I had let my feelings for her rise too much to the surface.

'Who deserves to fall in love,' he said matter-of-factly. 'Isn't that what you were about to say?'

He knew me too well. I didn't waste my time lying to him. 'It is.'

Andre's expression softened. 'You told me you were in love with each other last time she was here, so she has experienced love with a man.'

'But she has no recollection of it happening. I want her to know how it feels to be loved in that way.'

He sighed sadly. 'I know you do, but I won't stand by and watch you sacrifice yourself when all that might happen is the two of you will be executed.'

I finished my beer. 'I'll find a way.'

Andre didn't look convinced.

'I'm sure you'll do your best,' he said. 'But what if you fail?'

I shrugged. 'What if I don't?' I argued. 'I'll be doing it with Diana's help, don't forget. I'm sure that together we'll get Briar back to where she belongs.' She belonged in my arms, I reasoned. My mission was to return her to her mother and the relative safety that meant.

Andre sat back in his chair. 'And you believe the only way to make that happen is to give yourself in?' he asked scornfully.

'Hopefully not. But I will go to the castle.' I smiled at him. 'I've thought of a plan but I'll need your help.'

Andre laughed. 'Why does that not surprise me? Go on, what do you need from me?'

'I must have clothes a servant would wear. If I'm in disguise I will have a better chance of succeeding if I'm dressed appropriately.'

Andre gave my words some thought and nodded. 'Leave it with me.'

While my friend went out to find clothes, I wrote Diana a note telling her I would bring Briar as near to where she had disappeared as possible. I had no intention of letting any doubt put me off. I was also certain I had heard distant rumblings of thunder coming from the French coast while Andre and I had been speaking. I prayed the storm wouldn't die out, or bypass the island before it reached us. I knew I was attempting the near-impossible but had little option other than to try.

Chapter Thirty-Three

XAVIER

A few hours later, armed with a small bag of what appeared to be ground herbs hidden in my pocket, which Andre insisted could be used to induce sleep for several hours, I was inside the castle, thanks to a contact of his who exchanged his clothes for a bag of coins so that I could take his place serving dignitaries of the Lieutenant Governor that evening.

I waited outside the kitchen door as agreed and, spotting the man with a handkerchief hanging from his left trouser pocket, paid him the agreed amount and took the heavy server laden with a side of beef. Lifting it onto my shoulder, I fell into step with the other serving staff.

I had some idea of the layout from past experience visiting here as a privateer, when I had been in favour with the Governor and given an audience. I hoped that no one recognised me from back then. I knew the area of the castle where Briar would be held from my time as a captive. Now all

I needed to do was find a way to get down to the cells and locate her.

Later, when the guests were leaving and leftover food and drink were being cleared from the Great Hall, I executed the second part of the plan. I filled two jugs with leftover wine from the dregs of several others and, sneaking out of the room, ran down the first corridor, making my way hurriedly towards the cells.

'Who goes there?' a whiny voice demanded.

A couple of the guards had heard my footsteps, which was precisely what I had hoped for. I dropped a quarter of the herbal mixture into one of the jugs and an equal amount into the other, keeping half in case I needed it later. I then stirred the liquid with my finger, being careful to wipe it dry on my trouser leg and not put it near my mouth. After secreting one of the jugs in the shadows I rounded the corner to the main area outside the cells and handed the filled jug to the larger of the two guards.

'I can't recall his name,' I said, pretending to be annoyed, 'but one of your lot ordered me to bring this down here.' They swapped cheerful glances at the sight of the jug, seemingly convinced by my sullen behaviour, and, without questioning why anyone would send this treat to them, snatched the jug from me and began drinking greedily.

'Well?' the other guard said, glaring at me, one arm outstretched to his companion, trying to wrench the jug from him before he emptied it. He shoved me away from them. 'You've done what you came to do. Away with you before I have you locked in one of these cells.' He roared with laughter and it took all my determination not to slam him to the ground.

Thinking of Briar and feeling smug at their ignorance, I retraced my steps and stood by the other jug, waiting for the sleep-inducing concoction to work on the men. Andre had explained it would be about ten minutes but my impatience increased as the two men laughed at their good fortune. They joked about the Governor, mocking him and the attendees at the evening's event, as they took turns to guzzle the wine. Hearing belches and satisfied laughter, I paced back and forth, impatient for them to succumb to the sedative.

Eventually they fell silent. One began snoring. Satisfied, I stepped out of my hiding place and hurried back to them, kicking each hard in the ankles to ensure they were unconscious. I checked no one was coming before unhooking the keys from the shorter guard's belt. I made my way quietly through the corridors, recalling as clearly as my memory would allow the way to where the accused witches were kept when I had been imprisoned here.

I peered into the gloom of the cell, tormented by the sounds of weeping interspersed with groans of pain.

'Briar?' I whispered, desperate to find her while not alerting the others. It was an impossible task, but one I still attempted. I hadn't thought what to do about the other women when I did find her but would worry about that when I needed to.

I tried again. 'Briar, it's Xavier. Come to the door.'

I wasn't sure why I expected this vague plan to work, but moments later a hand I recognised, mainly because the skin was softer than that of most women I came across, reached out through the small, barred window.

'Xavier? Is that really you?' Her voice was fearful. She sounded weak, broken almost.

I clasped her hand in mine. 'I'm going to get you out of

here. We must be quiet if we are to make our escape before the others rampage through these corridors. When they do the guards will be alerted and call for help.' She waited while I tried several keys as quickly and as quietly as possible, tensing as they clanged together. I heard stirrings coming from Briar's cell.

'Oi, what's goin' on?'

'Someone's coming in,' a fearful voice replied. 'That strange girl is talking to him.'

I presumed they thought me to be one of the guards. Finally locating the correct key, I unlocked the door and pushed it open. Desperate to get a head start on the others and extricate Briar before others clambered to leave, I grabbed Briar's hand and pulled her behind me to shield her from the other inmates in case any of them reacted badly.

I raised a finger to my lips and hushed them. 'Listen to me. I will leave the keys with you on the proviso that one of you promises to unlock the other cell doors before leaving.' I kept my voice low but assertive.

'I'll do it.' A young woman came forward and took the keys from me. 'Bless you for your kindness and bravery, sir.'

'I'm happy to oblige. I beg you to be as quiet as possible. The longer it takes for other guards to be alerted the more chance you have of escape.' I turned to Briar. She was shivering and I wasn't sure if it was due to the cold in the damp dungeons or fear. Either would be understandable. I removed my jacket and held it out for her to slip her arms into. I took her hand in mine and gave it a reassuring squeeze. 'Let's go.'

We had one chance to make this work. I had no idea

whether it would work or if Diana would be waiting to rescue Briar, but I needed to try.

We ran through the corridors, past the sleeping guards, stepping back into the shadows whenever I heard footsteps coming in our direction.

Seeing a guard racing around the next corner I grabbed Briar around her waist and pulled her into a nearby alcove, holding her against me, knowing she wouldn't make a sound.

As we waited in silence for him and two others to pass, it occurred to me that if Diana's next attempt did work then this might be the last time Briar would be in my arms. She was still trembling slightly as she slid her arms around me. I silently kissed the top of her head, not daring to move much.

Screams came from behind us. Some of the women must have been captured already. The thought saddened me.

'Hey, you there,' a guard bellowed, his footsteps echoing noisily along the corridor as he came closer to our hiding place.

Briar tensed and clung to me. Just when I expected him to slam his hand onto my shoulder, voices from the freed women carried along the corridor, diverting his attention. He ran off after them cursing and shouting, giving Briar and me the opportunity to set off again.

We ran down corridors, passing through small rooms and startled servants, before escaping out of a door just before the kitchen. Finally, we stepped outside. It was raining heavily and I heard thunder. Relieved, I paused, pointing up at the sky. 'Do you hear that?'

She nodded, tears falling down her cheeks. 'There's a storm,' she whispered, looking up at me miserably when we stopped to catch our breath. All we needed to do now was round the side of the wall to the outside of the condemned cell.

'There is.' I couldn't tell if she was happy or sad about this. 'You'll soon be home and safe,' I said, hoping I was right, my heart breaking at the thought of parting from her again.

'You came for me,' Briar said quietly, her arms slipping around my waist and resting her head against my chest. 'I knew you would.'

I enveloped her with my arms, holding her tightly. 'We need to go where your mother will expect to find you,' I said, knowing I couldn't let my true emotions loose.

It took a few attempts to round the castle wall without being seen but we eventually reached the outside wall of the cell. Pressing ourselves back against it to keep as much in the shadows and out of the moonlight as possible, we took a moment to catch our breath.

'Xavier?' she whispered, looking up at me with her perfect green eyes.

'What is it?' I stared at her pale, beautiful face wishing things were different and I could spend the rest of my days with this brave woman who had changed my life in ways I never could have imagined.

'I'm sorry you had to risk your life for me,' she said. I opened my mouth to argue but she placed her fingers over my lips to stop me. 'I wish things didn't have to be this way,' she said, voicing my own thoughts. 'I want you to know I will be forever grateful to you, and I promise I'll never forget you.'

Unsure how much longer I could stand the tension between us, I tried to make light of the situation. 'All you need to do for me is stay safe and have the best life possible.'

'I just wanted you to know how I feel. How I'll always feel.'

She couldn't know that, I thought, immediately chiding myself for thinking that way when I knew in my heart that I would never forget her either. Realising time was running out for us and remembering the likelihood that she could disappear from me at any second, I took her in my arms. I had to make the most of what time we did have.

'I feel the same way,' I admitted, knowing that if I didn't share my feelings now I would miss the chance.

Her face brightened. 'You do?'

'Yes.' I smiled at her. 'I have for a very long time.'

She frowned in confusion. 'You have? Since when?'

I wanted to tell her that I had loved her for three years, but there was no time for that now. I also didn't dare risk her being hurt if she reacted badly to discovering that I had been lying to her by not telling her about her previous time here.

Unable to help myself any longer, I stared into her eyes. 'May I kiss you?'

'I can't help thinking I know you from somewhere.'

I feigned ignorance. 'From the 1940s,' I teased.

She gave a tight smile. 'No, from before.'

Shocked by her comment, and unsure how to answer without upsetting her, I lowered my lips to hers and kissed her. Unsure what to expect, I felt my heart racing as she hesitated briefly, then slipped her arms around my neck and responded with an intensity that surprised and delighted me. If only we had more time together.

A fork of lightning cracked against the other side of the castle, surprising us both. Desperate for more but not wishing to ruin Diana's attempt to take her home, I tried to move away from her and was surprised when she didn't let go of me. I smiled, enjoying her display of affection. 'We don't have any more time,' I soothed before raising my hands and gently taking hold of her wrists to lower them.

'I'm not ready to leave you.'

'Nor I you,' I admitted. 'But we have no way of knowing whether your mother is here, Briar, so we must take care not to touch this time,' I reminded her, regretting the necessity.

She sighed and brushed away raindrops from the end of her eyelashes. 'I know.'

Tears ran down her cheeks. She raised her fingers to her lips, kissed the tips and blew her kiss towards me.

I went to speak, but in the blink of an eye, she had vanished.

I stared at the place where she had stood a second before. Pressing my hand against the stones that her back had so recently touched, I attempted to pick up any warmth, but it was pointless: there was none. My lips still felt the pressure of hers on them and my heart ached as it had done that first time she had left me.

She had gone. This time forever.

Chapter Thirty-Four

BRIAR

Where was he? The realisation was like a punch to my chest. I barely had time to register anything else when a vice-like grip grabbed my shoulder and dragged me backwards behind the dilapidated wall of what had seconds ago been the cell.

I tripped backwards over something and almost fell. Then, righting myself, I noticed Pippin first, then Mum. She wasn't alone. 'Mrs Le Dain?'

Mum stepped in front of me and took me in her arms. She hugged me tightly, tears rolling down her face as her body shook.

'It worked, Babette, we did it,' she sobbed, pressing her hands over her chest. 'I would never have forgiven myself if we failed a second time.'

A second time?

'I can see that, dear.' Babette took a handkerchief from her sleeve and wiped her own tears away, then blew her nose quietly. I realised the effort they must have gone to and what they had risked making this happen.

I stared at my mother, my emotions conflicted – wanting to cry but not wishing her to see my distress at parting from Xavier. They had succeeded in saving me and I must be grateful. I was grateful. I pressed my lips together, still able to feel the pressure of his lips on mine. But at what cost. I had lost Xavier forever just when I had understood how much he meant to me. It seemed unbearably cruel, especially now I had discovered he felt the same way about me.

'You don't look happy,' Mum said anxiously. 'I only did what I thought best. What Xavier instructed me to do.'

At the sound of his name, I calmed slightly, remembering that saving me had been his intention all along. What we had both wanted. I thought about what she had just said.

'Xavier told you to do this?'

Mrs Le Dain picked up a large carpet bag, clearly impatient to get out of the storm. 'It's after curfew and we must return to our homes immediately if we aren't to risk being caught,' she whispered with an urgency that made us pay attention. 'I suggest you save any conversations until you're back in your home.'

She was right. 'We will. And thank you for helping Mum,' I said. 'For helping bring me back. I really am very grateful.'

They immediately began tidying away candlesticks and what seemed to be a tiny cauldron. I crouched to help. That done, Mum took my hand. 'Come along. Let's get you away from here. I'll tell you everything when we're back at the cottage.'

I hurried with the pair of them, ducking behind low walls and hedges when soldiers appeared nearby.

We parted ways with Mrs Le Dain at the end of our lane, exchanging discreet waves before hurrying on back to Honey Bee Cottage. Mum locked the front door behind us and rested her back against it. She sighed wearily. She looked exhausted, but smiled at me, her hand resting on her heart.

'I don't think I've ever been as frightened as I was this evening.'

'No?' Pippin settled onto my shoulder.

'She's missed you terribly,' Mum said. 'I've never known her to be so restless.'

'Poor thing. I'm not surprised.' I turned my head to look at the little familiar who was usually there for me. 'We're not used to being apart, are we?' She looked at me before flying back upstairs, satisfied that I was home again.

'I feel so responsible,' Mum said, taking my attention from Pippin. 'What if we hadn't managed to rescue you before … well, before.' She shocked us both by crying. Mum seldom cried. I was a bit disconcerted and unsure how to react.

Hating to see her in such pain, I went to her and gave her a hug. 'It's fine, Mum. You did do it. I'm here now.'

'You are. I can hardly dare believe it.'

We stepped back from each other. 'It's been an emotional evening.'

She gave a shuddering sigh. 'An emotional few days.'

She was right. Everything felt surreal. Barely an hour ago I had been in a dank cell with others like myself. It was a struggle to trust that I really was out of danger and back home again. I pictured Xavier's face as he gazed at me that last time and a sob escaped.

I covered my mouth, needing to contain my emotions. Mum had risked so much to rescue me and I didn't want her to think I was anything other than happy to be back home with her.

I went to the table, and it occurred to me that it was almost in the same position as the one Andre had in his home. I needed to help Mum feel better before I could indulge in self-pity. I pulled out her chair.

'You sit here and relax. I'll make us both a nice cup of tea.' There was little in the kitchen, which didn't surprise me, but I made us a slice of toast with a scraping of margarine and two weak teas. After the disgusting offerings in the prison, this was a treat.

'Here you go.' I placed the plates and cups on the table and sat next to her. 'What we both went through is bound to have an effect on us,' I told her. 'I'm sure we both need to catch up on our sleep. The most important thing is that I'm back now, so let's focus on getting back to normal.' Not that I was certain I knew what that was anymore.

'I can't forget what Xavier told me,' she said as if she hadn't heard me.

I realised it wasn't going to be easy to distract Mum until she had shared what she needed to. 'Which was?'

She looked at me aghast. 'You were arrested. And'—she pressed her lips together briefly—'there was a chance you could be burnt at the stake.'

'They don't do that here, Mum,' I reassured her.

'They don't now, or didn't then?'

I shook my head. However terrible it had been knowing I was to be tried for sorcery, I had discovered a couple of things. 'They usually strangled those found guilty of sorcery first.'

She frowned. 'They didn't burn witches at the stake then?'

I wished I had kept my thoughts to myself. I could see I

wasn't helping matters, but Mum would expect me to answer. 'They did, but unlike other places the powers that be here at least strangled or hanged those they believed to be witches to ensure they were dead before their bodies were burnt.'

Mum shuddered. 'That's still horrendous. How are you so calm about it?'

I wasn't sure. 'I suppose it all seems a little unreal now I'm not there.' I shrugged. 'That or I'm still in shock.'

Mum patted my hand. 'I think it's the latter.'

She was becoming agitated and I didn't want her to dwell on what might have happened when everything was fine now. 'I think we should talk about something else.'

'But, Briar, I need you to tell me everything.'

Realising she wasn't going to let up in her quest to find out more, I told her all that I could recall. As I spoke I saw what little colour there was in her pale skin fade. She was alarmed.

'I can't bear to think of a strange man and woman inspecting you like that.' She shuddered.

'I think I've said enough.'

She shook her head. 'No, I need to know every detail.'

'Why torment yourself?'

'Because I was the one who sent you back there.'

'No, Mum,' I said. 'That was my fault, not yours.'

She pushed her toast over to me. 'You're right, we should leave it. You must be starving. You need this more than me.'

I went to argue but she was having none of it. My stomach rumbled and I picked up one of the slices and took a bite.

She took a sip of her tea.

I looked around the room as I ate, picturing Xavier and Andre going about their day. My mood dipped as I pictured Ember arriving, her large presence demanding everyone's attention. I reminded myself how lucky I was to be safe. I needed to focus all my attention on the present, on my life with Mum, and try to come to terms with my misery at never seeing Xavier again.

After washing the filth off myself, I changed into my nightdress and went up to my room. I gazed out of the window up at the moon, desperate for a connection to Xavier. We might be seeing the moon three hundred years apart, but it was still the same moon we could both look at.

The thought soothed me slightly and I sent him my love. I got into bed and fell asleep within minutes. Immediately, I was back in that disgusting cell with all those women. I woke and, after shaking off the horror, calmed slightly, hoping they had all managed to escape. How typical of Xavier it was to want to rescue as many people as he could, not just me. No wonder Andre admired him so much. No wonder I loved him.

I must have dozed off again because I was back in Andre's house watching Xavier write something on a sheet of paper. He walked over to the hidey-hole and placed it inside.

I woke suddenly and sat bolt upright. The hidey-hole. Was my dream trying to tell me something? Had Xavier left me a letter in there? I desperately hoped he had.

Unable to resist checking, I got out of bed and tiptoed down past Mum's bedroom door, down the stairs to the living room. I lit the nub of a candle and stuck it on the spike of a candlestick. Then, walking over to the corner of the room, I lifted the rug and the cut floorboards to reach inside.

There was a sheet of paper but not Mum's pen. I wondered whether Mum might ever get her beloved pen back as I lifted the note from its hiding place, hoping it wasn't an old one I had already seen.

Relieved you are saved, Briar. This is the last note I shall
place here. I must leave the island for my own safety. You will be
forever in my thoughts and my heart. Xavier x

I sobbed as I reread his words several times. He was going away. I needed to respond immediately, hoping he hadn't already left, wanting him to know I was fine and thinking of him too.

Home and safe. Missing you. Thank you for helping me. I'll
never forget you and wish you safety, good fortune and above all
a happy life. I will savour every memory I have of you. Briar x

Irritated with myself for not thinking to leave a message as soon as I returned to the cottage, I quickly slipped the sheet into the hole and went to close the floorboards over it. Then, thinking back to how special it had been to receive Mum's fountain pen, I unfastened the small silver chain I always wore around my neck with the St Christopher on it that Dad had given me the first time I went to St Malo on a visit with Mum to see friends. I wanted Xavier to have something of mine to keep next to him. A St Christopher, the patron saint of travellers, seemed to be the perfect gift.

I lifted the small pendant to my lips and kissed it before lowering it onto the sheet of paper. Then, not wishing to miss him in case he was about to leave Andre's, I hastily replaced the floorboards and covered them with the rug. I would check tomorrow whether it was still there. If it was, I'd know Xavier had left without knowing how grateful I was to him.

I stared at the floor for a while, trying to imagine him walking past me and retrieving what I had left. It felt as if we were only separated by a thin veil of time. So thin I felt I could reach out and touch him if I believed hard enough. If only that were possible.

I yawned. There was nothing else I could do. I realised that if I was going to be anything other than an exhausted mess in the morning, I needed to catch some sleep.

I went up to my room and got back into bed. A strong urge to cry swept over me and I gave in to it. Then it occurred to me that this wasn't all about me. Mum was struggling to cope with what had happened too and I needed to be sensitive to her feelings. Dear, brave Xavier. I trusted that whatever he set his mind to he would accomplish it. All I wanted for him now was to stay safe.

Well, that and to be with him so I could kiss him again.

Chapter Thirty-Five

XAVIER

Ember glared at me from the doorway, hands on hips. 'What are you waiting for? Didn't you hear what I said?'

'I did,' I snapped, furious with her for being here instead of Briar.

'Then why aren't you running out of this cottage? You need to be as far away from this place as possible. They'll come for you at any moment after what you did.'

It took a moment for me to recall letting all the prisoners go free.

I heard the hysteria rising in her voice but was past caring about her feelings. 'Leave me be,' I shouted.

'Xavier, listen to me. I know you hate me for what I did to Briar but can't you see it was in your best interests?'

What? 'Have you lost control of your senses?' I was too emotionally drained to deal with this woman. 'Thanks to you, Briar could have been executed.' There was no remorse. No reaction at all. 'Don't you care how the things you do affect others?'

She shrugged. 'I regret you were foolish enough to break into the castle and rescue her.' Her voice rose. 'Why do you care more about her than saving your own life?'

'Because I do not care for the life I now have.' I was weary, tired of fighting.

There was someone else I cared about, though. 'I care for my family and Andre. I won't have my actions putting him in further danger.' I folded my spare shirt and pushed it into my leather knapsack.

'Then I'm glad you're leaving.' She turned on her heel and stormed out of the cottage.

I was relieved to see the back of her. She had been right about one thing, though: I must make haste and leave. By staying, I put my aunt and sister at risk as well as Andre. Just then, I noticed a small pebble Wren had found on the beach years ago. I picked it up but then accidentally dropped it. I watched as it rolled over to the corner of the room to Andre's hiding place.

I wasn't sure why but I had a strong urge to look inside. Determined to put my mind at rest and trying not to think of the disappointment I would certainly experience when I discovered there was nothing waiting for me, I knelt and took up the two floorboards.

Taking a steadying breath, I reached inside. My hand connected with something small. I picked it up and looked at the fine silver chain and pendant in my hand. I recalled seeing it around Briar's slender neck although I had no idea what it represented. My heart swelled. She had left something of hers for me.

Reaching in again, I found the sheet of paper I had left with my final note to her telling her I was having to leave this place forever. I read it, overcome with emotion to read her response. So that was it. We really had been parted forever.

Hearing stern voices down the lane, I quickly found Andre's quill and ink. I wrote a short note on the sheet and, putting it back into the hole, replaced the floorboards.

I fastened the chain around my neck, soothed to feel something of hers resting on my throat. I wasn't sure if I imagined it but the silver disk and chain felt warm to the touch. Had Briar only just taken this from her own neck? Or was I being fanciful, needing to feel closer to her?

Hearing voices shouting from down the lane, I hurriedly retrieved Wren's pebble and dropped it into my knapsack before securing the top of the bag with the leather strap.

Pulling on my jacket, I slung my rucksack over my shoulder and then left the cottage without looking back.

Chapter Thirty-Six

BRIAR

I sat on the floor with Xavier's note in my lap, unable to stem my tears. I reread it for the third time.

I must leave now. Live a full life, Briar, and know I will never forget you. X

'And I will never forget you,' I cried. One of my tears dropped on the ink making his kiss blur. I gasped, lifting the sheet of paper and blowing on it, desperate to dry it and stop further damage. It was all I had left of him. I needed to keep it as pristine as possible to affirm that what I had experienced with Xavier was real and not some crazed dream.

The front door opened. Shocked, I dropped the note and scrambled to reach for it.

'What are you doing?' Mum asked as soon as she had closed the door. I heard her put down her basket, her footsteps echoed on the wooden floor as she approached me. She crouched down and rested a hand on my shoulder. 'Briar?'

'This is his last message to me,' I said, my voice tight with emotion as I struggled to say the words and try to take in their meaning at the same time. I looked up at her. 'I'm never going to see Xavier again, am I?'

Mum sat on the floor next to me and pulled me into a hug. 'My sweet girl.' She waited a while as I sobbed into her shoulder. 'I suspected this had happened.'

'What?' I sniffed.

'If only you hadn't fallen in love with him.'

She pushed back a strand of my hair, then, taking my face in her hands, looked into my eyes. 'Nothing happened between you, did it? You know, intimately?'

I wasn't sure what she meant initially, then gasped. 'Mum, no.' I recalled his kiss and felt my cheeks heat. Seeing her look of shock, I decided to explain my reaction. 'We kissed, but that's all and only once.'

She sighed with relief. 'Good.'

'Good?' I couldn't help feeling irritated with her, despite her reaction being understandable.

Mum rose to her feet. 'Yes. I don't want my daughter's reputation tarnished.'

'Mum, this happened three hundred years ago, remember? Apart from me no one is still alive from my time there.' The realisation of what I had said hit me. Xavier wasn't alive anymore. How could he be?

My heart ached. I needed to be alone, so returned the sheet of paper to the hiding place, deciding it would be safest there, and replaced the two shortened floorboards and rug over it. I stood. 'I'm going to my room for a bit.'

She gave me a nod and looked as relieved as I did to have some time without me, probably to come to terms with what

I'd shared about my feelings for Xavier.

Once in my room, I closed the door, kicked off my shoes and then slumped on my bed. I thought of Xavier and how we passed messages across time. I decided that the only way I was going to find the strength to live any sort of life without him would be to focus on the tentative connection we did have, regardless of whether I understood how it worked. Not that there would be much chance of communication with him now that he had left Andre's home and lived in exile in France.

This was Ember's fault.

I thought of the tall, strong, strikingly attractive woman and a pang of jealousy hit me. She was everything I was not. Tall where I was only just over five feet two inches. Raven black hair, where mine was a light brown. She was charismatic and dramatic and demanded people do as she wished. She expected everyone's attention to be on her whenever she entered a room. She cared little for others' opinions of her. Unlike me, always wanting to please people.

Ember was magnificent, in her way, and a part of me couldn't understand why he'd chosen me over her, but I was glad that he had.

My satisfaction was short-lived when I remembered where I was and that Ember, although not in his favour, was still living in his time. It was plain to see that the only feelings Xavier had towards her still were ones of annoyance and disappointment. But she was cunning and clever and without me there to hinder any of her plans had free rein to do as she pleased. She didn't need to rush and could take her time if necessary. I sensed she wasn't finished with him yet. Her fury that Xavier no longer wanted to be with her was evident even if it did simmer just beneath the surface most of the time. I doubted Ember would rest until she had paid him back somehow for no longer having any affection for her. Worst of all, there was absolutely nothing I could do about any of it.

'Frau Le Gros.'

The sound of a German soldier addressing Mum as she opened our front door brought me back to the present. I still had to find a way to navigate my own situation and, regardless of my heartbreak, I needed to be present to support Mum. I wasn't the only one who had suffered.

I went downstairs to join her again. 'What did he want?'

'I dropped the two apples I bought at the store and he picked them up for me.'

'I see.'

I watched her unpacking the meagre supplies she had managed to buy that morning.

The reality of life here for us hit me, and I felt angry with myself for wallowing.

'Mum?'

She turned to me, eyebrows raised. 'Yes?'

'I'm sorry.' I crossed the narrow kitchen in two steps and hugged her tightly. 'I shouldn't take out my emotions on you. You're the one who rescued me, after all.' I looked at her. 'And regardless of how I'm behaving now, I really am happy to be back here with you again.'

Mum's hold on me tightened. 'That is a relief, because I can't put into words how grateful I am to have you back.'

'What can I do to help?' I asked as soon as she had let go. She handed me a knife and together we began peeling the few vegetables she had found for our lunch. It was a mundane task but it cheered me to be free to carry out these everyday chores as if nothing had happened.

As I worked, I thought of Xavier and wondered where he was and how he was doing. Remembering my plan to focus on Mum and our lives, I sent him my love across the ether, having to swallow to clear the lump in my throat.

I dragged my focus back to what I was doing. It occurred to me that all I could really do was trust in his strength of mind and body to survive as best he could, and hope he had an easier life now I wasn't there disturbing his peace.

It was a good plan, but not that simple to put into practice. I missed him more than I could have imagined. I had barely known him any time at all but was certain I'd never connect with another man like I had done with Xavier. I had no wish to.

Chapter Thirty-Seven

XAVIER

It was my fourth day hiding in a shelter up the hill from Rozel harbour. I needed a wash and was desperate to hear from Andre, who was doing his best to secure me passage from Rozel harbour to Portbail on the coast of north-west France. From there I hoped to contact acquaintances of mine and find a way to make a living.

The rustling of feet treading through long grass alerted me that I was no longer alone. I slunk back into the hedgerow, my senses alert and ready to defend myself should the necessity arise.

'Xavier?' I heard Andre whisper my name and slowly stood, careful should he have been followed and not realised it.

'Over here.'

He spotted me and, coming over to me, held out a small sacking bag. I took it and peered inside. 'You are a marvel,' I said, grateful for his thoughtfulness.

I sat and took the pie and stoneware bottle from the bag. Removing the stopper, I took a mouthful. Beer. Concentrating on drinking slowly despite my thirst, I raised my free hand in thanks.

'Good?' Andre asked, a glint in his eyes.

I nodded, taking another mouthful. 'You have no idea how good.' He seemed pleased with himself for some reason and, eager to find out why, said, 'I sense you have something to tell me.'

'I have a mission for you, as well as a way to escape from here. The captain of a boat is a distant cousin of mine. He's agreed to take you to France on the proviso that when you get there you help him locate a wretch who stole from his parents and track down the valuables taken by this man.'

'Tell me more,' I said, intrigued and relieved to be needed again.

'Unfortunately the mission won't take you as far as Portbail but will get you to Carteret where he was told the thief had been seen earlier this week.' It was good enough for me. Freedom and something to focus on, what more could I ask for? I slapped him on the back, thankful for his help.

'I would be grateful to be left anywhere off the island,' I admitted. Replacing the stopper in the bottle, I turned to the pleasant-smelling pie. I studied the golden crust with dried gravy around its rim. 'This is a sight for a hungry man,' I said half to myself. 'Thank you, my good friend. I will be forever in your debt.'

Andre laughed. 'I know.'

I held the pie in front of him 'Want some?'

Andre shook his head. 'I ate mine on the way here.'

He was such a good friend and I doubted I'd ever be able to pay him back for all his kindness. I took a mouthful, relishing the flavours. 'Mmm.'

'They're good, aren't they?'

'Delicious. Now, tell me more.' I took another bite.

'You must wait here until dusk. After that, make your way down to the harbour. The boat is the largest one there. It's *La Duchesse*.'

I finished my mouthful. 'You are good to me, Andre. The best of friends.'

We sat passing the time with memories of escapades we had experienced together. This was becoming a week of parting from people I was fond of. I thought of Briar. People I loved. I shook my head to banish thoughts of someone who was now lost to me forever. I needed to put all my energy into focusing on the task in front of me, saving my own life this time. I bade farewell to Andre and thanked him once more.

Five hours later, I reached the bustling small harbour. I remained hidden among the throngs of men loading boats and going about their business. I spotted *La Duchesse* easily, located the captain and handed him a note Andre had passed to me before we said our goodbyes. He read it before returning it to me.

'You will find your quarters below, next to my cabin. It is small but…'

'I am thankful for whatever space you can make available to me.'

Chapter Thirty-Eight

BRIAR

March 1946

I wasn't sure where the ten months since the end of the Occupation had gone. A lot had happened since the British Forces liberated the island on May 9th: repercussions, rebuilding of relationships and in some cases homes. Slowly the islanders were finding ways to get back to some sort of normality. It had been an interminably cold few months with more snow than usual. The upside was seeing friends who had been evacuated in June 1940 slowly returning and I enjoyed meeting up with them and exchanging stories. Not that I told anyone about what had happened to me or how I met Xavier.

I had always been happy in my own company prior to meeting Xavier, but since parting from him, I experienced deep loneliness for the first time. I longed for the summer months when at least it would be warmer, and the trees and flowers would blossom and bring colour to the island again. We needed help camouflaging some of the larger scars on our once beautiful landscape after five long years of Occupation.

It would soon be three years since I had last seen Xavier and I still recalled his kiss even though I couldn't picture his face very clearly anymore. I wished Mum and I had kept a camera in the house and not given ours up when restrictions had come in banning them. To have a photo of Xavier's handsome face to look at would have been such a treat.

As I hung out the washing in our tiny backyard, I wondered what had happened to him since we last saw each other. Whether he still remembered me. Whether he—? No. I wouldn't allow myself to think of him having been caught and executed. That was too much to bear, I decided as I took another wooden peg from the small bag.

I had checked the hidey-hole many times hoping to find a message from him, but to no avail. Had whatever means of connection we once had vanished? I didn't dare contemplate the worst that could have happened. I reminded myself that whether he had been arrested or not, no one could survive three hundred years. To me, though, he remained very much alive. I carried Xavier's memory in my heart and as long as I could I intended thinking of him as being larger than life.

There was a knock on the front door. 'Briar? You there?'

'I'm out the back,' I called, happy for Jeanne and any of our neighbours to walk through the house now there wasn't the risk of German soldiers wandering inside.

I finished fixing the last sheet to the washing line and picked up my empty washing basket and bag of pegs. 'Hi, Jeanne,' I said, seeing her at our back door. 'Is there something I can do for you?'

Since returning home after my escapade a few other things had changed. I could no longer dismiss my mum's coven, not after everything Mrs Le Dain, Jeanne and the other women had done to help bring me home. My respect for them and Mum's secret life had grown, though I had not yet joined them, mostly due to the strains of the final years of the Occupation. Our lives had become even harsher than before, and it was all we could do to find enough to eat and simply survive during those interminable months. With the success of the D-Day landings in June 1944, and the Allies working their way through Normandy and Brittany, they had successfully severed German supply routes through France causing us to be cut off from what little food, gas or electricity the Nazis had previously brought to Jersey. Everyone on the island was starving, even the Nazi soldiers.

We were free now, though, and I had recently recalled Xavier's suggestion that I should rethink my reluctance to join Mum and the other women and be initiated into the coven.

I led Jeanne back to the living room and, after taking the washing things to the kitchen and putting them away, returned to speak to her. 'Would you like something to drink?' I asked, glad to be able to offer tea after so long making do with whatever herbs we were growing.

She shook her head. 'No, thank you. Babette asked me to remind you there's a full moon tonight.'

I recalled Babette asking me to join them on a few previous full moons but had always found an excuse, deciding I wanted to spend more time considering whether or not I was ready to be enlightened.

I wasn't sure if it was because I missed Xavier more than

usual for some reason, but I decided it was time I relented. 'You can tell her I'll join you tonight.'

Jeanne's mouth dropped open. I realised she hadn't expected me to answer this way. 'You will?'

I laughed. 'I know I've taken my time deciding,' I said apologetically, taken aback by her delight, although unsure whether it was because she was happy for me – or simply because she was excited to pass on this news to her mother-in-law. Either way, I was glad I had given her cause to smile.

'I'll come along with Mum.'

I showed Jeanne to the door and thought of Mum's reaction. Now I had made up my mind I was beginning to feel more enthusiastic about the evening's meeting. I suppose, if nothing else, I was about to discover exactly what Mum enjoyed so much about being a part of a coven.

As I expected, Mum was delighted. And surprised.

'I can't believe you've finally succumbed,' she said pulling me into her arms and hugging me. 'I promise you, Briar, your life is about to be enhanced in ways you can't yet imagine.' She opened her arms wide, a beatific smile on her face, which appeared less tired as the months passed. 'I want to welcome you into my life fully. You already possess more power than you know and this is the perfect way for you to absorb the sights and sounds of the earth most people never have the chance to experience.'

'It sounds glorious.' I tried to imagine what she meant.

'It is.'

'I believe you.' I did. Whatever it entailed I knew my mother would look out for me. Hadn't she already shown how fiercely she protected me? There was no way she would allow any High Priestess or other witch to cause me pain or upset, of that I was certain.

'What worries you most about your initiation?'

I considered her question. Before going back to the seventeenth century I had worried that I'd be committing myself to something that I might then decide wasn't for me. Now, though, I knew without doubt that I needed to learn all the magick at my disposal and embrace what was meant for me since my birth. 'Nothing.'

'There must be something.'

I shook my head. 'Not anymore.' A thought occurred to me. 'Apart from maybe how much I still have to learn to make my spells as perfect as possible.'

She hugged me again. 'The most important part of any spell is the intent, Briar. Don't ever forget that.' She stepped back and took my hand. 'Come. Let me show you something.'

'Really, Mum. I really don't have any further reservations.'

'I believe you, but I have a gift for you. I hope you like it.' I hadn't seen her look this excited since the previous midsummer solstice.

'Is it your grimoire?'

She shook her head. 'It's the outfit you'll be wearing.'

Outfit? 'I don't understand.' I pulled back to make her stop walking. 'But you didn't know until now that I would agree to join the coven.'

She tilted her head to one side and gave me a sympathetic smile. 'Briar. You're my child. I know you better than I do any other person. You're sensible and careful, but above all you're inquisitive.'

'I am?'

She laughed. 'Of course. It's why you always have your

nose in a book. You're constantly fascinated by stories and learning new things. It was only a matter of time before you changed your mind and embraced your heritage.' She beamed at me. 'And now I can share the other part of my life with you.'

'I can't wait.'

'Neither can I.'

'Come along then,' I said. 'Show me this outfit you've been saving for me.'

Chapter Thirty-Nine

XAVIER

2 June 1646

Market Place was packed with cheering islanders. I wore a hat low and kept my head down, hoping not to be spotted by anyone. I was still a wanted man and the island was small enough for me to be recognised by one of the locals.

I was jostled from side to side, pressed between people as the cannons boomed noisily to celebrate Charles II being proclaimed King of the island. It was his second visit to Jersey but this time he arrived as our king rather than as Prince of Wales and the excitement was palpable. Bells had been ringing constantly from church towers all morning and I felt hope rise in me that maybe now things might settle down on our island.

Like others around me I was relieved to see the back of the Parliamentarians. We were weary from twenty turbulent years of changing hierarchy, from what we were used to with Royalist leaders, to Parliamentarian, then to Royalist and once again back to Parliamentarian rule. Enough was enough. At least we knew what we were dealing with, having the King back. Hopefully.

I also hoped that, if I could persuade Andre to find a way to put in a good word for me, I might be able to remain free long enough to be pardoned for my perceived betrayal, which was nothing more than a personal falling-out with our Governor.

Having seen all I needed I returned home to my aunt's cottage where I was hiding, enjoying the peace and quiet of her neat home. I had endured three long years away from the island living in a rural village and was in no mood for this much noise, and was looking forward to the tranquillity. As I neared Gorey village, I heard the familiar sound of bells ringing and music. Why hadn't I expected islanders to be celebrating on the outskirts of the island too?

I was passing Andre's home when the door opened. He spotted me, then, glancing from side to side, waved discreetly for me to join him inside.

As soon as the door was shut he patted me on the back. 'What a welcome sight you are, Xavier.'

I was glad he thought as much, and my humour improved immediately. 'It is good to see you again too, my friend.'

'Take a seat and tell me of your plans.'

Happy to do so, I waited while he fetched a jug of beer and poured out two beakers for us. We raised them in a toast to each other.

My thirst partially quenched, I listened as he questioned me about my life in France since we last met.

He raised an eyebrow. 'It's been a bit stormy of late. I wouldn't have wished to be on a vessel in that.'

I recalled the choppy sea and strong winds that lasted for days. 'It was a difficult crossing.'

We laughed at my struggles, both aware that rough seas weren't something that fazed me. Andre topped up our drinks. 'You look well, though.' He patted his stomach.

I grimaced at him. 'I do not have a paunch yet,' I laughed. 'Too busy working as a privateer for Captain Aubert these past few years to sit for long.'

'I heard as much.'

I should not have been surprised. Andre knew many people. His family was vast and one of his relations always seemed to have inside knowledge about locals.

'You are here for a while, I hope?'

I shrugged. 'I intend settling back here once more but only if I can find a way for my sentence to be quashed.' Our moods dipped at the reminder. I took a mouthful of beer and swallowed. I needed to find out whether Andre knew if someone could help me. 'Do you think that's possible, now that those in authority have changed again?'

'I would like to think so. As I mentioned to you in my last letter, there's word that Sir George de Carteret is willing to reinstate those privateers with experience,' he said, nodding thoughtfully. 'Now he's been appointed as our bailiff, once again he might feel generous towards you and your hope for clemency.'

I had wondered the same thing but was unsure how to go about making the request. I shared my concerns with Andre.

He thrust his hands out before him. 'I am your closest friend. Who else should do this but me?'

'That is kind of you, Andre,' I said gratefully, not that I had expected he would suggest anything less.

Andre stood. 'Now, I shall fetch food for us.' He narrowed his eyes. 'That scar below your right eye looks as if it must have been painful.'

My right hand went up to the scar that had taken weeks to finally heal. 'It was, more so because the edge of the filthy plate that had hit me caused the wound to become infected.'

'A fight?' Andre sighed.

I shrugged. There was no point dwelling on things that didn't matter. 'A drunken cook who lost all his wages gambling. I just happened to be in his line of fire. It has healed now.'

I followed him to the pan hanging over the fireplace and watched as he filled two clay bowls with a meat and vegetable stew. It smelt rich and I couldn't wait to taste it.

'You must have stories to tell about your exile,' Andre said.

'The vessel I crewed for was thought to be pirated by a French captain. He arrested the entire crew and threw us in jail for two months until our captain managed to find someone to stand up for us and produce proof that we were from Jersey.' I winced at the memory of the disgusting cells we had to inhabit for that time. 'I was thinner then.'

He turned back to me and handed me a bowl and spoon. 'Sit and eat. I want to hear more.'

I returned to the table and took my place. Eating my first mouthful, I closed my eyes, enjoying the salty tastiness of Andre's food. 'This is delicious. Thank you.'

'I'm glad you're enjoying it.' He ate some of his.

I stilled my hand halfway between my food and my mouth, sensing something was wrong. 'You seem concerned, Andre.'

Andre's expression clouded over. 'I have not seen nor heard from a cousin and her maid for over a year.'

'Who, Ember?' I had no wish to think of her but this was Andre and he had always been there for me.

He gave an anxious sigh and shook his head. 'Not her, no. Another more distant cousin. She is somewhat flighty but a good woman. I must admit to being concerned for her safety.'

I recognised the look on Andre's face and my cheerful mood dissipated. My friend was the best of men and was calling in a favour. A favour I could not refuse, because I owed him my life. And Briar's. I braced myself, suspecting what he was about to ask of me.

When he struggled to find the words, I spoke for him. 'You want me to find her, don't you?'

He lowered his gaze. This request was costing him a lot. 'With my help, but yes. Would you consider doing this for me? I would not ask if I wasn't desperately concerned for them, despite all the trouble she has caused her family by running away and becoming the mistress of a French count.'

I raised an eyebrow. 'She took her maid with her, you say?'

He nodded. 'Louise is a foolish young girl, but kind-hearted. Her maid is more of a friend to her than a servant and when the family holidayed in France last year, the two disappeared.'

'They have not heard from them?'

He sighed and rolled his eyes. 'Once to say she was to be married to this older man and not to worry about her, the second six months later telling her parents that he wasn't the man she imagined and she had been badly treated, and pleading for their forgiveness and asking to be allowed home.'

Intrigued, I asked, 'Did they give her permission?'

Andre nodded. 'They did, but she and the maid never

arrived back on the island. The parents, as I'm sure you can imagine, are frantic and begged me for help.'

They must be terrified for their daughter. I thought of how much I missed Briar still. Briar. A familiar pang squeezed my heart. I tried hard each day not to think of her. Even after all this time our last moments together tormented me. Missing her still felt like a physical loss.

'Xavier?' Andre's voice brought me back to the present. 'Would you do this for me?'

I didn't have to consider a moment longer. 'You know I'll do anything you ask of me, Andre. If it wasn't for you Briar might not have survived and I will never forget that.'

'Thank you, my friend.' He rubbed his tired face with his hands.

'It is nothing,' I insisted, unsure what troubles I had agreed to bring onto myself.

Chapter Forty

BRIAR

1946

The evening had come when I was to be initiated and I was almost breathless with excitement. 'Hurry up, Mum,' I called, wondering what was taking her so long. She was never late for anything and had waited and prepared her entire life for this occasion.

'I'm just coming,' she said, appearing in the living room. I went to fetch my coat to go out to make deliveries with Mum and was just buttoning it up when there was a knock on the door.

'See who that is, will you?' Mum grumbled, anxious in case we should be delayed further. 'And tell them we're on our way out.'

I pulled it open and was stunned to see a familiar face smiling at me. 'Henry?' It was Henry Pinel, a schoolfriend of mine who had left the island a month or so before the invasion to enlist with the Royal Navy. I stared at him, surprised to see him there. 'When did you get back?'

'Last week.' He smiled and I saw a confidence in him that he hadn't possessed when he had left. 'I hope you don't mind me calling on you?'

'Not at all.' It was good to see him again, especially as he appeared to have come through the war unscathed. 'You look well.'

He seemed happy with my response. 'I'm glad you think so. It was tougher than I had expected, but then it was for all of us.'

He had no idea quite how tough, I mused. He moved from one foot to the other and I realised he was hoping to be asked indoors. Remembering Mum's instruction, I said, 'I would invite you in for a cup of tea and a chat, but we're just about to go out.'

Mum came up behind me. 'Henry, is that really you?'

'Hello, Mrs Le Gros. How are you?'

'Very well for the most part.' She glanced at me thoughtfully. 'I'm afraid we're on our way out to, er, meet friends.'

'Yes,' I agreed.

He continued shifting from one foot to the other. 'I'm sorry, I don't want to keep you.'

Dear, sweet Henry. I hated to think we weren't being as welcoming as we'd like, seeing him again after all this time. Then again, we couldn't exactly tell him what we were doing, could we?'

Mum patted his shoulder. 'Would you like to walk part of the way with us? We can catch up on what you've been up to while we walk.'

I took the bag holding my robe and a few other essentials, leaving Mum to carry whatever she had secreted within her basket.

Henry seemed happy with that, so we left the house and began walking either side of him down the lane. I spotted a man lurking in the shadows and it threw me for a moment, reminding me of how Hauptmann Klein used to watch everyone's houses during the Occupation.

This wasn't any Nazi officer, though, I reminded myself, wondering how long it would take before I was completely used to being free again. Maybe the man was simply having a cigarette. I couldn't see his face, nor did I want to look at him for long in case he thought it was an invitation to come and speak to me.

'I was relieved to hear you weren't too badly hurt when your first ship was torpedoed and sank,' Mum said behind me.

I recalled her upset at the time. Mum had always liked Henry and, as I got older, kept insisting what a good husband he would make someone. I suspected she was thinking similar thoughts now, which was why she had invited him to walk with us.

'Yes, me too,' I agreed absentmindedly.

His head snapped in my direction. 'Really? You were concerned for me?'

I recalled our slight falling-out a few months before he enlisted. Henry had hoped to progress our friendship into something more romantic. I loved him but as a friend. It wasn't that he was unkind, bad looking or even bad company, only that I wasn't attracted to him. I had felt it unfair to lead him on when I didn't feel there could ever be anything of that nature between us, and had told him so – not expecting him to be as devastated as he had been.

'We all were,' I said, not wishing him to think my feelings for him had changed. 'We're all very fond of you, Henry, you must know that.'

'I see,' he said, seeming slightly disappointed. 'I broke an arm,' he continued. 'I was burnt on one shoulder but that was nothing compared to others who were killed or seriously maimed. I was very lucky really.'

We reached the bottom of Le Mont des Landes hill. 'I know you go up that way,' Mum said, pointing in the direction of Henry's home, 'so we'll part ways here, but don't be a stranger, Henry,' she said, taking his face in her hands. 'You must come around for tea one afternoon. I'll send Briar to sort something out.'

He beamed at her. 'I'd like that, Mrs Le Gros, thank you.' I noticed he didn't address me.

'We look forward to seeing you again,' Mum said. 'Don't we, Briar?'

I knew she was trying her best to help me settle down with someone but now wasn't the time to let her know, yet again, that it wouldn't be Henry. Not wishing to upset him I nodded.

'I can come further with you?' he offered.

'We wouldn't hear of it,' Mum replied quickly.

I noticed she didn't mention our intention to go as far as Anne Port, or that we would then continue up the hill to the woods to meet with our coven.

'I'll say goodbye here and see you both soon.' He watched me as he spoke this time.

'Yes, see you soon, Henry,' I said giving him a slight wave.

Not wishing Mum to give me the usual lecture about how

lovely Henry was, I drew her attention back to my initiation, a subject she loved discussing ever since I had relented and agreed to embrace my birthright.

'I still can't understand why I kept putting it off for so long,' I said, eager to reach the woods.

Soon we were there. I wore the white shift Mum had sewn for me for that special occasion, adorned with tiny embroidered splashes of briar around the hem, interspersed with small patches of violets. Violet was Mum's middle name. It was beautiful but it was another thing I felt guilty about, wishing I had known how much time and love she had spent creating this garment for me, and how long she had kept it packed away while I refused to accept my inheritance. I had every intention of treasuring it always.

I longed to remove my heavy winter coat, still the only one I owned, and the thin sweater and skirt Mum insisted I layer over my shift to hide it for our walk there and back home.

I gasped as an owl hooted, then spotted two shrews scuttling to the side of the path as we neared. It was the Spring Equinox and despite it being the twentieth of March it was still very cold. We greeted the other women. I removed all my outer clothing. Shocked by the sudden chill, I began shivering. Mum took my coat from me.

At first I couldn't see anything unusual and followed Mum through the trees and bushes that suddenly opened up to a space where a fire crackled, its flames dancing in the cool evening sky. It took a moment for me to notice that it was in the centre of a circle made up of the five witches still left in the coven.

Six of the women who had been evacuated prior to the invasion would soon be coming home, Mum had assured me earlier in the day. 'Then we'll be back to thirteen members,' she said, beaming at me.

I could see how much it meant to her, not only that I was finally here, but also that the coven would soon once again be back to how it had been before the war.

I saw Babette Le Dain, and her daughter-in-law Jeanne, and three other women I recognised from the village.

I realised how little I knew these women but saw how each seemed as happy as Mum as they stood around the fire, saying, 'We cast our circle to protect and shield our coven.'

After grounding themselves by closing their eyes and taking time to be at one with the nature around them: with the rich brown soil of the earth, the gentle whispers of the light wind through the pine trees, the familiar scents filling the air. The dusk of the darkening skies cooling the air around us was in itself magickal.

Babette raised her arms. The women began walking around the fire. Mum had explained to me that this was to cleanse ourselves, to remove any negative energy by walking through the smoke. I was finding the entire evening breathtaking, energised by the atmosphere.

Mum was beaming, a glint in her green eyes. I didn't think I had ever seen her this euphoric. She waved me forward to stand in the centre of the circle in front of the fire. I did as she asked, my nerves on edge in case I forgot the incantation Mum had taught me.

Babette gave me an encouraging nod. It was time.

I took a steadying breath. 'I ask to be initiated into the Gouôrray Coven and swear to support, aid and do my best in every way I can.'

The women responded as I breathed a sigh of relief.

'We accept Briar Le Gros into the Goûrray Coven and promise to support, aid and do our best for her to our greatest ability.'

Mum pressed her hands together and I could tell she was trying not to cry. She came over to me and hugged me. 'Welcome to our sisterhood, Briar, and to your birthright. Your grandmother, great-grandmother and our ancestors before you celebrate this special occasion with us.'

I hugged her tightly. 'Does this mean I can do magick too now?' I asked, thinking about my grandmother's grimoire and all the spells I imagined adding to it as I created ones of my own for her cherished book of shadows.

'It does. You can now make up for all the time you wasted thinking about joining us.'

I laughed, knowing she was only half joking.

'What are you thinking?' Mum asked quietly.

I beamed at her, looking towards the other women and enjoying how joyous they all were to welcome me into this secret world of theirs. How thrilled I was to finally be here. Xavier had been right to risk my anger when he voiced his thought that I was making a mistake in not joining this coven. I had only been a part of it for a few minutes but already a sense of coming home, of protection and of sisterhood enveloped me.

I couldn't wait to learn more about botanicals, their healing powers and different uses, along with candle spells for cleansing and especially for protection. I already knew some spells from living in a small house with Mum. Spells for protection, to fend off nightmares, for happiness. I already found solace being a witch and couldn't wait to put the knowledge I would learn from these women into practice.

We celebrated for hours, dancing, drinking mead and

enjoying the magick of the evening and the sounds and vibrations from being among the trees in the woods.

'Briar,' Mum said, tapping me lightly on my arm as I stared into the fire, now merely a glow on the ground. 'It's time to pack up. Fetch our coats while I help the others tidy everything away.'

I gazed up at the sky, surprised by how much lighter it was already, the horizon now a plethora of shades from dark ruby to orange.

'We need to hurry,' Babette said as I went to fetch our things. 'It'll soon be dawn and we don't need anyone spotting us arriving home after being out all night.'

'Now wouldn't that give the busybodies something to gossip about?' Mum joked, and a mischievous part of me wished they would see.

Chapter Forty-One

XAVIER

The storm raged, and on several occasions I feared the vessel taking Andre and me to France might sink. It was a filthy night. The high winds forced waves over the boat, soaking us. I would much rather have been back in Jersey in front of a warm fire than at sea again. I could no more leave this woman, Louise, and her maid to suffer than I could refuse to help my closest friend, though I hoped we would locate them and return them to their home in the speediest time possible. For all our sakes.

It took hours to find somewhere to drop anchor and wait out the storm. The protection of the bay where we sheltered went some way to help steady the ship. I was grateful not to suffer with seasickness like poor Andre, who had spent most of the time lying on a bunk and throwing up into a bucket on the floor next to him.

I wasn't sure who was more relieved to set foot on land, Andre or several other crew members who insisted they would never board a boat during a storm again. Thankfully it didn't take long for us to locate and hire two horses. We struck lucky soon after in an inn where we briefly stopped for a restorative mulled wine fortified with brandy and spices and where Andre found an acquaintance with directions to the chateau. After a few more hours shivering in the cold, our clothes still damp from the boat journey, the water receded from the salt marshes enough for us to be on our way to Saint Sauveur le Vicomte, where the women were being held. It was over an hour's ride away.

We arrived mid-afternoon. Andre, though exhausted from being so sick on the boat, insisted we continue until we found them. We tied the horses in the woods near Chateau de Saint Sauveur le Vicomte, planning to make our getaway as easy as possible. We travelled on foot to do a reconnaissance. After agreeing our plan we entered the arched entrance.

Once inside the echoing entrance hall we discovered to our relief that the nobleman and his entourage were out hunting boar. Glad to know fewer people were in the castle, we began our search for the women. After several false starts and almost being discovered twice, we located Louise and her maid Chantal in an annexe off the nobleman's private apartment.

For a moment I wasn't sure we were looking at two young women, their appearance was so shocking.

'Louise?' Andre whispered, his voice quiet. He seemed as distressed as I was to see the emaciated, battered body leaning against a wall next to a bed.

There was a whimper nearby and I ran to help Chantal while Andre untied Louise. The gags around their mouths were tight, bruising their lips. I looked at Louise, trying to imagine her stringy raven locks clean and coiffed. She caught my eye and lowered her face, trying to hide how puffy and discoloured it was where she had been struck several times. The sight of her was pitiful, and guilt at my earlier thoughts about not wishing to be there flooded through me. I wondered when they had last been given something to drink. I looked around the room and spotted a jug and a goblet. Going over to it I poured a little wine into the drinking vessel and handed it to Andre.

'Here, drink something.'

Louise began to argue, but Andre took her face in his hands. 'Now is not the time for pride, Louise. You need all the strength you can muster if you are to get out of here before that man returns.' She stiffened at the mention of her abuser. 'If we don't take you both from here soon, we will all be discovered, and it's clear to me that out of the four of us only Xavier and I have the energy to fight.'

He raised the cup to her lips and tilted it slightly so the liquid poured slowly into her mouth, then went to Chantal and did the same.

I kept watch out of the window, relieved to discover it faced the road from the village. It wasn't long before I spotted dust and saw eight horses cantering towards the castle.

'They're on their way back,' I groaned. 'We must go. Now.'

We each took one of the women and hastily made our way down the stone stairs, stopping each time we heard footsteps coming in our direction. Andre noticed a door to the side of the hall. With little choice, we made our way through it and along a passage on the other side, relieved to discover the door at the end led outside.

'Hide over there in those bushes until they've passed under the archway,' I whispered to Andre. 'We'll have more chance of escaping unseen if there's no one around to spot us going for our horses.'

We walked as fast as we could with the exhausted women, making our way towards the bushes, and crouched behind them. The movement made Louise groan in pain. I saw Andre cover her mouth to quieten her and looked down at Chantal. 'How do you fare?'

'I am well,' she lied, her voice croaky. She winced as she spoke and I dreaded to think what this poor, loyal woman must have suffered in that place.

Andre stood slowly and went to check the way was clear for us to move. When he was satisfied, he came back and took hold of Louise, as I helped Chantal to our horses. I waited for Andre to mount then hoisted Louise onto the back of his saddle before mounting my own horse and pulling Chantal up behind me. Once seated, I took Chantal's wrists and pulled her arms around me. 'Hold on tightly,' I said, wondering whether she had ever been on a horse before. There was no time to worry about such matters now, I decided, urging my horse forward and waving for Andre to follow.

With no time to waste we set off at a canter, deciding to cross fields wherever it shortened our journey. Remaining off the road would also keep our horses from kicking up clouds of dust for the nobleman's men to follow. The luck of the devil must have been with us because we were soon galloping towards Portbail.

'That was close,' I shouted, unable to hide my glee. I had almost forgotten how exhilarating it felt to make a narrow escape. We still needed to deliver the women safely back to Louise's family, and had at least another hour's ride before we would be free to return to the harbour.

'There,' Louise shouted later as we neared large gates a short way off the main road.

I was relieved to see a young boy, who must have been looking out for us, race back into the manor and return to the outside steps with several male servants and an older man I presumed to be Louise's father. At least we wouldn't need to spend any time locating family to help the women, I thought with relief.

Andre and I, released from our charges and carrying bottles of the best wine her father possessed, cantered from the home and on our way.

'We must hope the captain is still waiting for us,' I said, not wishing to be stuck in France long enough for the nobleman to track us down and take out his revenge on Andre and me.

'And that the tide doesn't turn before we reach the boat,' Andre added.

It seemed like no time at all before we cantered into Portbail and reached the harbour.

'The boat is still there,' Andre cheered.

I relaxed instantly when I saw he was right. 'Hurry, we have no time to lose.' I dismounted.

We couldn't miss the boat for any reason, I decided, though I was unsure whether she would even make it back to Jersey. 'You make for the vessel. Instruct the captain to wait for me if he can,' I said, not wishing to be left behind. 'I will be there as soon as I can but must return these horses to the stable yard first.'

That done, I ran to the boat. The crew were waiting for me and as soon as I stepped onboard they cast off.

Satisfied with our success and glad of a quieter evening, I smiled to myself as the boat pushed away from the harbour wall. It had been a long day but one filled with urgency. It dawned on me how much I had missed the energy that came with facing danger. I had also missed defending someone and fighting for them.

As the boat left the harbour, I heard orders being shouted and hurried to the stern of the vessel to see what all the fuss was about. Andre was there, laughing at the men in the nobleman's colours shouting and pointing towards us.

'We only just made it out of there in time,' Andre said, slapping me on the back.

He wasn't joking. 'We did.'

Exhausted from our jaunt, I decided to try and catch up on some sleep. There was little we could do until we reached Jersey. The women were safe now and so were we, I mused with relief.

Twelve hours later we docked in Jersey amid another noisy commotion on the quayside.

'I wonder what's happening this time?' I speculated to Andre when I joined him at the bow of the ship.

We casually watched as the crew secured the ropes. A young lad ran to the vessel, jumped onboard and stopped in front of me, staring up at me oddly before he turned, pushed past Andre, then jumped from the side of the boat onto the quay.

I watched as he ran quickly away. 'I wonder where he's going in such a hurry?' I said, intrigued.

The boy stopped at two guards and pointed towards the boat. Something wasn't right.

'I wonder what can be this important,' Andre muttered.

I had no idea but my instincts told me there was something odd about this scenario. I watched as one of the guards disappeared into a nearby pub, coming out soon after with two others. The four men ran towards the boat as the young lad vanished down a back street without a backward glance.

Andre and I straightened immediately as it dawned on us what was happening.

'Ember,' I said, suspecting she probably had something to do with what was going on. I had no idea how, but knew I was right. Andre didn't argue.

My luck had finally run out, I realised as they neared. I was about to be arrested.

'Dive over the side and swim away,' Andre insisted. 'Quick, I know you can do it. I'll cover for you.'

I ran across the deck and began climbing up the other side of the boat but before I was able to dive off the guards reached me and tackled me to the deck. Andre argued with them, insisting they had the wrong man.

Conscious that I had little choice but to give in, I shook my head. 'Do not cause trouble for yourself, Andre,' I insisted. 'Take care of my aunt and Wren for me.'

'Always,' Andre called after me as I was manhandled off the boat. 'I will do all I can for you too, my friend.'

I knew he would but doubted there was much he realistically could do. I had escaped rearrest for three years and Jersey was too small a place to get away with a death sentence like mine. My time was up and I knew it.

Chapter Forty-Two

BRIAR

I sat up with a jolt in bed, slowly becoming aware of birdsong and realised I was awake, and no longer under threat. I exhaled. I still sometimes woke expecting to hear soldiers outside the cottage. Whenever that happened, it took me a moment to realise I wasn't being sent back to the castle, that the island really had been liberated and I was safe at home with Mum.

Before the war I had thought it a bad day if a book I was waiting for hadn't been returned to the library. Now, having been half-starved for almost five years and forced to get used to living without everyday niceties like choices of food, new books, heating or even letters from acquaintances, it was taking some adjusting to not expect the worst to happen at any moment.

I got up and peered out of my small bedroom window. It was a grey, drizzly April morning. I was planning to find work either in one of the village shops or in St Helier. We needed money but now islanders were being repatriated to Jersey and the servicemen were slowly being demobbed; the vacancies were becoming fewer. I still had to try, though, because Mum and I were finding it difficult to live off the income we received from my occasional cleaning jobs and her sales.

The biggest improvement in my life was meeting up with the coven every first Thursday of the month. I had learnt more about special sabbat celebrations and looked forward to experiencing those events. For the first time in my life I felt a protection I'd only ever received from Xavier. I loved being a part of this sisterhood; it gave my life a new purpose and even though being a member of a coven wasn't something I could talk about with anyone outside the group, I felt less alone and no longer as if I was drowning in my own inner turmoil.

I brushed my hair and, pulling on my threadbare dressing gown, went downstairs to light the fire and prepare breakfast for Mum and me.

We were so much better off in many ways now, I thought, watching the first flames appear in the grate. I filled the kettle with water and put it on the range to boil. Having made two cups of tea, I placed two rashers of bacon in a frying pan and sat at the table waiting for them to cook before adding an egg for each of us.

My thoughts returned to Xavier as they often did. Reliving our kiss was always such a heartsore memory but I seemed unable to move on from my feelings for him, even though I knew how pointless it was to still be in love with a man I could never hope to see again.

I heard Mum's footsteps upstairs and was glad she would soon be joining me so I would no longer be able to wallow in my memories.

'Something smells good,' she said descending the stairs.

She looked at me. 'I would have thought you'd be dressed by now.' She narrowed her eyes. 'Or have you changed your mind about catching the earlier bus to town?'

'No, I thought I'd join you for breakfast first. We're so lucky to be able to eat decent food again, I want to make the most of each meal we enjoy together. I'll get ready and go after that. I don't have interviews, and we both know I'm probably wasting my time trying.'

'That's true.' She sighed and pulled her cup and saucer towards her. She lifted the cup, looking thoughtful. 'I suppose they do have to offer jobs to the men supporting families first.'

'What about families without a man like ours?' We had exchanged these thoughts many times, but as much as I understood the reasons why men were given work first, it riled me that women always seemed to come second, despite having suffered too throughout the war years.

Flipping the bacon to cook on the other side, I cracked two eggs and began frying them. While they were frying, I buttered two thick slices of toast and put them onto our plates.

'I think I'm grumpy because I have to go out in this miserable weather,' I explained. 'I was hoping you'd teach me a banishing spell.'

'Still having those nightmares then?' I nodded. 'We'll work on one later.' Mum took another sip of tea.

I served our breakfast and we ate, savouring each mouthful. 'This is the perfect start to a day, if you ask me.'

An hour later I was on the bus to St Helier, having checked first at the stores in the village for vacancies. As I sat on the full bus listening to local gossip and snippets of news about different families and those grieving loved ones who would never return, I knew Mum and I had escaped relatively unscathed.

I gazed out of the window as the bus slowed to let a car cross in front of it. I saw a man and couldn't help thinking his stance seemed familiar somehow.

Then he turned and looked up at the bus. His gaze went from window to window until he reached mine. Our eyes met and I felt as if I had been shot with a bolt of electricity. It was the man who haunted my worst nightmares. How was Roger Dankworth, the vile Witchfinder, here and why was he staring directly at me? My breath caught in my throat at the sight of him. For a moment I was sure I'd be sick. I chanced a look at him again, willing him to have vanished, a figment of my overactive imagination, but there he was, with a strange look on his face I couldn't decipher.

But how could that be? The bus moved on. Feeling lightheaded and breathless, I lowered my head into my hands. It didn't make sense. He was dead, surely. Died centuries ago. I swallowed the nausea rising in my throat, desperate not to be sick in front of the other passengers.

'You all right, lovey?' the lady next to me asked.

I struggled to explain my behaviour, not wishing to draw further attention to myself. 'I'm fine.' I forced a smile. 'I shouldn't have skipped breakfast this morning maybe.'

'That'll do it.' The bus stopped again, and she rose to disembark. 'You take care of yourself now. Buy something to eat as soon as you get off this bus.'

'I will.'

Relieved to be left alone, I looked out of the window. Not that I expected to see him there, because there was no way he could have kept up with the bus. Had I imagined seeing him? I hoped so because the alternative was too terrifying.

Chapter Forty-Three

XAVIER

Two months after my arrest, I was leaning against the cold granite wall of my cell going mad with frustration and hunger. There was little I could do to escape the interminable boredom of being incarcerated alone with only others' screams of pain from elsewhere in the castle as distractions. How powerful I had felt helping Briar escape with other prisoners that time – and now, here I was, languishing in this miserable place with no way of helping myself. I was beginning to wish they would hurry up and execute me. Put an end to this endless waiting.

I heard voices murmuring outside the cell. The door opened and Andre walked in. His gaze rested on me.

'Andre,' I said, glad to see a friendly face again. I strode over to him, not wishing to hug him, embarrassed at my own stench.

He brightened instantly, any joy vanishing when his eyes became accustomed to the dim light. 'They've beaten you.' It wasn't a question. 'I'm doing all I can for your release.'

His voice was thick with emotion he was struggling to suppress. We both knew his attempts would be fruitless.

'I feel better than I look,' I said attempting a little jollity.

'I wish I could believe you.' He looked me up and down. 'Your clothes are even worse than they were before.' His attempt to tease me was half-hearted. 'Xavier, I worry how thin you are.'

I rubbed my chin lightly, forgetting the punches I received that morning when I attempted to stand up for a much older man the guards were picking on.

'What have they done to you really?'

Not wishing our visit to be taken up with Andre's anguish at seeing me in this state, I forced a smile. 'Nothing I can't bear. Now, tell me, what are you doing here? Do you have news of —' I realised he wouldn't have news of Briar and I wasn't interested in Ember. 'What news of their plans for me?'

He folded his arms, frowning. 'My sources tell me you are to be brought before the court in the next fortnight. That is only a matter of process.' His eyes lowered. 'Xavier, you are to be executed this time. I fear there is no way out for you.'

I took him by the shoulders. 'Look at me, Andre.' I waited until he did so before continuing. 'I knew this day would come. I am prepared to meet my end.' He looked doubtful. 'We both know I have enjoyed an eventful life.' I thought of Briar. 'I met the love of my life, albeit only briefly, and have had you as my closest friend. How many men have been as lucky as me?'

I watched him consider my words, then sigh and glance at the door.

Turning his back to it, he withdrew a small flask. 'Rum,' he whispered. Out of another pocket he took a packet and handed it to me. 'Pie.'

Delighted with his offerings, I opened the flask and took a mouthful of the dark, sweet liquid, feeling its heat make its way deliciously down my throat and chest. 'This is good.' I drank more, relishing the strength it restored in me. I then pushed the flask into my trouser pocket to help dull my senses when my friend had gone. 'Tell me more while I eat,' I said. 'We haven't got long, the guards will be prowling again soon.'

'I bribed them.' He kept his voice low. 'I told them your father has not long on this earth and his dying wish was for me to deliver a message to you from him.'

'Clever, as ever, my friend,' I mumbled, then bit into the pie, determined to finish the tasty pork and jelly pie before the guards returned and snatched it from me.

'I'm going to attempt to send a message to Briar,' Andre said suddenly.

I almost choked in shock. 'How do you imagine you'll do that?' I coughed a few times to try and clear my throat, causing others to look over at us.

'Through the hiding place.'

I saw he knew as well as I did how unlikely his plan was to succeed. There was pain in Andre's eyes. He was grasping at anything he hoped might help me. Not wishing to upset him, I decided to play along.

'It's worth a try.'

His face brightened. 'You think so?'

'I do,' I lied.

Neither of us mentioned that it had been years since either of us had left a message in that place in his floor. I didn't even know if Briar still lived in the house or whether the Nazi regime had won the war. I didn't like to think what might have become of her, preferring to imagine the war being won by the

English, and that she had met a good man, married him and was now a mother of a brood of beautiful, rosy-cheeked children.

A familiar pang tightened in my chest.

'What's the matter?' Andre asked.

'I was thinking of Briar. I miss her.'

Andre's hand rested on my arm. 'I know you do.'

Poor Andre. I realised that as well as the pain of knowing his oldest friend was about to be executed, he still harboured guilt for his cousin's part in my death. If this was the last time we were to meet, I didn't want my friend to leave holding onto that pain.

'Andre, you have been the best friend a man could hope for,' I insisted. 'You have never let me down, my friend, and I am forever grateful.'

'Don't.'

'What?'

Andre's frown deepened. 'Talk as if we're never going to see each other again.'

'I don't mean to,' I said. 'I believe we will meet again.' I gave him a reassuring smile as I continued to lie. 'Many times.'

He seemed reassured.

The cell door opened.

'Time's up,' the guard bellowed.

Andre pulled me into a tight hug. I held him close, hoping we might see each other again.

'Go.' I needed him to leave before I made a fool of myself. 'Thank you for coming.' I patted my trouser pocket where the bottle of rum nestled against my leg. For everything.'

'I swear I'll do all I can to secure your release.' His eyes watery, he cleared his throat.

'I know you will, Andre. Now, go before they decide to lock you up in here with me.' I smiled. 'Then who would we ask to help us?'

We exchanged looks.

'Bye, Xavier.'

I tried to answer but couldn't find my voice. I waved for him to go, trying my best to force a smile that wouldn't come.

The rum helped me fall into a nightmare-filled sleep. I woke with a start, freezing cold yet with sweat dripping from my body. I tried to recall my dream, eventually remembering that I had lost something dear to me. What it was I did not know.

Later that day I was shocked to receive another visitor. I really was about to be executed if they were allowing family to visit me.

Wren walked in. She was trembling and her shoulders were slumped. I hated seeing her in this terrible place and wished she hadn't come.

'Wren, why are you here?'

I saw by her tear-stained face and puffy eyes that she had bad news for me.

'What is it?' I asked taking her hand in mine. 'Our aunt?'

She shook her head and sniffed.

I was resigned to hearing news of our aunt's passing though hoping it not to be the case. She had been unwell for months and it was Wren's turn as a young wife to take care of the woman who had taken her in, years before, after our parents died.

She shook her head slowly, a sob escaping as she wiped her

nose with a handkerchief. 'No. She's the same as she has been for a while now.' She wiped her eyes with the back of her hand. 'It's Andre.'

I heard the dread in her voice and my stomach dropped. 'Tell me,' I said, fearing that he had been the loved one I had dreamt about losing.

She stared at me for a few seconds. 'He's dying, Xavier,' she said, her voice tight.

I felt as if someone had punched me in the gut. 'But how? He was fine when I saw him yesterday.'

'He was set upon and beaten badly. The surgeon said he had no idea how he was clinging to life.' She broke into fresh sobs and, needing to comfort her more than I cared about my stench, I took her in my arms and held her tight. 'They don't expect him to survive, Xavier.'

Not brave, loyal Andre. I could barely believe what I was hearing. 'It must have happened last night,' I said, trying to keep my voice level.

She clung to me. 'He was accosted on his way home.'

An icy feeling shot through me. 'From visiting me?'

She sniffed and nodded.

I tried for Wren's sake not to give in to my anguish. 'Have they caught the perpetrators?' I asked, keen to know as much as possible before she was made to leave.

She shook her head. 'No.'

I saw something in Wren's eyes and sensed there was more. 'What is it?'

She moved back from me and looked me in the eye. 'Ember was seen leaving the public house near here just before Roger Dankworth.'

'Ember?' Surely even she wouldn't wish this on her cousin, however close he was to me.

'Yes. She ignored him outside, but I gather she was speaking to him for a long time inside.' She swallowed. 'I think she had something to do with it, Xavier. I know she and Andre were cousins but she hates you still. She's a vain, proud woman and I would be scared for you if—'

Her eyes widened as she broke off. 'If I wasn't already condemned to death,' I said, knowing that's what my sister had stopped herself from saying.

Her head drooped, she covered her eyes with one hand. 'Yes. Oh, Xavier there's something evil about her.'

'You are right, this is Ember's doing,' I said almost to myself.

Wren's tears began flowing afresh. 'I don't understand how she could do this to Andre.'

'I have a horrible feeling it's because she knows how much it will hurt me. I suppose she still resents him for trying to help Briar and me.' I groaned, my anguish threatening to overwhelm me. What a mess – and all caused by me not loving Ember.

I knew I was right. 'She has already taken everything from me, including soon my life.' Wren shuddered and I felt mean for speaking plainly. 'You must take great care, Wren. Tell that husband of yours to take you and our aunt to stay with family for the time being. Will you do that for me?'

She looked terrified. 'Yes.'

Ember really was the devil and if she was capable of doing this to Andre, heaven only knew what she might do to my sister given the chance. I needed to find a way to stop her. But how?

Chapter Forty-Four

BRIAR

I left Beghins shoe shop and walked along King Street, excited to tell Mum that I had been given the job. Maybe not as carefree as I would have been had I not seen that horrible man on my way to town. It had been a relief to have to focus on the interview and have something take my mind from dwelling on seeing him.

I needed to focus on my new start. Business on the island was slowly getting going again and I was proud to be joining a family business that was so well thought of and respected for over one hundred years. As the bus made its way back to Gorey, stopping to let passengers off and on, I stared out of the window imagining what a difference it would make to our daily lives for me to bring in an income.

Henry joined the bus at one of the stops but the seat next to me was taken so he simply smiled and said hello, taking a seat further back in the bus.

Relieved not to have to find things to say to him when my

mind was in such a turmoil, I stepped off the bus after thanking the driver and walked the few minutes to our home.

'I'm home,' I called as I walked inside, not spotting Mum straightaway. 'Mum?'

'Through here.'

I took off my coat and hung it up before going through to the small scullery where Mum was dicing a small amount of beef.

She stopped what she was doing and gave me a questioning look. 'How did it go?'

I beamed at her. 'I start work on Monday.'

She indicated the kettle with her knife. 'Well done, lovey. Make us a cuppa then and you can tell me all about it. Good shop, Beghins. They're getting some nicer stock in now that things are slowly getting back to some semblance of normality.'

I agreed, filled the kettle and set it back down to boil. Then, taking two cups and saucers from the shelf, I placed them on the worktop. *How normal this all seems*, I mused.

I must have looked more miserable than I thought because when I handed her her tea, Mum gave me a shrewd look.

'What's the matter?'

I shrugged and leant back against the worktop, crossing my arms. 'I was just thinking how ordinary my life is becoming.' I was, sort of. I was still shaken by the image of that man looking up at me when I was on the bus.

Mum frowned thoughtfully. 'Do you mean after all that has happened over the past five years and your, um—' She thought for a moment. 'All you went through?'

'I suppose I do.' It seemed so odd and rather mundane.

I told her my thoughts – the ones that didn't include Roger Dankworth.

Mum laughed. 'Both of us would have given our eye teeth for mundane and ordinary this time last year.'

She was right. It was silly of me to have said such a thing. 'I know. I'm sorry. After what everyone has suffered, you would think I'd be grateful that this is our life now.'

Mum put down her knife and slipped an arm around my shoulders. 'Briar, you're allowed to feel whatever you do. I'm sure you're not the only one to have confused thoughts.'

'Do you?'

She shook her head and grinned. 'No.'

'You see, it *is* strange.'

'It isn't.' She turned to face me. 'I might not have them, but I'm older and pretty exhausted from it all. To be perfectly honest with you, I'm just grateful that peace was restored to our island.' She sighed heavily. 'To the rest of the world. And that I have you here safe and sound.' She winked at me. 'And that you start your new job on Monday morning.'

'I'm being silly, I know that.'

Mum picked up her knife to continue with the peeling, then stopped. 'There's something else, though, I can sense it.' She waved the small vegetable knife in the air. 'And don't try to tell me there isn't because I know I'm right.' The intensity of her gaze made me turn and focus on making the tea. 'And it's more than you being worried about starting a new job.'

Why hadn't I been more careful about keeping my feelings hidden? I spooned tea into the teapot, poured the boiling water into it and replaced the lid. Mum had been through so much and was only recently starting to seem like the woman I remembered before the invasion. Was it right for me to unsettle her with another strange incident I couldn't explain?

'Briar,' she said without looking at me, 'I won't have you keeping things from me. Not important things. Surely you should know by now I'm not as fragile as I might seem. Tell me what's happened to unnerve you? I haven't forgotten you wanted to learn a banishment spell. We'll do that shortly.'

'Thanks, Mum. Actually I think I need that spell more than ever now and not just for my nightmares.'

She stopped what she was doing and turned to me. 'What's happened?'

I shuddered. 'I saw the man in my nightmares today. The Witchfinder.'

She gasped. 'What do you mean? Where did you see him?'

'He was looking up at the window at me when I was on the bus near Fauvic Common.'

Mum's face clouded over. She stared at me as she leant forward in her chair. 'Are you certain?'

I had hoped she would tell me it wasn't possible. I felt as if a cold hand was pressing lightly onto the back of my neck. 'You believe it could be him? The Witchfinder, I mean.'

She rubbed her forehead with the tips of her fingers. 'Well, you and Xavier travelled through time. There's no reason why a man with his contacts couldn't do the same.'

'But he tortures and puts people who practise sorcery to death,' I said, infuriated. 'How can he justify doing exactly what he executes others for doing?'

'He clearly has his reasons,' she said thoughtfully. 'And he must have the power to make people do all sorts of things for him.' She sighed deeply. 'As for why he's here, all I can think of is that he must want something very badly.' She rested a hand on her chest. 'Or have something planned.'

She reached out and took my hands in hers. I felt her trembling as much as me.

She stared at me silently for a moment. 'Unless there's another person who has come here from the seventeenth century having evaded his capture, I have a dreadful feeling in the pit of my stomach that you're the reason the Witchfinder has travelled to our time.'

I wanted to cry. 'I'm scared, Mum.'

She grasped my hand. 'So am I, lovey, and what's more, I sense our troubles are far from over. In fact, I have a terrible feeling our real troubles have only just begun.'

Chapter Forty-Five

XAVIER

It had been two days since my sister broke the devastating news about the attack on Andre and still I found it impossible to accept the news. How could someone, even Ember, wish this for him? He had always done his best for everyone around him. I willed him to keep fighting and survive this, unsure how to navigate a world where he no longer existed. Andre had always been the quiet, sensible one out of the two of us.

The frustration I felt being locked inside this damn cell when he needed me most was more agonising than any torture I'd experienced. Andre was my closest friend. He needed me now and I wasn't there for him.

As much as I hated Ember for her part in my arrest, this was something far worse. I struggled to believe she had it in her to instigate such a treacherous act and against someone she had always purported to love.

I shuddered. So much had happened and none of it good.

I sank to the floor, lowering my face into my hands, trying not to give in to my despair.

Hearing a young woman's voice pleading for mercy, I thought of my distraught sister, now a woman and thankfully not needing me like she once had. Wren had a husband who would look after her and their young child, as well as my aunt. The realisation soothed me slightly. I had always needed to look out for them, ensure they had shelter and food and were safe, but that role was mine no longer. In fact, I realised, the further away I kept from them the safer they would all be.

I recalled Andre's intention to message Briar asking her to help me then realised that as he was attacked on his way home from seeing me he wouldn't have sent it. Any chance I had of Briar or Diana's coven helping me was gone. Exhaustion washed over me and any fight I once had vanished.

I had never understood before how someone could give up, but now I was ready to go peacefully when the executioner's guards came to take me to the gallows. I yearned for release from this interminable grief.

I barely heard the clanking of the keys in the lock as a guard brought my ration of slop. I kicked it away, knowing from experience that it tasted foul. I no longer cared about keeping up my strength, for there was little point. I drank the water, which thankfully was cool and fresh, although on occasion the guards enjoyed playing tricks on the prisoners. I learnt quickly to look for amusement in their eyes before taking a large mouthful of water in case they had filled the jug with seawater instead of fresh stream water, or worse. Other inmates weren't as aware and shouted abuse, threw up and complained when it was their turn to be the butt of the guards' sick joke.

I leant back against the cold cell wall and, wanting my last thoughts to be of happier times, thought back to the adventures Andre and I had experienced together. The ones without Ember. I had no wish to think of her. My hate for her burned deeply. I had no wish to seek revenge on her either because I sensed it was what she was waiting for. No. I would do what she hated most and not give her the satisfaction of my attention.

She might not feel any guilt now, but she was young and chances were she had many years ahead of her to live with the knowledge that her closest relative's last moments were filled with pain thanks to her spitefulness. Yes, I decided, Ember's payback would be living with what she had done, even if the man who loved her like a sister did somehow survive against the odds.

I thought of Briar. Sweet, gentle, caring Briar. She would be heartbroken to know about Ember's revenge on me and Andre. I was comforted by the knowledge that she would never know.

Chapter Forty-Six

BRIAR

That night I dreamt of Xavier and woke suddenly, my heart racing, unable to ignore the feeling he was calling out for me. Needing my help. I tried to sleep again, telling myself it was just a cruel dream, but it was hopeless. My mind played tricks on me. I could hear Andre's voice calling out for me. Finally, unable to stand it any longer, I got out of bed and decided to make myself a hot drink, hoping it might calm me slightly.

I slipped on my dressing gown and crept downstairs. I pulled a chair closer to the banked fire and went to boil some milk. It seemed to take ages, but eventually I was able to pour the hot milk into a cup and took it into the living room.

I sat nursing the drink, my feet warmed slightly by the fire. It was too dark to read my book, so I slowly sipped the warm liquid and began to feel sleepy. I shivered, feeling a slight chill in the room that came from somewhere. The doors and windows were closed and the smoke was rising slowly up the chimney, so it wasn't coming from there. Unsettled, I placed my cup down on the small table next to the armchair and pulled my dressing gown tighter around me.

I thought I heard a faint whisper and stilled, shaking my head at my silliness.

'Briar.'

Someone had whispered my name. I looked around me but I was alone. I glanced up the stairs, wondering if Mum had come down, then realised it wasn't a woman's voice speaking to me.

My breath caught in my throat. What was happening? Who had whispered my name? I must be more tired than I imagined, I thought, taking a soothing sip of my drink.

'Briar.'

Chilled, I pulled my dressing gown even tighter around me.

'Who is this?' I asked, wondering why I was talking to myself. Maybe I wasn't up at all but in the middle of another dream. Yes, that's it. Calmer, I stood, deciding to return to my bedroom and try to get some sleep. Being overtired clearly didn't suit me.

I carried my cup through to the scullery, ran water into it and set it in the sink to wash up in the morning.

As I stepped back into the living room, I felt arms gently circle me from behind. I could barely feel the pressure but they were there. Strangely I didn't feel frightened. When the arms dropped away, I turned to see Andre – or what I believed to be Andre – standing in front of me. It was like trying to catch an image of someone in a dream. He was there, but not completely. His head seemed to be partly wrapped in bandages. My heart raced and my breath caught in my throat. I opened my mouth to speak but couldn't find my voice.

He smiled. 'I didn't mean to frighten you, Briar.' His voice as gentle as ever.

'Andre? What happened to you? Are you really here?' Did I miss Xavier so desperately that I had somehow conjured up his closest friend?

'Do not worry about me.'

I struggled to comprehend what was happening. 'I don't understand. How are you here?' I recalled how this used to be his home and wondered why I hadn't come across his spirit before.

As if he heard my thoughts, Andre answered, 'I was always here in some way, but things are different now.'

I tensed. Different? 'They are?'

'I need something from you now.'

'You do?'

He reached out without touching me. 'I need your help.'

'You know I'll happily give it, but how?' Dread seeped into the pit of my stomach. 'Why do you need my help, Andre?'

I heard a heavy sigh. 'You're the only one who can help save Xavier's life.'

Now I knew for certain this was really happening. Andre would only go to these lengths to help the closest person to him. I cried out, then quickly covered my mouth so as not to wake Mum, in case Andre vanished before I could find out more. 'Xavier? Why? What's happened?'

'He's in terrible danger.'

'Why?' I asked, my voice barely audible as I battled to control my emotions.

'He was arrested on his return from France, where he's been living for three years since you left.'

So their time moved at the same speed as mine. It was a revelation.

There was a sigh that seemed to come from the very depths of his soul. 'Ember, she was the one who instigated his arrest.' He raised a hand and indicated his bandages. 'And this.'

I whimpered, barely able to take in the enormity of what he was telling me. 'Why? How could anyone wish death on people they love, even if in Xavier's case that love is no longer reciprocated?' It was implausible.

'You're talking as a sane person, Briar. Ember's hatred for Xavier has sent her mind to a dark place. The only way I can save his life now is to beg for your help.'

My thoughts raced, jumbled in my panic. 'But the only way to do that would be to bring him forward in time again,' I replied, thinking aloud and trying to work out how he would cope with living here permanently. 'I'm not sure he'd want me to force him back here without giving him the choice.'

The temperature in the room cooled further and I sensed Andre's despair. 'He has given up all hope. He is being put to death in the next few days, Briar. Bringing him to you is the only chance left to him now.' His heartbreaking sigh sent shudders through me. 'I'm sorry I don't have the strength to stay much longer but I beg you to do as I ask. I know you have the power to do this.'

'I don't have powers, Andre. I'm only recently initiated.'

'You do. You're probably the only one who doesn't yet understand how powerful you truly are. It's why the Witchfinder is searching for you.'

'How do you know about him being here?'

He didn't answer my question. 'Briar, I need to know that you'll save Xavier.'

'But what about you, Andre?'

His head shook slowly. 'My life, if it continues, is here. I have family who love me but I will always be here for you if you need me. Promise me you'll do as I ask.'

'I promise I'll do everything I can.'

He gave a relieved sigh. There was a short silence. 'The Witchfinder is not yet in your home, but he soon will be.'

I flinched, recalling the Witchfinder, three hundred years before, slamming the door against the wall as he entered this same cottage.

'You have seen him,' he said, his voice urgent.

'Several times.'

'You must fear for your safety and that of your mother and the women of the coven. They are a threat to him that he will not tolerate.' There was a momentary silence while I tried to gather myself, then Andre continued, 'But you have the power to fight him. And the power to save Xavier... And you need to do it as soon as possible before it's too late.'

I squeezed my eyes shut, unable to take in the enormity of his warning.

'How am I supposed to do that?' I asked panic-stricken.

When I opened my eyes, Andre had vanished.

Chapter Forty-Seven

DIANA

'What are you working on?' I asked, entering the room and seeing Briar murmuring to herself as she focused on ingredients in the small copper cauldron that used to be my mother's, which I had come across in the attic.

Most days I found her hard at work perfecting her spells, and the sight never ceased to warm my heart. This is what I had imagined my precious daughter doing, ever since her birth. Picturing the two of us working side by side. Perfecting incantations and creating perfect spells was a dream I was beginning to worry might not come true, but here she was increasing her prowess and strengthening her magick more each day.

I thought of my mother holding Briar in her arms in the moonlight soon after she was born, telling me that the most powerful of all us witches had arrived. I had thought she spoke simply as a proud grandmother, but having watched Briar developing her skills at such a quick pace since her induction only a few weeks ago, I now suspected my mother knew something I didn't.

'I'm working on a banishing spell,' she said, bending closer to the cauldron and dropping another clove into the mixture.

'To rid yourself of the Witchfinder,' I said half to myself, saddened by his unexpected reappearance in Briar's life. As if her frequent torments from nightmares brought about by memories of the interminable hours she spent incarcerated in the stinking cell in the castle, and his terrifying interrogations weren't already enough for her to deal with.

Wanting to help in any way I could, I studied the selection of ingredients she had prepared and saw a small amount of dragon's blood, two more cloves and a jug of water, which I presumed was from the bottle she had left on the windowsill to be energised during the last visible crescent of the most recent waning moon.

'It isn't nearly powerful enough yet and it must be perfect. The Witchfinder is a determined man and I know we'll only have one chance to deal with him.'

'I suppose you could add some bay and hyacinth,' I suggested. Not wishing to take any chances, I added, 'We should probably consult the rest of the coven for their suggestions.'

She sighed and turned to me. 'I agree.'

I noticed the dark circles under her eyes and sensed this spell wasn't the only thing troubling her. 'There's something else, isn't there?'

'Let's sit down,' Briar suggested, then she proceeded to tell me about a visitation she had had.

I sat across the table from my daughter listening in disbelief, our untouched breakfast cold.

'I've experienced other spirits living here, but I don't think I've come across this ghost.'

'That's the thing, Mum. He's not a ghost. Well, he'll be dead now, of course, but in his time he's still alive, albeit barely from what I gathered.'

'You say he's a friend of Xavier's?' I asked, frightened by the enormity of what was happening.

'And mine. He helped save my life.'

I saw her attempt to hide her panic. The poor girl had been through so much but my sense that trouble was coming had been right. If this man's warning was correct, and I believed it to be, then Briar and I were in incredible danger.

'Even if this Witchfinder chap is here, Briar, there's nothing he can do to hurt us. People don't burn witches at the stake any longer, thankfully.' I saw the panic in Briar's eyes. 'And as far as Xavier's concerned, I thought you said he could settle in our time.' Then again, it sounded like he had run out of choices. 'I want to help him, too,' I admitted, conscious that the magick I had studied all my life was for the greater good – but how would that affect my daughter's life in the long term?

'We have to help him, Mum. We have no option.'

'I don't even know if I could bring him back a second time.'

She shrugged confidently. 'I can help this time, though, Mum.' Briar's eyes filled with tears. 'I've been practising my craft every day and I can feel my powers increasing. With your help and that of the coven's I know we can save him.'

I was taken aback to discover she still harboured such deep feelings for Xavier. I thought we were open with each other, but clearly not if my daughter had withheld her affection for this man from me all this time.

'Please, Mum, I won't ever ask you for anything again if you do this for me.'

I felt my resolve weaken. 'But no one seems to have asked Xavier what *he* wants. What if we bring him back, if that's possible, and he's unhappy with us doing so? Have you thought of that? Or what if he's resigned to his death?' I could tell by her expression that she hadn't considered any of this, but clearly Briar had no intention of giving up that easily.

'Why would Andre come to me begging for my help if that was the case?'

As I considered her question a thought occurred to me. 'Does he know Andre has spoken to you?'

She gave my question some thought. Eventually, she spoke. 'I don't know.'

I was about to reply, but she continued.

'You haven't met the Witchfinder, Mum,' Briar said, changing tactics. She lowered her head into her hands. 'He is the cruellest person I've ever met. My nightmares are still filled with women's screams from when he tortured them.'

Sickened to think of my daughter experiencing such horror, I distracted myself by picking up a piece of toast. I bit into it, looking forward to the taste of the crispy white bread covered in creamy Jersey butter, but instead it was like eating paper. I put the toast back onto the plate.

'How do you expect this time to be any different for Xavier?'

'Mum, this isn't just about Xavier,' she reminded me. 'Roger Dankworth terrifies me. Anyone determined enough to find a way to follow me through time has no qualms about taking chances. I've escaped his clutches twice. I don't believe anyone else has done that.' She shuddered and wrapped her arms around herself. 'He will have no intention of failing a third time, that much I do know.'

She thought for a couple of seconds as I let the seriousness of her words sink in.

'He wanted me to see him when I was on the bus that time. I hadn't realised it or why. But now it makes sense. And'—she hesitated, frowning—'I know without doubt that it isn't only Xavier's life in danger. I believe Andre is telling me ours are, too. All of ours, not just you and me but the other women in the coven, Mum. We owe it to them to do all we can to stop him succeeding.'

I couldn't miss the fear in her voice. I thought about this man who had been determined to put my child to death for being a witch. My feet tingled as my fear of the repercussions of her vision the previous night began to increase. I hated hearing her talk this way. Why did this have to happen? Hadn't we been through enough already these past few years? Obviously not.

'Mum.' Briar reached across the table and took my hand in hers. 'Whatever you may think, I believe we have no choice. I know I'll feel safer with Xavier here, never mind that I'll never forgive myself if he dies when I had the chance to save his life.'

I didn't like the tone of her voice and suspected she was about to say something that was meant to frighten me.

'Who knows what the Witchfinder has planned for me?' Briar continued. 'If he tries to take me back with him to the 1640s and succeeds, I know without any doubt he will make an example of me. This isn't a man who gives up on his prey. If you ever look into his eyes, I can assure you, you'll feel the same way I do.'

Nausea rose through my throat with such speed, I had to

cover my mouth with both hands and run to the bathroom to vomit. When I finished and my stomach muscles ached from dry retching, I splashed water over my face. Then, looking at my reflection in the mirror, I knew without doubt what I must do next.

I dried my face and returned to the living room to find Briar pacing back and forth. 'Are you all right, Mum?'

'I will be.' I motioned for her to sit and did the same. 'We need to make a plan and the first thing on our list is for us to confide in Babette.'

I thought of Babette's spell room. 'In fact there's somewhere I want to take you but I'll need to ask permission first.'

Chapter Forty-Eight

BRIAR

I waited while Mum wrote a note and handed it to me. 'Take this to Babette's home. Give it to her yourself. Don't leave it with another soul.'

'Why? What does it say?'

Mum rolled her eyes. 'I haven't put in anything I shouldn't.'

There was no time to waste, and I hurried as quickly as I could to Mrs Le Dain's home and rang the doorbell. Her maid answered. 'Yes?'

'I have a message for the Connétable's wife.'

The girl reached out to take it. 'Mrs Le Dain is otherwise engaged. If you leave it with me I'll see she gets it.'

I smiled politely. 'I've been asked to hand it to her personally.' I gave her my name.

The girl gave me an irritated look before turning on her heels. 'Wait there, I'll see if she has time to speak to you,' she said as she disappeared down the tiled hallway.

Within seconds, Babette appeared. She studied my face

briefly before she sent the girl off in another direction and came to speak to me. 'Briar. Is everything all right?'

I handed her the note. 'Mum wanted me to give this to you.' I lowered my voice. 'It's extremely urgent.'

I waited for her reaction as she read.

Her face paled. She looked at me, then back down at the short note, reading it once more. 'We won't discuss this here,' she said quietly, a tremor in her voice. 'You return home now. I'll follow as soon as I can. I have a few members of the WI here for coffee but shouldn't be long. Assure Diana I'll be with her in less than an hour.'

I thanked her and returned home. As I reached out to take hold of the doorknob the door drew back, and Mum frantically waved me inside. 'What did she say?'

'She has guests but promised she won't be long. Less than an hour.'

Mum groaned impatiently but we just had to wait. Twenty minutes later Babette arrived. She knocked once on the door before entering the cottage without waiting for an answer and immediately marched over to the table before we had a chance to get up to greet her.

'This is concerning news.' She took a deep breath. 'I've been thinking on my way here and one of the first things we need to do is see this Witchfinder fellow for ourselves, Diana.' She gave an involuntary shudder. 'Briar knows what he looks like but the pair of us don't.'

I tried to think of something that might make him stand out in her memory. Then it dawned on me. 'He always wears a leather glove on his left hand regardless of the weather.'

Babette rubbed the back of her neck wearily then raised her eyebrows. Something had occurred to her. 'I recall a story passed down through my family of a man of this name who blamed the coven for his sister's death. I seem to recall he wore a glove. It was said to hide a witch's mark given to him as a warning by someone.'

I was shocked she could know this. 'How was the coven to blame for that, though?'

'I gather the sister came to them for help, wanting a poison to kill her husband, but the coven decided they couldn't be a party to murder.'

Mum nodded. 'I remember hearing this from my grandmother.'

'What else did she say?' I asked, intrigued.

Mum continued. 'I believe one of the coven offered to take her and her children in but he found the girl packing to leave and killed her before they could get away.'

Mum and Babette exchanged glances as the enormity of Dankworth's hatred for the coven sunk in.

'That's right,' Babette said, all weariness vanishing. 'Didn't he threaten one of the witches and the others caught him and branded his hand?'

I gasped. 'They did that?' I could see why the repercussions of that act and the loss of his sister had led him to inflict so much pain and hardship on others.

'We really are in terrible danger, aren't we?' Babette said almost to herself.

They began talking frantically about a way to protect all of us. Not wishing them to forget about Xavier, I interrupted. 'Sorry, there's more.'

'More?' Babette grimaced at Mum. 'What else can there possibly be?'

I struggled to find the words to relay more bad news to this woman who had done so much to help Mum and me, but what choice did I have?

'I'm afraid so.'

'Go on.' The resignation in her voice saddened me.

As Babette listened, it became obvious to me that she didn't believe Xavier's presence could make any difference to our safety. It was frustrating, but I supposed it wasn't surprising, given how the coven and their mothers and grandmothers before them had ensured their safety through their traditional practices.

Babette shook her head. 'I'm sorry, Briar. We have too much to deal with as it is. I don't think we're going to be able to help this time.'

I turned to Mum but she kept her eyes downcast. 'Sorry, Briar. I have to agree with Babette.'

'Have to?' I accused.

She looked at me then. 'I do agree with her. It doesn't make sense to bring someone back here who, let's face it, has no idea we're doing this. What if he resents you for making this happen? Have you thought of that?' She looked at me silently for a moment, her tone gentle when she continued. 'What if his choice would be to stay where he is?'

I gritted my teeth in fury. 'I can't imagine he would choose what's happening to him right now.'

'And why might that be?' Babette asked frowning.

'Because he's about to be executed.'

I heard the women's sharp intake of breath and knew I'd shocked them. Good. If that's what it took for them to help me then I didn't much care.

Still, neither of them offered to help.

'Fine,' I said, breathless with anger. 'I'll do it myself.'

Mum glared at me. 'You don't know how to.'

That's what she thought. 'I've been using a reverse banishment spell I found in Granny's spell book. I believe I've almost perfected it,' I said, giving them a satisfied nod. 'If I'm to do this alone, then I'd better get going and finalise everything I need.'

Chapter Forty-Nine

BRIAR

That evening the weather was stormy but there wasn't any thunder or lightning. I struggled to contain my panic. Unless the weather changed, this wouldn't be the time to bring Xavier back. I decided to keep my concerns to myself.

The following morning Mum went out for several hours. I was still disappointed. So much for the coven having my back. For the sisterhood who would always be there for me. The first time I ask them for something important, and they reject my request. Never mind how upset I was with Mum for siding with Babette. I was relieved to be at home alone and not have to speak to her.

I took time to work on the spell, going through the worn pages of my grandmother's grimoire yet again to try and see how I might make the spell as powerful as possible. I loved Xavier and I intended doing everything in my power to save his life.

I was lost in thought, checking my incantation, when Mum

burst in the front door. I looked up when I didn't hear the door close again.

'Hurry, Briar,' she said, waving for me to join her.

I shook my head. 'I need to finish working on this.'

She walked over to me and picked up the leather-bound book.

'I need that,' I snapped, reaching out to take it back, only for Mum to hold it behind her back and hand my jacket to me instead. 'Put this on and come with me. Now.'

I knew that determined tone of hers. 'Fine.'

I reluctantly stood and did as she asked. 'I can't be long, though,' I argued. 'Anyway, where are we going that's so important?'

'Babette has invited us to her home. She wanted to show you her spell room.'

I didn't like to tell her that I wasn't interested in seeing it, because I was. We didn't have a designated spell area in our cottage; it was far too small with both of us living there. I was almost ready, when the opportunity came, to bring Xavier back, so I accompanied her.

A few minutes later, I stood at the entrance of Babette's spell room, entranced.

Mum put a hand on my back and pushed me gently forward.

I looked around me, stunned into silence by the spectacle.

'Well?' Babette asked, joining us. 'What do you think?'

This was like nothing I had ever seen before. The air was filled with scents I recognised like calendula, lavender, rosemary, pepper, but also others I didn't know.

'What is this?' I whispered to Mum.

'You'll see.'

I couldn't miss the excitement in her voice and it was a relief after the earlier tension at Honey Bee Cottage.

I gazed around me, mesmerised by the packed bookshelves lining the longest wall. Babette must have been working in here before visiting our cottage, because the cauldron hanging over the small fire in the inglenook fireplace had steam rising from it and smoke unfurled slowly up the chimney.

There was a long table laden with items grouped together. I walked over to have a better look and saw crystals, rose and clear quartz, lapis lazuli, turquoise, which I knew was for love, next to bloodstone, tiger's eye, obsidian, amber and amethyst. I gasped, unable to take in the wonder of the place.

Babette's willow wand lay next to several phials half-filled with an oil and what looked like herbs. There was a pestle and mortar with ground dried herbs still in it and various candles set in silver and wood candlesticks of differing heights.

'This is…' I couldn't find the words to convey how incredible I found this place. 'It's magickal. Every witch must want a place just like this one. I know I'd love one.'

'It's impressive, isn't it?' Mum said, clearly enjoying being there despite it not being her first time.

'I had no idea it was here,' I said, having never heard a snippet of a suggestion that there was more in the basement of this impressive house than anyone would expect.

Babette's pride at our impression of her secret room was obvious.

She pressed her hands together. 'I've heard there's another storm on its way in a few hours.' I wasn't sure why she was giving me this news. 'We've all had a chat and decided to do as you asked, Briar.'

Shocked, I took a moment to respond. 'You have?'

Mum nodded. 'Yes. We thought we should meet here where Babette has the best ingredients and prepare our spell for Xavier's return together.'

Covering my mouth to stop from crying out, I beamed at her, unable to hide my relief. 'Thank you, Mum. Babette. All of you.'

———

Several hours later Mum, Babette, Jeanne and I hunkered down in the ruin as we set out the candles and the small copper bowl with the ingredients I'd helped Babette prepare, ready to begin our chanting when the storm was overhead.

'It's much easier without soldiers patrolling,' Mum mused as Babette handed her phials of potions, a jar of salt and a candle from her carpet bag.

'We still need to keep watch for any passing locals,' Babette reminded her. 'None of us needs gossip going around about us. My husband couldn't stand the shame if he discovered exactly what I was up to in the basement.'

I helped Jeanne set up the rest of the implements in the cell. We then stood back to take our places in the circle with Mum while Babette cleansed the area, ready to carry out her spell.

We stood in a circle around the candles and began chanting our spell, repeating it over and over. We all needed this to work; our lives depended on it. As if my thoughts had been heard, a loud clap of thunder rumbled through the air around us, closely followed by an enormous crack of lightning.

The next thing I knew Xavier fell to the floor. I was elated to see him but quickly noticed a raw rope-like bruise around his neck, as if he had been wearing a noose only seconds before.

I cried out, horrified by how close we had been to failing. How near I'd been to losing him forever.

He opened his eyes slowly and looked about him, dazed. Wanting him to notice me there, yet not wishing to frighten him by making any sudden movements, I waited for Xavier to work out what had happened.

His eyes fell on me but instead of the elated reaction I had expected, his face fell and he glared at me, 'What have you done?' His voice was raspy and he looked devastated.

Stunned into heartbroken silence by his reaction, I thought of every time I'd played out this scenario in my head. I had imagined his reaction to be one of surprise, shock maybe, or delight to see me again. Not angry, like this. He was bewildered. I decided I would not allow him to see my hurt as I stepped forward and knelt next to him.

'You've come back to us, Xavier,' I explained gently, in case he was too much in shock to understand what had happened. I stroked his dishevelled hair back from his face, trying to hide my distress at his gaunt appearance. I didn't know why but it hadn't occurred to me he would be this thin and battered. It broke my heart to see how badly he had been treated. Andre hadn't exaggerated when he told me Xavier was going to die.

I shuddered to think of the consequences if I hadn't taken Andre seriously, or if there hadn't been a storm tonight. Xavier had been seconds away from death. No wonder he wasn't in good spirits. Who would be after what he had gone through?

Chapter Fifty

XAVIER

I looked around me at each of the women I never expected to see again, furious with them for bringing me back. For seeing me in such reduced circumstances. Ashamed of my weak state, I returned my accusatory gaze to Briar, who I knew must be behind this enforced travel through time.

'Why did you bring me back?' Another thought occurred to me. 'How did you know I would come?'

Diana made a sound like she had expected me to react this way. She raised her eyebrows. 'My daughter will tell you why we did this. As far as you allowing yourself to be brought here, I don't think you had much choice, did you?'

She was right, I thought, irritated. 'I imagine not.'

'You are here now, though,' Briar said, her gentle voice tight with emotion.

I locked eyes with hers, overwhelmed to once again be able to gaze deeply into them. Hating that my appearance had shocked her. Even I could smell the stink of me, now I was out of that rancid cell and among clean folk.

'You're really here.'

I wasn't sure how to answer. As much as I was happy to see her again, I still felt the pressure from the noose tight around my neck, then the drop. Yet instead of falling into an abyss of blackness, here I was. Why? My neck smarted and my shoulder ached from landing on it. 'Please untie my wrists.'

Two elderly women came up to the doorway and stared wide-eyed at me.

'Good grief, what's going on here?' one of them asked, leaning forward between Diana and her friend.

'Um, reenactment rehearsals,' Briar explained. 'We're working on the finer details.'

I was grateful for her quick thinking, as, I saw, were the other three women standing around me.

The older women nudged each other and nodded. 'Realistic costume,' one said to the other.

Believing I should do something to add credence to the charade, I got to my knees, trying not to groan, then to my feet. It took some effort, but once standing I gave a theatrical bow. 'I thank ye.'

'Very impressive,' the other agreed, beaming at me coquettishly. 'Dashing, too,' she added a little more quietly.

'Thank you, ladies,' Diana said with a forced smile. 'If you wouldn't mind keeping this to yourselves. We wouldn't want our secret preparations being shared before we're ready, would we?'

'Ooh, no, dear,' one of the women said, linking her arm with the other and leading her away. 'Come along, Gladys. Let's leave these good people to their planning.'

As soon as they were gone, Briar worked the rope until it dropped to the ground. I rubbed my wrists. 'Thank you.'

Babette and Jeanne began tidying away their tools into a carpet bag. Diana went to help. 'No, dear,' Babette said. 'I think you and Briar should take this poor man to your cottage.' She tilted her head in my direction.

'Yes, we'll go immediately.'

I hated that I had hurt her with my reaction, but I was still angry and needed to know what was behind this occurrence.

'We'll let you have a bath and give you something to eat and drink. I'll explain everything when you've had a chance to gather yourself.'

I heard Briar speaking but couldn't take my eyes from her delicate fingers as they took hold of my forearm. How could I be cruel to her? She was the sweetest woman; I was thankful to see her again.

'I know this isn't what you expected, or what you might have wanted, and this is probably very selfish of me, but I'm enormously happy you're here.' There was a haunted look in her eyes and I sensed something dark had happened. I studied her intently. Something frightening.

'What is it?'

Diana took my other arm. 'We don't have time for that now,' she said as Babette and Jeanne finished collecting and packing away various items. 'Not if we don't wish to attract any more unwanted attention. We can talk at home.'

Unnerved, I realised they hadn't done this without good reason. They had saved my life yet again. From the stress on these women's faces, their action had been concerned with something that affected all of us. I tried to hide my panic. 'Briar, has something happened to you?'

She slipped her arm through mine, hugging it to her side.

I was comforted to feel the warmth of her skin against mine. 'We have a lot to discuss. Like Mum said, it'll be better to talk properly at home.'

Chapter Fifty-One

BRIAR

I stared into his dark eyes. They seemed so much larger now than the last time I had seen him. As well as the torn skin around his neck, I couldn't help noticing how his ribs stood out and the boniness of his chest. Xavier had always been a well-built man, muscular as well as being strong. He appeared very different to that now and I could sense his humiliation at us seeing him in such a dreadful state.

There were several old bruises on his face, and his bottom lip had been split at some point recently – probably by a punch, I thought, furious that anyone could be violent towards someone unable to fight back.

He was shivering and I was about to say something when I realised he was smiling at me. 'I can tell by the look of your face how dreadful I appear.' He withdrew his arm from mine. 'I can smell myself, too. Maybe you should keep a distance from me until I have bathed and no longer smell this way?'

I started to argue with him but he shook his head.

'No, Briar. I have my pride. There will be time enough for us to talk.'

'He's right,' Mum said.

Babette picked up her bag. 'Jeanne and I will be running along now. Diana, I'll speak to you soon.' She looked Xavier up and down. 'I look forward to getting to know you once things calm down.'

'Thank you for all you've done for me.' He bowed his head. 'I'm sorry my reaction wasn't very gentlemanly.'

'You have no reason to apologise,' she said before leading Jeanne away.

'Come along now, the pair of you,' Mum said. 'Let's be getting this young man home.'

'Home.' I walked with them, unable to regulate my fluctuating emotions. They alternated between relief that Xavier was safe with me now and dread that I still had to tell him about Andre coming to me, and how gravely ill he was. I hoped Xavier already knew but had no way of knowing if he did until we talked.

Despite Xavier's wish not to be held, due to his filthy state, Mum and I had to support him to help him on our walk back to the cottage. He was frighteningly weak and, although terribly thin, still heavy. Never mind telling Xavier about Andre, I mused as we walked, I also needed to tell him about the Witchfinder being with us and why Mum had agreed to bring him back here.

For now, though, I just wanted Xavier safe and warm at the cottage.

Once inside, Mum took off her coat and hung it up. 'Sit down, Xavier, while I fetch clothes for you and run a bath.'

She turned her attention to me. 'Heat up some of that stew I made earlier and make the poor lad a hot drink.'

'I'd rather something cold, if you have it,' he said, raising his hand to his throat.

I glanced at Mum and wondered if the same thought had occurred to her as it did to me. 'Your throat must smart?'

He nodded. 'I think it's bruised inside as well as outside. From the noose.'

I shuddered at the thought, wondering why the noose hadn't travelled with him but the rope tying his wrists had. I imagined the shock of the executioner and the crowd, if there had been one, as they saw him vanish and a swinging empty noose left behind.

'You must be parched,' I said, wanting to focus on other things. 'We have some beer left in the scullery cupboard.'

'Yes,' Mum said. 'From the celebrations last Christmas. Fetch him a bottle, Briar. If that's what you'd like, Xavier. Or maybe you'd prefer water.'

He smiled. 'May I have both? One to quench my thirst and the other for the taste.'

'I'll fetch them right now,' I said, glad he could still muster his sense of humour.

After handing him a glass of water and a bottle of beer, I returned to the kitchen and gave the bubbling stew a stir. He really was here, I told myself, hardly daring to believe it. My mind raced. I had prayed for this moment many times over the past three years and now it had finally happened. Xavier had returned. Although it had been a close thing, he was still alive, and I hoped he would never have to leave again.

'May I do anything to help?' he asked from the living room.

I poked my head around the door, thinking how surreal it

was to have him here. 'No, thank you. Mum would go mad if she thought I wasn't being the perfect hostess. You sit there and relax. This stew is almost ready for you.'

I sliced two pieces of bread and spread a thick layer of yellow, creamy butter over them before popping them onto a plate. Then, serving a bowl of steaming stew, I picked up some cutlery and carried Xavier's food to the living room.

'There you go.' I stood and watched him take a mouthful of bread, then he smiled up at me. 'I'll fetch you a napkin.'

He reached out. 'No. Please sit with me. I want to look at you while I'm eating this delicious food.'

'Look at me?' I wasn't sure what he meant.

He took a mouthful of stew and ate it. 'Let it sink in that I'm here and not in my stinking cell dreaming this is happening.'

I saw such deep sorrow in his eyes and wanted to soothe him, so I stretched out a hand. He stared at it briefly before taking it in his.

'You're really here.' He closed his eyes. 'I suppose I'm the one who's come to you, aren't I?'

As I sat opposite him, I noticed more about him and understood much better what he must have gone through. He hadn't only lost weight and clearly been beaten, probably several times, but there was a fragility about him I hadn't seen before. What had they done to this poor man whom I loved and dreamt about to almost break his spirit? Almost.

'Don't worry about me.' His voice was quiet but determined.

'What do you mean?'

'At this moment I might be reduced in vigour and not the

man you once knew, but I will return to my old self, I promise you.'

I believed him. 'You just need rest, nourishment and the chance to come to terms with everything,' I said, wondering if I was trying to persuade myself as well as Xavier. Unable to help myself, I asked, 'Do you think you can settle here? Permanently, I mean?'

He picked up the glass of beer. 'I have little choice.' I must have looked sad as Xavier gave me a reassuring smile. 'We have much catching up to do and hopefully all the time in the world in which to do it, thanks to you, Diana, Babette and Jeanne.'

'Xavier?' I began wondering if now was the time to tell him about Andre.

'Your bath is ready,' Mum called from upstairs. I wasn't sure if I was irritated with her interruption or relieved. 'Come up as soon as you've finished eating,' she added.

I stood. 'I'll make up a bed for you.'

He shook his head. 'Please, wait for me to finish this.'

I settled back onto the seat, wondering if he was frightened that if I left the room, he might never see me again. It was probably an odd thing for someone to think if they hadn't experienced all that we had, but I understood his reasoning perfectly.

'Take your time. I can always add more hot water to the bath if it cools too much.'

Shortly after, Mum came down the stairs. 'Oh, good, you're eating.'

'It's delicious, Diana. Thank you.'

'I'm glad you think so,' she said looking pleased. 'We still can't buy everything we want but we're much better off than when you were last here. I've left a towel, soap and a toothbrush for you in the bathroom. There's no rush, though. I want you to make yourself at home with us here. You'll also find your clothes in Briar's room where you slept the last time.' She looked at me. 'I've moved some of your things into my room.'

'Thanks, Mum.' It was going to be wonderful knowing Xavier was sleeping under our roof once more.

'I have a feeling you're going to sleep well tonight, young man.'

He didn't seem convinced. 'I hope so. I've barely slept since being arrested.'

'When was that?' I asked without thinking.

'Briar, I think we leave questions until tomorrow. Give Xavier a chance to feel a little more like himself again.'

She was right. 'Yes, sorry.'

He winced as he swallowed his food. 'I'm happy for you to ask me anything.'

I shook my head, thinking of the Witchfinder and of dear, sweet Andre. We didn't have as much time as we might hope, but now wasn't the time for me to worry about that. 'Today we concentrate on looking after you.'

He finished a last mouthful of bread and downed the rest of his beer before slowly getting to his feet. 'I already feel much revived. I shall leave you both to take my bath.'

Mum and I watched him walk to the stairs, glancing at each other in concern when he winced as he took the first step.

When he had gone, I waved her into the kitchen. Once inside and certain we couldn't be overheard, I kept my voice low. 'Oh, Mum, he's in such a terrible state.'

She sighed. 'Poor man has obviously been through hell.

We should give him a few days at least before we trouble him with everything.'

I agreed, wishing the sole reason he had been brought back here was because I wanted to save his life.

I washed his dishes and served a bowl of stew each for Mum and me. As we ate, I listened for any sound that he might need help coming downstairs. I decided that whether he believed me or not, the most important thing right now was that Xavier was safe. He was no longer being beaten or starved or staring death in the face. For now, that was all that mattered.

Chapter Fifty-Two

XAVIER

I had been back with the Le Gros family for under a week but already felt more like my old self. The first time I saw my reflection in the bathroom mirror I was mortified to think the woman I loved had seen me this way. I tried to reason that should the circumstances be reversed I would not love her any less.

I suppose my dramatic fall from grace stung my pride, but there was little I could do about that, apart from working to build myself back to the man I had once been. I still struggled to come to terms with Andre's demise, and hadn't yet shared this tragic news, or Ember's part in it, with Briar. There would be time enough for that.

This morning, though, as I had washed my face and cleaned my teeth, I was pleased to see that their tender care and good food were already making an improvement.

I was still much weaker than I was used to being. I was unaccustomed to the lack of food, of sunlight and of exercise.

I shook away the memory and decided to look to the future. I was here, working to regain my fitness.

Briar and Diana hadn't said much but I hadn't forgotten Briar's haunted expression when I arrived. I knew there was a reason for me being here. She would never have brought me back just because she wanted to see me again. Briar was not a girl to do anything for selfish reasons. Several times their conversation had stopped abruptly when I entered a room, and I hadn't missed occasional furtive glances between them. I trusted that they would tell me whatever it was as soon as they felt the time was right.

My bruised feet barely hurt now, and my muscles ached and cramped less. The cuts I had sustained during beatings in the prison were healing too. I decided it was a good time to go out and start building up my stamina.

I found Briar and Diana in the living room. Briar was standing by the front door with a basket over her arm.

'You're going out?' I asked unnecessarily.

'Yes,' she said giving me a welcoming smile. 'We need a few things from the shops. Would you care to join me?' She had told me how grateful they were about the war ending and how difficult times had been for the islanders especially in the final year. 'If you'd rather stay here and have breakfast, please do. I shan't be long.'

Not wishing to miss the opportunity of spending time alone with her, I walked over to where the coats were hanging. 'I'll gladly join you.'

I took my jacket from the hook by the door and put it on, noticing Diana's cheerful demeanour as she turned and went to the kitchen. She was happy for us. It was good to know she didn't hold any resentment against me for my part in what had happened to her daughter.

Briar linked arms with me as we walked. 'You're looking much better as each day passes.'

I lowered my head closer to hers. 'It's thanks to my hostesses and their excellent care of me.'

She hugged my arm a little closer. 'I'm glad you think so.' She rested her cheek against my upper arm for a moment. 'I can't tell you how wonderful it is to have you here, Xavier.'

I kissed the top of her head. 'I still worry I'll wake up and be back in that cell.'

She looked up at me, concerned. 'I was the same after I returned. You're never going back there, and I hope that soon you'll stop having nightmares about it.'

Briar spoke from experience, and I believed her. Soothed by her insistence, I relaxed further. 'Where are we going?'

We visited two shops and after much persuasion Briar allowed me to carry her heavy basket laden with packages.

The greengrocer followed us out of the shop. 'Oi, Briar, love,' he shouted, a wide smile on his cheerful face. 'Would you mind coming here for a second? The wife has something she wishes to ask you about one of those books you and she like reading.'

She looked up at me. 'You don't mind, do you?'

'Of course not,' I assured her. 'I'll take the shopping to the cottage and see you back there.'

'Thanks. I won't be long.'

I was crossing the road at the edge of the village when a man stepped out around a corner from between two houses and slammed into me.

There was something familiar about his stance but he was lurking too far in the shadows for me to make out his face.

I noticed he had dropped the fruit he was carrying in our collision and bent to pick it up.

'It is no matter,' he insisted.

Shocked by the phrase he used, I stiffened. The way he had spoken, it wasn't from this time. Bracing myself, I straightened and moved closer to him, horrified when he stepped forward. My heart almost stopped at the realisation that I was looking straight into Roger Dankworth's dark eyes. How in the hell was the Witchfinder here?

A chill ran through me. Something was going on. Was this why Diana and Briar had been behaving oddly? Did they already know? Had they decided for some reason to withhold the information from me? I couldn't understand why they would do so.

My mind raced as I tried to decide whether to show recognition. I knew surprise was the best tactic when fighting but couldn't fathom whether this man recognised me as I had done him. He didn't appear to have done. I decided to err on the side of caution and immediately looked down at my provisions. I noticed that two of the packages had been knocked out of my basket onto the road. I hoped whatever was inside hadn't broken. I bent to collect them.

'You are unhurt?'

'Merely surprised.'

I couldn't tell whether he was referring to his surprise at being slammed into, or at seeing me. I decided not to stay and find out. There would no doubt be time enough to do that. First, I needed to confront Briar and Diana. Now that I thought about how they were acting, I suspected they knew he was lurking in the village, and I wanted to know why I hadn't been told.

I walked around him and continued on my way without looking back, anxious to come to terms with what had happened. I wanted to return to the cottage as quickly as possible but showing I was in a hurry would make him suspicious. Checking behind me that I hadn't been followed – for I had no wish to lead that man to Briar and Diana's door – I finally reached the cottage and went inside.

'You're back,' Briar said, coming from the kitchen and reaching out to take the basket, shocked when I didn't let go. She laughed, but when I didn't do the same her expression changed. 'Whatever's the matter?'

I gritted my teeth. I hated lies. 'You knew, didn't you? Is he the reason you brought me here?'

Realisation crossed her face. She glanced down at her feet briefly before returning her gaze to me. 'You've seen him, haven't you? Roger Dankworth.'

I stared at her, wanting to find words that weren't too harsh. 'Why didn't you tell me he was here?' She tried to take my hand, but I withdrew it from her. I needed an answer.

'Why, Briar?' I slammed the basket onto the table. I was more deeply hurt than I could have imagined. 'I believed you when you told me you had brought me back to save my life and because you wanted to see me again. I didn't imagine it was because I was useful.'

Her face fell and she grabbed my arms. 'Xavier, you must know it's not like that.'

I thought of the previous time I had seen him. 'How did he come to be here? Surely the Witchfinder wouldn't deign to ask for a witch's help?' I asked, voicing my thoughts aloud.

My mind raced. I heard nothing, felt nothing but shock for a moment as something occurred to me.

'If Roger Dankworth is here now it's because he's after you, isn't it?' An icy sensation shot through me.

From the look on her face, I had struck a chord. We stared at each other as the enormity of what we had to contend with sank in.

She looked away and I sensed she was hiding something else. 'What is it?'

Briar stared at her hands, her fingers clasped.

'You brought me here to defend you and your mother's friends?' I shrugged. 'You must know I would do all I could to help all of you.'

'Would you hate me if I told you it was?'

Recovering from my self-indulgence, I reminded myself that I was willing to do everything in my power to keep them safe. I was the obvious person to help them.

'Never.' I pulled her into my arms. She was trembling. It was cruel of me not to have put her at her ease far sooner. 'I could never hate you, Briar.'

She wrapped her arms tightly around my waist and rested her head against my chest. 'You're such a good man.'

I laughed quietly. 'You clearly don't know me as well as you think.'

'I don't care what you might have done in the past. All I know is what you've done for me and how you are with those you love.'

She was so kind-hearted and innocent. I lifted her chin with my finger and pressed my lips to hers in a kiss, grateful that someone still thought of me this way.

'Never worry about telling me anything ever again,'

I insisted. 'I will always do what I can for you and for those you love.'

Briar flung her arms about my neck, surprising me, then kissed me. 'I love you, Xavier.'

I loved her too. Very much, although I wasn't worthy of such an incredible woman. I didn't reply, just held her tightly to me and kissed her again.

If I needed any incentive to build myself back to my former strength, this was it. These women had gone out of their way to save my life. I had every intention of doing my utmost to protect them from this twisted bully whose life's work seemed to be to ruin as many women as possible by branding them as witches, then sending them to the most brutal death.

Diana and Babette were witches and I realised Briar must now be one, too – giving the Witchfinder far more reason to wreak his revenge on her. She was far too precious for me to stand by and let anything happen to her.

Chapter Fifty-Three

BRIAR

The following day was warm and sunny. Xavier had been outside turning the ground in Mum's vegetable patch for over an hour while I continued working through my grandmother's spell book, fascinated by all the different spells and eager to try some of them out. Xavier had been a little more subdued since discovering that Roger Dankworth had travelled forward in time and I suspected he was making the most of having time alone to think about how best to deal with the man who had caused both of us so much trauma.

I got to my feet to go and offer him something refreshing to drink when Mum arrived home.

'Working on your spells, I see,' she said proudly.

I took her coat from her and hung it up. 'I'm enjoying learning so much,' I said, catching that yes-well-we-both-know-you-could-have-been-doing-this-three-years-before-if-you-weren't-so-stubborn look of hers I had seen on her face a few times.

I watched as she went to check the kitchen before she waved for me to join her on our worn sofa.

'It's all right, Mum, Xavier is outside, he won't be able to hear you.'

She raised an eyebrow. 'I hope he doesn't touch my herbs.'

I grinned. 'He knows not to. He just needed time alone with his thoughts and I think the gardening helps.' I waited but when she didn't elaborate on why she needed to speak to me in private I thought I'd better ask. 'What is it?'

'I bumped into Babette outside the bakery. She said she saw you and Xavier out yesterday and we agreed that although he probably feels strong enough to confront that Witchfinder, Xavier is still far too weak to take any chances just yet.'

'He's getting very frustrated, though,' I confided, keeping my voice low. 'I'm not sure how long I can persuade him to wait. After all, now we've presumed Dankworth is here to take me back as some sort of act of revenge we're all waiting for him to strike.' I wasn't sure what was worse, my paranoia about being watched or waiting for Dankworth to do his worst. The thought of him catching me alone and unawares terrified me, and I suspected Xavier and Mum too. 'And he's not the only one.'

It wasn't only the thought of Dankworth doing something dreadful that was driving me crazy. Being under the same roof as Xavier was getting a bit too much. He hadn't kissed me again, not like he had done that first time, and all I wanted to do was be alone with him. I sensed he was finding our closeness a bit of a strain too.

I thought of Xavier's need to confront Dankworth and decided to defend him. 'He's much stronger than you imagine, Mum.'

She gave me a knowing look. 'That's as maybe, but we'll only have one chance to rid ourselves of that dreadful man. We can't afford to take any risks. We're going to find a way to catch him off-guard and Xavier will need his wits about him as well as all his strength.'

She had a point. 'Fine, so what are you suggesting?'

'We continue to do our best to nurse Xavier back to full health both mentally and physically. Babette insisted on sending Jeanne here later with the best cuts of meat and fresh fish to build his strength.'

Insulted to think others didn't believe Mum and I could look after Xavier well enough by ourselves, I folded my arms and glared at her. 'We don't need her to do that. We're already giving him all the nourishment he needs.'

Mum rested a hand on my forearm. 'Don't be like that, Briar. She's only trying to help. That man being here frightens her as much as it does us. I must let her feel like she's doing something to contribute to Xavier's recovery.'

What she said made sense and I felt silly for overreacting. 'You're right. Sorry.'

'You continue to help him by walking further with him each day, maybe take more hills to strengthen his legs, that sort of thing. Fresh air and exercise are your job. I've been adding my own little something to each of his meals.'

I thought of the additions I'd been making too and grimaced.

She narrowed her eyes at me. 'Oh, Briar, I do hope we haven't been doubling up on the dosage for that poor man. What have you been giving him?'

'Nothing harmful,' I said. 'Only a little basil to help with his insomnia, calendula and aloe vera for his wounds and thyme for any iron deficiencies from his lack of food in jail as well as its healing qualities.' I smiled, amused. 'Don't worry, I didn't overstep and give him any of your tinctures. I notice you putting drops into his meals.'

She nudged me and laughed. 'Be quiet. I know what I'm doing.' Her smile faded. 'Have you broached the subject of his friend Andre yet?'

I shook my head. 'Not yet,' I admitted recalling Xavier's insistence that I should never worry about telling him anything.

'Briar, you must tell him.'

I sighed. 'I know, but he is so damaged by all he's gone through in the castle. I've caught him staring into space. I don't know how well he'll take it.'

Mum took my hand in hers. 'He's been through a lot, but he's tough and resilient. You need to do it and soon.'

I decided to take Xavier for a walk on the beach, wanting him away from the house and the risk of visitors interrupting at an inopportune moment. I went outside and watched him work for a few minutes. He had removed his shirt, and as he dug the fork into the ground I was transfixed by the muscles in his arms and his broad back, already bronzed from the past few days being in the garden. The urge to go over to him and run my hands over his warm skin was intense but I resisted, not wanting to surprise him when he was deep in thought. He really was starting to look more like the old Xavier.

He must have sensed me watching him because he stopped what he was doing and turned, his face lighting up when he saw me standing there. 'What was that sigh for?'

I felt my cheeks heat, mortified, unaware that I had made a sound. 'Sigh?'

He grinned and I sensed he knew what I was thinking. 'Did you want me?'

I did, but not in the way he meant. I reminded myself what I needed to do. 'How would you like to go for a stroll on the beach?'

'I'd like that very much.' He stabbed the fork into the earth and retrieved his discarded shirt from the top of the wall. 'I'll need to wash first, though.'

'I'll wait for you by the front door.'

'I won't be long.'

Minutes later we were walking hand in hand the short distance to the beach. It felt good having my hand in his once more. Comforting, as if we were both finally where we should be.

'It's a good thing we're going straightaway,' he said. 'It's still sunny out here but I happened to notice when I was drying myself near the window that rain is on its way from France. We might have another hour or so before it reaches the island.'

We reached the beach and after a brief discussion about whether to walk along the promenade or the sand, Xavier decided for us. 'I'd prefer to feel the sand beneath my feet.'

'Then the beach it is.'

We took off our shoes and, carrying them, walked down the nearest slipway. Reaching the warm, fine pale gold sand, Xavier stopped and dug his toes in, smiling. 'I dreamt of doing this many times when I was chained up in that place.'

We both looked up to our left at Mont Orgueil castle, looming high on the hill above the terrace of Victorian houses and Gorey pier. The castle looked so majestic yet we both knew only too well the horrors deep inside the dungeons that had been inflicted on each of us.

I shuddered. 'I've always loved that castle but now I can't shift the sense of foreboding that seeps into me whenever I look at it or think of it.' It was a shame but true.

'I'm also reminded of my time there whenever I see the castle. I know it was centuries ago now, but in my reality it has only been a few days.'

It saddened me to think that this special place had been marred forever in my heart. 'Maybe we should think about moving away from Gorey?'

He frowned, clearly confused by my suggestion. 'Move away? I don't understand.'

Of course he didn't. I had spoken without thinking. In my fantastical world I imagined the pair of us married and living on a sweet little farm elsewhere on the island, probably in the north-west in St Ouen. But how could I admit that to him? I gathered my thoughts. We weren't here to discuss my dreams, but his best friend.

I took his hand in mine waiting for him to pass the shoes he was carrying into his other hand. 'Xavier, there's something I must tell you. I brought you here so I could make sure we were alone when I did. Let's walk down to the shoreline where we can be sure no one will overhear us.'

'I suspected as much.' He knew me well.

We began walking as I considered how to share what I knew. I hated to think of him being hurt again, but what choice did I have? Eventually I gathered my thoughts.

'I need to tell you about Andre,' I said finally.

He stopped and frowned. 'Andre?'

I heard the concern in his voice and tensed at the thought of how he might react. 'He came to me, Xavier.'

'I don't understand.' I felt his hand tense in mine. Then he lowered his eyes. 'He's dead, I know.'

'He is?'

Xavier closed his eyes for a couple of seconds. 'Wren told me he'd been attacked and wasn't expected to live, that he was about to die.'

I tried to work things through in my head. 'When was this?'

He thought briefly. 'Two days before you brought me back here.' He shook his head. 'I'm not sure why the timing matters.'

I looked up into his eyes, confused. 'I'm not sure he did die after his attack. He was definitely alive the night before I brought you back, because I spoke to him.'

He took a step back. 'How?'

'I have something I need to tell you, Xavier. Shall we sit there where the sand is dry?'

He let me lead him several yards back from the water's edge. Once seated, I explained how Andre had come to me that night. Xavier didn't speak.

'That was how I knew your life was in danger,' I continued. 'Andre begged me to help you and of course I was only too willing to do as he asked.'

'Andre came to you as a ghost?' He seemed to be talking to himself despite the question directed at me. 'In the cottage?' he added. I hoped the notion comforted him.

'That's what I thought at first, but he wasn't dead.' I pictured Andre that night. 'He had a bandage around his head and told me he was unconscious, but he wasn't dead.' When

Xavier didn't respond, I added, 'I know it sounds far-fetched, but then so is us two travelling back and forth in time.'

He lay back on the sand, his hands behind his head, and stared up at the sky. 'I feel as if the world and all of us in it have gone mad.'

I knew the feeling. 'You wouldn't be alone in that.' I lay next to him resting on my elbow, my cheek on my right palm. 'I'm aware this is a lot to take in.'

He turned to me. 'How did Andre seem when he visited you?'

I thought back to that evening. 'He wasn't as distinct as if he was here with us now, but it was just like speaking to the man I met with you that first time. His kindness and love for you came through clearly. All he wanted was to warn me and make sure I understood the urgency of rescuing you before you were executed.'

'Typical Andre.' He wiped one of his eyes with the back of his hand.

'Are you all right?'

He looked away and cleared his throat. 'I am.' Turning back to me, he added, 'Andre is, was, the best of men and didn't deserve what happened to him.' He narrowed his eyes. 'Did he tell you who was behind the ambush?'

I hesitated for a moment, trying to recall everything Andre had told me that night.

'He told me of his suspicions, yes.'

There was an underlying darkness to his eyes. 'Was it Ember?'

I still couldn't believe what she had done. 'He thought so but I couldn't understand why. She loved him. He was her cousin, for pity's sake.' When he didn't react, I continued. 'She had no reason to hurt him, let alone have him almost killed.'

He looked at me with an intensity and hatred on his face I didn't recognise. 'Wren visited me and told me about Andre and her suspicions that Ember was the instigator of the attack on him. I don't know why I'm shocked that her loathing of me ran deep enough for her to do such a thing to him.' He closed his eyes momentarily before opening them and adding, 'I hope she spends the rest of her life regretting that choice.

'When I heard what she had done, at first I wanted to hunt her down and kill her with my bare hands. Then I realised that even if I was free to do that, it is exactly what Ember wanted, my attention.' He shook his head. 'Someone once told me the worst thing you can do to someone is nothing at all. And so that is all I will do as far as she's concerned.' He rested a hand on my shoulder. 'All I can do now. Anyway, her family were good people. They loved Andre and won't have taken this well. She will have been made to face her actions. If I knew them at all she will have been cast out of the family, and probably the island.'

I sensed there was more. 'He told me she was the reason you were locked up and finally about to be executed,' I said.

He gave a bitter laugh and I listened in shock as he told me how Ember had arranged for his arrest on his return to the island.

'She really is a monster. Or was,' I reminded myself.

'You have no argument from me on that score,' Xavier said.

Chapter Fifty-Four

XAVIER

We finished our walk invigorated by the fresh salty air. It still surprised me to see the impressive stone pier above Gorey harbour and below the castle with houses spanning the length of it. So different to how it had looked to me days before when I had been back in my own time. The atmosphere was like nothing I'd experienced before, calm, carefree even. I could get used to living this way. I glanced down at Briar with her tanned shoulders exposed by her summer dress and her shiny hair streaked with strands of gold by the summer sun.

I didn't even mind too much that I had no boat to sail in despite being this close to the sea. We held hands, relishing every moment together, and made our way back to the cottage. She seemed relaxed, as much as she could be knowing Roger Dankworth was lurking. Where he could be staying, I had no idea, but I didn't bother searching for him. I could hardly confront him if I didn't want locals to start asking awkward questions about where I had come from.

At least now I knew that my friend wasn't dead. I felt oddly soothed to discover Andre had appeared to Briar. Touched to know that even in his pain my friend made that effort to rescue me. I had worried about telling Briar of Andre's death, remembering she was fond of him, but now that wasn't necessary.

I watched her from the corners of my eyes as we ambled across the sand. She was so beautiful. And while I was just happy to be living in the cottage with her, I had caught her looking at me in a way that showed me she was finding it hard that we couldn't spend time alone together.

We arrived back at the cottage. Diana was out and I saw a glint in Briar's eyes that I was sure mirrored my own.

'Alone at last,' she said coyly. I suspected she was saying this now because she felt that I had recovered emotionally, or maybe she had also seen the longing in me that I had seen in her.

I watched her mouth move as she spoke and all I could think of was that I needed to kiss her again. I led her into the kitchen so that if Diana returned early and interrupted us we would have some warning. Briar smiled up at me and I saw she wanted this as much as I did.

Taking her in my arms, I slipped one hand behind her head and drew her to me, kissing her. Briar's groan intensified my passion for her even more. I felt her arms go around my neck and her soft, warm body press against me, making me wish we lived alone in the cottage.

'I missed you so much,' I whispered in between kissing her.

She immediately responded, her kisses as urgent as mine. She kissed my neck and I kissed the tanned skin over her collarbone. My body reacted instinctively. I wanted her badly.

My hand clasped her bottom and pulled her against me as we kissed. Briar murmured something and, suddenly aware of what I was about to do, I snapped back to reality.

'What am I thinking?' I whispered, my voice tight.

'What's the matter?' she asked, looking hurt.

I held her slightly away from me. 'When I love you'—I hesitated, wanting to say 'for the first time' but knowing she had no recollection of her initial visit to my time—'properly, I want it to be perfect.' Briar wasn't experienced in the ways of men. I didn't want to instigate something she might later regret. 'I shouldn't have taken advantage of you like that. I'm sorry.'

Her expression changed to one of annoyance. 'Stop being so honourable, Xavier.'

'I'm not sure "honourable" would be the best way to describe me.'

She took my face in her hands and leant in closer to me. 'I don't care what you've done in your past, Xavier. I wish you'd believe that.' I went to argue but she pressed the tips of her fingers lightly on my lips to stop me.

'Listen to me, Xavier. We have experienced many terrible things both together and apart, yet still you see me as an innocent.' Her cheeks reddened, this time in temper. 'I admit in some ways that might be true, but I've experienced enough of life. I've spent three years yearning to be with you again, and I know I want only you.'

Stunned yet relieved, I struggled to find words to reply. Eventually, my mind calmed. Briar was right. She had seen more than I knew and, more importantly, had survived everything that had been thrown at her. What right had I to decide what was best for this amazing woman? None. I smiled, unable to help myself.

'What?' she asked, the beginnings of a smile on her face too.

I pulled her into my arms once again. 'I'm sorry for presuming I could make decisions for both of us when you are more than capable of making your own choices about your life.' I kissed her lightly on her pouting lips.

Her expression softened and she returned my smile. 'I'm glad we're finally in agreement about that, Xavier Givroye.'

I let go of her and bowed low before straightening up again. 'I'm at your service, my lady.'

'And that is exactly as it should be,' she teased.

Loud banging on the front door startled us and we sprang apart.

'I'd better see who that is,' Briar said, kissing me briefly once more before hurrying to the front door.

I didn't hear what the neighbour said, leaving them to their conversation, but shortly after I heard Briar's tone change as she thanked the woman and closed the door loudly behind her.

Alarmed, I stepped out of the kitchen to ask whether she was all right and found Briar slumped on a chair, her hands over her mouth, eyes wide.

I rushed over to her, crouched and placed my hands on her knees. 'What's happened?'

She took a moment to respond. 'It's the Witchfinder, Xavier,' she said, her voice trembling, a haunted look in her eyes. 'He's ransacked Babette's secret spell room.'

'They've caught him?' I had no idea what or where this

secret room might be but hoped the police had arrested the man.

She shook her head. 'They don't know.'

I didn't understand. 'Why not?'

I listened as she explained about Babette's husband being the current Connétable of our parish. 'Connétable Le Dain knows his wife has a craft room in the basement, but not what it's really used for.'

I was stunned. 'You mean Roger Dankworth has broken into their home?'

Her eyes filled with tears. 'It was well secured with bars on the windows and not easy to find if you didn't know where to look.' She sniffed. 'It was such a magickal room too, Xavier. I only knew of its existence when I was invited there recently.' She began to cry. 'Poor Babette. Mum has gone there and they need me to help restore the place as much as possible.'

'Will I be able to join you, do you think?' I asked wanting to see for myself the damage this man had caused. 'I can help lift anything heavy for you.'

She nodded. 'I'm sure they wouldn't mind.' She wiped her eyes with her sleeve. 'After all, you know about us all being witches, which is more than any other man does.'

As we made our way to the Le Dains' home, my thoughts raced about Dankworth and why he had needed to cause this trouble for the women.

We arrived and were greeted by Diana and immediately shown down to the devastated room. I stood at the door trying to take in the extent of the damage. 'This is a message,' I said intuitively.

'It is?' Babette asked holding her arms wide. 'What could he possibly be trying to tell us by making this mess?'

I sighed. 'He's proving to you that you're not safe from him however careful you are,' I said, hating that my words would trouble them. 'He wants you to know that he will be returning, maybe not here, but he will find what he's looking for and take it with him.'

'Me, you mean?' Briar asked in a quiet voice.

I gave her an apologetic nod. 'I believe so, yes.'

Diana put an arm around Briar's shoulders. 'What can we do to stop this obsession he has with Briar?'

'I'm unsure yet, but I believe that with your powers and my help we will find a way to keep Briar and the rest of you safe from that man.'

Briar came to stand next to me. I felt her arm slip around my waist and put mine around her shoulders, hoping to comfort her.

'What are you thinking?' she asked.

'Does your coven meet openly?' She seemed confused by my question. 'Are your neighbours aware of your practices? Do you keep your meetings secret from non-members?'

Babette nodded. 'We're very secretive about everything to do with it.'

'Then Roger Dankworth will have a hold over you all. He will make it his business to discover what he can, then blackmail you because you won't want your secret becoming common knowledge.' Briar began to speak but I continued, determined to say my piece. 'All he needs to do is threaten to make your secret known, Briar. I've seen your local paper. To put a piece in the *Evening Post* would ensure the entire island knows your business.'

She blanched. 'That would be disastrous, especially for Babette. Mum and I are used to people whispering about us, but she has standing here. It would ruin her marriage, and I can't have that on my conscience.'

I looked in turn at Babette, Diana, Briar, Jeanne and a fifth woman I'd heard one of them call Winnie. 'If we are to find a way to stop him, we must be completely open with each other. No secrets.'

Briar gave me a reassuring smile. 'That man almost succeeded in having me killed in the worst possible way.' She shuddered and I tightened my hold on her to remind her I was there for her and not going anywhere. 'I still have nightmares about him,' she admitted quietly.

I hated to think she was tormented by that man even in her sleep.

'We will find a way to stop him, Briar,' Babette insisted.

I nodded my agreement. 'I'm sure we will.'

Chapter Fifty-Five

BRIAR

Back home at the cottage, Xavier and I sat outside, each with a mug of tea. My hands travelled slowly over his back and I could tell that, even though he was finally regaining some of the weight he had lost during his incarceration, he still had a way to go to return to his former fitness. But there was no more time left for his recovery, not now Dankworth had shown that he would soon be coming for me.

'Briar, you do trust me, don't you?'

I saw the earnest look on his face and nodded. I trusted him with my life. That calmed me slightly. 'You know I do, Xavier. With all my heart.'

He seemed satisfied. 'I'm happy to hear you say so.'

Someone knocked on the front door, making me jump.

I was about to answer it but Xavier rose. 'I shall see who has come.'

I waited anxiously for him to answer the door. It wasn't a familiar knock, and Mum had just let herself in. It had been a heavy knock too, I realised, and probably a man's.

I watched as Xavier opened the door, but I was unable to see the person because Xavier's body blocked my line of vision.

There was a momentary silence. 'I'm looking for Briar Le Gros,' a voice I recognised said, sounding suspicious, probably because he wondered why a man he didn't know was answering the door.

'Henry, is that you?' I called, standing and going to join them. 'Xavier, this is my friend. Come in, Henry. It's wonderful to see you again.'

The men looked each other up and down before Xavier stepped back and gave Henry space to enter the cottage.

'Would you like something to drink?' I asked, noticing their mutual distrust. 'Or maybe to eat?' I motioned for Henry to take a seat at the table but he shook his head. For the first time I realised his expression was serious and also that it had little to do with Xavier.

'No, thank you,' he said, looking at Xavier again. 'If you wouldn't mind, I was hoping to speak to you alone.'

Henry and I had something of a personal nature to discuss, so I felt this was something he could relay to me in front of Xavier.

'Xavier is a very old friend of mine,' I explained, although from the look on Henry's face he was dubious. 'I don't mind you speaking in front of him.'

He hesitated and looked from Xavier to me. 'In that case, I've come to warn you about someone.'

Surprised, I pressed my right palm to my chest. What now?

He paused before continuing. 'I've spotted a man watching you on more than one occasion. I asked my mother whether I might be overreacting in coming to tell you, but when I described him she admitted he sounded like the man who had stopped her on a lane a few mornings ago and pushed her into a ditch when she went to walk past.'

Horrified, I exchanged glances with Xavier. 'Oh, my word, is Winnie all right?' I thought back to seeing her at Babette's and realised that although she looked unharmed, she did seem very nervous. I had put that down to seeing the damage to the spell room.

'She is,' he said, glowering. 'If I get my hands on the man I'll have something to say to him.' He clenched his fists and I guessed he didn't mean to exchange words. He stared at me. 'You've also seen this man too?'

I nodded. 'As has Xavier.'

He looked at the pair of us aghast. 'Do you know who he is then?

'He's not from here,' I said, not wishing to explain much more about him. 'His name is Roger Dankworth and you're right, he is trouble.'

I glanced at Xavier but his face remained expressionless. I assumed it was because he didn't think it right to share everything we knew.

Henry frowned and studied Xavier for a moment. 'Is that why you're here? To protect Briar?'

'Yes, partly,' Xavier replied.

I rested a hand on Henry's arm. 'Thank you for coming to tell me. It's lovely to see you again. Are you staying here in Jersey for a while?'

'I'm not sure what I'm doing just yet, but I won't be leaving too soon. I want to spend some time with Mum before I move on anywhere.' He smiled, pushing his sandy hair from his eyes. 'You seem to have everything in hand, but do let me know if you ever need my help.'

'I promise I will.' I leant forward and kissed his cheek. 'And thank you for being a true friend.'

'Always. You mean too much to me for me to stand by and do nothing.'

'I know.' And I did. Henry was a kind, sweet man and I knew he had feelings for me – had always done, but I couldn't reciprocate emotions I didn't feel, especially having met and fallen for Xavier.

My mother had mentioned a couple of times how Winnie had confided to her that thinking of me had kept Henry going during the war. Henry had never told me this himself and I guessed he would be embarrassed if he found out I had been told about it. But we all knew now that life was too short for pretence, especially when it came to matters of the heart. I hoped Henry would meet someone else to fall in love with and enjoy the future he yearned for, one that I couldn't give him.

'It was good to meet you, Xavier,' he said.

'Likewise,' Xavier said.

'I'll leave you both to your day then,' Henry said before leaving without another word.

'Poor man,' Xavier said, staring at the door Henry had pulled shut. 'He's in love with you.' He sounded forlorn.

'I believe so.'

Xavier turned to me. 'If you have feelings for that fellow, Briar, I want you to follow them. Your heart is precious, and we both know I'm not the person your mother would choose for you.'

I stared at him in frustration before punching his left arm.

Had he not listened to anything I'd said about my feelings for him?

'Ouch.' He grabbed hold of his arm and laughed. 'That hurt.'

'Don't you ever say anything like that to me again. I love you very much and have done ever since I met you. I'm fond of Henry, like I was of Andre, like a brother. There's no comparison between how I feel about him and how I feel about you.'

His dark eyes peered into mine with an intensity that almost made me forget my train of thought.

Xavier needed to know in no uncertain terms that he was the only man for me. 'Even before your return, when I assumed I had lost you forever, there was only one man for me, Xavier, and that man was you.' I laid my hand on his cheek. 'I would rather be alone than be with anyone else.'

His hand covered mine. 'I know you're saying this to make me feel better,' he said, his voice hoarse. 'But it upsets me to hear that you might have ended up without anyone to love you.'

'I'm not saying this to please you,' I insisted. 'I'm telling you this because it's how I feel.' I stood on tiptoe and kissed him. 'I'd rather be lonely than with a man I didn't love.'

A thought occurred to me. 'I'm not sure whether to be concerned that others have also seen Dankworth watching me. Or do you think it's a good thing that we're not the only ones who've seen him?'

'I do. It's also reassuring to know they don't trust him either.'

He had a point.

Chapter Fifty-Six

XAVIER

I knew Briar meant every word. Struck by the intensity of her love for me, I wanted to devote my life to forging a future for us, but she deserved so much more than I could give her. I kissed her several times.

'What's the matter?' she whispered, when we eventually stopped.

'Your feelings for me are a weight I am unsure I can bear.'

She frowned and took a step back from me. 'What do you mean by that?'

Hating to think my words had unintentionally hurt her, I tried to take her in my arms once more but she slapped them away. 'No. I want to know what you meant.'

I decided to speak my mind. 'I love that you reciprocate my deep love for you.'

'Go on.'

I saw suspicion in her beautiful eyes and forced myself to continue. 'I have done many bad things, though, Briar.' She went to speak but I continued before she managed to say anything. 'No, listen to me. You know the private me, the Xavier I share with you. But you've never seen me kill someone.' I saw her wince and wanted to stop and take back my words but I needed to be open with her, for I was certain I would never love another as completely as I did Briar. 'It's true, my love. I have done bad things.' I thought of Henry and his earnestness. 'Not like your friend. Unlike him, I am not worthy of your love, Briar. I want to be, but I worry that I can only bring you pain, loss and inevitably a lonely future.'

She stared at me thoughtfully and for a moment I thought she was about to cry. 'Are you trying to tell me you want to return to your own time?'

Shocked she thought such a thing, I shook my head. 'What? No. Never.'

Her gaze hardened. 'All these things you've said about yourself might be true,' she said, surprising me. 'You might have done bad things, but you've also done the most incredible things, mostly for other people. You've rescued me, twice.' She rolled her eyes. 'And I hope I will do so for a final time when we banish Roger Dankworth forever.' She shrugged. 'You spent time in France rescuing those women.

'I've also witnessed Andre's love for you. Andre, bless his soul, was a truly decent man, one of the best I've met. A man like him could never love the man you believe yourself to be.'

I mulled over her words. She was right about Andre being decent. I couldn't bear for her to discover one day something about me that killed her love for me. Hoping to force her to understand what I meant, I held out my hands. 'These have killed many men, Briar. They are stained with blood. Even though it might not be visible to you now, I still feel it.'

She frowned. 'Don't you think Henry has killed people too,

Xavier? He's also fought in a war.' She threw her hands in the air. 'If I was a man I would have done so too. You can't hold on to that guilt.' Briar leant forward and, placing her hands on her hips, brought her face closer to mine. 'If you love me, then good. If you don't, be honest about it, because me loving you is unconditional.'

'You don't understand.'

'I do. I've lived through a war, don't forget. I would have done anything to save Mum during the Occupation. Things I'd never probably consider doing during peacetime. Anyway, if something happens to you, I'll survive. I won't want to, but we both know I can because I've done it before when my mother and Babette brought me back just before I was to be executed.'

Briar's words reminded me of her incredible strength and fortitude of character. She was also right. I was using her love for me as an excuse not to give in to my feelings for her – not completely. I realised she saw through me and all my insecurities.

'Xavier, I love you, but I don't need you. If ever there comes a time when you no longer wish to be with me, all it will take is for you to tell me and I'll walk away.'

'That easily?' I couldn't hide my shock.

She laughed. 'No, it would be anything but easy, but I would do it. I don't want my love being a burden to you. I am an independent woman, Xavier. This isn't the 1640s, this is 1946.'

'It is strange to me that so much has changed for women in the past three hundred years.'

'That's as maybe. Women are more independent now than they have ever been. We've had to help keep this island running, as have women in other countries, like they did in the

Great War. We can do anything we put our minds to.' She jutted her chin proudly. 'Well, almost anything, but you should know by now how forceful a woman can be.'

I knew by the determined look in her green eyes that our conversation was at an end. I loved how her delicate beauty belied her strength. She was a surprise in so many ways. I hoped we did have a future together because I knew without doubt that it would be endlessly fascinating.

Chapter Fifty-Seven

DIANA

I was still shocked by Winnie's experience with that Roger Dankworth fellow. He was becoming bolder in his vengeful destruction, and I worried what he might do next.

Briar had been spending a lot of time with Xavier over the last few days, taking longer and longer walks on the beach. I decided to make use of that. She would be safest in his company while I worked with Babette, Winnie and Jeanne to come up with a plan to rid ourselves of this dreadful man – something that was becoming more urgent with every passing day. The very thought of him in our village sent shivers down my spine.

'That there could still be someone around with such hatred in their heart who wants to hurt us all simply because of us practising our craft shocks me,' Jeanne declared when the coven gathered one night in the woods.

'I'm just grateful Briar spotted him. I was shocked to my core when my Henry told me he'd noticed him watching her, too,' Winnie said, clasping her hands together. 'Even more so, though, when he shoved me into that ditch.'

I put an arm around Winnie's shoulders, hating to see her in distress.

'Briar can't have mentioned anything about him being a Witchfinder, though. Or maybe she did and Henry worried about sharing that bit with me? What do you think, Diana?'

'I believe she kept it from him because she knew it was up to you to let your son know if you are part of the coven,' I suggested, believing that to be the case.

Winnie sighed. 'That's a relief. I wouldn't want him to know. He's a lovely boy, my Henry, but people sometimes don't take information like this as you would hope.'

We all nodded our agreement. Hadn't I been guilty of keeping my practices secret from my own husband? I only confided in Briar when she was old enough to join us at eighteen, although she had known some of it, having grown up helping me forage and prepare some of my spells. My heart warmed to think how she instinctively knew to keep my practices to herself.

She was one of us now, though, and I was relieved. Or at least I had been until this man Roger Dankworth made an unexpected entrance into our lives.

'Enough chatter, ladies.' Babette clapped quietly. 'We might feel safe in this area of the woods, but it's never sensible to be complacent, especially now we all know he's one to lurk in the shadows.'

Each of us looked about us into the trees, shoulders tensing.

Keeping her voice low so that only we could hear, Babette continued. 'We have urgent business – a plan to rid ourselves and our beautiful island of this man and put an end to his viciousness and his threats against Briar and all we stand for. We need to ready ourselves to take action now that young Xavier Givroye has recovered enough to help us.'

'I agree,' Winnie said. 'But how are we going to do it?'

I felt compelled to speak. 'I'm certain we'll have only one chance. According to my daughter he has many years of experience preying on women. If we mess up in any way, then who knows what permanent damage he can do to us.'

The others winced at my words, which might have been harsh but as far as I was concerned were completely necessary. If they couldn't listen without being intimidated, then how would they cope facing up to the man?

'Diana is right,' Babette said. 'We have no time to waste. First we need to create an identical talisman for each of us for protection against his evil, and a protection spell. We'll make one for Xavier too, as I presume we will need him to join us. Then we work on finding the right spell to send him back through time.'

One of the other women agreed. 'I sense this man's power is far greater than anything we have come up against before.'

'How shall we begin?' Jeanne asked.

I listened as Babette gave each of us orders of different herbs and items that needed to be collected. I couldn't dispel the dread seeping into my bones. At least Briar and I were among friends I could trust completely. I needed to save the coven but my greatest task would be to ensure Briar's safety. She had escaped this man's clutches before; someone like him would have felt his humiliation keenly and would not rest until he had meted out his revenge.

I wondered how people had reacted to Briar's disappearance under his watch. Not once, but twice. Surely his integrity must have been questioned, which could only have added to his fury? If so, how would that have affected a man who valued his power over others? Had they feared him less? All my questions just made me more certain that he would not stop until he had destroyed my daughter. My heart raced.

'He might want to ruin us for the imagined slight to his sister centuries ago,' I said, reminding them of the story we had discussed recently. 'Mostly, though, he knows how badly we would feel should he kidnap Briar and take her back with him.' As I spoke I heard others murmur their fears. I knew I was right. 'He wants to use her as an example of what he is capable of to anyone who dares to defy him.'

I became lightheaded with the realisation and lowered my face into my hands.

Winnie rested a soothing hand on my back. 'Now, now, Diana. Don't distress yourself in this way. We are all in this together. We are strong and powerful women and now is not the time to doubt what we can do.'

'Yes,' Jeanne agreed. 'And I think we've all seen how quickly Briar is learning her craft,' she said, sounding impressed. 'I believe she has powers far exceeding most witches.'

I thought of my mother's prophecy for Briar once again. 'I have a feeling you could be right, Jeanne.'

Chapter Fifty-Eight

BRIAR

The following day, Xavier and I finished dropping off a couple of parcels to Mum's clients and, after going for one of our regular walks, returned to the cottage to find Mum and Babette sitting at the table. They weren't smiling and I knew instantly this wasn't a social visit but something far more serious.

'We've been waiting for you,' Mum said, her tone sombre.

'What's happened now?' I asked, dreading her response. I wasn't sure why I was asking when I had a good idea already.

'Sit down, the pair of you,' Mum said. 'Babette and I have something to talk to you about.'

We did as they asked, waiting to hear more.

'There's a storm forecast,' Babette announced. 'It's due tomorrow night.'

'Which is good,' Mum said. 'Because we'll be able to work under the cover of darkness.'

Shocked, I caught Xavier's eye. 'Sorry,' I said, asking what I guessed might be on his mind. 'Are you saying we'll need to put our plans into action tomorrow night?'

As much as I longed for Roger Dankworth to be banished from our lives, I couldn't help being frightened by what might happen.

'What choice do we have?' Mum replied impatiently. 'We must grab the chance when he least expects it.'

Xavier took my hand under the table and rested it on his thigh. 'I agree. We have no choice but to take advantage of the weather,' he said gently. 'Who knows when the next storm will come, and what damage he might have achieved by then.'

'But Xavier, you're not nearly strong enough yet,' I insisted, conscious that he would sacrifice himself for me if necessary and frightened to lose him if anything went wrong.

'He's right, Briar. We must work with what we have,' Babette insisted. 'I know the timing isn't ideal but there's no time to waste.'

I felt him tense. 'I'm happy to do whatever you need.'

Anxious for his safety, I couldn't hold back my concerns. I looked at Mum, then at Babette. 'He isn't strong enough to deal with that madman so soon.'

Xavier's hand tightened slightly. I frowned at him. 'You're not, Xavier. We both know that.'

His eyes were gentle as he stared at me. 'I'm stronger than you suppose. Anyway,' he added when I went to argue, 'I've spent years fighting, and, as the ladies have said, what choice do we have?'

'Neither of us wishes any harm to come to Xavier,' Mum said. 'But we've weighed up the pros and cons and the only conclusion we came to is that it must be tomorrow night.'

My temper and my fear for Xavier were rising and I could

barely remain seated and listen to their arguments. Pulling my hand from Xavier's, I stood up so quickly my chair screeched across the tiled floor. 'Don't any of you care that Xavier will be risking his life?'

I glared at Mum and saw she had already considered this eventuality. I gasped. 'He might die, Mum,' I said, my voice thin with fear. 'Or end up being sucked back in time with that dreadful man, whose cruelty knows no bounds.' Mum went to speak but I carried on, determined to say my piece. 'Because if either of you thinks Roger Dankworth is going to go quietly then you're mistaken.'

'I'm sorry, Briar. We really don't want to put Xavier at any risk but if we are to be free of this man we have little choice.'

Unable to bear listening anymore, I ran out of the cottage needing to be alone. I looked left then right, unable to decide which way to go – not that it made any difference.

I heard the cottage door slam and knew Xavier had followed me. Refusing to look back, I hurried away with little thought about where I was headed.

'Briar, wait.'

I didn't slow down, too angry with him for giving in to their preposterous idea. His hand took my arm and slowed me down. I stopped and turned on him, beside myself with fear.

'Don't try to persuade me this is a good idea.'

Looking around us, he led me down one of the small entryways between two cottages. When we were alone, he pushed me gently back against a house wall. For a few seconds we just stared at each other. I breathed in his familiar scent, agonised that the future I yearned for with him could be taken away so soon.

'Briar,' he said quietly, kissing me lightly on my forehead, his voice gentle and low. 'I understand why you're angry, but we both know I must do this.'

I looked up into his beautiful dark blue eyes and my temper vanished. He was right. I wasn't angry with Mum, Babette or him, but with Roger Dankworth and the universe for allowing that vile man back into our lives. My fear for Xavier's safety, and for the loss of what we had only just rediscovered, overwhelmed me. 'But I love you too much to let you go again.' I began to cry.

He placed a finger under my chin and gently raised it. 'I'm also not ready to let you go,' he whispered. 'But I'm more frightened about him kidnapping you when I'm not there and taking you back in time where I can't reach you. As far as I can see, I have no choice but to act when I have the opportunity.'

He took me in his arms and held me against him, stroking my hair and kissing my forehead. 'I promise you I will find the strength to fight this devil.'

'I believe you will do your best,' I admitted. 'But what if he manages to take you back with him somehow?' I sniffed. 'They'll execute you immediately this time and there'll be no chance of you being brought back here again.'

'That won't happen,' he said soothingly. 'I'll make sure it won't.'

I wanted to believe him. 'And how do you suppose you'll do that?'

He thought for a couple of seconds. 'The four of us will make a plan. You mustn't worry.' He kissed me again. 'I think we should return to the cottage. I left your mother and Mrs Le Dain aghast when I ran after you. It was impolite of me to leave without bidding them goodbye.'

I smiled despite myself. 'Whether you like to think so or not, Xavier,' I teased, 'you really can't help being a gentleman.'

He smiled. 'Sometimes I surprise myself.'

Chapter Fifty-Nine

DIANA

'Try not to fret about Briar,' Babette said. 'I'm sure that strapping man of hers will do his best to talk sense into her.'

'I hope so.' I was also concerned for Xavier. He might have only lived with us a relatively short time but he made my daughter happy as well as more settled. He even felt like part of the family now. I completely trusted him as far as Briar's safety was concerned. I didn't wish to see anything happen to him, or for him to end up departing again and leaving Briar inconsolable.

As far as I could see we had little choice, and, going by Xavier's reaction when we explained about the storm, he was in agreement with us.

'While we wait for Briar and Xavier, we must work on our plan to trick Roger Dankworth and get him to the castle just before the storm hits the island.'

'I have a feeling there's only one person he's desperate enough to catch who can do that for us.' I heard the regret in

Babette's voice and knew she meant Briar. 'As much as I struggle to think of Briar acting as bait, I know it is our best option.'

'What are you talking about?' Briar asked, surprising us by her appearance.

I looked at Xavier. He waited for Briar to sit down with him. 'I think the idea is that you entice the Witchfinder up to the castle, and once he's there the coven do their work, while I ensure he doesn't escape.' He addressed me and Babette from across the table. 'Is that correct?'

Hearing Xavier speak so matter-of-factly steadied me slightly. I watched Briar consider the plan.

'You don't have to do anything you're not comfortable with,' I assured her.

Briar sighed. 'I have no hesitation in doing it,' she said. 'None of us can get on with our lives properly while he's hanging around.'

'Don't feel you have to,' Babette said.

Briar shrugged. 'If you're all putting your safety at risk then I should too. After all, this man is here because of me.'

'He's here because of what he perceives our coven to have done to his sister,' Babette said. 'You just happen to be the most important witch among us because you and Diana are the only two in the coven who are related. And as your mother's closest friend and your High Priestess, you are important to me, too. That is what makes you so valuable to him.'

Briar pursed her lips. 'I probably want him gone even more than you do having seen first-hand the depths he's capable of sinking to.' She sat back in her chair. 'Please, tell me the rest of the plan.'

Unsure whether to be relieved or concerned, I focused on

talking her and Xavier through our plans. 'Babette and I have been tweaking your grandmother's ancient banishing spell with Winnie and Jeanne. It's almost ready. Most importantly we'll need two mirrors to set a portal to send him back, just in case the ruin's magickal elements aren't strong enough for some reason.'

'No problem, I'll get those.' Briar beamed. 'I'm excited to be using Granny's spell. I'll feel safer knowing her magick is around us when we do this.'

The idea comforted me, too.

Briar frowned thoughtfully. 'We need to track him down so that I can set him up to follow me. He has to believe this is his idea or he won't take the bait.'

'That makes sense,' Babette agreed. 'Each of us can spend time apart around the village and send a message to you when one of us finds him.'

'Yes,' Briar said. 'I'll then go there with Xavier and pretend to be shopping or just walking or something.' She rolled her eyes. 'We all know Roger Dankworth enjoys lurking in shadows. I'll make my journey to the castle known.' She bit her lower lip as an idea occurred to her. 'I can say I'm going up there to try out a spell by myself.'

Xavier beamed at her proudly. 'That's an excellent idea. He won't be able to resist catching you in the act. It'll confirm his belief that you are a witch.'

'Then that's what we'll do,' I said, satisfied that we had all agreed.

'Winnie, Diana and I will be up at the castle with you,' Babette assured her. 'The three other members of our coven will be in the woods. They'll be increasing our powers by tuning in to what we're doing and chanting and casting their own spells to add strength and protection to yours.'

I had an idea. 'You'll need to be believable, Briar,' I said as my idea took shape in my head. 'When you get there take your tools out of your bag and set everything up for the spell. Then, when Babette arrives, everything will be in place for us to cast the spell.'

'Sounds good,' Briar said.

'We need to ensure everything is ready for when the storm strikes and the electricity in the air is at its strongest.'

'That's right, Diana,' Babette agreed. 'When it's at its height, we'll strike. It'll ensure we have the most power behind us. You, Xavier, will bar him from leaving the ruin if he gets wind of our presence. You can also ensure this man doesn't drag Briar back to the seventeenth century with him.'

I shuddered at the thought. 'There must be no margin for error where that's concerned, Briar. Do you understand?'

'Yes, Mum. Don't worry, I have no wish to go back there either. Last time was enough for me.'

I saw her turn to Xavier. 'We'll look out for each other, won't we? If each of us plays our part well we stand a better chance of succeeding.'

'We have no choice but to succeed,' Xavier said, giving her a comforting smile. 'Then we can relax and finally start living our lives.'

I noticed something pass between them. An unspoken agreement – as if they had already talked about their hopes for the future.

I liked the idea. I had loved my husband very much and wanted more than anything for my sweet daughter to experience happiness as I had. I realised that having an ex-privateer from the past as a son-in-law wasn't anything I could ever have expected, let alone hoped for. But Xavier had proved himself to be a truly decent man and above all he loved my daughter with a passion that was unmistakable. I trusted he would protect her. It was enough for me.

'Now we're all in agreement,' Babette said, 'I think we should go through everything step by step. We can't afford to leave anything to chance if this is to go perfectly.'

'Good idea,' I agreed.

Xavier leant forward, resting his elbows on the table, his fingers intertwined with Briar's. 'You can do this, Briar.'

'I know I can,' she replied with a certainty I had never seen before.

Chapter Sixty

BRIAR

That evening the storm still hadn't arrived. I checked and rechecked the spell finding it difficult to contain my frustration.

'Stop fretting over that spell, Briar,' Mum grumbled. 'If you need to keep busy come and help peel these potatoes with Xavier.'

Happy to work next to the man I loved, I put my spell book down, telling myself I would not forget the incantation, however terrified I was when I found myself in the Witchfinder's company again.

Xavier helped Mum and me prepare supper in our cramped kitchen. We talked him through the plan yet again, he listened patiently, and I began to feel a little calmer.

'You'll be fine,' he whispered when someone knocked on the door and we were left alone.

'I hope you're right.'

'I am.' He gave me a puzzled look. 'I understand your

trepidation about confronting him, but I have a feeling you don't have the confidence in yourself that others have in you to carry out the spell.'

Xavier's comment bolstered me. The women in the coven did believe I could cast the spell successfully. 'You're right, they do trust me to do this,' I said with conviction, 'and I have no intention of failing them.'

'I'm so proud of you,' he said as he placed his knife and potato on the worktop. He wiped his hands on a tea towel before resting them on my shoulders. 'Briar, I know almost nothing about witchcraft but even I can sense a power in you that's out of this world. I honestly believe you'll be fine.'

I wrapped my arms around him, resting my head on his chest, relishing being held tightly by him. 'Thank you for believing in me.'

'Always.' He kissed the top of my head just as Mum entered the room.

'Henry's here,' she said, giving me an odd look.

I looked up at Xavier, unsure why Henry would come to the house this late, and we followed Mum back into the living room. Henry did look very serious about something.

I tensed. 'Nothing else has happened to your mum, I hope?'

He shook his head. 'No, it's not that.'

He seemed sort of sheepish yet somehow determined, and I was intrigued to discover his reason for coming.

'I overheard Mum and Jeanne speaking earlier and I know what you're planning to do, Briar.'

Mum looked at me, widening her eyes just enough for me to realise what she was thinking.

'I assume you know to keep this to yourself,' Mum said.

'Of course. I wouldn't tell a soul.' He glowered at her. 'Anything that can be done to rid this island of that man is fine by me. In fact, that's why I'm here.'

'Go on,' I said, intrigued.

'I want to be there when you banish him.'

'No.' I hadn't meant to sound sharp, but apart from his mum being pushed into the ditch by Roger Dankworth, Henry had nothing to do with what we had planned. 'Sorry, Henry.'

'Briar, please.'

I shook my head. 'There will be enough of us there, and any more might cause suspicion among other islanders who might be passing.'

He was about to argue, but Mum stepped forward, one arm outstretched to lead him to the door. 'Henry, if you wouldn't mind, we need to continue preparing our supper. I'm sure Winnie will tell you what happens when the spell has been cast and she returns home.'

Henry and I both knew from experience Mum's tone meant she wasn't open for argument. He looked over at me, then at Xavier, gave a nod and left quietly.

'How does he know about Winnie being a witch?' I asked, surprised. Winnie had always made a point of not telling her son, often reminding us that she didn't want him to know.

'Winnie told me that on his return to the island Henry admitted seeing her cast a spell before he went to war. She was a bit taken aback but is apparently fine with him knowing now.' She looked at me. 'Briar, I understand you not wanting unnecessary people when we do this, but Henry is one of your dearest friends and we both know all he wants is to help ensure your safety. I think that's very sweet of him.'

'It is, Mum.'

'Well, I don't know about the two of you, but I'm hungry. Shall we get on with making our supper then?'

'That sounds like a good idea,' Xavier said. He finished peeling the last potato and put it down on the watery mess next to the damp newspaper on the worktop where we'd been collecting the potato peelings.

Then he looked at us both very seriously. 'Briar has seen some of what Roger Dankworth is capable of, but not everything. I can assure you he is extremely cunning and dangerous.'

Mum shot a panicked look my way.

'I'm not exaggerating, Diana,' he insisted. 'I worry that if Briar goes into that ruin alone with him, there's no way she's coming out again. At least not in this century. He wants to take her back to his time and have her executed as a witch as retribution for all he blames your coven for doing against his sister, and as payback for Briar humiliating him by twice escaping his clutches.'

'What are you trying to say, Xavier?' Mum clasped the wooden spoon tightly in her hand, unaware that meat juices from the roast lamb were dripping onto the floor.

I was about to argue that I would surround myself with a protection spell but realised Xavier hadn't finished.

'Even with my experience fighting,' Xavier continued, 'I couldn't say for certain that I will be able to ensure your safety.'

'I'm not sure the plan is safe enough now,' Mum said crossing her arms, her lips pressed together, showing me she wasn't going to listen to any argument from me.

Irritated with Xavier's outburst, I groaned. 'What exactly are you trying to say?'

'Only that it might be a good idea to have Henry there as backup, just in case the Witchfinder overpowers me.'

I realised Xavier really was very frightened for me. 'Fine,' I said agreeing that having Henry there was probably a good idea. 'You can tell him he's allowed to join us, if you like.'

Chapter Sixty-One

XAVIER

I couldn't recall the last time I felt unsure of my ability to overpower someone. I was almost back to full strength but I had no intention of risking Briar's life. She was far too precious to me to take any chances. I was relieved when she agreed to allow Henry to come along, and was cheerfully walking up the hill to his and Winnie's home, longing for the entire sordid banishment to be over with.

I reached the black front door and knocked.

'Coming,' Henry called, seconds before he pulled back the door. 'Xavier! What are you doing here?'

'May I come in?' I asked, not wishing to be overheard.

He seemed surprised. 'Yes, of course. Please do.'

I followed him into a living room, shaking my head when he asked if I wanted to take a seat or have some refreshment. 'No, thank you. I'll only be a short while.'

His face coloured. 'I'm sorry if you felt I stepped out of line last night. It's only that, well, I care for Briar deeply. Always have done.' He turned to face the empty fireplace. 'You're the last person I should be admitting this to, but the truth of it is that I love Briar.' I wasn't surprised, having seen the desperation on his face the previous evening. He turned back to me. 'I'm sorry, Xavier, but that's just how I feel.' He raised a hand. 'I'm under no illusions that she reciprocates my affections, though. As much as that saddens me, it's impossible to miss how in love you both are and I'm glad she's happy.'

I waited to be certain he had said all he needed to. 'Henry, I am aware of your feelings for Briar. Or at least I suspected this to be the case.' I smiled to show I bore no ill feeling towards him. 'She is a special woman and we are lucky to know her,' I said, not wishing to dwell on the fact that we both loved her, although I was the man she had chosen to be with.

He pushed his hands into his trouser pockets. 'I'm sorry – I don't mean to be rude but I don't understand why you're here.'

I smiled. 'I've spoken to Briar and Diana and they agree with me that we should take you up on your offer to be there when the spell is cast.'

His face lit up. 'You did that for me?'

I laughed. 'I did it for Briar's sake, and probably for mine too.'

He withdrew his hands and, taking my right one in both of his, shook it vigorously. 'Thank you, Xavier. You are a good man. I appreciate this.'

I returned to Honey Bee Cottage and told Briar how grateful Henry had been to hear the news.

'That's a relief.' She took my hand in hers. 'I also have news.'

'You do?' I asked, intrigued to discover what had happened in the short time I had been away from the cottage.

'Yes. The forecast is for storms tomorrow evening and I need you to accompany me into the village. Jeanne has popped round to let us know that Roger Dankworth was seen walking past the stream by the edge of the green.'

I thought of the green that stretched halfway along the side of the village, and the ducks that paddled about in the stream. 'Then that's where we need to go for a walk and chat about your plans for this spell you're casting.' I gave her a wink and kissed her, trying my best to appear jovial despite my concern for her safety.

Just as Jeanne had reported, we saw his tall slim figure walking slowly by the side of the stream. I spotted the subtle change in his stance when he noticed us as we turned the corner. Not wishing him to think we were trying to entice him, we went right onto the green instead of in his direction, certain he would end up following us.

As soon as I was satisfied he wasn't far behind I put the first part of our plan into action.

'I'm just not happy about you doing this, Briar,' I said sounding angry.

She gave me a fleeting look of surprise at my tone, then looked ahead and continued the act. 'That's just too bad, Xavier. I've been working on this spell for a while now and whether you like it or not I'm going to be practising it up at the ruin by the castle tomorrow night.'

'But what if someone sees you there?'

'I'm not reckless,' she said, giving an annoyed sniff. 'I know to be careful.'

'Won't you let me come with you?' I pleaded.

She stopped walking and I heard the crunch of Dankworth's feet as they stopped unexpectedly on the gravelly pathway. I caught the glint of amusement in Briar's eyes and had to concentrate not to give in to my own. It felt good to fool this man, but I had to be careful not to let him perceive that this was a trap.

'I've told you several times now that I want to do this by myself. I've not been a witch for long and need to practise. I can't do that with someone looking over my shoulder.'

'Fine,' I said, glowering at her.

'Fine,' she snapped, marching off ahead of me. I waited a moment before following. We reached halfway along the green and turned right into the lane, giving me the opportunity to take a peek through the trees to see if he was still behind us. He wasn't.

'Do you think that worked?' she asked, linking her arm through mine.

I grinned. 'I certainly do.'

Chapter Sixty-Two

BRIAR

Xavier and I were lying on the bed in each other's arms. Every time I was alone with him the temptation to take things further became more intense, as did our kisses. No doubt our passion for each other was intensified by our fear that tonight's events could possibly part us forever.

'You're trembling,' he said, holding me closer to him, my head resting on his chest. 'I promise I will do all I humanly can to protect you.'

'I know.' I also knew that if his love was all it took to keep me from Dankworth's clutches then I would never be unsafe again, but life wasn't that simple. 'I'm grateful to have you but also to know Mum and her coven will be working their hardest to make sure everything goes according to plan.'

He bent his head down as I looked up at him and our lips met in another kiss.

There was a knock at the door. Shocked to realise Mum was home when we hadn't expected her back from her rounds for another hour at least, we sat up and scooted over to the edge of the bed.

I hurriedly straightened my clothes and ran my fingers through my hair while Xavier did the same. He leapt to his feet and stood by the door.

Mum knocked again. 'I know you're in there.'

I gave Xavier a nod and he opened the door. 'Diana, I—' he began but she shook her head. 'No time for that,' she said clearly unfazed by us both being in my bedroom.

'It's tonight, isn't it?' I asked fearfully.

'I'm afraid so,' she whispered. 'The storm should be reaching its peak around seven or seven-thirty. We're to meet up at Jeanne's first, across from the castle green. When we know that man has followed you up there, we'll be right behind him.'

Butterflies began swooping and crashing into each other in the depths of my stomach. The reality of what I was about to face washed over me. 'I'm nervous,' I admitted. 'Terrified', was more accurate, but I didn't want to make Mum worry any more than she already was.

She came further into my room and sat on the edge of my bed next to me. Taking my hand in hers, she smiled. 'We've gone over and over the plan and everyone knows the part they must play. There's no need to worry.'

'I must admit I am frightened about how this will pan out.'

'Don't forget, with your help we've perfected the banishing spell. In fact,' she said, looking at Xavier, 'I need the pair of you to join me downstairs, please. I've made something for you both to wear. I'm taking no chances.'

I could tell Xavier wasn't sure what Mum had prepared for us but suspected he would do as she asked. We followed her to the living room and watched as she picked up an amulet in each hand. Both were made with two crystals. She held them up and I could see they were as similar as crystals could be.

I took one of them by its thin silver chain from which the two crystals hung. 'Bloodstone and amethyst, if I'm not mistaken,' I said, giving her a kiss on the cheek. 'For protection, am I right?'

'You are. Yours is the same, Xavier. I want you both to wear them from now or at least until tonight's events are concluded.'

I slipped mine over my head and saw him do the same.

'Thank you, Diana.'

Satisfied, Mum brushed her hands together. 'There. That should do it.'

I trusted our spells but suspected Mum had needed to do this to be confident that she had thought of everything where my security was concerned. She liked Xavier and Henry, but I knew she didn't trust anyone with my safety as much as she would herself, or the women from the coven.

'I'd better hurry if I'm not going to be late to help Xavier and the others take Babette's tools up to the castle.'

The room lit up as distant lightning struck somewhere out to sea. Xavier pulled me against him in a comforting hug. 'You'll be fine. I'll be there every minute and will not let anything happen to you.'

He put a finger under my chin and raised it to give me a light kiss on the lips. 'I love you and will be ready for every eventuality.'

'Thank you.' I didn't actually know how he could promise that, but I found it reassuring to hear him say the words.

His intentions were good. I knew without any doubt that if anyone could ensure my safety it would be him.

Mum gave me a knowing smile as she buttoned up her coat. 'We must hurry if we are to catch up with everyone. Briar, you slowly make your way to the castle, and Xavier, you follow behind Dankworth at a safe distance.'

I couldn't hide my amusement when Xavier turned to Mum. 'Diana, I promise you I've done this sort of thing before. I won't mess it up.'

'Henry is pretending to go out to meet friends but will wait to follow the pair of you there, taking a different route.'

'I'll see you both up there when this is all over.'

Mum pulled me into a tight hug. 'Don't take any chances, Briar.'

'I won't, Mum.'

She walked outside and I noticed Xavier was waiting to have a moment alone with me. 'Your mother is right, Briar. Do not under any circumstances risk that man getting what he wants. Keep your back to the door, so he must pass you to leave. If it's the other way round he'll be able to block your exit.'

'I'll remember.'

He wasn't finished and took hold of my arms. 'Keep him in your line of sight at all times. If you're uncertain or become frightened, run out of the cell door.'

'Xavier, I promise I'll do these things. Now leave. We don't know whether he'll follow me from the cottage, and I don't want you putting him off by still being here.'

I watched him go, confident he wouldn't be far away, then went the opposite direction towards the village and up the hill to the castle for the ten-minute walk to the ruin. I was banking on Dankworth's arrogance and determination to catch me alone but I had no idea if he was behind me at that moment.

A loud clap of thunder deafened me, followed seconds later by a shard of lightning smacking into the sea midway along Grouville Bay. The storm was coming closer, and my fear was increasing with each passing second. I forced myself to keep going, not wishing to let the others down now, not when we were this close.

The thunder continued. I wasn't sure why the sound made me anxious but presumed it reminded me of the noise from all the bombing we heard during the war when St Malo was blasted endlessly by the Germans.

The light rain that had begun just after I left home was becoming heavier.

Another fork of lightning lit up the sky, catching me off-guard and making me shriek. *Calm down, Briar*, I thought, annoyed with myself for being so jumpy. I had no idea whether I was alone. I certainly felt as if I was.

My breath caught in my throat as another fork of lightning slammed into the earth behind the castle. I was scared for my safety. The storm was ferocious, and I doubted Dankworth was foolhardy enough to risk staying out in it on open ground this high up.

Not caring whether he was following me or not, I began running as fast as I could towards the ruin.

Chapter Sixty-Three

XAVIER

Henry and I had made good time and as I waited inside the rundown cell Henry hid somewhere in the darker recesses outside. It was still odd to think how this ruin had once been my jail while I awaited execution.

My head ached as I listened for any sign that Briar was on her way. I tried to ignore my concern that Roger Dankworth wouldn't follow her up here.

The man was canny. I worried that he might suspect Briar was up to something. Then again, I mused, he was also arrogant and supposed himself to be far cleverer than others. It wouldn't surprise me if the man followed her without question, amused at her silliness in risking an encounter with him alone without anyone to look out for her.

I knew Babette, Diana and Jeanne were somewhere nearby and hoped they remained hidden until it was too late for Dankworth to escape. Supposing Briar must be almost at the castle, I crouched low behind a row of stones, out of sight, until she and, hopefully, the Witchfinder entered the ruin.

Hearing voices, I took a calming breath before exhaling slowly. The time had come for me to show my worth to the Le Gros family. They had helped me in many ways and I had no intention of letting them down even if it meant that I ended up returning with Dankworth to my own time.

Briar walked in, carrying a bag with the tools for the spell Dankworth was expecting her to cast. I watched, her being careful to keep out of sight, as she drew a circle in the soil, then unpacked the candlesticks, candles, two mirrors, a jar of some mixture and a couple of coloured stones that she placed inside the circle.

The sound of the rain and wind was loud and I was unable to make out what Briar was chanting to herself as she prepared for the spell. I was wondering where Dankworth might be, when he stepped into the ruin. Briar didn't appear to have registered his presence. I hoped she was pretending to focus completely on her task in hand, but wasn't certain.

'I never thought I would catch you in the act of sorcery,' Dankworth said, a look of triumph on his pinched face.

Briar tensed and continued what she was doing for a moment longer. She had her back to him and I wasn't sure why until he walked around her so he was facing her and she was between him and the entrance.

I smiled to myself, proud of her for remembering my advice to do exactly that, and crouched lower as Dankworth looked at the space around him.

How the man didn't connect where he had been on his arrival to the cell where he once held his captives I had no idea. Only a man as arrogant as he could be tricked this way.

'What are you doing here?' Briar asked feigning surprise. 'How did you know where to find me?'

'I have my sources,' he lied.

'What do you want with me?'

He laughed. 'You do not know?'

She didn't speak immediately. 'I suppose you want to take me back with you, is that it?'

'Clever girl.' Briar must have given him a look that annoyed him because he added, 'You do not appear to be as frightened as I imagined you might.'

'Well, I am. But I can't help thinking that when I disappeared from the seventeenth century – *for the second time*,' she emphasised, I presumed to rile him as much as possible, 'people might have thought your powers rather wanting.'

'In what way?' His tone grew darker, and I tensed, ready to spring into action. 'Are you mocking me, girl?'

'I wouldn't dare do such a thing,' she insisted. 'It's simply that I'm aware how your ability to instil fear in the islanders must surely depend upon their fear of your wrath. My escaping from you at all, let alone for a second time, must have sullied your reputation.'

'You have no power to cause damage to me in any way.' He laughed, but I could tell it was forced.

I smiled to myself, impressed with Briar's bravery in confronting the man who had terrified her. Then I heard a whimper and guessed he must have taken hold of her in some way. Tempted to intervene but knowing that might endanger everything that had been planned, I remained where I was, barely able to contain my fury.

'You are a silly young girl caught up in matters you cannot comprehend.'

'You don't believe me guilty of practising witchcraft then?' Briar asked.

'You're too pretty to have enough thought in your head to engage meaningfully in matters such as those,' he mocked.

I cringed, imagining how Briar would hate to be referred to as empty-headed.

I heard a rumble of thunder and then a flash of lightning lit up the area. Careful to keep out of sight, I tensed when Briar gave a small shriek. Was she play-acting, conforming with his perception of her? I had to assume she was. The women had made me swear to do exactly as they asked, only deviating from the plan should an emergency arise, or when it was the right time for me to confront this man.

'Let go of me,' I heard her growl. She sounded infuriated but not scared.

'I have no intention of doing that.' A demonic chortle filled the cell. He was laughing. 'Did you truly believe I thought you empty-headed?' He laughed again.

'You bastard. You knew I was leading you here on a pretext, didn't you?'

'Finally, you begin to understand me. I never expected to be able to come here, or wherever you had vanished to. I went looking for you and that oaf who is besotted with you to bring you back with me, but mostly to ensure that you led me to other witches who still dare to continue their heathen practices here.'

Briar groaned. 'You're mad. What if you'd died coming here? Did that ever occur to you?'

'I had little choice, silly girl. I was in the cell one minute, there was a clap of thunder, and the next moment I was in a ruin and everything around me appeared to be different. Naturally I was shocked but I soon recovered and decided to continue my quest to make all witches suffer.'

'You're disgusting.'

He yelped and I hoped Briar had bitten or kicked him. Good for her.

'I determined to track you down and here I am.'

'Why? What is wrong with you that you couldn't leave me to get on with my life? It wasn't as if my living now could affect you in your time.'

'Time is immaterial. Not only was I determined to revenge my sister, but you stupidly thought you could escape me. When you vanished, I vowed to make you all pay. And that fool convict, who I know was involved with your escape somehow.' He gave a satisfied sigh. 'I was about to arrest Andre Touzel but that slut of a cousin took matters into her own hands and relieved me of my need to do so.'

At the mention of Andre, and Ember's part in his being beaten, I clenched my fists, desperate to drive them into his face. But I contained myself; I had promised not to deviate from Babette and Diana's plan.

'How did you know I'd disappeared and not just escaped from the dungeon?' she asked.

'You were seen. Two soldiers reported what had happened. At first I took them to be drunk, and they were, but even sober they insisted that one minute you were there, the next you'd vanished.'

There was a brief silence before Briar spoke. 'You're going to a lot of effort on my behalf.' I heard amusement in her voice. 'Should I be flattered?'

'You think I don't know you're the strongest, most dangerous witch on this island?'

Briar laughed, a strained sound that hinted at something I couldn't decipher. Then it dawned on me: she was probably wondering whether this was why her mother had insisted she be here to step in and add her powers to the banishment.

'I expected you to deny this, but I can smell the intensity of your powers on you. You are like no other witch I have ever come across before. And even if I did not already sense your powers, why would all these people go to such efforts if not to protect someone they needed? You are worth much to them.'

There was a moment's silence. When Briar didn't respond, he added, 'Even you cannot deny what I'm saying. The proof of your powers and what they mean to your coven is in the actions of other witches. And that, maiden, is why I have no intention of ever letting you escape.'

'That's ridiculous.' The fear in Briar's voice was obvious.

'I intend ridding the world of your ungodliness if it's the last thing I do. And,' he said, excitement in his tone, 'if I manage to destroy others in your coven while I do it, all the better.'

I couldn't believe what I was hearing. The man was insane. His obsession with these women had driven him mad.

My leg began to cramp. I bore it for as long as I could. Then, stretching out my foot, slowly and silently I began to massage the contorted muscle. Inadvertently I knocked a small stone from the broken-down wall.

'What was that?' I heard Roger Dankworth say. 'Someone is here?'

'I didn't hear anything.'

The tension in the storm was palpable as it intensified.

I heard a slap and Briar moan and realised he had hit her. I couldn't wait for the women to give me the sign to move. Unthinking, I leapt from where I'd been hiding.

Chapter Sixty-Four

BRIAR

My cheek stung from his backhanded slap, infuriating me further. I heard a shout, and Dankworth's hold on me relaxed slightly. Making the most of the opportunity, I started to free myself from his grasp, but he grabbed my arms and clung tightly to me.

For the first time, I heard chanting, and realised that Mum, Winnie and Babette must have been doing so all along. I looked to my right to see them crouching, each holding a mirror, repeating over and over the incantation we had created from Granny's spell book.

'Be gone, be gone, send him far, with air and water, earth and fire, remove this man's hateful desire. With harm to no one and protection to all. Great spirit, hear us, hear our call. So mote it be.'

It seemed almost as loud as the thunder and rain.

I spotted Xavier coming towards Dankworth and me, then cringed as a sharp blade nicked the skin on my neck. Damn the man.

'Let her go, Dankworth.' Xavier's face was as thunderous as the storm raging all around us. I tried to catch his eye, not wanting him to risk his life for me. He was too focused on the Witchfinder to notice.

Henry appeared at the entrance and looked from me to Xavier and then at Mum, Winnie and Babette chanting as if their life depended on it – or, I supposed, mine.

'I know what these witches are doing,' Dankworth screamed, spittle flying from his mouth. 'I've dealt with evil like yours for years.'

'You're the evil one,' I retorted. 'To go to such lengths to pay us back for something we had no part in doing.'

'Briar, hurry,' Mum shouted as she and Babette raised their mirrors, moving to hold them on either side of Dankworth – and me, because he was holding on to me.

'If I go, you're coming with me,' Dankworth screamed, almost deafening me.

'Briar, listen to me,' Mum yelled.

Realising they needed my help to energise our spell fully, I kicked him in the shin. He groaned and cursed me but held onto me. His blade cut me and made me wince.

Then, as if in slow motion, Xavier leapt forward and seemed to grasp Dankworth's hand that held the knife. 'Move, Briar!'

Stunned by Xavier's retaliation, I froze. Henry stepped forward and took hold of me just as Xavier smashed his fist down on Dankworth's hand, forcing his hold to loosen on my arm and giving Henry the opportunity to grab me and pull me outside.

'Briar,' Mum shouted. 'We need you to help us.'

I struggled to unscramble my thoughts, then, recalling the

incantation, joined them in their chanting, leaving Xavier to battle with Dankworth.

'Be gone, be gone, send him far, with air and water, earth and fire, remove this man's hateful desire. With harm to no one and protection to all. Great spirit, hear us, hear our call. So mote it be.'

Finally managing to knock the Witchfinder to the ground, Xavier stepped past Mum, Winnie and Babette and came behind me. He took hold of me and held me tightly against him as I continued to chant, my heart racing as I became aware of a maelstrom of dust swirling in the ruin, despite the heavy rain falling in through the gaps in the roof.

Spurred on by the realisation that Dankworth was becoming fainter somehow, I continued chanting in unison with the other witches, our voices strong despite our exhaustion. I was beginning to feel lightheaded, hysterical almost, when Dankworth opened his mouth and let out a scream of fury.

Then he was gone.

There was a second's silence, as if the world had paused. I didn't even hear the thunder or feel the stinging in my neck as I stared at where Dankworth had stood seconds before.

'Briar? Are you all right?' I heard Xavier's voice and slowly realised that he was still holding me. I winced.

Xavier turned me to face him, his eyes lowering as shock registered on his face. 'You're hurt.'

I reached up to touch the stinging and my hand was wet. I looked down at my fingertips to find them covered in blood. 'I thought my neck hurt,' I said in a pathetic attempt at humour.

'She's bleeding,' Winnie announced, causing Mum to get to her feet and start fussing over me.

'I'm sure I'm fine, Mum,' I assured her, wanting to be left to gather my senses.

'Let me see how bad it is,' Xavier said, peering at my neck. He kissed me lightly. 'You'll live, it's only a tiny cut.' He took his handkerchief from his pocket and pressed it lightly against my neck. 'Hold that there for a while. It's not deep and should stop bleeding soon.'

'Thank you,' I said, looking around me to check Dankworth had vanished and I hadn't imagined it. 'He's really gone.'

'He has,' Xavier soothed. 'You were very brave.'

We stood in each other's arms. I was trembling all over but felt safe once more with Xavier holding me.

'We did it,' I heard Mum say.

'I knew we would.' Babette laughed, her voice rather high-pitched.

'That was like nothing I've ever seen,' Henry said putting his arms around his mother's shoulders and gazing at her proudly. 'I never would have believed this if I hadn't seen it with my own eyes.'

Winnie beamed up at him and I could tell she was basking in his admiration.

It wasn't surprising Henry was shocked by what had happened. I suspected it would take even me a while to come to terms with what we had done. I smiled.

'What's so amusing?' Xavier asked.

'We're all ordinary-looking women whom no one would ever expect to be this powerful,' I said. 'I would think that too if I didn't know these witches as well as I did.'

Xavier laughed. 'There's nothing ordinary about you, Briar Le Gros, or these ladies.'

'We should leave here before anyone sees us,' Babette interrupted. 'You take your mum home, Henry. There's nothing more we can do here but risk getting struck by lightning.'

Henry and Winnie left and I helped Mum and Babette pack away our tools and erase the circle so that nothing was left in the ruin for anyone to find suspicious.

'Let me carry those for you,' Xavier offered, picking up the large bag, his free hand draped over my shoulder.

We silently made our way back to the village, each of us stunned by what we had experienced.

At the edge of the village, Mum turned to me.

'You two go and rest.' She took the bag Xavier had carried down the hill for us. 'I'll accompany Babette back to her house and help her unpack everything.'

'All right, Mum,' I said, assuming the women needed to talk and come to terms with the incredible thing we had achieved. 'We'll see you later.'

Xavier and I arrived home exhausted. Having changed and made hot drinks, I noticed a cut on Xavier's forearm.

'You never mentioned he had cut you too.'

He shrugged, glancing at it and smiling. 'It's nothing.'

Determined to look after him, and knowing that without his intervention I would not have left the ruin barely unscathed, if at all, I took out our first-aid kit and cleaned and bandaged his arm. Then, exhausted, we got a blanket and snuggled next to each other on the sofa.

'I can't believe it's over,' I said, resting my head on his chest, happy to be warm, dry, and safe once again.

Chapter Sixty-Five

XAVIER

It was a few days later, and Briar was humming to herself as she gathered Diana's jars and placed them neatly under the brown paper packages in her wicker basket, ready to deliver to clients. I smiled, happy to hear her. I didn't think I had ever seen the woman I loved more relaxed, or felt happier in myself. The cuts and bruises we had sustained from the tussle with Dankworth were healing well, thanks to a salve Diana had given us.

Life seemed perfect. Or as perfect as it could be after what we had experienced.

I accompanied Briar while she made the deliveries and, once we were finished, walked hand in hand with her down to the beach for some precious time alone.

We lay next to each other on the warm sand. Unable to help myself, I rolled over and kissed her, my hand resting on her warm hip. 'I need you to marry me.' I hadn't planned to voice my thoughts but when I saw joy light up her face, I was glad I had.

'Marry you?'

'Don't you believe we know each other well enough yet?' I teased.

She smiled. 'I think we know far more about each other than most couples do when they get married.' She laughed. 'We probably know what we're both capable of better than people who have been married for decades.'

I agreed. 'We've travelled through time, battled adversaries… I could not imagine ever doing such things with anyone else.'

Briar kissed me. 'Let's hope neither of us ever has to face anything that alarming again.'

'You haven't answered me,' I said after we kissed once more.

She pursed her lips. 'Haven't I?' I shook my head.

She placed her hands on either side of my face and with her mouth almost touching mine, whispered, 'Of course I'll marry you.'

'Soon?' I didn't like to sound impatient but realised I had.

She grinned. 'As soon as we can possibly make it happen. I too want to spend every night in your arms,' she said, proving how well she knew me.

We lay in each other's arms gazing contentedly at the dark blue of the sea interspersed with diamond-like glints, caused by the sun beating down on the gentle waves.

'You don't mind being married to a witch then?'

I shrugged. 'As long as you don't mind being married to a convicted ex-privateer.'

'I think I'll be fine. At least if any other nasty people come forward in time bearing a sword, I know I'll have you nearby to defend me.'

'I don't think that'll be necessary,' I said, kissing her shoulder. 'Don't forget I've seen how powerful your magick is. You won't need my sword when you can cast one of your spells.'

She leant over me, sending shivers through me as she kissed the skin on my chest, then my neck and finally my mouth. I wrapped my arms around her, holding her against me tightly, wondering how I ever thought my life was full before meeting this incredible woman.

Unable to stand it a moment longer, I got to my feet and reached down to help her up.

'What's wrong?' she asked, looking confused.

'I think we should go and speak to Diana. I need to ask her how soon I can marry her beautiful daughter.'

'Let's go,' she said, laughing.

I took her hand in mine and together we ran up the slipway and down the lane to Honey Bee Cottage, hoping Diana was at home. We both knew we didn't need her permission, because Briar was over twenty-one, but I wanted to do what I felt was right and respect the woman who had done so much for me.

We stopped at the front door with our hands clasped. 'I can't wait to marry you,' I whispered, kissing her again.

'And I can't wait to be Mrs Givroye.'

We went inside and found Diana in the kitchen tying twine around a small bunch of lavender. She looked up and saw us. 'Am I right in suspecting you're here to ask me something important, Xavier?'

Unable to help myself, I smiled. I realised that living with two witches was going to be rather interesting. 'You are.'

'You'd better leave us for a moment, Briar,' she said, waving Briar away with both hands.

'I'll go and freshen up then.' Briar blew me a kiss. 'Love you.'

'I love you too.' I watched her go then realised Diana was waiting to speak to me.

'Diana—' I began but she raised a hand to interrupt. 'While we're alone there's something I've been wanting to ask you,' she said, making my stomach tense nervously.

'I see.'

She seemed calm but I sensed she was about to ask me something serious.

'Would I be right in thinking you knew my daughter before you first arrived here?'

Shocked to be asked about that first occasion when Briar had gone back to my time – since I had never mentioned it to either of them – I nodded.

'You were already in love with my daughter when you arrived that night during the Occupation, weren't you?'

'How did you guess?' I asked, taken aback.

'Call it a mother's intuition.' She peered past me to check we were still alone, then pushed the door closed and lowered her voice. 'That and me noticing how different Briar seemed when I returned from England after staying with family for a few weeks. I worried what might have happened to her, because something most definitely had changed in her. I expected her to tell me when she felt ready but she never did. Then you came into our lives and I sensed your heartbreak when she didn't know you.'

'You could tell how I felt?'

'I saw the way you searched for signs while you were here. Your desperation to see recognition in her eyes was unmistakable.'

I couldn't speak, shocked that she had seen the depths of my feelings for Briar.

She rested a hand on my arm. 'I'm so sorry, Xavier, I suspect you probably intend telling Briar about that first time she travelled through time.' I nodded. 'I've given this a lot of thought and believe the right thing to do is keep this between ourselves. One day Briar might remember what happened and that she had met you before, but for now I think she's experienced enough trauma.'

'You think we should let her be?' I asked.

'I do. It's enough for her to think she's been back that one time with you, don't you think?'

I nodded. Neither of us wanted Briar to have to come to terms with something she couldn't even remember. 'I agree. She's been through a lot.'

'You both have.'

'All I want is to be with Briar and build a future with her. I have no wish to look back.'

'And neither do I,' Briar said, pushing the door open and walking in to join us. 'I presume you gave Xavier your blessing, Mum?'

I swapped glances with Diana and from her calm smile I realised our secret was safe and that Briar was referring to our marriage.

'Of course I have, darling girl,' Diana said stepping forward and enfolding Briar in a hug. She looked over her daughter's shoulder at me and I saw a twinkle in her eyes when she added, 'And what's more, I know you'll both be very happy.'

Briar flung herself into my arms and pressed her lips to mine in a kiss. 'I never imagined that the man I was destined to marry would come from a different time, or that my life could ever be this perfect.'

'Nor I,' I said, wrapping my arms around her and kissing her once again. The only thing that mattered to me now was that Briar and I finally had the chance to be together forever.

Author's Note

Dear Reader,

I'd like to thank you for choosing to read *The Witching Hour*, and I hope you enjoyed getting to know Diana, her daughter Briar, and Xavier. I've loved writing this book, especially setting it in two timelines. I chose 1643 and 1943 as the start dates for the book because this was partly when the witch trials on the island took place, as well as mid-way through the Occupation of Jersey, and therefore two dark times in the island's history.

As always, I aim to keep historical facts as exact as possible, but there are a few instances where I've used poetic licence here. For example, although Xavier mentions that he's heard of tea in 1643, tea wasn't introduced to England until the 1650s. I also mention when King Charles II arrives on the island and is celebrated. I have this as happening in 1646 so that it fits into the story, but it actually happened in 1660.

In *The Witching Hour*, Babette Le Dain's husband is the Connétable (Constable) of the parish, and I thought I should explain a little about his position in the parish. There are twelve parishes in Jersey. Each parish elects a Connétable, the head of the parish who also represents the parish in the States Assembly. Then there's the Chef de Police, a Centenier, who is an elected officer in the Honorary Police. This is the voluntary service that has been part of island life for hundreds of years maintaining law and order for the parishioners. The rest of this honorary police force is made up of Centeniers and Vingteniers, and until the 19th century these people provided the only civilian law enforcement on the island.

I use the term 'magick' instead of 'magic' because my witches in this book are traditional witches, and this is how they refer to their craft. It also differentiates traditional witchcraft from the sort of magic we might see from illusionists on the television or on the stage.

The witches in my book only practice their craft for good, or to protect those they love. They use what they can source from the nature around them, as well as the seasons and power of the weather to help with their spells.

Thank you again for choosing to read *The Witching Hour*. I hope you enjoyed reading Diana, Briar and Xavier's story as much as I've loved researching and writing this book. Please consider leaving a review and maybe tell your friends about the book.

You can subscribe to my monthly newsletter (deborahcarr.org/newsletter) where I share special offers, giveaways and behind the scenes news. I also have a YouTube channel (youtube.com/@DeborahCarrAuthor) where I post a weekly video about what I've been doing, my book news and my reading recommendations. My three dogs occasionally make an appearance there, too.

With my very best wishes,
Until next time,

Deborah x

Acknowledgements

I'd like to thank my amazing editor, Charlotte Ledger, for her continued belief in me and for suggesting this change in direction for my writing. I have loved researching and writing *The Witching Hour* so much that I've already written another paranormal romance.

My thanks also to the rest of the One More Chapter team. From the editors who have worked on this book and helped make it the best version of itself, to the cover designer and the marketing team for sharing my books and bringing them to readers' attention.

Thanks must go to my wonderful family, who are a constant source of support, amusement and love.

I might spend my working days by myself, but that doesn't mean I don't have constant support from many author friends. There are many I'd like to thank, and one of these amazing women is Christina Jones, who has been a huge supporter of my writing for the past twenty years. Thanks to my dear friends Amber Raven and Christie Barlow, who came to stay at my home here in Jersey for a few days – I don't think there was a moment when one of us wasn't talking. Also, my lovely Blonde Plotter besties, Gwyn Bennett and Kelly Clayton, whom I speak to each day.

To everyone who has shared my posts on Instagram, Facebook and TikTok, and all my subscribers to my YouTube

Channel (youtube.com/@DeborahCarrAuthor) and my monthly newsletter (deborahcarr.org/newsletter/) – a big thank you.

Last but certainly not least, my thanks to you, dear reader, for reading *The Witching Hour*. I hope you enjoyed getting to know Diana, Briar and Xavier so much that you want to read my second witchy book coming out in a few months' time.

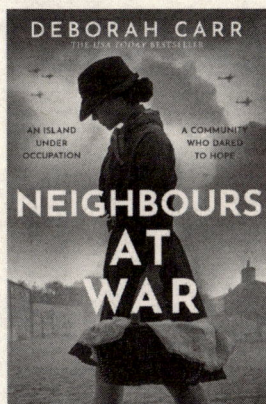

When everything is at stake, how far would you go to save your neighbour?

When German forces invade the Channel Islands and the citizens of Jersey are cut off from the rest of the UK, the islands' residents bond together to resist the enemy.

East London native Helen Bowman was never meant to be here, but when she found herself alone and pregnant her beloved aunt's home in Jersey was the only place she could go. But now, as the enemy start rounding up anyone not born on the island to be sent to a camp on the continent, Helen is forced to rely on the kindness of strangers, like her new friend Peggy Hamel, to keep herself and her son hidden.

But as the Nazis' net closes in, it's soon more than just detection that is at stake for Helen and Peggy – it's their very lives…

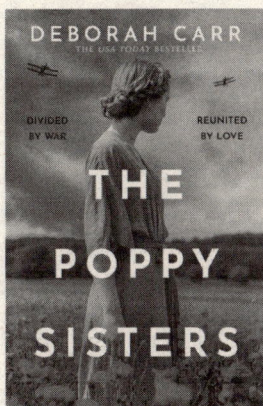

Divided by war. Reunited by courage.

Phoebe is a volunteer nurse at a Base Hospital in Étaples, France, treating men who've served on the Western Front. Their courage and resilience inspires her, and though she's meant to keep her distance, Captain Archie Bailey soon captivates her heart.

Her younger sister Celia is a nurse at a POW camp on the island of Jersey. These men fight for the forces that bombed her brother and parents, but long hours spent healing them shows her they aren't the monsters she expected.

Despite the miles between them, both Celia and Phoebe come to see the commonality in their experiences – the sense of community and friendship, the unexpected moments of love and laughter, and a bond so strong that even war can't break it…

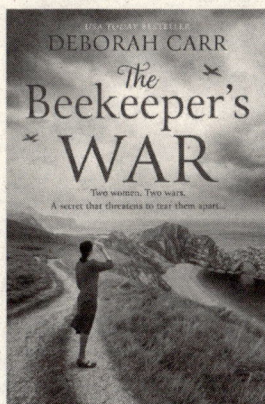

Two women
Two wars
A secret that threatens to tear them apart

1916

At the onset of war, Nurse Pru le Cuirot left her home in Jersey to care for injured soldiers at Ashbury Manor, Dorset. She wanted to do her bit but she never expected to meet American pilot, Jack Garland, so unlike any man she has ever met.

1940

Another lifetime, but another war and Pru's daughter Emma comes to Ashbury Manor. As Jersey falls to the Germans, Emma is fearful for her mother back home. And when she meets the mysterious beekeeper who lives in the grounds of the manor she finds herself caught up in a web of lies. As past and present collide, will the secrets of her mother's life finally be resolved?

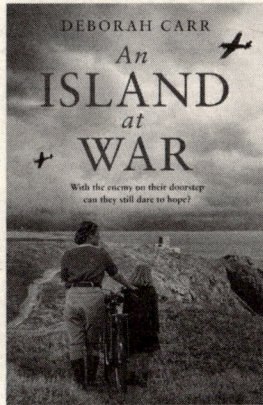

This is a story of courage, resilience and everyday acts of defiance from ordinary people forced to live in an extraordinary time.

June 1940

While her little sister Rosie is sent to the UK to keep her safe from the invading German army, Estelle Le Maistre is left behind on Jersey to help her grandmother run the family farm. When the Germans occupy the island, everything changes and Estelle and the islanders must face the reality of life under Nazi rule.

Interspersed with diary entries from Rosie back on the mainland, the novel is also inspired by real life stories from the author's own family who were both on the island during the occupation and in London during the Blitz and is a true testament to the courage and bravery of the islanders.

ONE MORE CHAPTER

YOUR NUMBER ONE STOP

FOR PAGETURNING BOOKS

The author and One More Chapter would like to thank everyone who contributed to the publication of this story…

Analytics
Imogen Wolstencroft

Audio
Fionnuala Barrett
Ciara Briggs

Contracts
Laura Amos
Inigo Vyvyan

Design
Lucy Bennett
Fiona Greenway
Liane Payne
Dean Russell

Digital Sales
Laura Daley
Lydia Grainge
Hannah Lismore

eCommerce
Laura Carpenter
Madeline ODonovan
Charlotte Stevens
Christina Storey
Jo Surman
Rachel Ward

Editorial
Janet Marie Adkins
Kara Daniel
Charlotte Ledger
Jennie Rothwell
Tony Russell
Sofia Salazar Studer
Emily Thomas
Helen Williams

Harper360
Emily Gerbner
Ariana Juarez
Jean Marie Kelly
emma sullivan
Sophia Wilhelm

International Sales
Peter Borcsok
Ruth Burrow
Bethan Moore
Colleen Simpson

Inventory
Sarah Callaghan
Kirsty Norman

Marketing & Publicity
Chloe Cummings
Grace Edwards
Katie Sadler

Operations
Melissa Okusanya
Hannah Stamp

Production
Denis Manson
Simon Moore
Francesca Tuzzeo

Rights
Ashton Mucha
Alisah Saghir
Zoe Shine
Aisling Smyth
Lucy Vanderbilt

Trade Marketing
Ben Hurd
Eleanor Slater

**The HarperCollins
Distribution Team**

**The HarperCollins
Finance & Royalties
Team**

**The HarperCollins
Legal Team**

**The HarperCollins
Technology Team**

UK Sales
Isabel Coburn
Jay Cochrane
Sabina Lewis
Holly Martin
Harriet Williams
Leah Woods

**And every other
essential link in the
chain from delivery
drivers to booksellers
to librarians and
beyond!**